Praise for *The Marx Sisters*

"A fine morsel . . . There is no lack of suspense and no lack of skill in the presentation. More, please, Mr. Maitland."
—*The Washington Times*

"One of the most intelligent, intriguing and well thought-out debut crime novels I have read in a long time."
—Marcel Berlins, *The Times* (London)

"Completely chilling . . . An accomplished work, which is surprising because this is Barry Maitland's first novel; if he only gets better—as novelists tend to do—mystery readers will be enjoying his work for years to come."
—*The Mystery Review*

"Engrossing . . . Maitland's deft depiction of his idiosyncratic characters, his evocative portrayal of Jerusalem Lane and his clever use of Marxist theories and history make this nothing less than a Kapital read." —*Publishers Weekly*

"A deceptive little tale indeed . . . Kathy and David make a good team, and if their future stories are as smartly constructed and as well written as this one, readers will have a wonderful new series to look forward to."
—*Booklist*

"A notable first." —*The Observer* (London)

"Mesmerizing . . . Maitland's subtle treatment of the potentially tired setup of an inexperienced female sergeant and a formidably impatient male inspector is the book's best surprise. One hopes for a long and fruitful relationship between these two."
—*The Houston Chronicle*

"A clever, flavorsome debut with a particular knack of pulling the rug out from under you in between chapters, just when you think you're safe." —*Kirkus Reviews*

ABOUT THE AUTHOR

Barry Maitland, recipient of the Ned Kelly Prize (Australia's Edgar), was born in Scotland, raised in London, and now lives in Australia where he is Dean of Architecture at the University of Newcastle. *The Marx Sisters* was shortlisted for the British Crime Writers Association's John Creasy Award for Best First Mystery.

THE MARX SISTERS

A Kathy and Brock Mystery

BARRY MAITLAND

PENGUIN BOOKS

*To Margaret
for unflagging encouragement
and with special thanks to Anna*

PENGUIN BOOKS
Published by the Penguin Group
Penguin Putnam Inc., 375 Hudson Street,
New York, New York 10014, U.S.A.
Penguin Books Ltd, 27 Wrights Lane,
London W8 5TZ, England
Penguin Books Australia Ltd, Ringwood,
Victoria, Australia
Penguin Books Canada Ltd, 10 Alcorn Avenue,
Toronto, Ontario, Canada M4V 3B2
Penguin Books (N.Z.) Ltd, 182–190 Wairau Road,
Auckland 10, New Zealand

Penguin Books Ltd, Registered Offices:
Harmondsworth, Middlesex, England

First published in Great Britain by Hamish Hamilton 1994
First published in the United States of America by
Arcade Publishing, Inc., 1999
Reprinted by arrangement with Arcade Publishing, Inc.
Published in Penguin Books 2000

3 5 7 9 10 8 6 4 2

Copyright © Barry Maitland, 1994
All rights reserved

ISBN 0 14 02.9176 8
(CIP data available)

Printed in the United States of America
Set in Sabon

Part I

I

'Something ain't right.' Meredith glared at her two sisters, sitting facing each other at the far end of the table, in front of the window. Eleanor looked at her carefully, recognizing the pouted lip that signified she was being stubborn.

'Well, your apple sponge was beautiful, as always, dear.' Peg dabbed her mouth meticulously with her napkin.

'What do you mean, "Something isn't right"?' Eleanor said.

'The way the Kowalskis decided to up and leave, just like that, all of a sudden. They should have discussed it.'

'They're retiring, Meredith. They don't have to discuss it. They're getting on, and the bookshop couldn't have been making them much of a living.'

'Adam Kowalski is a hopeless businessman, that's true,' Meredith conceded ungraciously. 'Anyone could have made a better job of selling second-hand books than Adam Kowalski. But what about Konrad Witz next door? His camera shop has been doing well enough. He told me so, after the Christmas season last year.'

'He's at an age to retire too, dear. They sold together to get a better price, so someone can knock the two shops together if they want. That's what Mr Hepple said. You remember.'

'I don't like empty shop windows, Eleanor. It gives me the creeps.'

Looking at her two sisters, Meredith was struck by how little they had all changed since they were girls. Eleanor, the youngest, was the same headstrong child she had been then, always certain she knew best, all elbows and knees, head in the clouds and holes in her socks. Meredith was irritated to find herself wondering, exactly as her mother had done sixty years before, whether Eleanor had remembered to put on fresh knickers that morning. And Peg was still the neat, sweet little girl who could always find a way to get other people to do things for her.

'Adam Kowalski looks more and more like a beanpole every time you see him,' Peg piped up.

'Have you ever noticed,' Eleanor said, 'how he always runs his hand over the plaque in the wall beside his shop, every time he passes? I wonder if he is a secret believer.'

'No.' Peg shook her head. 'I saw him do it and I asked him why, and he said he did it for luck. He said that Karl Marx might be the most famous man in the world, and he, Adam Kowalski, the least, but Marx was dead and he was alive, and that, in the end, was all that really counted.'

'That,' said Eleanor severely, 'is a matter of opinion.'

Peg suddenly gave a little shiver. Meredith, thinking of the electricity bill, snapped, 'It's not cold, Peg. Look at the sun out there.'

It was true. The golden light was gleaming on the chimneys and slate roofs of the buildings on the other side of the Lane.

'It is a beautiful day, dear,' Peg replied wistfully. Then impulsively she added, 'Why don't you come with us today, Meredith? Just this once?'

'Why should I want to go for a walk in a flippin' cemetery?' Meredith sniffed. 'I'll get there in a box soon enough, I dare say. No, thank you, I'll put me feet up as usual and have me glass of port and forty winks.'

'Come on,' Eleanor said to Peg, getting to her feet. 'We'll clear the table and do the washing-up before we go.'

2

Kathy came running down the stairs to the mortuary feeling like a school kid late for classes. *This is ridiculous,* she thought, *it's my case,* and stopped to get her breath. She pulled her sweater straight over the pleats of her skirt and ran a hand across the fair hair pulled to the back of her head, then stepped forward and pushed open the plastic swing doors.

There were half a dozen people in the room. She recognized the pathologist, Dr Mehta, standing by an open filing cabinet, writing on a clip-board, while his assistant, green-overalled and already kitted out with rubber gloves and cap, was sorting through nasty-looking tools on a stainless-steel tray. The anxious woman in the dark suit was probably from the coroner's office, and a photographer sat near her, looking bored and hung-over.

In front of Kathy, and with his back to her, a big man in a surprisingly smart suit was leaning forward, peering at the table in the centre of the room. His hands were clutched behind his back, and from their fingers hung the straps of a Polaroid camera. *Less like a Legend of the Yard,* she thought, *than an overdressed tourist.* He straightened as the doors flapped closed behind her, and turned, peering at her over the top of the half-lens glasses perched on the end of his nose. She hadn't expected the almost boyish thatch of hair, and the beard. Both hair and beard were grey, almost blue-grey in the cold fluorescent light.

'Detective Sergeant Kolla,' she said brightly, extending her hand, expecting some put-down for being late, knowing his reputation among the junior officers at Division. But he just beamed at her, a big bear of a man, twice her weight,

5

and took her hand, introducing himself disarmingly without rank. 'David Brock,' he said in a low growl.

They both turned their attention back to the body.

The old woman looked smaller and more frail here, naked on the table, than when Kathy had seen her yesterday, lying peacefully on her bed in her woollen cardigan and skirt and thick stockings. Now her face was tinged grey on one side, and her eyes seemed to have sunk back into their sockets behind the wrinkled lids. Her dowager's hump was quite pronounced, forcing her shoulders forward as she lay on her back on the stainless-steel surface. Kathy's eyes skipped quickly down her body, over the withered breasts, the pubic hair ginger unlike the silver hair on her head, to the feet gnarled with arthritis.

Dr Mehta broke the silence. 'You'll make the identification, Sergeant?'

'Yes. This is the same woman I saw yesterday at 22 Jerusalem Lane, WC2, at' – she consulted her notebook – '16.56.'

'How do you spell your name?' he asked. She told him, watching Brock bend lower again until his nose was within a few inches of the old woman's face.

'I'm damned if I can see any spots, Sundeep,' he muttered.

'On the scalp, just inside the hair line, Chief Inspector. In any case,' he continued, addressing himself to Kathy in his precise, formal manner, 'petechial haemorrhages don't prove anything. They can be a sign of smothering, but they're also seen in other conditions of terminal lack of oxygen and congestion, such as heart failure, so they're not diagnostic of asphyxia in the forensic sense.'

He returned to filling in his form.

'Her skin is pretty tough,' Brock remarked.

'Yes. I'd say she spent some years out in the sun, in a warmer climate than we are blessed with in these blighted shores.'

'Oh now, it hasn't been a bad summer,' Brock murmured absently, continuing his detailed inspection of the corpse. 'What about these faint bruises on the upper arms? Could somebody have held her down?'

Dr Mehta shrugged. 'Perhaps she got so excited watching the gee-gees on TV she gripped her own arms too tightly. They bruise very easily, these old dears.'

'But you've got the bag?' Kathy broke in, and turned to Brock. 'We found a plastic bag in her kitchen rubbish bin which had moisture inside, and a couple of silver hairs.'

'Oh yes, I've got it,' said Dr Mehta, 'and of course we'll test it against the swabs. Anyway, we'll have a good look at blood fluidity and, of course, the condition of the heart, dilatation of heart chambers, oedema of the lungs, congestion of organs, et cetera, et cetera, but I'm not in the least *sanguine*, Sergeant, that in the end I'll even be able to establish the *cause* of death, let alone provide you with *clues*.'

He turned to Brock. 'As you know, Chief Inspector, evidence of asphyxia is often uncertain, and if it was a plastic bag . . .' He shrugged. 'And to tell you frankly' – he lowered his voice and switched off the tape recorder that had been running at his elbow – 'I find it difficult to have much confidence in the judgement of her doctor, whatever his name was, who called us out, although I couldn't say that at the time.'

'He was a bit of a character.' Kathy smiled and the pathologist rolled his eyes, returning to his paperwork.

After a while he put the clip-board down and pulled a packet of rubber gloves out of a drawer. Kathy knew the procedure – first the Y-shaped incision on the front of the body, from shoulders to crotch, and the taking of blood from this cut for alcohol analysis before opening the body cavities; then the systematic opening of skull and body cavities and inspection of organs in place, and their removal in turn for individual examination. Just thinking about it

7

seemed to drain the thing on the table of what was left of its humanity, as if its soul were shrinking from the approaching knife.

'You all right?'

Kathy started, then nodded at Brock. 'Yes, sir. I was in Traffic for two years.'

'Ah, yes. Blood enough for a lifetime. All the same, not much point in our hanging about, eh?'

He waited for her to agree before speaking to Mehta. 'We'll leave you to it then, Sundeep. Anything occurs to you, we'd appreciate an informal opinion.'

'I always oblige when I can, Brock. But this time, I would *not* hold my breath.'

They left, closely followed by the woman from the coroner's office.

It was a fine September morning, and after the chill of the mortuary the city seemed soaked with warmth and life by the glittering sunlight, although the leaves of the plane trees were already curling yellow and showering down with each gust of breeze. Traffic was heavy, and Kathy made slow progress across town.

Her passenger said nothing for a while. She wondered what she had done to deserve this; there was enough to think about in running a murder investigation without having a Detective Chief Inspector from Scotland Yard's Department SO1 – the Serious Crime Branch – following your every move, let alone one with Brock's reputation. Inspector McDonald had been evasive when he had called her in this morning, and that wasn't like him. She had heard detectives at Division discussing Brock in the past. People who made a practice of remaining studiously unimpressed by senior officers apparently had difficulty doing so in his case. He was good, it was said, but difficult, often secretive, ferociously cranky and impatient. He didn't look that way now, she thought, as she glanced at him out of the corner of her eye, slumped comfortably in his seat, a benign look on his face, enjoying the sun through half-closed eyes and sniffing at the autumn smells through the open window.

'So you feel convinced it's murder?' he said suddenly.

'Not yet.' Kathy was cautious. 'But I could be. The whole set-up was rather odd. I had the same reaction as Dr Mehta to the woman's doctor – Dr Botev.'

'He called the police in the first place?'

'Yes. She was found by her two sisters who live in rooms upstairs in the same house. They called Dr Botev and he then phoned us after he had examined her. A patrol car responded, and they called in CID. I arrived with DC Mollineaux about twenty-five minutes later – maybe three-quarters of an hour after she was found.'

'That would have been soon after 4, then.'

'Yes. The sisters had been out since about 2 on a Sunday afternoon outing to the cemetery to visit departed relatives. Apparently they did that quite often. They'd said goodbye to their sister Meredith when they left, and when they got back they looked in on her and found her lying on her bed, not breathing. They called their doctor. When I got there, one of the sisters had gone upstairs to her room to lie down – in shock, apparently. The other was with Botev and quite coherent, although upset of course. The doctor insisted there was nothing wrong with Mrs Winterbottom's heart – she'd had a thorough check-up only recently. He was quite stroppy about it, and I thought a bit unnecessarily so in front of the sister. It must have been upsetting for her to hear him demanding a post-mortem, and telling me to get on to the coroner's office, although she stayed quite calm. Actually she was rather good. Seemed a lot more sensible than he did. I asked her to make sure her sister was all right, and then argued a bit with him, about people dropping with coronaries ten minutes after being told their heart was perfect, but he wouldn't hear of it. Eventually I did as he asked.'

'You had no choice.'

'That's what I thought. Dr Mehta arrived at 5.40.'

'Between one and a half and three and a half hours after she must have died.'

'Right. He took her temperature straight away, and he did seem surprised that it was as high as it was. But it was a warm afternoon, and she was well wrapped up.'

'Do you know what the temperature was?'

She shook her head.

'It'll be in his report. After asphyxia the body temperature can actually rise for a while before it begins to drop.'

'He didn't tell me that.'

'Sundeep enjoys being a sceptic – and keeping his cards close to his chest.' He growled at the car in front trying to make an illegal right turn and blocking their lane. 'You checked the place over, of course.'

'Yes, Mollineaux and I had a look round, and then the scene-of-crime crew arrived and did it properly. There was no sign of forced entry, but there wouldn't need to be – the place was wide open. The sisters habitually leave the front door on to the street on the latch apparently, and Meredith's door to her apartment was the same. Also there's a fire escape at the back, and the window on to that was open, too. A couple of drawers in her bedroom were open, but apart from that nothing looked disturbed. It all looked so peaceful, as if she'd just lain down for a nap after lunch with a glass of her favourite tipple, and then passed away. Dr Mehta will analyse the drink of course, but it was hardly touched.

'Apart from the plastic bag in the kitchen, there was one other thing that made me begin to wonder if Botev was right. Meredith's shoes were on the carpet at the foot of the bed, toes pointing away. There's an end-board, so she couldn't have sat on the edge and taken them off. They would have to have been taken off somewhere else and placed there. But if she'd done that, she would have held them by the heels and put them down with the toes pointing towards the bed, most likely. On the other hand, if she lay down with her shoes on, and someone tidied things up afterwards, that person might reach across the end-board, slip them off, toes pointing towards them, and set them down that way on the floor.

'At least,' she said, taking a deep breath, 'it seemed a possibility at the time. Maybe it's a bit far-fetched.'

'Hmm,' Brock grunted non-committally, 'worth bearing in mind, anyway. SOCO's printed the shoes?'

'Yes, and the glass of port beside the bed, and the rubbish bin in the kitchen, and all the usual places.'

Brock smiled. 'Sorry.'

Kathy flushed and was quiet as she turned the corner into Marquis Street and pulled up on to the pavement against the bollards that closed the south end of Jerusalem Lane.

Barely a dozen paces wide and a hundred long, the Lane crossed a city block, from Marquis Street through to the tube station on Welbeck Street to the north. Because of its skew angle however, and because its alignment gave a little kick to the right halfway along its length, it wasn't possible to see directly through from one end to the other. Like most of the buildings around the perimeter of the block, those facing on to Jerusalem Lane were built of yellow London stock bricks, faded and stained black by over a century of smog and soot. But whereas the terraces around the perimeter formed orderly rows with uniform roof lines, the buildings on the Lane were much more varied in height, as if no two neighbours had been able to agree on whether they should have two storeys or four, or even whether their plots should be laid out to the line of the surrounding streets or to the angle of the Lane. Despite this they were packed together as tightly as the perimeter terraces, and the sense which this gave of jostling anarchy beneath the common surface of blackened brickwork was confirmed by the explosion of chimneys, parapets and cross-walls which burst through the dark slate roofs against the sky. Glancing casually at this disorder, someone passing the end of the Lane might assume that it had been built as a service alleyway or mews, yet a second look would show that the shop fronts at the base of every building were original, and that it had always functioned as a thoroughfare. It was in recognition of this that a local by-law was enacted in 1893 to erect the bollards at the south end of the Lane to close it to wheeled traffic, and to repave it in York stone slabs. That was the last, unsuccessful attempt to gentrify Jerusalem Lane.

'It must be twenty years since I was last in this street,' Brock said as he got out of the car. 'And it doesn't seem to have changed at all. I'm sure that was there then. Just what I need in fact.'

He was gazing at the window of Rosenfeldt's Continental Delicatessen, which stood a few metres up the Lane on the left.

'Yes. That's number 22. The sisters live upstairs.'

'I'll interrogate Mrs Rosenfeldt after we've seen upstairs, then.'

'She was closed yesterday. She lives on the other side of the block.'

'About her sausages, I meant.'

'Yes, sir.' Kathy smiled as Brock strode purposefully to the shop front, pulled out his glasses and peered through the window. After a moment's inspection he turned regretfully and grunted, 'Come on, then, let's visit the scene of the alleged crime.'

They pushed open the front door, a bright pillar-box red, and climbed up to the first-floor landing. The carpet was threadbare in places, and there was an old-fashioned, homely smell in the air, a mixture of teak oil, lavender and fried onions. A very young uniformed constable stood by the door to Meredith Winterbottom's flat.

'Everyone's finished up here, sir. DC Mollineaux told me to wait here for you, case you needed anything. He's with the door-to-door team. The two old ladies are upstairs if you want them. And Dr Boter left a message that he can see you after his morning surgery at 10.30. His rooms are just down the street at number 11.'

'Botev,' Kathy corrected him. 'All right, we won't need you. We'll lock up after we're done.'

He handed her some keys and left with a salute aimed tactfully at neutral ground between the two of them.

The flat was as Kathy had described, cosy, peaceful and unruffled, and immediately improbable as the scene of a violent crime. It was tidy, but not obsessively so, and the two half-opened drawers in the main bedroom might easily have been left that way by Meredith. The clothes inside had not been disturbed, and there were no empty cash boxes or purses hidden among them. The furniture dated mostly from the fifties and sixties, with a few more recent things such as the large TVs and videos in both the main bedroom and the living room. There was no sign that anything was missing. In the small spare bedroom a filing cabinet contained only household accounts and personal papers. There were no books.

'She liked German sausage too, sir,' Kathy called from the kitchen.

'Perhaps Mrs Rosenfeldt did it,' Brock grunted. He was leaning out of the living room window and taking a photograph of the synagogue which stood facing on to Marquis Street on the other side of the entrance to the Lane. Although built of white Portland stone, it had turned the same grey-black colour as the brick buildings around. It was surrounded by a narrow yard fenced in by stone pillars and iron railings.

Brock came in and settled himself at the kitchen table.

Kathy sat opposite him. 'I don't know. I'd half convinced myself yesterday, but coming back again today, it doesn't feel much like a murder scene. I've heard of fatal accidents with plastic bags, and suicides too, but no plastic bag murders.'

'It was a favourite murder weapon of the Khmer Rouge,' Brock said. 'Very cheap. Well now, I suppose she might have had a pile of cash or something hidden somewhere, that someone knew about, let's say in her bedroom, and let's say she wakes up while they're taking it. But then there would have been signs of a struggle, and bruising, and surely they would have used the pillow, say, or thumped her on the head, or strangled her. Where would the plastic bag have come from?'

Kathy opened her mouth to speak, but Brock continued.

'Yes, all right, the money was in the plastic bag . . . And maybe she just began to wake up, and they panicked, tipped the money or whatever it was out and slipped the bag over her head before she could begin to struggle.' Brock screwed his eyes up at the ceiling and scratched his beard.

'How long would it take, I wonder? We'd better speak to Sundeep.

'Alternatively,' he continued, 'there was no secret treasure, and the killer came specifically for her. Someone who knew her, maybe. In which case again, why a plastic bag? And why not make it look more obviously like someone had broken in, someone without prior knowledge? In fact that applies in both cases.'

Brock nodded and got to his feet. 'All the same, I wouldn't give up yet, Kathy. Dr B may just be right. Let's go upstairs.'

One door on the landing on the top floor had a neat label *Peg Blythe*, and the other *Eleanor Harper*. Kathy picked the latter.

With her dark hair, straight posture and bright, attentive eyes, she looked younger than her sixty-nine years. Her flat was much smaller than Meredith's, occupying only the rear half of the building, and it was simply and economically furnished so as to make full use of the space of the main room, which served as a living, dining and study area. One wall was completely lined with bookshelves. Books and papers were piled on the desk against the window which looked out on the jumble of outbuildings, fire escapes, brick walls and ramshackle extensions which had grown up in the rear court of this west side of Jerusalem Lane. Kathy noticed that the room hadn't been dusted for some time, and that Miss Harper too looked in need of a scrub. Her hair was dull, and Kathy had the thought, of which she was slightly ashamed, that the old lady's underwear probably wasn't all that clean.

The women sat on two ancient leather armchairs, stuffed hard with horsehair, which stood on each side of the gas fire, while Brock pulled over an upright chair from the small dining table by the door to the kitchenette. Eleanor sat stiffly upright, her hands clasped on the lap of her dark wool skirt.

'Peg is lying down at present, officers, but I'll wake her if you wish. She didn't sleep last night.' She spoke with a low, firm voice and articulated the consonants precisely.

Kathy answered, 'We'd prefer to speak with you first, Miss Harper. Perhaps we can see her later. I'm sorry to have to disturb you again so soon. You must be very tired, too.'

They could both see the dark shadows under her eyes.

'Detective Chief Inspector Brock here is from Scotland Yard. He's an expert . . .' – she hesitated a moment – 'from the Serious Crime Branch.'

Her expression didn't change, but the hands twitched on her lap. 'I find it so hard to believe,' she said. 'I really don't know what to make of Dr Botev's notion. Are you certain that he's right?'

'No, we're not. We want to be sure, one way or the other, so to begin with we'll look into it as if it's a real possibility.'

'Poor Meredith. On her own . . . There's no point in it, I know, but I keep thinking over and over that if only we'd stayed home with her yesterday.'

'You saw her just before you went out?' Brock asked.

'Yes. The three of us had lunch together in Meredith's flat – we usually do on a Sunday. Meredith likes to cook a roast, and afterwards apple sponge and custard. She's been making the same Sunday lunch for years. First for her husband, Frank, and then, when he died, for us.' She frowned, then shook her head and continued, in a voice quieter and more strained than before. 'Afterwards Peg and I often like to go for a walk, and Meredith likes to watch the races on the television. Yesterday she said she was very tired. She hadn't been sleeping very well lately.'

'Had she complained of feeling tired before this?'

'Yes, because of not sleeping well, you see. That's why we insisted Dr Botev give her a complete check-up. He gave her some medicine, but said she was basically quite fit.'

'Could she have been worried about something?'

'She had been unsettled. I believe she had got herself into a pattern of broken sleep, waking up after a few hours and not being able to get back again, and then feeling tired all day – you know. So yesterday she said she would rest after lunch, and she looked so drained we insisted she take one of Peg's sleeping pills to make sure she had a good rest.'

'You didn't mention that yesterday, Miss Harper,' Kathy said.

'Didn't I? It was all such a shock yesterday.'

'Did she not have sleeping pills of her own?' Brock asked.

'No, she was like me. She didn't really like the idea of them. But she did take one yesterday, and took her glass of port with her to lie down. We closed the door of her flat behind us, got our coats from up here, and went straight out. Oh dear.' She looked at them suddenly. 'How rude of me. I should have offered you something. Would you like a cup of tea, Chief Inspector, or coffee?'

'Coffee would be splendid, thank you, Miss Harper.'

While she was in the kitchenette, Brock got to his feet and peered at the book titles. The fiction was grouped at one end, a mixture of classics – Hardy, Dostoevsky, Blake – and more recent writers – Isabel Allende, John Fowles and Günter Grass. The rest of the wall, about two thirds of the shelf space, was taken up by non-fiction titles on socialism, economic history and politics.

They heard a noise of breaking china from the kitchen, and Kathy went to investigate.

'I dropped a cup. It doesn't matter.'

Close up Kathy could see the tension lines around her eyes and the working of the muscles in her jaw.

When they returned with the tray of coffee cups, Brock was examining a framed photograph on the wall. It was a portrait of a young woman with the same strong, almost masculine, features as Eleanor Harper, with dark hair pulled back from her face in a similar simple style. She was wearing a dark velvet dress with a white lace collar, and a pair of spectacles was hanging from a cord round her neck. She was smiling gently at someone off to the left of the frame.

'A relative, Miss Harper? I thought I could see a family resemblance there.'

Her tired features relaxed with pleasure. 'Do you think so, Chief Inspector? She was our great-aunt. A wonderful woman. I would consider it a very great compliment to be compared to her.'

'Miss Harper,' Kathy asked, 'can you think of anyone who might want your sister dead?'

She looked shocked.

'Certainly not! Meredith was a wonderful person, full of life and vitality. She was interested in everyone in the neighbourhood, always trying to help people who needed it. No one would want to harm her.'

At that moment the door from the landing opened and

the Queen Mother entered the room, or so, for a moment, it appeared to Brock. She was shorter and plumper than Eleanor, dressed in a pale pink silk blouse and angora cardigan, her silver hair recently permed, and with a gracious, if somewhat vague, smile upon her lips. She paused in the doorway as if to orient herself, and Eleanor got up quickly and went to her side.

'Come in, dear. I thought you were still asleep.'

'I heard voices. Who is it, Eleanor?'

'It's the police, dear. You remember Sergeant Kolla from yesterday, don't you?'

It was evident that she did not. Eleanor led her to the armchair and fetched her a cup of coffee, while Brock brought another of the dining chairs over for Kathy.

'Are you all right, dear? Would you like the fire on?' Eleanor looked at her sister with concern.

'No, no.' Peg smiled regally at the visitors. 'I just had a little rest. I feel much better, thank you.'

'We won't bother you for long, Mrs Blythe,' Kathy said. 'We were just talking about yesterday afternoon. You said yesterday that you returned from your walk about 4.15, Miss Harper?'

'Yes, I suppose it must have been around then. We came upstairs and called through the door to Meredith when we reached her landing.'

'The door was open?'

'No. Closed, but on the latch. That's how we usually leave our doors during the day, so we can call in on each other. When she didn't reply we thought she must be asleep, so we went in to check. At first, when I saw her lying down on her bed, I assumed she was asleep, but then, I don't know what it was, she was so still . . .'

Eleanor bowed her head for a moment. Peg was sitting with the same vague smile upon her face, gazing benignly at the sunlight gleaming on a wall outside the window, and then, suddenly, she closed her eyes and gave a moan.

Eleanor looked at her with concern. 'Are you all right, Peg?' She got to her feet and went to her sister's side. 'Peg?'

'I don't think I want this coffee, Eleanor,' the old lady whispered at last, and held up the cup. Eleanor nodded and took it away, while her sister pulled out a small embroidered handkerchief from the sleeve of her cardigan and pressed it to her nose.

There was silence for a minute, then Kathy spoke again, gently.

'I am sorry. Only a couple more questions and then we'll leave. Do you remember touching her shoes?'

Eleanor looked perplexed. 'Her shoes? I don't remember her shoes.'

Peg sniffled noisily.

'No, that's all right,' Kathy said. 'And how about the drawers in her room, or the window, do you remember touching them?'

They both shook their heads.

'Did you touch Meredith?'

'Yes, I did,' Eleanor said. 'I shook her shoulder, gently. Her head ... was loose. It didn't seem natural. I couldn't see or hear her breathing.'

'So you called the doctor?'

'Yes. Peg was upset' – a sob of confirmation came from Peg – 'so I sat her down and I waited on the landing for Dr Botev to arrive. He lives just up the Lane, at number 11.'

'All right.' Kathy looked at Brock, who shook his head. 'We won't need to disturb you any more just now. Would you like us to call someone to be with you?'

'No,' Eleanor said firmly. 'No, thank you.' She drew herself up straight and led them to the door. 'You will get to the bottom of this, won't you?' she said. 'I would hate to think that Dr Botev was right.'

'We should know more by tomorrow.'

'What about the funeral? When can we bury poor Meredith?'

'The coroner's office will be in touch with you, Miss Harper. They will be as quick as they possibly can, I know.'

She smiled gravely at them and let them out.

The corridor outside will be no match for a ... Miss Harper. They will contain as strong a shape as they can however, I concluded; and so I went down and looked out.

3

There were neither patients nor receptionist in the waiting room of Dr Botev's surgery. As the jarring note of the door buzzer died away, a dusty silence settled back over the room. Under the glare of a bare fluorescent ceiling light, public health posters about smoking, osteoporosis and safe sex curled on the walls where they had been roughly pinned, and a small pile of tattered and outdated magazines spilled across a low table surrounded by six chairs, each of a different height and design. After a moment there was a noise from the other side of a glass-panelled connecting door, and the doctor appeared, nodded briefly and waved them through into the next room.

He presented an unlikely appearance for the family physician. Short, thick-set and muscular, he squinted at them through bottle-bottom glasses. He was swarthy in complexion, and his grey hair was cropped to short bristle not much longer than the grey stubble on his chin. Over a khaki shirt and a tartan tie he wore a brown, short-sleeved sweater with several large holes.

'Well,' he barked, 'what does the police doctor have to say?' His voice was pitched unexpectedly high.

'We don't know yet, doctor,' Kathy answered. 'Could you just go over again for the benefit of the Chief Inspector here what your assessment was yesterday, and in particular why you were so convinced Mrs Winterbottom hadn't died naturally?'

The doctor turned and stared at Brock for a moment.

'Miss Harper phoned me yesterday about quarter past four in the afternoon. I was here, upstairs. That's where I live. I have been the doctor to the three sisters for over ten years.'

Kathy stared at the powerful hands clasped on his blotting pad. They were disproportionately large for his body, with thick stubby fingers matted with black hair. They were the hands of a bricklayer or a farmer. She stopped herself trying to imagine him giving the old ladies internal examinations.

'She said she needed me straight away. There was something wrong with Meredith – Mrs Winterbottom.'

'What were her exact words, doctor?' Brock asked.

'"Please come at once. I think Meredith is not breathing." Something like that. It only took me a few minutes to get my bag and go down the street to the house. Eleanor was waiting on the landing.'

'And Mrs Blythe?'

'She was sitting in Meredith's bedroom. She seemed to be in shock.'

'Could you describe her?'

The doctor frowned.

'I didn't take much notice of her, not at first. I was more concerned with Meredith.'

He stared up at the ceiling, recalling the scene.

'Peg was sitting on an armchair beside the window, looking at the bed. I don't think she moved or said anything all the time I was examining her sister. Later, after I called the police, I had a look at her and checked her pulse. She was trembling and showing signs of shock. Eleanor and I took her upstairs to her room. I gave her two secobarbital tablets and Eleanor stayed with her until the detectives arrived.' He nodded at Kathy. 'By that time she was asleep.'

'I understand you were already prescribing sleeping pills for Peg,' Brock said. 'Is that right? Eleanor told us that they gave Meredith one of Peg's sleeping pills after lunch yesterday to help her rest.'

'Really? I'm surprised she took it. Yes, I did prescribe sedatives for Peg from time to time. The last time would be . . . oh, two months ago, perhaps. She was complaining of

22

sleeping badly and I gave her a prescription to last her two weeks. I suppose she didn't finish them.'

'All right, tell us about Meredith.'

Until this point Dr Botev had been speaking slowly and cautiously, but now he clutched his big hands into fists and said fiercely, 'She was a fine woman, a strong woman.'

Brock waited for him to elaborate on these qualities, but he sat in silence, eyes staring unblinking behind his thick lenses.

'She was seventy-four, doctor.'

'So? I am seventy-six.'

Brock raised his eyebrows in surprise.

'People don't die of age, Chief Inspector. Death has a cause – natural or unnatural. There was no reason for Meredith to die.'

'You had examined her recently?'

'Yes. For some months she had been sleeping badly. Unusual for her. She came to see me for help.'

'How long ago?'

The doctor peered down at a patient record card on the desk. 'The first time in early June, just over three months ago. Apart from a fall she had two years ago it was the first time I'd seen her professionally, although I knew her well. Everyone in the Lane did. Of all the people who live here, she was the most alive, the one who was always keeping up with things. It took her a lot to come and see me in June, I could see that. She wasn't the sort of person who goes to the doctor just because she's had a few sleepless nights. But I could see she wasn't well. She said she didn't have her usual energy, was run down. Said she wanted a tonic. Something about a bottle of iron medicine her mother gave her as a girl.'

Dr Botev paused and repeated 'iron medicine', shaking his head. 'When we talked some more, it appeared there were other symptoms: no appetite, constipation, dry skin. She was also troubled by stabbing pains in the lower back.

Also, she seemed to have lost interest in what was going on in the Lane. I noticed that in particular, because it was so unlike her. I remember that she didn't seem to be at all interested in the Kowalskis selling their bookshop and moving down to the coast.

'I gave her the usual check-up here, and sent her down the road for blood tests, but I was fairly sure what it was. My diagnosis was depression. She claimed she wasn't worried or upset about anything in particular, that nothing had happened to make her anxious in the past few months, but to me she was presenting the symptoms of depression.

'When the results of the tests came back I had her in to see me again and told her I was going to give her some pills to help her. She didn't like the idea. She said she wouldn't take sleeping tablets or tranquillizers because she believed they were addictive – she'd seen something on TV about it. So I told her these were like iron tablets, only more modern.'

'What did you prescribe?'

Dr Botev consulted his card again. 'Plustranil, 200 milligrammes a day. It's a tricyclic antidepressant.'

'It worked?'

'Yes. It took a week or so before she started to feel better, but after three weeks she came back to thank me. She had all her old bounce again, and said she felt much better and had stopped taking the pills. I told her she had to keep taking them for a couple of months and gave her a repeat prescription.

'A couple of weeks later she came back to say she was getting new symptoms – palpitations, occasional dizziness, and the constipation had returned. These are quite normal side-effects for this type of drug, but from her remarks I could see she was worried there might be something wrong with her heart. Well, postural hypotension can be a side-effect of Plustranil too, and that can be a problem for someone with a bad heart, so I suggested she had a thorough check-up and she seemed quite relieved. I also reduced the Plustranil to 150 milligrammes a day.

'She attended the cardio-vascular unit at the hospital on . . . August 12th. I got the report three weeks ago. She had a complete set of tests, and she was absolutely in the clear. There is no history of heart disease in her immediate family.

'So' – he glared at Kathy through his lenses – 'while it is not impossible for someone to walk out of their doctor's surgery with a clean bill of health and to drop dead with a heart attack ten minutes later, it is highly unlikely. Also, she didn't *look* as if she'd suffered a heart attack. No warning chest pains, no signs of distress.'

'What about a "silent coronary", while she was asleep on the bed?' Brock persisted.

Botev turned his glare back to Brock. 'I don't believe it. Come back when your police doctor has something to persuade me to change my mind.'

'But do you know of any reason why someone should want to kill her?'

Botev didn't reply, but only glared more defiantly over Brock's head.

'Or have any suspicion who it might be?'

Again no reply.

'What about Eleanor? Have you been treating her?'

He shook his head. 'She never needs a doctor. She is strong, too. Quite different from Meredith. But a fine woman.'

As Brock and Kathy got to their feet the doctor spoke again. The tone of abrasiveness had gone, and the curiously high pitched voice suddenly sounded plaintive.

'I will never forget how good she was to me when my wife died. I was helpless . . . like a baby. She saved my life then. You *must* find who killed her.'

4

They stepped out into the little square which was formed where Jerusalem Lane changed alignment halfway along its length. Across the way the proprietor of the Balaton Café was taking advantage of the warm morning sun to set a couple of tables outside on the stone flags. A powerful rich smell of roasting coffee beans came from Böll's Coffee and Chocolates next door, and on the near corner of the square, tubs of cut chrysanthemums and roses stood outside the front of Brunhilde's Flower Shop.

Brock's nose twitched at the smell of the coffee. 'We're early for the solicitor,' he said, 'let's have a break,' and set off with his big rolling strides towards the café. Kathy stopped to speak to two detectives making house-to-house inquiries before she followed him, and when she got to the table he was already deep in conversation with the owner about the Hungarian lake after which he had named his business. They ordered short blacks.

'This is very civilized.' Brock stretched back in his chair expansively. 'I could live here quite easily. There's everything you'd need on your doorstep: Mrs Rosenfeldt's bratwurst, Mr Böll's fresh ground coffee, the Balaton Café, and Dr Botev to prescribe Plustranil if it all gets too much. Shame about Kowalski's bookshop, though.' He nodded at the empty window up towards the north end of the lane.

'Mind you, I see there are other services available here to compensate.' He indicated a small handwritten card taped discreetly to a corner of the café window, offering 'Swedish massage' and an escort service. 'Probably the same old dear who was giving "French lessons" here twenty years ago.'

'Yes,' Kathy nodded, 'this is a *real* place, isn't it? I've never been here before, and yet it all seems quite familiar, homely.'

'It's real, all right. Not like that yuppie tourist kitsch they've turned Covent Garden into,' Brock grumbled. 'That used to be real once, too.'

'Although . . .' She hesitated.

'What?'

'There's an element of strangeness about this place, too. Maybe that's part of what makes it real. I noticed it yesterday. There are odd things that are difficult to interpret. Over there' – she waved her hand towards a shop window beyond the door of the doctor's surgery – 'there's a framed photograph in the window of some elderly gent, edged in black, and draped with a flag I've never seen before. And that enormous empty flagpole on the top of this café building! And there's a poster or sign up in that window on the second floor next door, which you can hardly see from down here, as if it's aimed at the house across the street. Or' – she looked around with a frown – 'that building over there with all the window boxes of geraniums, as if you were in Austria or something, except that they're all dead, except for just that one window. It's almost as if the people who live here are all frantically signalling to one another, without letting on to the people passing through on the street.'

Brock laughed. 'Yes, I like that. And you don't think the signals are friendly?'

'I don't know. I feel I don't know the code.'

Brock looked up at the aggressive Gothic lettering on the sign for the Balaton Café, and the unlikely clashes of colour on some of the front doors.

'Whatever it is, I suspect it's not in English,' he said. Then, changing the subject, 'I can see how Sundeep didn't hit it off with Dr Botev.' He smiled, thinking of the distaste with which the dapper, fastidious Indian had referred to the Slav.

'He's a rough diamond, isn't he?' Kathy said. 'Those hands! But this time I thought he was rather sweet.'

'"Sweet" wasn't exactly the word that sprang to my mind.'

Kathy smiled. 'I think he was in love with Meredith. His voice softened a little each time he mentioned her name.'

'Yes, now you mention it, that could be. But that just makes his opinions about her death all the less reliable. He didn't really give us anything. I wouldn't be surprised if he has a theory, but he wasn't game to try it on us. Not yet, anyway.'

The offices of Hepple, Tyas & Turton were next to the Balaton Café, above a small tailor's shop which appeared to have closed down some time ago. The solicitors' brightly polished brass nameplate was set beside a door which opened on to a staircase leading straight up to the first floor.

A large woman in her mid-fifties was sitting at the reception desk, opening mail. She beamed at them through ornately framed glasses and invited them in to an inner office.

'I'm Sylvia Pemberton,' she said, 'Mr Hepple's secretary. He hasn't arrived yet, I'm afraid, but he shouldn't be long. I spoke to him myself about your appointment at 12. Probably stuck in the traffic – his other office is in Croydon.'

Her manner was confident and jovial, and gave the impression that she was much more likely to know what was going on in the office than Mr Hepple. There weren't many indications, however, that much *was* going on. The photocopier and typewriter in the front office were both ancient, and the general air of tidiness seemed to owe as much to a lack of activity as to Ms Pemberton's efficiency.

'Can I get you coffee?'

'Thank you, no,' Brock said. 'We've just had a cup at the café downstairs.'

'Yes, I think they pay Mr Böll to fill the Lane with the smell of freshly ground coffee. I've become a passive coffee drinker just living here – I live in the flat upstairs.' She gave a hearty chuckle and then frowned. 'But look, that was terrible about Mrs Winterbottom. So sudden. I was shocked to see the ambulance there yesterday, and the police. People are saying there's some doubt about how she died.'

'Too early to say yet,' Kathy replied. 'We're just checking things.'

'Oh dear. She was so much a part of everything around here. It's difficult to imagine the place without her. She just . . . I don't know . . . kept everyone up to scratch, in touch with the latest. Always ready to step in and help if things went wrong. She really was . . . well, the life and soul of the place. Mind you, the way things seem to be going around here –'

The sound of the street door stopped her.

'That'll be Mr Hepple now. I know he'll have a coffee. Are you sure?'

Kathy shook her head, but Brock relented and she went out to meet her boss.

They heard his voice as he came puffing up the stairs. 'Ah, Sylvia! Traffic was terrible, terrible! Visitors here? Mr Böll has given me a terrible thirst for one of your splendid coffees.'

He burst into the room, a diminutive round figure in a pinstripe suit, thinning dark hair plastered down over a pink cherubic face, tossed a briefcase on to the empty desk, and shook their hands.

'Sorry, sorry. I only get over here once a week now, and each time it seems to take a little bit longer to get through.' He threw himself on to the chair behind the desk and took a deep breath. 'Terrible business about Mrs Winterbottom, terrible. And I understand you suspect foul play. Appalling. The Lane has been quite untouched by all the burglaries and muggings one finds elsewhere. And now this.' Suddenly his mouth opened and a look of revelation lit up his face. 'Brock! The famous Inspector Brock!' he cried. 'The

Manchester Poisoner! The South London Granny Killer! And that most recent thing – the murder of those two young policemen. Oh, most unfortunate. What was it? The "City Securities Slayings", the press called it. Oh, indeed, we are honoured to have you on this case, sir. The authorities must view Mrs Winterbottom's death with considerable disquiet!'

'We're not sure of the cause of death at this stage, Mr Hepple,' Brock answered. 'An autopsy's in progress at present.'

'Quite so, quite so. But one must be extremely concerned for the others who live here now if there is some violent murderer on the loose. Miss Pemberton, for example.' His eyes widened in alarm at the thought of Miss Pemberton in danger.

'There were no signs of violence.'

'Ah!' His eyes widened further as this sank in. He continued in a hushed voice, 'You mean, she may have known the culprit? Oh dear.' They could see his mind running over the possibilities. 'Oh dear, oh dear.'

'We really can't say yet. But we'd like to get some background information on the lady. You've been the family solicitor for some years, I believe.'

'Indeed, yes. Hepple, Tyas & Turton have been here in this office since my father founded the practice sixty years ago, in the same month as the Wall Street Crash. A propitious beginning!' Despite his concern over Meredith Winterbottom's death, it was apparent that Mr Hepple was unable to resist the telling of a good anecdote. 'I have been acting for Mrs Winterbottom and her family ever since she moved here with her husband in 1967. Well, earlier actually, because I did the conveyancing on the house when Eleanor bought it earlier in that year.'

'Eleanor?'

'Yes. Meredith and her husband Frank Winterbottom were in Australia at that time. They went out there as soon as they got married, after he was demobbed at the end of the war. Twenty years later they decided to come back and asked Eleanor to choose a house for them in London. He had made a bit of money in Australia – import and export, I think – and I imagine he had in mind a comfortable suburban villa in Sevenoaks or Amersham. Instead Eleanor bought them number 22 Jerusalem Lane, WC2. It was a bit of a shock at first. Frank's first words to me when they arrived were to put the place on the market again because they weren't stopping.'

Mr Hepple chuckled at the memory. 'However, it was an extraordinary thing. The house didn't attract any buyers for a while, and by the time one came along they didn't want to sell any more. Meredith was the first to fall for the place. She started to get to know the people living here, and soon found herself caught up in it. Frank discovered that it was quite convenient for doing business in the city, and then gradually he started to feel part of it, too. It is an extraordinary little corner of London, this. I always feel I'm coming home when I walk down the Lane. Are you familiar with it, Chief Inspector?'

Brock shook his head and Mr Hepple beamed, heaped two spoonfuls of sugar into the cup which Sylvia Pemberton placed on his desk, selected a ginger crunch biscuit from the plate she offered round, and leaned back in his chair.

'It looks quite scruffy, wouldn't you say? No buildings of great architectural merit. The scene of no great historical events. A bit of a shambles. Yet it is unique, and, to my mind at least, a place redolent of the sort of history which we tend all too often to ignore.

'The area which we know as Jerusalem Lane is really the whole of this city block, which is divided into two irregular halves by the line of the Lane itself, apparently all that remains of a rural track which once ran from somewhere around what is now King's Cross down to Holborn. Do you know that the peculiar kink in the middle of the Lane is probably a corner where four fields met and the track had to change direction round them? I think that's rather wonderful, isn't it, that we should still have to walk along the boundaries of odd-shaped fields that disappeared hundreds of years ago.

'Now although the block lies in the middle of thriving commercial districts – the City to the south and the railway termini at Euston, St Pancras and King's Cross to the north, and in the other direction, Bloomsbury to the west and Clerkenwell to the east – despite this, Jerusalem Lane has remained largely untouched by development since it was first built up, in a haphazard fashion, by small builders and speculators in the late eighteenth and early nineteenth centuries.'

Kathy tried to catch Brock's eye, wondering how she could return the solicitor to the present, but Brock, attentive and contentedly munching on a chocolate digestive biscuit, seemed happy to let him continue.

'This lack of attention from developers was due not to its location or potential, you understand, but rather to the confusing complexity and multiplicity of freeholds, leaseholds and tenancies which established themselves within the block, and which frustrated the most determined attempts to replace the warren of small buildings with something more coherent and profitable. There is that one row on the west side of the block, where an Edwardian developer managed to buy up about half of the street frontage and build that rather flamboyant red brick and stone trimmed office building seven storeys tall (thanks to the recent introduction of Mr Otis's patent safety lifts), but the rest of the block remained as we see it, a jumble of fragmented ownerships, uses, floor levels and building forms.

'Now' – Mr Hepple leaned forward over the desk and looked intently at them, as if he was getting to the point of his story – 'because of this, rents in Jerusalem Lane have remained low throughout its history, and within a generation of its construction it had established itself as a small haven for poor newcomers to the city, and in particular immigrants and refugees from Europe. The first such wave was of Russian Jews, fleeing the pogroms of the 1830s, and we can still see the traces of their early occupation of the area in the synagogue at the south end of the Lane, opposite Mrs Winterbottom's house, and by the name of the public house, *The Wandering Jew*, across the road in the next block to the north, and of course by the name of Jerusalem Lane itself.

'After the disturbances in the year of revolutions, 1848, political refugees from Germany, France and half a dozen other European countries found their way to the Lane. Did you by any chance notice the engraving over there by the door?'

'I did,' Brock said. 'It looks like a Doré.'

'Quite right, Chief Inspector! It is one of Gustave Doré's scenes of Victorian London, and it is actually a view of Jerusalem Lane as it was in the decades after that influx of refugees from the continent.'

Brock and Kathy got up and had a look at the drawing hanging in its black and gold frame. It showed a narrow street teeming with hawkers, beggars, handcarts and ragged children.

'Among those refugees, and the most famous of our former residents, was Karl Marx, who lived for most of 1850 with his family in the house of a Jewish lace dealer at number 3 Jerusalem Lane, which most recently has been Adam Kowalski's home and bookshop. You can see a plaque, mounted in the wall outside the shop a few years ago to record the fact that the Marxes lived there.' Mr Hepple chuckled and a twinkle came into his eye. 'It was not a period which the Marx family was to look back on with much nostalgia. They lived in great poverty in two rooms on the second floor, one of which was shared by the whole family: Karl, his pregnant wife Jenny, their three small children, and their maid. The other room was used by

33

Karl alone as his study, chaotically untidy and invariably filled with a fog of tobacco smoke so thick that it stung the eyes of anyone who ventured in. There he worked late into the night on his researches into British capitalism and composing his *Address of the Central Committee to the Communist League*.'

Mr Hepple beamed as he showed off his knowledge. He paused to gulp down some more coffee, and Kathy, seeing that Brock was showing no sign of wanting to interrupt him, made to speak. Hepple sensed this, however, and got in first.

'Cramped, cold and spartan as their accommodation was, it at least had the advantage of being only a short walk to the British Museum, for which Marx gained a reader's ticket in the June of that year, and where he spent the next three months immersed in back numbers of the *Economist*. Soon after they moved into Jerusalem Lane, Jenny became ill and, fearful of losing her as they had lost their fourth child not long before, Karl sent her to stay with friends for over a month. It was during this period that the maid became mysteriously pregnant and gave birth to a baby boy towards the end of that year. Soon after, around Christmas time, the family was evicted for not paying their rent, and, with the help of Marx's friend Engels, moved on, firstly to lodgings in Soho, and later, when they inherited money, out to the new suburbs of Kentish Town and Hampstead.

'A hundred years later, in the period after the Second World War, Jerusalem Lane was largely unchanged, and was still providing shelter to refugees from European upheavals, as waves of Latvians, East Germans, Hungarians, Czechs and Poles made their way westward. For most it was, as for the Marxes, a temporary stage on their route to prosperity in the suburbs of the Home Counties, but others stayed, setting up small businesses in the buildings which had once housed the Russian-Jewish clog maker, butcher and lace trader. The key to the success of these small businesses (and I would count my father's practice among them) was Jerusalem Lane itself, which provided a short cut for people travelling from the tube station at its north end to the northern parts of Holborn and to the hospital of Great Ormond Street. Each day the ebb and flow of these travellers have irrigated the cash registers of Witz's Cameras, Kowalski's Old and New Books, Brunhilde's Flower Shop and all the rest, while the Balaton Café and Böll's Coffee and Chocolates have tempted people to linger before moving on to the noise and traffic of the surrounding streets, where a somewhat greyer style of trading – office supplies, photocopy services and travel agencies – has taken over.

'However, none of the children of these refugees of the 40s and 50s have remained in the Lane; they have moved out to the suburbs, returning occasionally to visit their now ageing parents, still living above the shop, still without cars (for there is nowhere to put them), and still performing their good-natured, if sometimes fiery and increasingly eccentric, revue of Central European politics of a generation ago.'

Brock roused himself. 'Mrs Winterbottom had children?'

'A son, yes.' But Mr Hepple hadn't quite finished the broad picture. 'The Winterbottoms didn't really fit this pattern. They weren't refugees, unless from Australia,' and he gave a self-deprecating little laugh to avoid the possibility of offence. 'They weren't Central Europeans or Jews. They were simply Londoners returning almost by accident to this area. But they became, and Meredith especially, the linchpins of the place.'

'I met the son yesterday evening, sir,' Kathy said. 'Terry Winter. Lives in South London. Eleanor phoned him and he came to the house.'

'Winter?' Brock queried.

'Yes, he was particular about that.'

'He dropped the "bottom",' the solicitor interjected, anxious to resume his role as principal storyteller. 'Meredith was rather annoyed when he did it. Quite disgusted in fact.

35

I rather gathered it was his wife who was behind it, so to speak.' They all showed their appreciation of his little joke.

'No other children, then?' Brock asked.

The solicitor shook his head.

'And the sisters? How do they go in ages?'

'Now, let me see. Meredith was the oldest certainly, and would have been in her mid-seventies. Peg was next and Eleanor youngest. There are only a couple of years between each of them, so Eleanor must be sixty-nine or seventy, although I must say she doesn't look it, wouldn't you say?'

'Have they all been living there since 1967?'

'No, no. In those days Peg was a buyer for one of the big department stores – I'm not sure which one – and Eleanor was an assistant librarian at the British Museum. They were both single ladies, and had their own flats somewhere.'

'Wasn't Peg married?' Kathy asked.

'Only briefly. She was widowed before Meredith and Frank returned to England.'

'So, they came back.'

'Yes, and lived together at number 22 for ten or twelve years. In those days it was an ironmonger who rented the ground-floor shop. Terry only lived with them for a year or so, because he was nineteen or twenty at that stage and went off to technical college or something, and got a place of his own.

'Then Frank died. Cancer of the bowel. That would have been about ten years ago. By this stage Peg had retired, and Eleanor was coming up to it as well, and so Meredith had the alterations done to the top floor and made them their own flats for them to come and live at 22 with her. I must say that I was very doubtful about it. They're so different the three of them, I thought they'd never get on living together.'

'In what ways different?'

'Well, in every way. Their personalities, their tastes, and above all in their politics.'

'Politics?'

'Oh dear me yes. Meredith, well she didn't really have any politics; I mean she might have voted Tory, but there again it might have been Liberal or Labour if it suited. She was a business woman, like Frank. They rented the newsagent's on the corner next door – what's now Stwosz's – just for something to occupy Frank when he wasn't doing business with his stockbroker. And they made a real go of it, too. Special pipe tobaccos and cigars ordered for individual customers, special deliveries of the foreign financial papers to the offices around here, you know. They were really entrepreneurs – what the other two sisters would call *petite bourgeoisie*, I dare say.'

'They were of a pinker persuasion, I take it?' Brock said.

'Pink? Oh dear me no. Red! And very red at that. Eleanor is what she calls a "scientific socialist", which I think is some form of extreme Marxist, and Peg is a Stalinist.'

'Stalinist?' Brock and Kathy gaped at the solicitor, trying to reconcile this information with the vision of the Queen Mother they had met at number 22.

'Indeed!' Mr Hepple beamed, delighted at the effect of this titbit. 'Staunch member of the Party. Used to go every summer to East Germany and other delightful parts of the workers' paradise, at the invitation of the comrades. And still believes in it all. Quite unyielding. She was telling me only the other day. "They've lost all sense of discipline," she said. "You'll see what a mess there'll be now they've abandoned the Party." And I said, "You must be the very last Stalinist left in Europe," and she said yes, she thought she might donate her body to the British Museum to be stuffed and displayed as the last member of an extinct species, when they decided to do away with her.'

The smile slowly faded from his chubby pink cheeks as he registered his own words. 'Oh dear,' he murmured, 'oh dear, oh dear.'

'Mr Hepple,' Brock said, taking advantage of his moment

of confusion, 'I wonder if you would be able to help us in the matter of Mrs Winterbottom's will.'

'Well, I am her sole executor, so I don't see why not, under the circumstances. She made it out some time ago, but I can recall the gist.'

'She didn't alter it recently, or talk of doing so?'

'No, no. In fact I hadn't really seen her for a while. As I say, I don't get up here so often now. The main beneficiary of Mrs Winterbottom is her son, with small legacies for his two daughters – some pieces of jewellery and a little cash. Unless her circumstances changed substantially in the last year or so, her estate really amounts to some shares and other savings left by her husband, which she had been gradually eating into for her income over the past ten years, together with the property, number 22. However, she had me establish a trust to administer the property after her death for the period that either or both of her sisters survive her, to allow them to continue to remain there for as long as they wished, rent-free. Once they leave or pass away, the property reverts unobstructed to the son.'

'Could he challenge that?' Kathy asked.

The solicitor examined his fingernails. 'No, I think that's unlikely.' From his tone Kathy felt he had considered this possibility quite carefully. She suddenly wondered if he was more devious than he looked.

'And is he aware of the terms of his mother's will?' she asked.

'I believe so,' he said vaguely, then suddenly looked worried. 'You're surely not suggesting . . .'

'These are just standard lines of inquiry in these sorts of circumstances, Mr Hepple,' Brock said soothingly. 'I'm sure you understand.'

'I see.' He still looked worried. 'I must say my familiarity with murder investigations is somewhat limited. The last time I came up against such a thing was many years ago. A client in Southwark, I believe . . .'

'We'd best be getting along, sir,' Kathy broke in hurriedly, and rose to her feet.

'Of course, quite so.' The solicitor got up and hurried round his desk to show them out, making a particular point of shaking Brock's hand. 'If there's anything you want to know about the people around here, Miss Pemberton is the person to speak to. She's been living here for some years now, and she does the books and VAT returns for quite a few of them. We shall be very sorry to part company with her.'

'She's leaving?'

'Well, we both are in point of fact.' He shrugged his shoulders and spread his hands in regret. 'We do so little business here,' he said, lowering his voice to a discreet whisper. 'It really doesn't make much sense – hasn't for several years now. So we're selling the property, and Miss Pemberton has her own plans to retire.'

From the car phone they arranged to interview Meredith Winterbottom's son at his home later that afternoon. Kathy had to return to her divisional headquarters near by, where an incident room had been set up in an office adjoining her own, to check on the progress of the three other detectives who had been working their way round the neighbourhood that morning, interviewing potential witnesses. As she was about to leave, she hesitated a moment and then turned to Brock.

'Sir, do you think I might be able to knock off by 7 tonight? I was at it till fairly late last night, and I sort of had something arranged for this evening. Of course, if you feel it's important . . .'

'Not at all,' Brock replied genially. 'We should have done for the day well before then. And, anyway, it's your case. We'll do as you say.'

As she left, she thought uneasily that this certainly wasn't the Chief Inspector Brock she'd heard about. *Maybe he's getting soft,* she thought. *Or maybe he's like this until you make your first mistake.*

Having arranged to meet her at 3, Brock strolled back to Rosenfeldt's Continental Delicatessen. The shop smelled as good as it looked. Cheeses, wursts, breads, salamis and pickles filled it with layers of intriguingly delicate and pungent odours which varied subtly from corner to corner of the small space. Mrs Rosenfeldt came out from the rear in response to the tinkling bell over the door. She was a small woman in her late sixties, dressed simply in greys, who looked as if she might have suffered from some serious illness in recent years, or perhaps, further in the past, a spell in one of the Third Reich's more horrific institutions. Her silver hair was drawn tightly back into a bun, emphasizing the lack of flesh on her skull. Her throat and wrists were corded and criss-crossed with what appeared to be pale scars. Yet the eyes that glittered through her steel-framed glasses were needle-sharp.

'Good afternoon,' Brock said amiably. 'I am very interested in your bratwurst, and possibly some cheese, but perhaps you could give me a small guided tour of your specialities.'

Mrs Rosenfeldt gave a little smile and began to outline the things under the glass display cases. Brock settled for some pumpernickel, Westphalian ham, a jar of pickled herrings which he knew he should avoid, a dozen bratwurst (having established that freezing wouldn't spoil their flavour), a large slice of Allgau cheese, some sliced poltava salami and a small tub of black kalamathes olives.

As she wrapped these up and placed them in a plastic carrier bag, Mrs Rosenfeldt said, 'You're one of the police looking into Mrs Winterbottom's death, aren't you?' The way she said it suggested that death was a familiar fact which didn't have to be hedged around with euphemisms or hushed tones. Her voice was low, almost masculine, and with a strong German or Central European accent.

'That's right. I understand you weren't in your shop here yesterday?'

'Yes. I spoke to a detective this morning.'

'But you must have known Mrs Winterbottom well?'

'She was my landlady.'

'She seems to have been very popular in the neighbourhood.'

'Oh, she knew everybody. Liked to know everything going on.' The tone suggested some reservations about people who liked to know everything going on.

'You mean she might have been a bit too concerned with other people's business?'

41

'I didn't say that. I was very fond of her, myself.'

'But others weren't?'

She hesitated. 'All I'd say is' – she stared intently at Brock – 'when I heard that she might have been murdered, my first thought was, they should speak to those Nazis in the Croatia Club.'

'Nazis?'

She shrugged her shoulders. 'I've said enough. I have to live here, you know. I said what I said. Maybe it's a clue for you, maybe not, I don't know.'

Brock picked up his carrier bag and thanked her. As the door tinkled shut behind him he turned and looked back through the shop window. She was standing motionless in the shadows at the back of the shop, a pale wraith, watching him.

On the drive down through South London to Kent, Kathy told Brock what the door-to-door inquiries had produced.

'It's extraordinary, isn't it, in a street like that, with the net curtains twitching every time we appeared this morning, that nobody admits to having been by a window overlooking either the front or the back of number 22 yesterday afternoon. Not one.'

'Always the way. Anybody remember seeing any strangers in the block?'

'Well, the thing is that there are always strangers passing through, so no one takes any notice unless they do something odd. It's like living next to a railway line. After a while you just don't hear the trains any more. The only outdoor areas you'd call private are the yards behind the buildings. Mr Hepple parks his car in one of them when he comes, and there's a jumble of sheds and open yards with an access passage from Carlisle Street on the west side of the block. But no one remembers seeing anybody there yesterday afternoon. It's all very frustrating. Inspector MacDonald said he wanted Mollineaux and the other two for another job, and I couldn't really argue.'

'Never mind. Perhaps Mr Winter-without-the-bottom will break down and confess when we beat him about the head and shoulders with a bratwurst. Did you get some lunch, by the way?'

Kathy shook her head and accepted Brock's invitation to help herself from his bag while he told her about Mrs Rosenfeldt's 'clue'. She groaned. 'Geriatric Nazis are all we need. The press'll get to hear of it, and then the whole thing will blow up in our faces when we discover the old lady had a heart attack after all.' She peeled off several slices of salami and took a few olives.

'But you don't really think so, do you?'

Kathy paused, and then said 'No, sir, I don't. I don't know what it is, but I felt it was wrong when I first went into that flat yesterday, and the feeling's never left me since. I know it sounds weak in the circumstances.'

'Not at all, Kathy,' Brock said. 'I always have feelings about cases. I think you may be right. It's just doubly important to check everything.'

'Sir, can I ask you about something that Hepple raised? It's bothered me too. This case, it's not exactly the Manchester Poisoner, at least not yet. I was surprised the Yard wanted to get involved. And then when they said it would be you – well, it just seemed unlikely.'

Brock smiled. '"The Yard moves in mysterious ways, its blunders to perform" ... Actually, I never really know what they'll put me on next. Part of the attraction. I agree that this didn't sound too promising at first, but I'm rather enjoying it. Don't mind, do you, me tagging along?'

'Oh no! Of course not. It's great being able to work with someone like you. It was just – well, after your last case, I mean this isn't the same sort of high-profile thing at all.'

Brock's previous case, the 'City Securities Slayings' Mr Hepple had referred to, had been in the headlines for weeks. Two young police officers had been shot dead in the City by a gang escaping with the contents of a bank's security boxes. Brock, in charge of a team drawn from the Serious Crime Branch and Robbery Squad, had eventually identified the gang leader as Gregory Thomas North, a professional criminal with a record of violent robberies, known as Upper North because of his dangerous habit of psyching himself with stimulants before a job. On the point of arrest, North had disappeared, surfacing a few days later in South America, beyond the reach of extradition.

'Everyone in Division got really worked up over that,' Kathy said. 'Half of us had been on the case, anyway, doing leg work for the Yard, and when it turned out the way it did . . . You must have felt terrible, sir.'

'Yes, well, we may yet have a little surprise in store for friend North,' Brock grunted. He said no more, and they continued in silence through the southern boroughs until they came out among the oak and silver birch woods around Chislehurst Common.

Terry and Caroline Winter lived in a house called Oakdene, which was separated from the road by a lawn, rose beds and a red-brick drive, much of which was obscured by expensive silver German cars. The house belonged to the Tudorbethan school of suburban domestic architecture, built in the thirties when Lutyens' models were still fresh and were copied with some substance and conviction. Wall panels of herring-bone-patterned red brickwork were framed by dark, heavy timbers and sheltered by a wide gabled roof, whose clay tiles were now dark green with algae nurtured by the broad overhanging boughs of oak and ash. A light visible through the diamond-paned leadlight windows of the ground floor shone out against the gloom of the afternoon.

Brock parked in the street and they walked to the front door, breathing in the damp, lonely smells of autumn woodland. Terry answered the door and led them across a dark panelled hall into the lounge. The central heating was up high, and he wore a black shirt and jeans, both with conspicuous designer labels. The sleeves of his shirt were loosely rolled back on his forearms, exposing a heavy gold chain on one wrist and an expensive-looking gold watch on the other. He looked younger than his early forties, with a lean, tanned face and thick, dark wavy hair. He indicated casually towards the new leather suite and flopped into a director's chair on a swivel base.

'Well,' he said in a neutral voice, 'what's the story?'

Kathy answered. 'We still aren't sure of the cause of your mother's death, Mr Winter. We hope to have that established soon, but in the meantime there are procedures we work through which are designed to help us clarify the situation. We interview neighbours, close relatives . . .'

'And solicitors, apparently,' Winter interrupted smoothly. His eyes flicked quickly, appraisingly over Kathy, and he gave her a wolfish smile. 'I've just had Mr Hepple on the phone. He seemed to feel that, since he'd told you the contents of my mother's will, he might as well let me know too.'

'Weren't you familiar with the terms of your mother's will before then?' Kathy said quietly, holding his eyes.

'In general terms. Mum had told me what she had in mind.'

'And were you happy about the arrangements? I'm thinking about the term that allowed your aunts to stay at 22 Jerusalem Lane in perpetuity.'

His face became expressionless, his eyes cold. He stared at Kathy rudely for a while, examining the dimple on her chin. Then he shrugged and, rocking slightly in his chair, which gave a little squeak, he turned to Brock.

'Up to her. It was her house. She always felt kind of protective towards Eleanor and Peg. I think she felt the old ducks didn't know how to look after themselves. Not really practical like, in business matters.' He turned back to Kathy and grinned deliberately at her.

At that moment his wife entered the room. She was an

attractive strawberry-blonde, carefully groomed to a casual wind-ruffled look, and dressed in a silk shirt and loose linen trousers. She glanced at her husband, took in his leer at Kathy and walked over to the two officers to shake their hands.

'We're sorry to disturb you and your husband, Mrs Winter,' Kathy said. 'It must have been upsetting for you both.'

'Oh, yeah.' Like her husband, her accent was broad cockney, which she had made huskier over the years, especially with strangers. 'It was unexpected. Even though she was over seventy, she was always very lively. She was a real character.' The way she narrowed her eyes and pursed her lips might have been taken to mean that 'character' was the most charitable word she could find for her mother-in-law.

'I felt so helpless, too, when Eleanor phoned, not being able to find Terry, and then having to tell him such a dreadful thing over the phone, when he did eventually ring in.' She looked angelic as she laid this out so sweetly. Her husband's chair squeaked more loudly, and a frown passed briefly across his face.

'Your husband was out yesterday afternoon?' Kathy said easily, girl to girl.

'Yeah,' Terry Winter broke in. 'I often am on a Sunday afternoon. That's when I go round the salons, checking stock for the next week. It's the only chance I get.'

'What salons are those, sir?' Kathy asked.

'Victor Haircare. I franchise five salons in the south-east.'

'Oh yes, I know them.' Kathy smiled. 'That's where I go, on the Finchley Road.'

'No, that's not one of mine. Mine are all south of the river. Lewisham, Forest Hill, Peckham, New Cross and Deptford.'

'So you drive round all of those on a Sunday afternoon?'

'Yeah. The managers leave out their stock books for me and I order up for the next week. I don't let them do that.'

'What time did you leave home yesterday?'

'About 2.'

'More like 1.30, wasn't it, darling?'

Caroline smiled sympathetically at her husband, then turned to Brock. 'He works so hard.'

'Maybe,' said Terry, shrugging.

'And Eleanor phoned when?'

'Oh, about 5.30. There was a programme I'd been watching on holidays in the Pacific. It had just ended. Well, first I tried Terry's car phone, and there was no reply, so then I started phoning round all the salons. But there was no reply at any of them, either. I was getting really worried.' She turned to Kathy who noticed her startling violet eyes, and wondered whether she was wearing coloured contact lenses.

'I thought, what if Terry's had an accident, just at the time when his mother's had one too. Wouldn't that be just too awful?'

'I was at Deptford, the last one.' Terry's words cut across the end of her sentence. 'Before I went in I parked the car and went to the café next door for a cup of coffee. When I got through in the salon I got into the car and thought I'd better ring Caroline to let her know I was on my way.'

'At what time?'

Terry looked as if he was uncertain, but Caroline smoothly answered, 'Oh, well after 6. I was going round the twist. Well, I'd phoned all the numbers twice by this time and I didn't know what to do. I was on the point of calling the police, you know?'

'Oh Christ, Caroline, you're exaggerating. It wasn't that long.'

'So after you eventually spoke to your wife, sir, you turned directly back towards the City and went to your mother's house?'

'Yeah, sure.'

'Arriving there' – Kathy consulted her notebook – 'at 6.33.'

There was a moment's silence, and then Caroline got to her feet brightly. 'I'll make some tea,' she said. 'OK for everyone?'

Kathy got up too and said, 'I'll give you a hand, if that's all right. I'm always nosy to see other people's kitchens, actually.'

'Oh well, you've come to the wrong place then,' Caroline said as they went through a panelled connecting door. 'I'm about to have all this redone.'

Kathy looked around at the gleaming appliances and crisp white ranges of cupboards and units. 'Oh! It's beautiful.'

'No.' Caroline curled her lip. 'It's all wrong. I've never liked it much. There's much better equipment on the market now. And I'm going to have it all done in oak – to go with the house, you know?'

The worktop on the island unit in the middle of the room was covered with open magazines of kitchen designs, but there was no sign of food or recipe books.

Kathy looked round as the door from the hall clicked open and a young woman stood in the opening. She stared at Kathy in surprise.

'Oh, this is one of our two girls, Sergeant. Alex, say hello to the Sergeant – I'm sorry, I've forgotten your name.'

'Kolla. Kathy Kolla. Hello, Alex. How are you?'

The girl muttered something indistinct and ducked her head. Kathy judged her to be hardly out of her teens. Beneath thick spectacle lenses her eyes looked red and blotchy, and her mother went over to her, crooning sympathetically.

'All right, luv?' She turned to Kathy as she put an arm round her daughter's shoulder. 'She was really cut up about her gran, weren't you, luv?'

Kathy saw the girl wince under her mother's grip. She seemed the most unlikely of offspring for the Winters, physically awkward, socially uncomfortable and apparently

48

uninterested in her appearance. She stood for a moment, ungainly and morose while Caroline dug her long painted nails into her arm, then pulled away and ran back across the hall and up the stairs.

'She's upset.' Caroline screwed up her cute little nose. 'You don't need her, do you?'

In the living room, Terry got to his feet. At first it didn't look as if he knew why, then he pulled out a packet of cigarettes and offered one to Brock, who shook his head. Terry pulled out a small gold lighter and lit up, inhaling deeply on the first drag.

'This ain't easy,' he said. 'You can understand how someone feels when their mother's just died. Especially if people are suggesting she might have been murdered.'

'Of course,' Brock said. 'I remember when my mother died. She was in hospital. When I left I got on a bus to go home, and it reached the depot before I realized I'd gone in the opposite direction.'

Terry nodded.

'The Sergeant wasn't trying to be intrusive about her will,' Brock said, his brows knitted with concern. 'But it was a natural thing to wonder, when we heard the conditions. I suppose I might have been a bit annoyed with my old mum if she'd left me something, but then said in effect I couldn't have it for, well, who knows? Twenty, thirty years?'

Terry looked at him suspiciously. 'My aunts are entitled to feel some security at their time of life. I don't begrudge them that.'

'They're quite a formidable pair, your aunts, aren't they?' Brock said.

'Mad as hatters,' Caroline replied, bringing in the tea, and then, seeing the expression on her husband's face, corrected herself. 'No, they're sweeties really. I get on well with them, especially Peg. I think Eleanor disapproves of me sometimes.'

She giggled and poured out the tea.

6

As they were driving back into London against the evening tide of traffic, Dr Mehta came on the phone. 'I thought you might like a preliminary report, Brock.' The disembodied voice of the pathologist filled the car interior.

'How does it look?'

'Well, lots of nothing, frankly. First the heart. No significant narrowing of the coronary arteries, heart muscle healthy and no inflammation, no lesions of the heart valves, aortic valve in good shape.

'Then the brain. No arterial blockage, no intracerebral haemorrhage, no brain artery aneurysm, no subarachnoid haemorrhage, and no tumours, abscesses or other brain lesions.

'I'm still waiting for the chemical analyses, so some form of poisoning can't be ruled out at this stage, but I don't think it's likely.

'Of course there are other natural causes of sudden death. Anaphylaxis for instance. She could have had an acute reaction to some antigen she was sensitive to. There was no marked swelling of the lining of the larynx, however, or oedema of the lungs. I've spoken to her doctor again, and there's no history to suggest anaphylaxis, or for that matter epilepsy, asthma or insulin medication.

'Then there's smothering, say with the plastic bag your Sergeant found, if the tests match the swabs. All right, there were petechial haemorrhages on the lungs and the pericardial sac – Tardieu's spots – which certainly suggests terminal lack of oxygen, but not necessarily asphyxia – heart failure produces the same result. Again, the fluidity of the blood and some blue discoloration of the skin were also consistent with asphyxia, but blood fluidity and cyanosis aren't certain tests, either.

'So, as things stand, I couldn't say that she died of asphyxia, only that the evidence is consistent with it. As you know, Brock, in about ten per cent of cases we see we simply cannot establish a cause of death from the forensic evidence. I think this may be one of those.'

'Ten per cent!' Kathy exclaimed.

There was a momentary pause while Mehta identified her voice, and then he crackled back, 'Yes, Sergeant. Any experienced pathologist will tell you the same: no cause of death can be demonstrated either anatomically or by toxicological analysis in approaching one in ten cases. If they tell you otherwise, then they're making guesses not justified by the evidence.'

'Sundeep,' Brock said, 'if she was smothered by the plastic bag, how long would she take to die, and wouldn't she have shown signs of a struggle?'

'Not necessarily. Do you have Jaffe's *Guide to Pathological Evidence for Lawyers and Police Officers* in your office?'

'Yes, I'm sure we do.'

'Well, there's a photograph in there of a young woman who died by accident, while she was on the phone, when a plastic bag accidentally slipped over her face. A simple lack of oxygen isn't distressful. If it's sudden, unconsciousness comes very quickly. What is distressing in choking, say, or smothering, is when the exhalation of carbon dioxide is prevented. That's what causes the panic we imagine with that kind of death. I'll get back to you when the test results are available, but I think the coroner will have to reach a decision on this one without me.'

'Thanks, Sundeep.'

When he'd rung off, Brock added, 'Cagey as always. Still, it looks as if you were right, Kathy.'

'Yes.' She sat in silence for a moment and then said quietly, 'I'd like to phone DC Mollineaux, sir. Get him to check that Terry Winter had a cup of coffee in the café next to his salon in Deptford, as he said. Then he can start interviewing the managers of each of the salons to see whether they can produce any of the paperwork Winter's supposed to have done over the weekend.'

'You didn't like him?'

'No, I didn't. I thought he was full of himself. But worse than that, I thought he was the sort of man who expected to get his own way with women, and wouldn't think twice about lying, or if necessary using violence, to make sure he did.'

She spoke quietly, but with an intensity which made Brock glance across at her.

'Can you tell?'

'His wife had what looked to me like bruising around her left eye.'

'Really? I didn't notice.'

'She'd pretty well covered it up with her make-up, and the swelling had mostly gone down, but when I was near her in the kitchen I spotted it.'

'Hmm. You may be right. Anyway, you can relax tonight and feel reasonably satisfied.

'I hope he's taking you somewhere nice,' he added.

She looked sidelong at him and said nothing at first. Then, as she picked up the phone and started to press in the numbers she replied, 'I'm taking *him* somewhere nice, actually. It's his birthday.'

'Ah, lucky chap,' Brock murmured, switching on the windscreen wipers and apparently concentrating on weaving through the traffic on the approaches to Waterloo Bridge.

He dropped her off outside Charing Cross Station and continued on down Whitehall towards the Yard. Kathy went into the entrance to the station and took the stairs down to the tube. They had got back into town earlier than she had expected, and the corridors were crowded with home-going commuters. She took the Northern Line northbound, but instead of continuing all the way to her home stop at Finchley Central, suddenly changed her mind after Tottenham Court Road and got off the train at the next stop. It was dark when she reached the street, the shop lights reflecting from wet pavements. By the entrance to the Underground a news vendor was pulling a clear plastic sheet down over one end of his stall to protect it from the cold drizzle which was beginning to blow in earnest from the east.

Jerusalem Lane was deserted. The two lamps which served as street lighting for its length had just switched on, giving an ineffectual dim white light as they struggled to warm up. The shop fronts at this north end of the Lane were all in darkness, and any lights in occupied upstairs rooms were heavily curtained against the night. Kathy thought of the Doré etching in Hepple's office, with its teeming mass of humanity seething down this street. All ghosts now.

She walked towards the door of Hepple's office, and was rewarded by the reflected glow of the windows of the Balaton Café, facing into the little square ahead, and the smell of cooking. There were two front doors beside the brass plate, one for the solicitor's office, and the other for Sylvia Pemberton's flat. Kathy pressed the buzzer beside the second. After a moment an unrecognizable squawk came from a small speaker on the wall.

'It's Kathy Kolla, Miss Pemberton, from the police. We met this morning. Could I trouble you again for a minute?'

Another squawk came from the box and the front door gave a click. Kathy pushed and went in. The stairs rose in front of her in two straight flights to the second floor, where Sylvia Pemberton stood waiting for her.

She left her wet coat in the hall and they went into a snug sitting room, filled with furniture as ample as their owner.

'I'd just settled down with my usual G and T, wondering whether to chance the Balaton's goulash or put up with frozen chicken in front of the TV, so I'm very pleased to be intruded upon. I'll call you Kathy, shall I? Sergeant seems rather formal in front of your own gas fire, don't you think? And I'm Sylvia. Let me pour you one. It doesn't taste the same if you're with someone who isn't drinking, and you're not going to arrest me, are you? Not yet, anyway.' She roared with laughter. Relaxed, her cheeks rosy with the heat of the fire and the gin, she seemed larger than life.

'It was something you started to say this morning, Sylvia,' Kathy began, easing back into the plump cushions carefully so as not to spill anything from the generously filled glass. 'Just as Mr Hepple arrived. Something about the way the neighbourhood was going downhill or something. I just wondered what you meant.'

'Ah, yes. It's been in the back of my mind for months, and poor Meredith Winterbottom going like that just seemed to bring it all into focus. The place is changing, and the weird thing is that nobody seems to have noticed it. I mean normally the slightest thing happening in the Lane would go round like wildfire. But over the past year things have been going on that seemed ... well, reasonable enough on their own, but taken together ...'

'What sort of things?'

'Well, the most obvious were the Kowalskis selling up and moving away, and then Mr Hepple deciding to sell this place too. They both have long connections with the Lane, and two of them closing down is a big change for this area, which has really been very stable in the past. Then there's Konrad Witz going too, and on top of all that, lots of smaller things I noticed. I do the books for several businesses around here, so I get to know how things are going, and everyone has been doing reasonably well lately, certainly no worse than before. But I noticed odd things.

'First, Brunhilde Capek cancelled her plans to renovate her flower shop. Now she'd been going on about it for so long, and at last had actually got a builder ready, that I couldn't believe she'd changed her mind. She said she'd run into some problems with the council over the drains, but I didn't see how that would stop the whole thing.

'A bit later I noticed that a couple of places seemed to be running down their stock. And then when I did Stwosz's books last year I saw he'd started paying rent, even though he owned the place before. When I asked him, it turned out he'd sold his shop, and was leasing it back. But he didn't really want to discuss it. Like Mr Hepple or Adam Kowalski, when you ask why, they explain it in terms which make sense for them, which is fair enough, because they're all getting older. But so many, all at once . . .'

'I see. Yes, that is odd. Mr Hepple did mention that he was closing down here, but he didn't say anything about the others.'

'No, well . . .' Sylvia Pemberton hesitated, then said, 'Actually, he's not all that keen to talk about it, I've found. He even told me at one point not to discuss the matter with anyone in the Lane. But they're all the same. Everyone's been so secretive, keeping it all to themselves, and even more peculiar, they're not much concerned at what the others are up to, and that just isn't like the Lane at all. It's almost as if everyone had just suddenly lost interest in the place.'

'What about Mrs Winterbottom, was she considering selling?'

'Not as far as I know. I didn't do her books – she still goes to the accountant her husband had when he was alive. But she often used to have a chat to me about things she was considering, and ask my opinion.'

'What would have been the most recent things she talked to you about?'

Sylvia Pemberton sipped her drink, thinking, and then suddenly chuckled.

'Oh well, I remember one day, maybe six months ago, or perhaps longer, we stopped and had a chat in the street. I asked how her son and his family were. She was ever so proud of them. The older granddaughter, Alex, was doing very well at university, and Louise getting ready for her O levels. And Terry, her son – oh, he was doing so well, running five hairdressing salons in South London, and he and his wife were going off for a wonderful holiday to some place in the Indian Ocean, or something. Only Terry has cash-flow problems, Meredith explains, like all successful businessmen do, because they're maximizing their resources. This is what she tells me, and it's obvious they're Terry's words. So Terry has suggested to his old mother that it would be an excellent idea all round if she would mortgage her house in the Lane, and lend him the money so as to ease these temporary cash-flow problems.'

Sylvia roared with laughter.

'She looks at me carefully after she's told me this, and says what do I think? Well, I told her. Let Terry look after his own cash-flow problems, and keep the house free of debt, the way her husband left it to her. She seemed quite relieved, I think. It had been worrying her.'

'Someone else said that Meredith had seemed worried about something lately. Would that be the reason, do you think?'

'I don't know, Kathy. I hadn't really seen so much of her lately, to speak to. She seemed to keep a bit more to herself.'

'Did everyone like her really, Sylvia? I mean, after someone dies, everyone says nice things about them, but no one gets through a lifetime without falling out with a few people. Particularly in a close-knit street like this, I should think.'

'Well, Meredith was a very gregarious sort of person, and couldn't help herself getting involved in other people's lives, especially if they were in trouble and needed a helping hand. I suppose sometimes people like that are a bit annoying. I mean, when you're not in trouble they still like to come round and organize you. I can still remember one day ages ago when Mr Hepple offered to take Meredith and me out to the new shopping centre at Brent Cross for the afternoon. As soon as we drove off she started, "Oh, you'd go this way to Euston Road, would you, Mr Hepple?" and "Turn left here, George" and "I always think the Edgware Road is better than the Finchley Road, but you know best, I suppose". Mr Hepple didn't say a word, but when we got home, he said to me, "She's a wonderful woman in many ways, Sylvia, but that is the first and last time that I will ever have her in my car."'

Kathy joined Sylvia's laughter. 'Yes, I have an uncle like that.'

'Top you up, Kathy? Yes, come on, you're not driving and you're off duty now. As I said, I don't mind drinking alone, but it feels bad to drink with someone who isn't.'

'All right.' It had been a long day, and more of a strain doing it with Brock alongside her than she'd realized. 'Just a small one, though, Sylvia. I have to go out tonight.'

'Oh. Someone nice?'

'I think so.'

'Lucky you. Maybe he's got a nice older brother going spare. Actually, I don't think I'd know what to do with one any more.' They laughed again. 'No, I'm looking forward to moving down to Tonbridge when Hepple, Tyas & Turton closes down. I've got friends down there who play eighteen holes every day, 365 days a year, rain, hail or shine.'

Kathy smiled, visualizing four ladies of Sylvia's build ploughing round the fairways, year after year.

'You won't miss this place?'

'Oh yes, but time for a change.'

'Did Meredith ever have a more serious tiff with anyone, though?'

Sylvia thought. 'I suppose the thing with Adam Kowalski did get a bit tense. Have you met him? No. Well, they've gone now, although I did see him up here at the weekend, come to think of it. Still clearing things from his shop, I suppose.

'Anyway, it was a day when some royalty or other was getting married or something, and there was a street party in Jerusalem Lane. The bunting was out, and there was music and they were doing their polkas and mazurkas out there in the square. Meredith was talking to Marie Kowalski, Adam's wife, who I think might have had one or two vodkas. Anyway, Meredith was going on about how wonderful her granddaughters were, with Alex going to university, and Marie comes out with the fact that at one time Adam had been the youngest and most brilliant professor in the University of Cracow, which was the second-oldest university in Europe, or something like that. So Meredith says, why is he selling second-hand books now then, and Marie says that he had been made professor just before the war, but during the war terrible things happened, and afterwards things were such a mess, he never got back to the university, he had enemies in the new government, and eventually they left and came over here.'

'Well, of course Meredith wouldn't leave it at that. She says, well, if he's such a brilliant scientist or whatever he was, he should have been in a university here, and his talents should have been recognized. She started talking about writing to the newspapers about it. Well, Marie started to get worried at this point apparently, and tried to get Meredith to let it alone, but Meredith starts saying how she'll get Mr Hepple to have a word with a judge he knows who's the chancellor of some university or other.

'Well, eventually, when Marie can see that things are getting out of hand, she confesses to Meredith that the reason Adam was kicked out of the university was that during the war he'd been forced to collaborate with the Germans. Apparently they had told him that either he collaborate with them or else Marie would be taken away to the camps, and so all through the war he had been reporting to the Gestapo on his students.'

'Oh my God.'

'Yes. After the war the Poles didn't punish him, but he found he couldn't get work, and the whole family was completely ostracized. It's a very sad story. But the terrible thing was that Meredith still wouldn't leave it alone. She thought it was shocking that they should go on being punished for something that had happened so long ago. She wanted to get him the recognition he deserved for his early genius, and started telling the story to other people. Adam was appalled. I mean, it might seem like it happened a long time ago to us, but to some of the people here, it's still very fresh. Mrs Rosenfeldt, for instance, she was in Auschwitz. She lost all her family there. The Kowalskis had come here to escape from everyone who knew their story, and now Meredith was opening it all up again. It must have seemed like a nightmare. Adam was devastated. He pleaded with her to be quiet. I believe he threatened her, too. Her sisters came to her defence, and then his friends pitched in.'

'The Croatia Club?'

'Yes, Konrad Witz mainly, who had the camera shop on the corner up by the tube station, and other old drinking mates. They were a bit abusive to the sisters for a while, I believe.'

'Mrs Rosenfeldt called them Nazis.'

'Oh, no. I mean most of the people who have come here since the war have been running away from communist countries, so they don't like Peg and Eleanor's politics, but they don't go around painting swastikas on the synagogue or anything like that! But they are a funny lot, you know, so intense. They'd give each other their last pound, and then have a raging argument over some crown prince or general or something who died fifty years ago. They forget nothing. Did Mrs Rosenfeldt tell you about her dog?'

'No, I didn't know she has one.'

'She hasn't, not for twenty years. But the story of Mrs Rosenfeldt's dog is one of the sagas of the Lane. Are you sure you want to hear it?'

Kathy smiled. 'Go on.'

'Mrs Rosenfeldt has been here longer than anyone. She met her husband in one of those refugee camps after the war and they came over here soon after, so by the time the others arrived, the ones escaping from the communists, she'd already been here a good few years. I can remember her quite well when I first started to work here for Mr Hepple, in 1969. She was a widow by that stage, and she used to walk up and down the Lane, chatting to everyone, pretty much as if she owned the place, and with her she would take her dog. He was one of those little pugs, you know? The kind that looks as if it's walked into a brick wall.

'It was a snappy little beast, and it seemed to have a knack of sharing its owner's prejudices about people, giving the ones that Mrs Rosenfeldt didn't like a hard time. It would bark at them and bite their heels, and leave little messages on their doorsteps. Mr Witz especially. It used to drive him mad, stepping out of his shop and straight into one of the dog's little messages. Well, one day someone left a message for Mrs Rosenfeldt. She opened the shop door one morning, and there was the dog, dead. It might have been run over, but Mr Stwosz next door saw it, and he said it looked more like as if someone had whacked it, here' – she pointed to her forehead – 'with a hammer. Poor Mrs Rosenfeldt. Everyone felt terrible for her, although there weren't many people sorry to see the back of the dog.'

'Who did it?'

'No one knows. Mrs Rosenfeldt didn't make a fuss or anything. She didn't accuse anyone, and she didn't let anyone see that she was upset. But she was much quieter after that, and stayed indoors more.'

Kathy nodded. 'Nasty. What about the other problem, Sylvia, between Meredith and the Kowalskis? How long ago did that happen?'

'Last year, I think. When Prince whatsisname got married. The time goes by so quickly now.'

Kathy left soon after, and made her way back to the tube feeling considerably more relaxed than when she had arrived. When she stepped through the front door of her flat, the light on the answering machine was blinking. She replayed the message, swore, stomped into the kitchen and slammed a frozen chicken dinner into the microwave.

7

Brock's home phone rang just after 7 the next morning. It was Kathy.

'Sir, I'm sorry but I just looked in my diary and realized I'm supposed to be giving evidence in court this morning. With everything going on yesterday I just forgot all about it. I should be through by 11.'

'Not to worry. I've got some things I could be doing at the Yard. Anything you want me to follow up for you?'

'Well, I went back and spoke to Sylvia Pemberton, the solicitor's secretary, on the way home last night, and there are a couple of things we could follow up.'

She outlined Sylvia's account of property changes in the Lane, and of Meredith Winterbottom's falling out with the Kowalskis and their friends.

'All right, I'll see what I can find out. Get an officer to ring me at the Yard when you're called, and I'll come over and pick you up.'

When he arrived in the office at 9, Brock phoned George Hepple at his Croydon office, leaving a message for him to return the call when he arrived. He rang back shortly before 10.

'Sorry to bother you again, Mr Hepple. It occurred to us that with you and the Kowalskis selling up, there might be other property movements going on in Jerusalem Lane. Are you aware of any?'

There was a pause.

'Yes. I don't think it's any secret that there is, in point of fact, a proposal for some redevelopment in the Jerusalem Lane area before the council planning committee at this moment.'

'A council development?'

'No, it is a commercial project, by a private development company. Do you want their name?'

'Yes please.'

Again a pause.

'First City Properties.'

'How many properties in the block have changed hands over the past few years, would you say, Mr Hepple?'

'I really couldn't say, Chief Inspector.'

The solicitor seemed considerably less loquacious this morning.

'An estimate. Ten per cent?' Silence. 'Fifty?' More silence. 'Ninety?'

'I'm sorry, I really can't say,' the solicitor said at last. 'I think you will find that quite a few residents of the area, getting older, have decided to take advantage of a buoyant property market to retire elsewhere.'

'I see. And Mrs Winterbottom? Had she considered such a move?'

The solicitor's conversational speed seemed stuck in its slowest gear. There was another pause while he considered the question.

'She had considered it, yes.'

'She sought your advice?'

'No.'

'You gave her advice?'

'I really don't think this is of any relevance to your inquiries, Chief Inspector. Any such conversations between Mrs Winterbottom and myself are a private matter.'

'No, Mr Hepple, they are not. And the coroner I think will take the same view when an inquest is held. However, I believe you've answered my question. Good morning.'

The phone went down at the other end without a reply.

Brock tucked himself into a corner between a sandstone wall and a cluster of pink granite columns which carried the ribs of a Victorian Gothic vaulted ceiling. He kept out of the way of the streams of people hurrying across the echoing hall to the various waiting rooms and the courts. After ten minutes he saw Kathy emerge from a corridor on the far side of the hall, then pause to talk intently to a man in a pinstripe suit. Brock didn't recognize her at first. The fair hair which she had worn yesterday drawn back into a band was now brushed loose. She was wearing a smart black houndstooth jacket and short black slim skirt, and he had taken her for a solicitor or officer of the court.

The man she was talking to had his back to Brock, who could make out thick dark hair curling over a white collar. The man was relaxed, poised, in contrast to Kathy, who seemed agitated, her hands gesturing impatiently. All the same, Brock thought, with some little stab of envy, they made a fine-looking couple. Young, fit, confident, vigorous . . . His left shoulder, which had been giving him trouble off and on for years, chose this moment to get cramp. He groaned, straightened away from the cold stone and reached over with his right hand to massage the pain.

Kathy was shaking her head, and suddenly the man reached down and took hold of her hand and held it. He half turned towards Brock, who could see that the face, though handsome and intelligent, was not quite as young as the thick hair and well-tailored figure had suggested from the back. There was a slight chubbiness about the jowls and under the eyes, and lines around the mouth.

'Martin Francis Connell,' Brock muttered to himself. 'Solicitor, squash player, father of four. Married to Lynne Connell, daughter of Judge Willoughby.'

He eased himself out from his niche and walked quickly down the broad flight of grey granite steps to wait for Kathy outside in the sunshine.

'How'd it go?'

'Oh fine. Formality, really. Where are we going?' Kathy asked.

'Mayfair. To the offices of First City Properties. It seems they've bought up most of Jerusalem Lane, one way or another, over the past couple of years. Oh, and Detective Constable Mollineaux seems to have been doing a good job stirring up Terry Winter. He phoned demanding to know why Mollineaux was pestering his managers, and when I told him, he went rather quiet and asked if he could see us again. I said we'd see him at your office at 3.'

'Great. I've a feeling we're going to nail him.'

She said it with some vehemence, and Brock glanced across at her.

'Possibly, but not necessarily for doing in his old mum. And how did your dinner go last night?'

'Oh.' Kathy stared balefully ahead at the traffic. 'It didn't. Something came up.'

'Sorry. Nothing serious?'

She shot him a look which made him grunt and change the subject.

'Fill me in on Adam Kowalski, then. A collaborator, you said?'

Kathy nodded and began to fill out the brief account she'd given Brock over the phone.

The plate-glass door to the developers' offices had no handle and was locked. As they pushed it tentatively, a female voice issuing from the chrome grille in the marble wall panel instructed them to enter.

The door slid open, revealing a small marble-lined lobby. Ahead of them was a narrow, open lift. They got inside and eyed themselves in its smoky glass walls as it rose to an upper floor. Reception was lined with the same dark marble. Its impressively sombre effect was spoilt by the display on the walls of some rather garish watercolour impressions of modern office blocks. A young woman sat at a large toughened glass table, her long legs crossed beneath a surface on which nothing much appeared to be happening. She looked as if she wasn't long out of some expensive private school.

She eyed them coolly, like a face from the cover of *Vogue*.

'Mr Slade's secretary will be along in a moment. Would you like to take a seat?'

Brock and Kathy subsided into soft black leather cushions. Recessed downlighters in the smoky silvered ceiling picked them out in pools of light, so that they felt like scruffy artefacts on exhibition in an upmarket gallery. Copies of *The Estates Gazette* bound in clear perspex covers were to hand on glass side tables.

Mr Slade's secretary was considerably more mature and more functional than the receptionist. She led them down a timber-panelled corridor and knocked at an unmarked door.

'Come.'

Derek Slade was in his shirtsleeves, his tie loosened at his neck. He was a powerful-looking man in his mid-thirties, who looked each of them directly in the eye, shook hands firmly, sat them down courteously and ordered coffee.

'Have we met before, Chief Inspector? Your face looks familiar. No? Well, this is an unusual visit.' His voice managed to sound both circumspect and quietly forceful. 'I don't believe I've ever been interviewed by detectives from Scotland Yard before.'

Both Kathy and Brock were trying to process his accent in the automatic English way, without success. It seemed both classless and placeless.

'Yes. Thank you for seeing us so promptly, sir,' Brock led off. 'We're conducting inquiries into a possible murder, and you may be able to give us some background information on the circumstances of the victim.'

'Really? Is it someone I know?'

'Meredith Winterbottom.'

Slade looked puzzled, 'I don't think the name rings a bell.'

'Of 22 Jerusalem Lane, WC2.'

Slade's expression didn't change. He just stared for a moment at Brock.

At that moment the phone at his elbow burbled discreetly. He lifted it.

'No calls, Valerie . . . Oh? All right, I'll speak to him.' He smiled apologetically at Brock. After a brief exchange he hung up.

'My solicitor. A colleague of his wanted to warn me that you might be calling on me. Intriguing. So, how can I help?'

'We understand,' Kathy said, 'that your company has been buying property in the area of Jerusalem Lane. Can you tell us how much of the block you've actually acquired to date?'

Slade frowned. 'We have agents who act for us in property acquisitions. If you want to talk about that, I would prefer to have them present.'

'Oh, is that necessary? Surely you would know which properties you actually own?'

'They act under our instructions, but we may not have a complete record of transactions to date here in this office. If you want an accurate picture I'd really prefer to get them in. They're only round the corner – Jonathan Hockings.'

'You think Mr Hockings might be available?' Kathy asked.

Slade smiled at her. 'Jonathan Hockings are the company. You've probably seen the name on letting boards. They're an international firm. Their Quentin Gilroy works for us. I'll try him.'

He picked up the phone and placed the call through his secretary. Gilroy was available, and promised to come round immediately.

As they sipped their coffee, a look of recognition suddenly came over Slade's face.

'Brock! Of course. You were in charge of that recent shooting case, weren't you? That's where I've seen your face. On TV.' He smiled and sat back in his chair staring at Brock appraisingly.

'Look, could I have your autograph for my son? He was following it all.'

Brock dutifully took the offered pen and notepaper and wrote, 'Best wishes from Detective Chief Inspector David Brock, Scotland Yard.'

'Splendid. Could you maybe put his name at the top – to William Slade?'

As he added this, Brock said, 'I understand you're planning a bit of development around Jerusalem Lane, Mr Slade?'

Slade gave a little smile. 'You might say that. Come, I'll show you.'

They went through the secretary's connecting office to a long, windowless room with a boardroom table. At one end stood a large architectural model. Three granite-clad towers with pyramid roofs, ranging from fifteen to twenty-five storeys in height, stood in a landscaped plaza.

Slade gestured with open hand: 'Jerusalem Lane, mark two.'

'Good God!' Kathy exclaimed. 'Where's the Lane?'

'We've kept the name in a bistro planned in the podium here.' Slade pointed. 'Sunlight, space and greenery. Like the squares of Georgian London. Well, the Prince won't think so. All the same, a big improvement on what's there at the moment, yes?'

At that moment the door opened and a tall young man stepped soundlessly into the room. 'Derek,' he murmured, and then shook the others' hands as Slade introduced them.

'This is the famous Inspector Brock, Quentin. You remember? That shooting of those policemen.'

'Oh, right, yes.' The young man smiled languidly at Brock. He had the casual assurance of a public school education and three years at Oxford, and the sharp eyes of a dozen years in real estate.

'Have you come across a Mrs Longbottom, Quentin?'

'Winterbottom,' Kathy corrected.

'Believe I may, Derek. Jerusalem Lane?' He nodded at the model.

'Right. Seems the lady is deceased, and the Inspector is interested. Any clues?'

'Last spoke to her about four months ago, I'd say. Not interested in selling, I'm afraid. It's in the monthly print-outs.'

'How much of the block does First City actually own now?' Brock asked the agent.

Gilroy raised an eyebrow at Slade, who nodded.

'Pretty much all of it, number 22 excepted. And 83–87 Carlisle Street is still with the lawyers. Braithwaite's still playing silly buggers, Derek. I've told him to get his bloody finger out, but he's the same as always. I think you should give him a blast. The synagogue's still in limbo, but it seems pretty certain now that the Minister will declassify it.'

'But surely,' Kathy broke in, 'if 22 doesn't sell, the whole thing will be stopped.'

Slade smiled indulgently at her. He reached across to the model and lifted out a small section of the podium near the base of the tallest tower. 'Phase five,' he said. Beneath the removed section was the outline of the plan of 22 Jerusalem Lane. 'They can stay if they want. Of course it'll be a worthless piece of real estate if they do. Unsaleable.

'You have to understand,' he continued, fixing Brock with his unblinking eyes, 'that this has been the outcome of a long and painstaking process. The key to the redevelopment of this run-down area of London has been land ownership. For hundreds of years no one has been able to assemble the land to redevelop it. Now we have. It's taken a long time. We bought our first property in this block thirty years ago, and we've hung on to it through boom and bust, and gradually added to it and waited until within the last year the whole block matured like a ripe fruit, ready to go. I didn't know Mrs Winterbottom, and I'm sorry to hear about her death, but her decision wasn't going to make any difference to this development, one way or the other.'

'Couldn't she have objected to your planning application?' Kathy asked.

Slade shrugged. 'As I said, it would have made no difference.'

'Mr Gilroy,' Brock said, 'who else have you negotiated with over number 22, apart from Mrs Winterbottom?'

Again the agent looked to Slade, who gave an imperceptible nod.

'I did speak to the family solicitor. I thought he might have been able to help Mrs Winterbottom to get a balanced view of the advantages of our offer.'

'And her son, Mr Terry Winter?'

'Yes, the solicitor mentioned him. I had a word with him on the phone one day. Didn't do much good, though.'

'But he was receptive to your proposals?'

'He listened to what I had to say.'

'May I ask what you were prepared to pay for number 22?'

'Do you recall, Quentin, or do you need to look it up?'

'No, Derek, I do remember. We offered Mrs Winterbottom two hundred K. I believe I indicated to Mr Winter that we might go to a quarter million.'

As they stepped out through the sliding glass door on to the street, Kathy took a deep breath. 'Poor Meredith,' she said, 'and poor Peg and Eleanor.'

8

Terry Winter was waiting for them in an interview room when they got to divisional headquarters. He looked sulky.

Kathy began, her face expressionless, voice neutral. 'Well, Mr Winter, what can we do for you?'

'I wondered if there were any developments.'

'Oh we've made some progress. We believe that your mother did die of asphyxia. And we've discovered that you didn't have a cup of coffee in the place next to your Deptford salon, as you informed us yesterday.'

Winter rocked a little in his seat and blinked. 'Yeah,' he said hoarsely. 'Well, that's what I came here to talk to you about, wasn't it?'

'Could you speak up, sir? Just so we don't miss anything.'

'Look, I didn't tell you the exact truth yesterday.' He spoke aggressively. 'I was in sort of a difficult position.' He shrugged, as if that explained it.

'Go on.'

'I spent most of Sunday afternoon with a friend ... a woman friend. My wife doesn't know.' He tried to address himself to Brock, but the Chief Inspector had opened a newspaper and appeared to be ignoring the proceedings.

'Yes,' Kathy said without any hint of surprise. She thumbed through a file of papers on the table in front of her, as if the whole sorry mess had already been written up. 'Name?'

'Is ... is it going to be necessary for this to come out?'

'Is she married?'

'No, divorced. I was thinking of my wife.' His voice tailed away. He swallowed. 'Could I have some water?'

Kathy poured him a glass. He took a gulp. 'Can I smoke?'

'No. I'd rather you didn't. It's these new smoke-free zones, you know.'

'Jesus.' He shook his head and shoved the packet back into his jacket pocket. 'Her name's Geraldine McArthur. She's the manager of my New Cross salon.'

'You were with her between what times?'

'From about 2.15 till around 6.'

'Can anyone else vouch for that?'

'No. No, I don't think so. We were alone in her flat near the salon at first. Then we went out for a drive in the Merc, up to Greenwich. We took a walk in the park, but I don't remember seeing anyone in particular there. We returned to her place for a cup of tea, then I left.'

'No one phoned her while you were in her flat?'

He shook his head. He was fingering the gold chain round his wrist impatiently.

'And you've discussed this with her, and told her you were coming to see us?'

'Yes.'

'All right. We'd better get her over here straight away. Where will she be?'

Winter gave Kathy a phone number and she left the room. They waited in silence, Brock slowly scanning the pages of his newspaper, until Kathy returned with a young woman constable.

'We're going to videotape you. Is that OK?'

'I suppose . . .'

'Fairly normal now. Just to make sure we get it right. Now, you realize that, having lied to us once, you have now given us an explanation of your movements during the afternoon your mother died which depends on one other witness, with whom you have since had the opportunity to collude, and with no likelihood of corroborating evidence. So' – Kathy sighed and put her papers to one side – 'the only way we can test your statement is to take a detailed account from you and another from Ms McArthur, and see if they match.'

'I've told you what we did . . .'

'I said a *detailed* account, Mr Winter, minute by minute, of what you did. Who did what, to whom, in what order, and for how long.'

Winter stared at her, startled. He glanced at the police-woman in the corner, head down, writing furiously, and at Brock who turned the page of his newspaper absently.

'You're not serious!' Winter was agitated, his fingers working overtime.

'Only way, sir. So let's get on with it. You arrived in your car at what time?'

Winter began haltingly with the innocuous details of his arrival. He described parking the car round the corner because it was so conspicuous among the wrecks in her street, the walk to her front door, how many times he rang the bell, the sound of her footsteps running to the door. His attempt to maintain a neutral flow of words was disturbed by vivid pictures of what he was describing – Geraldine's face glowing with pleasure at his arrival, her arms around his neck.

'Was that before or after you closed the front door?'

'After.'

'Then?'

Pause.

'I said, "Let's go to bed."' There was an edge of defiance in his voice.

'You said, or she said?'

'She said.'

'You first said that you said it.'

'No.' Confusion. 'No, she said it.'

'Then?'

'We went into the bedroom. Geraldine drew the curtains. We got undressed.'

'Did you undress each other, or what?'

'No. Each on our own side of the bed. Quickly.'

'Did you put your clothes on a chair? What were you each wearing?'

Winter was becoming flustered, but he stuck gamely to his account, the mental images of private passion so at odds with this drab room and his indifferent questioners that he kept losing the thread. He saw his lover's naked belly, smelled her perfume. He lifted the glass of water again and saw that his hand was trembling.

'And then we made love.'

'How?'

'What?'

'How did you do it? What position?'

'I don't know, several.'

'You made love several times?'

'No, once. But we had several . . . positions.'

'Describe them.'

'Well . . . to begin with face to face . . . then later, her on top.'

'Did you have oral sex?'

'Yes . . . no, I don't know.'

'You don't remember?'

'No . . . I can't remember.'

Kathy raised her eyebrows incredulously. 'What about anal sex then? Do you remember that?'

Winter's face had turned bright red and there were drops of sweat on his forehead. He turned to appeal to Brock, but he was now engrossed in the crossword.

'No, certainly not that, because . . .'

'Because?'

His jaw was clenched tight and for a moment it looked as if he might explode. Then he burst out, 'Because we used to do that, but we had to stop after Geraldine saw the doctor.'

His chest was heaving, his eyes fixed on the floor. But what he saw was not the grey sheet-plastic flooring, but the look on Geraldine's face when she had told him that time that it was hurting.

'All right, Mr Winter.' Kathy's voice was mild, reassuring. 'Don't worry. You're doing fine. Just have a little break. Have another drink of water. Perhaps you'd like tea, no?'

They started again, patiently opening up Winter's Sunday afternoon, moment by moment. They discovered the form of contraception used, whether Ms McArthur was having her period, and what colour the pillows were. Then they moved from the bedroom to the bathroom, to the kitchen and the lounge.

An hour after he had arrived at his girlfriend's flat, the two had gone out to his car and driven to Greenwich. They walked through the park, where there might or might not have been small boys playing football on the grass, families picnicking beneath the trees and tourists queuing to see the Queen's House. They established that the affair had been going on for six months, and that the Sunday afternoon assignation had been a regular event for over four. The only questions which Winter evaded concerned the future – whether he was intending to divorce his wife and marry his lover.

'I don't see the relevance of that,' he said.

'It would be expensive, wouldn't it? That nice house in Chislehurst, the cars, the overseas trips, maybe some of the business. You'd lose quite a bit.'

Winter shook his head and shrugged. 'I don't know. It could all be worked out.'

'You think your wife would be reasonable, do you?'

Winter looked queasy.

'When did you suggest to your mother that she mortgage her house and lend you the money?'

For a moment Kathy thought Winter was going to pass out. His expression was stunned, his eyes unfocused. Then he recovered himself and gasped, shaking his head.

'That ... that was nothing to do with this. After I

opened the fifth salon last year, I needed extra cash. It was just a suggestion to Mum, in passing. It wasn't serious.'

'Well, she seemed to have taken it very seriously. She was very worried about it.'

'I . . . I didn't know.'

'Yes, well perhaps you'd know what had been worrying her lately?'

'Lately?'

'Yes. She was worried, depressed about something. For the past three or four months, maybe longer. She'd been getting antidepressants from the doctor.'

'I had no idea. Really, I didn't know. She never said.'

'Maybe you'd been putting pressure on her to sell her house.'

'Dear God, no.' Winter bowed his head, his hands between his knees, palms together, and began to rock back and forward.

'Come on, Mr Winter. You wanted her to sell the house, didn't you?'

'Yes, yes. I wanted her to get rid of that place. It was always needing maintenance. It needs rewiring. The roof needs complete reslating. I wanted her to get a nice little place on one level she could cope with. A modern flat with central heating. Maybe nearer to us. She had got a good offer. And her solicitor told me that everyone was selling up and leaving there. She would be left there in the middle of a building site. It was crazy.'

'And did the agent for First Properties also tell you that if she didn't sell soon, the place might end up being unsaleable?'

Winter looked at her with a mixture of grief and despair on his face.

'Yes,' he whispered, 'he told me that.'

Winter was taken out to wait in another room while they interviewed Geraldine McArthur.

Brock got to his feet and stretched. He groaned. 'Oh dear. I need a coffee before we get on to her. The things we have to do! I'm glad I had a decent breakfast this morning. I couldn't have stood that on an empty stomach.'

'You think I was too rough on him, sir?'

'No, no. Exactly what he deserved, really. You wonder why he bothers, don't you?'

'How do you mean?'

'Well, hauling himself off every Sunday afternoon to bed down with some woman whose every bump and wrinkle must be as familiar as his wife's by this stage. I mean if he can't even remember the next day whether she gave his dick a suck – sorry, Constable.' The WPC in the corner smiled and stirred her coffee. 'You can understand it at first, the excitement, the irresistible temptation, showing off in a big flashy car to some impressionable girl, but by this stage it must be getting a bit of a chore. And it's going to cost him plenty, one way or another. Probably already has – that new kitchen, for instance.'

'You think the wife knows?'

Brock shrugged. 'I mean, I know I'm getting old, but where's the point at this stage? I suppose the other woman must have her claws sunk deep into him.' Kathy opened her mouth to object, but Brock carried on. 'What do you reckon she's like? Have to be a stunner, I suppose. Glamorous.'

'That's a bit of a stereotype, isn't it?' Kathy realized she sounded irritable.

'Yes, maybe. "The other woman." Could be an intelligent, sensible, attractive woman like ... well, like you, Kathy.' Brock ploughed on, relentless, pretending not to see the look on her face. 'But unlikely. Why would such a woman go for a sleazy married man like Terry? Almost bound to be some glamorous, vain young thing. Hairdressing salon manageress. All hair and boobs. Let's take a bet on it.'

Brock lost his bet. Ms Geraldine McArthur was older than Caroline Winter, and not nearly as striking. She had a wide mouth with a generous smile, and wore her dark brown hair in a plain straight bob. She was obviously very worried, but more self-possessed than Winter had been. She also had a better recollection than he had had of the detailed events of Sunday afternoon, which she related to Kathy without protest, and with some considerable, if embarrassed, dignity. Her account of the past tallied with his in every significant respect, although her version of the future seemed rather clearer than his.

'Terry has been working out with his accountant how things can be settled with Caroline, his wife. It's complicated, you see, with the loans outstanding for the businesses and the cars leased, and so on. It's taking him a long time to work out just the best way to do it, so that everyone comes out of it all right. He wants to have that all worked out before he tells Caroline that he wants a divorce, to make it as painless as possible. I think he's right about that. Only the accountant is being very slow.'

Kathy's eyes narrowed.

'His two girls are quite grown up now, so it shouldn't be too hard on them. I have two boys, six and nine. My husband married again not long after we were divorced, and because he and his wife have a nice home with a garden for pets and so on, and good schools near by, we agreed that the boys would live with them. My flat isn't really suitable. But when Terry and I get married, I shall apply for custody of the boys.'

'I see.'

Kathy seemed temporarily lost for words. The rustle of writing in the corner stopped, and for a moment a heavy silence hung in the room.

'Did you ever meet Terry's mother, Ms McArthur?' Brock asked at last.

'No. I would have liked to. But it didn't seem possible.

She would have been very upset to learn that Terry's marriage was a failure. Although I think we would have got on after she'd got over the divorce. She was very fond of Terry, and she would have seen how much in love we are. I think she was a generous person.'

'In terms of money?'

'Yes. I don't think she had a lot, but she was very independent, and she was always buying things for Terry and his family. Terry used to complain about her being too generous.'

'And did Terry ever talk about getting financial assistance from his mother – for his business, or to help with the divorce, for example?'

Geraldine McArthur frowned. 'No, he never said anything about that.'

'Or about the possibility of her selling her house?'

'Yes, he did talk about how unsuitable it was for her, and how she should sell it. She was quite stubborn, I understand.'

From the window of Kathy's office, Brock looked down on the figures of Winter and his girlfriend as they emerged on to the street. They spoke briefly and then parted, walking away in opposite directions.

'It doesn't really settle anything, though,' Kathy said. 'They could have been describing the Sunday before last. Say Winter left her after an hour or so, and went to call on his mother to have another go at persuading her to sell the house. He went in to 22 and found her fast asleep on her bed. Just looking at the cantankerous old bird snoring away there, he knew she'd never change her mind. She was going to sit it out and he'd see his quarter of a million crumble to dust. He's fuming. He goes into the kitchen for a drink of water, and he sees a plastic bag. He's seen warnings on the TV about how easy it is to suffocate by accident with a plastic bag. He takes it back into the bedroom and discovers that they're right, it is easy. Then he goes back to New Cross.'

'So you see him as a villain?' Brock smiled.

'Damn right.'

'And her too? I owe you a drink by the way. Not at all the scarlet woman.'

'No. I think she'd protect him, but she wouldn't murder. I think he returns in a state. He tells her that when he went to see his mother he found her lying dead on her bed with a plastic bag over her head. He thinks she killed herself. He says he took the bag off and put it in the kitchen bin, but then worried that he shouldn't have. He panicked and left. He's in a state of shock. He begs her not to contact anyone until he's had time to think it through. He delays until he hears from his wife that his mother's been found and the police are on the scene. Now he tells his girlfriend that he can't admit that he was there, and anyway there'd be no point. She agrees to cover for him.'

Brock nodded. 'Plausible.'

The pathologist's report arrived shortly afterwards. Analyses of blood and vital organs had revealed no poisons. The moisture on the inside of the plastic bag was confirmed as Meredith Winterbottom's saliva, and the hairs were also hers. Dr Mehta's conclusion was as he had indicated on the phone the previous day – cause of death unable to be determined by anatomical or toxicological analysis, but evidence compatible with asphyxia of some form. The coroner had now agreed to release the body to the family for cremation on the following day.

'Fair enough.' Brock got to his feet. 'Well, I've had my fill of life's tangled web for one day. I think I might go back to the Yard and play with my computer for a while. All right with you?'

'Of course, sir. I thought we might go down to the seaside tomorrow, to visit somebody else who was in Jerusalem Lane on Sunday afternoon – Adam Kowalski, former professor of Cracow, now resident of Eastbourne.'

9

As on the previous evening, Kathy went by Jerusalem Lane on her way home. This time she saw it not as the temporarily emptied setting for the Doré etching, but rather as a piece of nineteenth-century London in the final moments of its life. Suddenly its presence appeared incredibly robust and indelible, every angle and texture an essential part of the reality of the neighbourhood, like the presence of an old and characterful relative whose imminent passing seems inconceivable.

She walked to the south end of the Lane, where number 22 stood close to the junction with Marquis Street. She had thought of checking on the two sisters, but when she saw the light on in Mrs Rosenfeldt's deli, she went there instead.

The skeletal figure of Mrs Rosenfeldt responded to the bell. She recognized Kathy and acknowledged her with a tight smile.

'How are you, Mrs Rosenfeldt?'

'Well enough.'

'How about Peg and Eleanor upstairs? Have you seen them today?'

She nodded. 'I've been up a couple of times. So have Mrs Stwosz and Miss Pemberton. I think they've had enough visitors. They'll be better after the funeral tomorrow.'

'Yes, well, they're lucky to have plenty of good friends.'

'Ah . . .' Mrs Rosenfeldt clucked her tongue. 'And what about . . .' She nodded her head up the street.

'Sorry?'

'Witz and Kowalski – those people in the Croatia Club. I told your Inspector about them.'

'Yes, we're checking on that. There are a number of

things we're looking into. When was the last time you saw Mr Kowalski?'

She shook her head. 'Couple of weeks, I don't know.'

'Well,' Kathy said, 'let me know if you hear of anything else we should know.'

She turned to leave, and as she pulled the door open she noticed a point of light, like a candle flame, flicker briefly in the dark corner of the synagogue, where its back butted up to the end of the terrace on the other side of Jerusalem Lane.

'That's funny. I thought I saw a light in the synagogue yard.'

'That'll be Sam,' Mrs Rosenfeldt said. 'Lives in a cardboard box in the corner there.'

'We never saw him when we were going round the block talking to people.'

'He's not usually there during the day. He doesn't like to be disturbed. He's been around for six months or more. I think it's shocking that people should have to live like that – in a cardboard box!' She snorted. 'More and more of them now. It's like the thirties again. Meredith used to talk to him. And Eleanor, too. Not since Sunday, of course. They would sometimes take him food. He liked the Balaton's goulash, poor old soul. Like the thirties again.'

Kathy bought a take-away portion of goulash at the Balaton and walked quietly back to the synagogue. She could dimly make out the pile of cardboard in the corner of the yard, behind the railings. She went through the open gates and over to the boxes, opening the lid of the goulash tub so that the smell filled the night air.

'Sam,' she called.

There was a snuffling sound, and then a voice.

'Mer'dith? El'nor?'

'I'm Kathy, a friend of Eleanor's.'

Sam crawled out of his box. The flame of a gas lighter briefly illuminated his face. He looked old. A battered hat was pulled low on his forehead and a dirty white beard filled much of the rest of his face. Kathy made out a sore on the end of his nose.

'I've brought you this.'

He nodded and took the container from her. Untroubled by its heat, he pushed the food quickly into his mouth with a plastic fork. Kathy let him finish, and then as he turned to crouch back into his box, she said, 'Sam, Meredith died on Sunday.'

He stopped and turned to her. 'Died?'

'Yes. In the afternoon. Were you around here then? Did you see anyone visit her on Sunday afternoon?'

He crouched, lost in thought for some time. Then he spoke. 'Bow tie.'

'What?'

'Man with a bow tie. Rang Mer'dith's bell on Sunday afternoon. Went inside.'

'Have you any idea what time it was?'

Again he pondered. 'Sun was shining on the front of Mer'dith's house. When he came out it wasn't any more.'

'You're sure it was Sunday?'

He snorted. 'The bells of St James was ringing.'

He turned and crawled into the box.

On her way back, Kathy checked with both Mrs Rosenfeldt and the people in the Balaton Café, but no one knew of anyone who wore a bow tie.

Kathy ran to the front door, reaching it before the chime of the bell had faded in the small space of her hallway. He grinned at her and threw a bouquet of flowers behind her on to the hall table. He took her in his arms.

Before or after the door is closed? she thought.

'Happy birthday, darling, for yesterday.'

She kissed him.

'Am I forgiven, then? Good. Let's go to bed.'

He felt her body stiffen with sudden annoyance.

'What's the matter?'

'Nothing. Yes, come on.'

After they made love, she lay curled against his side, smelling his expensive after-shave. *Not the one I gave him,* she thought to herself.

Aloud she said, 'Are you beginning to find it a chore, coming here?'

'Oh, come on, Kath. I explained what happened last night.'

'Not about last night. It's been just over six months' – she meant to say it lightly, matter of fact, but she could hear it coming out petulant – 'and I thought you must know me so well now that the excitement might have gone for you.'

'Has it for you?'

'No. For me it's just as exciting as it was the first time. It always has been.'

'Well, then.'

Trust a lawyer never to answer the question.

'Have you had a bad day at work? You seem tense.' He stroked her cheek.

'Not bad, really. A bit frustrating in some ways, and I've found it difficult trying to lead a case with a Detective Chief Inspector from Scotland Yard breathing down my neck. I wanted to tell you about it last night.'

'Who is it?'

'David Brock.'

'Oh, Brock. That's interesting. He's quite a big gun. You must have a pretty important case.'

'No. Just some old lady who was probably suffocated while she was asleep. He said the Yard assigns him to odd things from time to time, and it looks as if I'm this week's oddity.'

'What's he like?'

'Oh . . . quite sexy, really. If you go for older men.'

'I meant to work with.'

'He seems very relaxed, almost detached. Not what I expected at all.'

'Maybe they're assessing you for promotion, or a transfer. Inspector Kolla of the Yard. I like it.'

'Piss off.'

'He led the hunt for Gregory North recently, didn't he?'

'Yes. Everyone we've questioned seems to know about it. One suspect today got him to give him his autograph for his son.'

'Did he talk about the North case at all?'

'Only briefly. Said it wasn't over yet.'

'Really? I wonder what he meant by that? North escaped to some place in South America, didn't he? Where they can't extradite him.'

'I don't know. He said something about having a surprise in store for North. Let's have a glass of wine. I've opened a bottle of the special Italian red for your birthday. You remember the Barolo?'

Kathy's lips moved seductively up his shoulder to his neck. But she could feel the tenseness in his arm around her. *If he's looking at his watch I'll bloody kill him.*

'I have to go, love. I'm sorry. Let's have a glass while I get dressed.'

'You've only just arrived.'

'Don't say it like that, Kath. I told you what the score was tonight.'

Kathy stomped out to the kitchen and returned with the two glasses of wine. She sat, naked, on the end of the bed and watched him as he did up his shirt buttons, pulled on his trousers.

'You ought to get Brock to talk about the North case. It's very interesting.'

'Bugger the North case.'

'No, really. Try to find out what kind of surprise they've got lined up for him. Maybe they've got around the extradition thing.'

'Why are you interested? He's not a client, is he?'

'Of course not.'

The extra-special-super-charming smile, the one kept in reserve for new judges, not to be used too often in case it gets shop-soiled.

'Just professional curiosity. It's an opportunity for you to see how the big league works. But suit yourself, anyway. Oh God, I must fly.'

'Flap, flap.'

'Come on, darling, this isn't like you.'

He took her in his arms again, kissed her gently on the mouth. 'I do love you, you know that.'

'I love you too,' she whispered. 'I really do.' And then he was gone.

Kathy felt good the next morning as she drove over to Scotland Yard to pick up Brock for their trip to the coast, as if she were escaping from school for the day. But before they set off there was one chore to be done. She parked at the north end of Jerusalem Lane and the two of them walked over to the camera shop on the corner. Fluorescent pink posters stuck to the grubby shop front announced a closing-down sale.

'Mr Witz?'

'That's me.' He came out from behind his counter towards them.

'We're police officers, investigating the death of Mrs Winterbottom.'

'I thought so.' He smiled affably at them. 'I already told your detective what I was doing at the time.'

'Yes. You were in church.'

He beamed. 'At my niece's wedding in Northwood, twenty miles away, taking the wedding photographs. You want to see the pictures?' He was teasing her.

'No, thank you. We'd like some information on a quarrel between Mrs Winterbottom and the Kowalskis next door. Concerning his past in Poland during the war.'

'Who's been telling you that rubbish?' He was suddenly angry. With his pink cheeks and white hair growing in big tufts around, and out of, his ears, he looked like a burly and malignant little gnome. 'There was no quarrel, just a small misunderstanding, which some busybody women in this street like to blow up for mischief.'

'Who?'

'Ach!' He turned on his heel and stamped back to his place behind the counter.

'Believe me,' he waggled his finger at them, 'you're wasting your time if you think Adam Kowalski, or anyone else for that matter, would kill Mrs Winterbottom for such a stupid reason.'

'Wasn't that the reason the Kowalskis were selling up?'

'What?' He looked at her incredulously. 'Of course not! Adam sold his place on the same day I sold mine, and for the same reason, because it is time to retire, and take things easy. He should have done it long ago.'

As they turned to go, Kathy suddenly stopped and asked him, 'Can you recall anyone around here who wears a bow tie, Mr Witz? Someone who visits, someone's relative maybe?'

He shook his head, still grouchy. 'Bow ties aren't that unusual. But I don't remember anyone special.'

'All right. Thanks for your help.'

He shook their hands with a better grace.

'When did you both sell, Mr Witz?' Brock asked.

'Back in February. It was a sunny day like today when Adam finally made up his mind.' The gnome snorted. 'But it took him another three or four months before he finally managed to get permission from that Marie to come to the pub with me to celebrate.'

He suddenly frowned and scratched his ear.

'What's the matter?'

'That's funny. That day . . . when he was about to close up the shop to go out to celebrate, Adam had to serve a customer. I remember how impatient it made me, waiting outside in the Lane. And I remember the man was wearing a bow tie.'

Kathy's spirits rose the further they got from central London. It was a bright, clear day, the sun gleaming off the paintwork of cars, sparkling off their chrome. As they got closer to the sea, the sky became imperceptibly more brilliant, lightened by reflection from the sheet of water which lay ahead. Kathy took a pair of sunglasses from her shoulder bag and put them on. It was the sort of day that always seemed to come towards the end of the summer holidays when she was a child, glowing and bright, made achingly poignant by the knowledge of the dark autumn, dark suburbs and dark school to which she must inevitably return.

Brock was in good form, chatting amiably about the eccentricities of his colleagues and his computers, and then, when they were past Tunbridge Wells and into the woods and farmlands of the Sussex Weald, lapsing into silence as they absorbed the unfamiliar scenery. The Kowalskis had bought a small house on the east side of Eastbourne, on the Pevensey road. A two-storey semi-detached on a 1930s estate. Its upper storey enjoyed a limited view eastward down the English Channel, towards the Strait of Dover. Severely pruned rose bushes struggled in beds on the small patch of lawn. Mrs Kowalski opened the front door.

'Good morning.' Brock beamed. 'Splendid day! We phoned yesterday from London. Metropolitan Police.'

She glared suspiciously at them, and they felt obliged to produce their warrant cards. She led them into the front room.

Mrs Kowalski was a small, peppery woman who appeared to be highly protective of her husband. 'What do you want to see him for?' she shot at them as soon as they sat down.

'Perhaps we could explain when he arrives. Is he not at home?' Kathy, her good mood broken by the woman's antagonism, spoke with careful politeness.

'He can't walk. He's hurt his foot. He's upstairs and can't come down. Ask me your questions.'

'Perhaps we could go upstairs to him, then,' Kathy persisted. They faced each other in obstinate silence for a moment, until Mrs Kowalski snorted and got to her feet.

'Come, then.'

The front upstairs room was furnished as a small sitting room, which became uncomfortably overcrowded with the four of them in it. Adam Kowalski was seated in a cane chair by the window, which had a shallow bow front and was hung with heavy dark curtains. Beside him stood a telescope trained at the shimmering sea on which hovered several long grey ships. The gauntness of his frame was emphasized by the length of his right leg which stuck out stiffly to one side, the foot encased in plaster. As Brock and Kathy entered the room, he tried to struggle to his feet and the newspaper on his lap slid to the floor.

'Don't get up, don't get up.' Brock went over and shook his hand, despite an attempt at a blocking move from Mrs Kowalski.

The two visitors sat together on a sofa while Mrs Kowalski positioned herself on an upright chair between them and her husband.

'You follow the shipping movements up the Channel, then?' Brock indicated the page of the newspaper lying on the floor.

'Yes.' Kowalski gave a faint smile. His eyes were rimmed with pink, and his skin was like pale, translucent parchment. He spoke slowly, with a scholarly precision. 'The novelty of a view of the sea.'

'We've never lived beside the sea,' Mrs Kowalski broke in. She seemed to feel it necessary to underscore his account with her own more combative statements. 'That's why we came here. A complete change. Why not? It's what we've always dreamt of.'

Kathy looked around at the awkwardly furnished room. 'What did you do to your foot, sir?' she asked, hoping to return the conversation to Adam Kowalski.

'*He* didn't do anything to it,' his wife intervened once again. 'It was that clumsy son of ours who dropped a box of books on it and broke a bone.'

'It was a small accident.' Kowalski fluttered long fingers to mollify her bad temper. 'But painful.' He smiled bravely at their visitors.

'Would that have been at the weekend, then, sir?'

He frowned. 'Yes.'

'Perhaps I should explain why we're here.'

'About time,' Mrs Kowalski said crossly.

'Did you know that Mrs Winterbottom in Jerusalem Lane died on Sunday?'

This stunned Mrs Kowalski into silence. She turned and looked at her husband, as if to see from his face whether he knew and could therefore be accused of not keeping her informed. But there was no sign of foreknowledge. In fact, no sign of anything.

'The circumstances of her death aren't clear at the moment, and so the police were called in. We are interviewing everybody we can find who was in the area of Jerusalem Lane between the hours of 2 and 4.15 last Sunday afternoon. We understand that applies to you, Mr Kowalski.'

'You mean . . . somebody killed her?' Mrs Kowalski spoke in hushed tones, her eyes round.

'We're not sure yet.'

'But why else are you involved? Oh, my God! Meredith Winterbottom!'

'You had no idea about this, sir?' Kathy inquired.

'Of course he didn't. Are you blind?'

Kathy bit her tongue, and turned to Brock. 'Sir, the news has probably been a bit of a shock. Maybe if you and Mrs Kowalski went and made some tea . . .'

Mrs Kowalski looked with horror at the big frame of Brock. 'I stay here!'

'Marie,' Adam Kowalski said wearily, 'we must be hospitable to our guests. They have come all the way from London. Make a cup of tea . . . please.'

Grumbling, his wife left the room.

'She means well,' Kowalski said without much conviction to Brock, who stayed where he was. Then, turning to Kathy, he said, 'No. I didn't know. I'm sorry for the lady, and for her sisters.'

'Could you tell us what you were doing in London?'

'We went up to clear the last of the stuff from my shop. We actually sold it about six months ago, but the new owners allowed us time to remove the stock. They said they weren't ready to let the place again yet, so they didn't mind as long as I was responsible for insurance of the contents.'

'Excuse me, sir, you said "we went up". Was your wife with you in Jerusalem Lane, too?'

'Yes, we both went.' Kowalski shifted his gaze around the room as he spoke, avoiding eye contact. Every so often he would look at the window, as if considering an escape out into the sunlit morning. 'We'd arranged to sell the last boxes of books to a dealer in North London, so Marie and I went up to town on the train last Saturday and stayed overnight with our son, Felix, in Enfield, and then he helped us sort and pack on Sunday morning and load up the van he had hired. We delivered the boxes to the dealer, and then returned to the shop to tidy up. Then we went to the station and caught the train home. We left the shop at about 4, because I remember we worked out that that would give us plenty of time to catch the 4.46.'

'So your son was also in the area on Sunday afternoon?'

'Yes.'

'Do you remember seeing anyone, anyone at all, in Jerusalem Lane between, say, noon and 4 that afternoon?'

Kowalski thought, his eyes travelling back to the window. Eventually he shook his head. 'No, we were in the back room of the shop for most of the time till 1 and then we left, and returned around 2.30, I should think. I don't remember seeing anyone in Jerusalem Lane. It's very quiet on a Sunday afternoon.'

'A man in a bow tie?'

He shook his head.

'Do you remember *ever* seeing a man wearing a bow tie in the area?'

Kowalski shrugged. 'No.'

'A customer, in your shop? About two or three months ago?'

He looked startled. His eyes darted to Kathy and then veered away again quickly when he saw her staring intently at him. 'Oh. A customer, you say? Well, you may be right, I do seem to recall ... Was there something special about him you were interested in?'

'Just tell us about him, please, Mr Kowalski.'

The pale skin of Kowalski's head coloured slightly. 'I do seem to remember a customer with a spotted black and white bow tie, some time ago. I think ... that he came back later, perhaps.' He looked hesitantly at her.

She nodded, as if she knew this. 'Go on.'

'Oh, six or seven weeks ago, I'd say.'

'What was his name?'

'I'm afraid I don't know.' His expression had become vague.

'What did he want?'

'Well, I seem to remember that he bought something the first time.'

'And the second?'

'I'm not sure. I think not.'

'If he did buy something the first time, you might have his name on your books?'

Kowalski looked doubtful. 'Oh, I don't think so, not unless he particularly wanted me to look out for something for him.'

'But if he used a credit card?'

'I wouldn't have a record of that now.'

'Well, could you describe him?'

'No, I don't think so. I just remember the bow tie.'

'Young, old? Tall, fat?'

'Youngish, I think.' He shook his head, 'I'm sorry, I can't really remember.' He was becoming slightly flustered. He seemed to search in his mind for something to give her, to satisfy her. 'When he came in the first time he was looking for something . . . travel, no . . . art . . . No – architecture books, that was it, architecture books.'

'And you sold him some?'

He shook his head. 'I'm not sure.'

His wife bustled back into the room, carrying a tray with four cups of milky instant coffee.

'You like sugar?' she asked Kathy, thrusting a cup at her.

'No, thank you.'

'Well, don't stir it, then.'

Her husband's gaze shifted uncomfortably away back to the window.

She answered Kathy's questions about their visit to Jerusalem Lane curtly, confirming her husband's account. Like him, she could remember seeing no one in the area, and she knew of no one who wore a bow tie. She hadn't been in the shop when the man her husband remembered had called.

'I wouldn't say anything against the departed' – Mrs Kowalski's thinking had evidently moved on while she had been in the kitchen. – 'but it doesn't really surprise me.'

'Oh?' Brock prompted mildly.

'She could drive you mad, that woman.'

Her husband opened his mouth to protest, but she cut him off. 'Oh, Adam won't say it, but she nearly drove him into the grave last year, spreading vicious stories about him. He nearly had a break-down. Our friends tried to persuade her to stop. Felix spoke to her. But she was so stubborn! Wouldn't be told. It was one of the reasons we began to think about leaving the Lane. Oh yes, I can quite imagine she could have driven somebody to do something desperate!'

'Your family had a serious quarrel with her, then?' Kathy asked.

'No, no,' Adam Kowalski broke in anxiously. 'She had meant to help me. It was all most unfortunate. She dragged up things from the past which were best forgotten. She didn't understand what she was doing.'

'She wouldn't be told! She was a stubborn old busybody who liked to organize other people's lives.'

'Marie!' her husband protested. 'She's dead!'

Mrs Kowalski snorted and lifted her coffee cup to her mouth. When she returned it to the saucer, she raised her chin defiantly, her pose of righteous indignation somewhat spoiled by a skin of milk sticking to her upper lip.

'When was the last time either of you had any contact with Mrs Winterbottom?' Kathy asked.

Mr Kowalski shook his head. His wife said, 'It was months ago. I don't think we could have exchanged words since Easter.'

'Didn't you say goodbye to them when you left the Lane?'

'No. There was a little farewell party for us in the Croatia Club, but they didn't come.'

'What is the Croatia Club, Mrs Kowalski?'

'Oh, it's just a social club which people started years ago, when we first came to the Lane. It wasn't only for Yugoslavs – that was just a name. It was for anyone in the Lane who wanted to have a chat or play a game of cards. It has a room over the Balaton.'

'Does everyone in the Lane belong?'

'No, no. In recent years not so many people go any more. People have left or passed away, you know.'

'Who came to your party?'

'Oh, the Bölls, Mr Witz, Brunhilde Capek, Dr Botev for a while. I don't know, people came and went.'

'Mrs Rosenfeldt?'

'No, she wasn't there.'

'Did Mrs Winterbottom discuss you selling your property, or talk about selling her own?'

Both the Kowalskis looked surprised. 'Oh no,' Adam said. 'I'm sure she wouldn't do that.' He smiled confidentially, modestly pleased with himself. 'We were approached to sell, along with Konrad Witz, by someone who wanted to combine our two properties into one. We got a good price, you know, but the buyer asked us to keep it to ourselves, about selling, for as long as possible. We didn't tell anyone we were going until a month or so ago. Certainly not Meredith.'

Kathy put her half-finished cup down. 'Well, we've taken up enough of your time. If you remember anything else, you will call us, won't you? Here's my card. And we'll need to talk to your son. Can you give us his address and telephone number?'

Adam Kowalski wrote down his son's details on Kathy's pad. 'He's a lecturer at the London Polytechnic. Probably he could speak to you after work. Maybe in the shop. He still has the key.'

'Yes, we'll arrange something. It must have been difficult for you moving books with your hurt foot.'

'Fortunately we had nearly loaded the van.' Kowalski smiled ruefully. 'Felix was inside, pushing the boxes around to make room, and one of them fell off the back on to my foot. It was very painful, but I thought it was just bruised until I went to the doctor on Monday and he made me get an X-ray and they found one of the little bones was broken. So, I shall be stuck here for a few days.'

'Weeks more likely, old fool,' his wife muttered.

Kathy took a deep breath of fresh air when they reached their car. Seagulls wheeled in the sun overhead, the air pungent with salt and seaweed.

'What a bitch. "Don't stir it, then"!'

Brock laughed and turned the car to take the road inland to the A27.

'He must have spent fifty years regretting that he hadn't handed her over to the Gestapo,' she went on. 'In her case at least they probably would have done the right thing.'

'It's appalling, isn't it, how the Kowalskis' whole life has been controlled by that moment, the decision to protect her.

96

What else could he have done?' Brock scratched his beard. 'But then follow the years of betraying his students, losing his career, being forced out of Poland, and now being forced out of Jerusalem Lane. And odd too that it was she who let the secret out to Meredith.'

'Yes, I must say that if I were Adam Kowalski and I were thinking of bumping somebody off, it would have been Marie Kowalski who wound up with a plastic bag over her head, not Meredith Winterbottom.'

They turned off the main road on the way back and stopped at a pub for lunch. Brock ordered paté, green salad and a tomato juice for Kathy, a pint of bitter and a ploughman's lunch for himself. He poked at it when it arrived. 'No ploughman ever survived on these scraps,' he grumbled, pushing a lettuce leaf to one side. 'Still, the beer's quite good.' He took a big gulp and licked his lips.

'Yes, and I don't suppose old Adam's ever even had the opportunity to get a few brief moments of relief with some lady hairdresser in New Cross or whatever. Wife living over the shop, never letting him out of her sight. They probably developed the siege mentality back in Cracow and have been cultivating it ever since. I wouldn't be surprised if she was responsible for dropping the box on his foot, to stop him straying out of her sight.'

Kathy spluttered into her tomato juice, laughing. 'Oh, I thought you were saying yesterday that you couldn't understand how anyone could be bothered to have an affair. Now you're conceding that it might be a good idea in some circumstances.'

'Not really.' Brock toyed with the pint mug on the beer mat. 'I believe that things badly begun end badly.'

'Oh golly.' Kathy stared at him, still smiling. 'That's a bit Old Testament, isn't it? Do you really believe that?'

'Yes, I do. But then, first marriages are doomed these days, anyway. And so are people who get tangled up in them.'

'You really are a cynic, aren't you, sir?'

'A realist, I think. Do you know any first marriages you'd want to be in?'

'Yes . . . All right, no.'

'Too inexperienced, taking too much for granted, held together by the kids. Mind you, that can blow up in your face, too.' He was now gloomily drawing small patterns with beer slops on the shiny table top.

'Is that what happened to you?'

'Me?' He looked up. 'No . . . No kids in my case. No, I was thinking of Mr Gregory Thomas North again, my former quarry. Sorry, it's difficult to forget about old enemies sometimes.'

'He has children?'

'One boy. Six years old. North dotes on him. His only redeeming feature. We assumed that he would try to get Mrs N and junior to follow him out, but it seems the wife doesn't fancy a life on the pampas. Delighted to see the back of him in fact, because she has other arrangements in hand, and a homicidal husband doesn't figure in them. Only the little boy has just been diagnosed as having leukaemia. Three months to live. The missus is keeping it quiet in case North tries to come back to see him.'

'Oh God, how awful.'

'Yes. I almost feel sorry for the animal. However, he may find that he gets to see his little boy after all.'

'Oh?'

'Mm. We've been having unofficial discussions with our friends over there – exchanging information on things generally, you know, the best buy in data banks, thumb screws, flashing blue lights, the things coppers like to talk about when they're together. I was over there last month, as a matter of fact. Private visit, of course. It seems they don't like villains who kill coppers any more than we do, whatever their politicians say. The politicians are, however, very sensitive about foreigners who import drugs.'

'Is North doing that? He must be crazy.'

'Of course not. He doesn't need to with all that money in the Swiss bank accounts. However, it'll be difficult for him to explain that to them when a large stash of heroin is found in his cellar in a couple of weeks' time, him not even having learnt the language yet.'

'Wow. And you'll be waiting for him at the airport.'

'*Moi*?' Brock raised his eyebrows in mock innocence. 'I know nothing.

'Anyway,' he added with a weary sigh, 'how wonderful to have no part in the whole dreary mess – scheming wives, unfaithful husbands, desperate plans leading nowhere. How wonderful to be like you, Sergeant Kolla, young, beautiful, single and free.' He raised his empty glass. 'And if you're sticking to tomato juice, you can drive us back to Meredith Winterbottom's funeral, and I can have another pint before we go.'

II

Just as at the end of her remembered childhood holidays, the sky was clouding over and becoming darker as Kathy drove them back towards the familiar urban landscapes. On the way they phoned Felix Kowalski and arranged to meet him at his father's former bookshop at 4.

Traffic was heavy in central London, and when they reached the crematorium the service for Meredith Winterbottom had already begun. They waited in the car, parked so that they could view the front of the chapel. A faint smell of smoke permeated the air. Heavy drops of rain began to fall.

After five minutes the chapel doors were opened by a man in a dark suit, and people filed out under the portico, forming stiff little groups beneath its shelter. Most were elderly, and Kathy recognized a number from Jerusalem Lane. The members of Meredith's family remained by the chapel doorway, as mourners came up to offer their condolences. The figure of Eleanor was distinctive, dressed in black, erect and sombre, her face pale against her dark hair. Beside her and a head shorter, Peg struck a considerably brighter note, in a scarlet coat with a pink scarf, matching gloves and wide-brimmed hat. From the car they could see the hat tilt graciously this way and that to acknowledge the sympathetic words of friends. On the other side of the chapel doorway, the Winter family formed an awkward group. Terry looked uncomfortable accepting the condolences of those who approached them, and his wife Caroline's smiles of acknowledgement seemed thin and unconvincing. Kathy recognized the elder daughter, Alex, hovering in the background, morose, her shoulders stooped. Her teenage sister stood beside her, scuffing her feet impatiently.

No one was wearing a bow tie.

'Do we go out and ask them?' Kathy inquired doubtfully. The rain was falling steadily now, and one or two people were beginning to hurry out from the shelter of the portico towards the car park.

'Not here.' Brock wrinkled his nose. 'Let's try a long shot. Have you got the developer's number?'

Brock dialled, and was passed from the receptionist to Slade's secretary and finally to the man himself.

'Hello, Chief Inspector.'

'Sorry to bother you again, Mr Slade. A quick one. The architect for your project, does he wear a bow tie?'

'Herbert Lowell? Never seen him in one. Why?'

'We have to trace everyone who was in the area when Mrs Winterbottom died. Someone thought they'd seen a man in a bow tie, possibly an architect, youngish man.'

'Not Lowell. Sounds more like Bob Jones. He used to work for The Lowell Partnership, on this project actually. But they parted company a couple of months ago, so I don't know why he'd have been around the place.'

'Probably not him, then, but we may check. Do you know where we could reach him?'

'He set up on his own. You could try Lowell's, or the Institute of Architects would have his address.'

'Yes, fine. Thanks for your help.'

'No problem. And thanks again for the autograph. My boy was over the moon. Goodbye.'

Kathy smiled. 'He'll be even more delighted when he sees your picture on the front page arresting North. You should start a fan club, sir.'

'Thank you, Kathy. Just concentrate on getting us to Jerusalem Lane, would you, while I track down our phantom in the bow tie.'

He placed three more calls – one to directory inquiries, one to the Royal Institute of British Architects, and the third to the office of Concept Design, off Tottenham Court

Road, less than half a mile west of Jerusalem Lane. Bob Jones agreed to meet them at his office at 5.30 that evening.

Through the empty shop window they could make out a light at the back of the bookshop. Eventually Felix Kowalski answered their knock, but not before they had become thoroughly wet waiting at the door. He led them through a succession of cramped rooms, their walls lined with empty shelves, the pages from old books scattered on the floor like the detritus of autumn. The musty smell of the departed books permeated the place. Without them the building looked forlorn, like the old lady's body on the mortuary slab, a form abandoned by its content.

At the back of the shop was a tiny kitchen, with a small table and three rickety bentwood chairs. A green plastic shade hung over the light bulb suspended above the table, the electric light a welcome contrast to the dim greyness of the sky beyond the kitchen window, through which a small walled yard was visible.

At first Felix Kowalski was civil in his offers to take their wet coats and make them comfortable, but beneath the words Kathy soon began to feel the same bristling antagonism that had surprised her in his mother. His references to the meagre facilities of his father's shop were scornful, and soon this bitter edge to his voice hardened into a constrained anger. He had, it seemed, a number of things to complain about, and it wasn't long before he began to air them.

'Yes, I work at the Polytechnic, for what it's worth these days. Although it's difficult to see the point sometimes when a lecturer with seven years' fulltime study and a Ph.D. behind him is paid little more than an eighteen-year-old police constable on his first day on the beat.'

He glared at Kathy, as if challenging her to provoke him further. His eyes, disconcertingly, didn't quite look in the same direction, so that it was difficult to be sure whether the intensity of his stare was due to aggression or an attempt to focus. He was about forty. Damp black hair was pushed back from his forehead, his face puffy and flushed. She thought she caught the sweet smell of whisky on his breath.

'Do you work in the same field as your father did when he was a professor?'

His lips pursed and he twitched his head back and forward in a gesture that might have been meant to indicate scorn.

'Yes, I rather thought it might come round to that. My father isn't well, you know. It's a pity you found it necessary to bother him the way you did this morning. He found it very stressful.'

'Really? That wasn't the impression we got. He seemed quite happy to help us.'

'And I resent you raking up things from his past that have nothing whatsoever to do with the case you're supposed to be solving. Your approach just seems to be to charge in and stir up the mud and then grab at whatever comes up. Hardly scientific method, I should have thought.'

Kathy found his angry sarcasm all the more irksome because there was an element of truth in what he said. She imagined how devastating it would be to be one of his students faced with this choleric venom.

'I take it,' she said, as icily calm as she could make herself sound, 'you're referring to the dispute which your family had recently with Mrs Winterbottom, who, in case your mother didn't mention it, we believe may have been murdered on Sunday afternoon last.'

'If you're suggesting that I or either of my parents had anything to do with Mrs Winterbottom's death,' he exploded, 'you'd better come right out and say it now, so that I can get a solicitor down here straight away.'

'Oh dear, oh dear.' Brock, who had taken no notice of this exchange, was stooping in a corner of the room. He straightened with a grunt and turned toward the table, adjusting the glasses on the end of his nose and squinting at the spine of a small red-covered book which he'd picked up from the floor.

'A Baedeker!' He opened the cover. 'Southern France and Corsica, 1914.' He flicked through the pages. 'Maps still there, quite good condition. You don't want to lose this, Mr Kowalski. They're worth a few bob these days, aren't they?'

'What?' Kowalski turned to Brock, a look of irritation on his face, as if he was having to deal with some imbecilic first-year student who had lost track of the argument. 'I wouldn't know. Second-hand books aren't my field.'

'So you're not in the business with your father? We rather thought, when you were helping him to sell his stock, that you might have been involved.'

'No . . . I was simply giving him and my mother a hand. Look –'

'Tell us exactly what your movements were on Sunday, would you, Mr Kowalski?'

With bad grace he began to do as Brock asked. The three of them had left Enfield after breakfast, catching the train into central London – 'because my wife decided at the last possible minute that she needed the car'. Once in London, his parents went to the shop, while he took a bus to Camden Town, where he had arranged to rent a van for a few hours. He drove it to Jerusalem Lane, into the yard behind the bookshop, and helped his mother and father pack and load the last of the books into the van. They finished soon after 1, and ate a packed lunch his wife had made for them.

'That was after your father had the accident with his foot?'

'Yes. We were nearly finished when that happened. My mother knocked the box off the back of the van on to his foot.' He shook his head. 'Typical. Anyway, after that I drove to the dealer in Notting Hill who had bought the last of the stock.'

'You drove alone?'

'No. My father had to come too, to conclude the sale with the man, but there wasn't room for my mother. She stayed at the shop.'

'And you returned when?' Kathy asked.

Kowalski looked her in the eyes and answered calmly, '2 o'clock, I should think. Yes, 2.'

'Was your father not in pain with his foot? It seemed pretty bad when we saw him.'

'It wasn't so bad at first, after he got over the initial shock. The corner of the box seemed to land on the ground, taking most of the impact, and then the edge caught him. When we set off he said he was all right, but by the time we got back he was pretty uncomfortable.'

'What did you do then?'

Kowalski shrugged impatiently, 'My mother was doing some last-minute sweeping, and I helped for a bit. Then I took the van back.'

Kathy opened her mouth, but he anticipated her question, 'Mum came with me. We left Dad to rest his foot. He could hardly walk by this stage.'

'Times?'

'Oh for God's sake, I don't know. We weren't away long. We got the tube back from Camden Town on the Northern Line to the station round the corner. We stayed a bit, to finish up. Then I went back to the tube station to call a cab for my parents from the phones there, and when it arrived we all left. I walked back to my station. It must have been around 4.'

They put on their coats and went outside briefly to see the yard in the failing light. By the time they came back inside, Kowalski had stoked up his anger once more.

'I just want it to be understood that I resent this intrusive pressure on elderly people who, God knows, have had enough to put up with. One shudders to think how you lot would behave if we'd actually done something wrong.'

'We have to speak to everyone who may have seen something of significance on Sunday last,' Brock said smoothly to him. 'It's a little difficult to see why you seem to feel so threatened by that, Mr Kowalski. If everyone we spoke to was as defensive, we might end up having to pay our constables even more extravagant wages than we do at present. Anyway, thanks for your help, and don't forget your Baedeker.'

It was dark outside as Brock and Kathy ran back through the rain to their car, which was parked beneath a no-waiting sign at the north end of the Lane.

'Sorry,' Kathy said as Brock got the heater going on the steamed-up windscreen. 'I didn't seem to be able to get anywhere. You were much better with him than I was.'

'I wonder if he's like that with all women. His girl students must get a hard time.'

'Yes, I thought that. But it was my fault, too. I just found it impossible not to be riled by him. All that anger and self-pity – his job, his little digs at his wife, his rudeness . . .'

'And his lies.'

'Yes. The only time he sounded half civil was when he was obviously lying – about the time they returned from Notting Hill. He said 2, whereas his father this morning said 2.30. We can check that, but I'll bet the father was right. Which means that the mother was on her own in the Lane for half an hour during the period the sisters were out.'

'And the father was on his own for most of the following hour, lame or not. And we don't really know for sure that the son didn't find some time on his own that afternoon either, say when he went out to call the cab. We'll have to go back over it all again, and talk to Sylvia Pemberton about when she saw Adam Kowalski that afternoon. But it's interesting that Felix Kowalski should have felt it necessary to lie about the period that his mother was on her own.'

12

The office of Concept Design stood at the end of a cul-de-sac, off a narrow rear access street in a block behind Tottenham Court Road. It occupied a two-storey brick building which had been built in the twenties as a warehouse at the rear of a retail store. On both sides were pre- and post-war commercial buildings about eight storeys high. Behind a large plate-glass window the name of the firm was spelled out in miniature red neon letters. Stepping inside, Kathy and Brock found themselves on a steel bridge, which spanned a large hole in the ground floor and offered a view of the main draughting area in the basement below. Ahead of them, suspended over the draughting floor, was a reception area with glass walls screened by narrow grey venetian blinds.

'Hello.'

A figure climbed up a spiral steel staircase from the level below.

'Secretary's gone home. My name is Bob Jones.'

He was in his late thirties, of medium height, with a mop of tousled black hair. He wore a black sweater, grey trousers, red shoes, and a spotted black and white bow tie. He smiled at them and held out his hand. Then, seeing it was covered with black ink, apologized and withdrew it.

'Pens always play up at the worst moment. At least it's not all over my shirt this time. Come through into the conference room, will you?'

They passed the empty reception desk, made of charcoal-grey laminate, and went through into a room behind the louvred screens. It was lined with grey pin-board, to which a number of coloured free-hand sketches had been attached.

Track-lighting overhead threw spots of light on to the walls and on to a grey table that stood in the middle of the room.

'How can I help?' He offered them seats. 'Has there been another break-in next door?'

'No, sir,' Kathy said. 'Nothing like that. Could you tell us if you were in the vicinity of Jerusalem Lane, over on the other side of Bloomsbury, on Sunday last?'

Jones's expression changed abruptly. He blinked a couple of times and swallowed.

'Oh.' He stared at the table.

'Sir?'

'I'm sorry. Yes, yes, I was there, on Sunday afternoon.'

'On your own?'

'No, with a friend.'

'What were you doing there?'

'We'd gone to visit someone we knew.'

'Who was that?'

'A Mrs Winterbottom. Look, could you tell me what this is about?'

'Mrs Winterbottom is dead, sir – you don't look surprised.'

'No.' Jones's voice had dropped to a whisper. 'No. I read about it in the paper last night, a short report. I only noticed it by accident. It said her funeral was today. I . . . half wondered if that was what this was about.'

'The newspaper report also said that the circumstances of the death were suspicious and that the police wanted to speak to anyone who had been in the neighbourhood on Sunday afternoon. Why didn't you get in touch, Mr Jones?'

'Oh my God,' Jones muttered. They could see that he was breathing in short shallow breaths, like someone in mild shock, keeping his hands pressed to the table so that they wouldn't shake. 'I know I should have. I wasn't sure if it was . . . necessary. Whether it would achieve anything at this stage. But I think I would have.' He looked at them anxiously. 'But how did you get hold of me?'

'Someone answering your description was seen entering Mrs Winterbottom's house at about the time she died.'

'Really? It was about then she died, was it? Oh God. I didn't actually see her, but Judith said she was asleep. I felt really we shouldn't have gone in, but we had arranged to see her at 3, and when she didn't answer our ring at the front door bell, and we saw it was open, Judith said, well, let's make sure she hasn't just taken a snooze after lunch. So we went upstairs, and again her front door was open.'

'When you say open . . .?'

'On the latch. She usually left it like that when she was at home.'

'How do you know?'

'She'd told us.'

'So you just walked in?'

'Yes. I didn't feel right about it, but Judith had a plane to catch back to the States later that afternoon, and she was so keen to see the old lady. I waited in the living room, and Judith put her head around the bedroom door. She said that she was asleep.'

'Did either of you actually step into her bedroom?'

'No . . . I don't think so.'

'Why can't you be sure?'

'Well . . . We weren't sure what to do. We were talking in hushed voices, you know. We didn't know whether to go away for a bit and come back, or wake her, or just forget the whole thing. Then Judith suggested I go upstairs and knock on her sisters' doors, to see if they were in. I tried, but there was no reply at either.'

'And Judith stayed in Mrs Winterbottom's flat while you did that?'

Jones nodded.

'What is Judith's full name please?'

'Dr Judith Naismith.'

'A medical doctor?'

'No, Ph.D.'

'And she's an American?'

'No, but she works there, at Princeton University. Has done for . . . oh, fifteen years.'

'And why were you visiting Mrs Winterbottom?'

'Oh gosh . . . Do you want the short answer or the long one?'

'We've got all night, Mr Jones. Tell us the whole thing.'

'Well, in that case I'm going to need a cup of coffee. There's a percolator next door going all the time. An intravenous drip would be easier, but it gets in the way when you're drawing.'

He winced at his own attempt at humour, seeing the stony look on both their faces. 'Sorry,' he whispered, and got shakily to his feet.

Jones left the room and came back a little later with a tray of coffee mugs.

'I'm really not sure whether any of this is relevant, you see,' he began.

'Just tell us the whole story and we'll decide.'

'Where to begin?' He thought for a moment. 'Well, I suppose . . . One morning, it would have been three or four months ago maybe, about the end of June, I think – I could check my diary – there was a meeting here with a client of ours. He's a developer, called Derek Slade, Managing Director of First City Properties in Mayfair. That would be the first time I was aware of Jerusalem Lane, except I didn't realize it was Jerusalem Lane then. Sorry, I'm not explaining this very well.'

Jones ran his ink-stained hand through the mop of his hair and took a sip of coffee. He was calmer now as he concentrated on his account.

'You knew Mr Slade well, did you?' Kathy asked.

'Yes, we'd done a few jobs for him in the past. Nothing big, but he's a very well-respected developer, and we'd always hoped for something more substantial. The thing was, we'd recently done a number of speculative designs for them, sketch designs to explore the potential of a site, without charging a fee, and our senior partner, Herbert Lowell, was getting a bit impatient that none of them had come to anything. He was the other person there at the meeting that morning. He'd come up specially from the main office in Basingstoke to see Slade, and he made it clear right at the start of the meeting that there was a lot of other work around at that time, and what he called "no hay, no pay" jobs weren't very high on our priorities. He's a pompous twit, actually, and he seemed to have got out of bed on the wrong side that morning, I remember. I wasn't much better, to tell the truth. We'd been doing a competition for a big project in Paris, and I had been up most of the previous night finishing it off.

'Anyway, Slade is a very cool operator, and he just gave his little smile at Herbert's blustering and said he mustn't worry, this time what he had was certain to come off, and it was big, very big indeed. That silenced Herbert. When it comes to architectural judgement, "big" is Herbert's bottom line. Slade explained that over a period of time First City Properties, his company, had been buying small buildings in an old city block in central London. He said his father, who founded First City, had actually bought the first one over thirty years before. Recently the company had been stepping up their acquisitions, and they were now getting close to consolidating their ownership of the whole block. When that happened, he wanted to be in a position to act fast, to have a preliminary development proposal ready to go out immediately for planning permission, and to fast-track the project from then on. He had already organized substantial finance for the scheme, and some likely pre-lets to a big institution of some kind.

'The thing was, though – and he kept returning to this – until all the acquisitions were complete, the essence was secrecy. Apparently the ownership pattern was such a tangle that it had been an enormous effort to get as far as he had.

He'd been buying through intermediaries, and in a very low-key way, and he was paranoid that it could still fall apart. For that reason he couldn't tell us where it was, but he did say that completion on the final key contracts was very close, and it was going to be a very significant project indeed – a "landmark" development, he said, one of the most important in central London.

'Herbert was very alert by this stage, and his eyes lit up at the word "landmark". He promised that Slade would have all the resources of the practice behind him when the time came. He was getting quite excited.'

'Weren't you?' Kathy said. 'It must have sounded like a great opportunity.'

Jones hesitated. 'No, not really, to tell the truth. I was pretty jaded after the competition, I suppose. But, anyway, the thought of doing a big office development for First City didn't fill me with much enthusiasm. They're a solid company, but their work is very run-of-the-mill. Dead dull, actually. I quite like Slade, and in many ways he's an ideal client – he's straightforward and pays his bills on time. It's just that he's not interested in architecture. If you try to talk about it, you get the feeling he's indulging you. Which is a bit sad for someone putting up buildings all over the place.

'Anyway, Slade then said that he didn't want us to wait, he wanted us to start work designing the buildings straight away, which knocked Herbert off his perch a bit. "How can we, Derek, if we don't know where they're going to go?" he said, which seemed to me a pretty reasonable question. "Why not?" Slade came back at him. "People design cars and ships and aeroplanes that way all the time, don't they?"'

Bob Jones laughed and shook his head as he remembered.

'It was preposterous, but he meant it. He opened his briefcase and produced a drawing which his surveyors had prepared, of the outline of the site. It was really nothing more than a rough rectangle, about ninety metres in one direction and a hundred and twenty in the other. In one corner was a tube station, which he said would give an opportunity for some underground specialty shopping levels. The predominant use was to be commercial offices, about a million square feet in all, mostly in central core towers preferably, with net floor areas of ten thousand square feet per level. He didn't want any housing of course, but he could accept a small amount of non-commercial space as a sop to the planners if there was some convenient corner for it.

'The words "a million square feet" did something to Herbert's synapses, and he went quiet at this point, so I chipped in that it really would be impossible to do anything worthwhile without more information. Buildings aren't like ships and planes, they're rooted to the spot, they impact on one specific place, they sit alongside, overlook, cast shadows on, generate traffic around, a specific set of neighbours. To tell the truth, I still wondered if he was pulling our legs, but he was studying his fingernails in that very patient way he has, so I tried again. I explained we had to consider the context of our buildings right from the first concept stage as much as later on in the details. They have to take their place in their streets in a civilized way. Apart from anything else, the planners would insist on it.

'Slade let me finish, then let silence fall. I'd seen him do this before. It's his most reliable and effective technique, to let the opposition talk itself out, show its arguments, run out of steam, and then to wait for a moment in tense silence before he finally utters his verdict.

'"The site is in central London, Bob," he said at last. "You know central London. The present buildings on the site are all rubbish, with the possible exception of a small synagogue which I'm currently getting heritage advice on. The surrounding buildings are a mixed, undistinguished lot. You design your ideal solution to the brief I've just outlined for you – God knows it's loose enough, I should have thought. I always thought you architects were begging for a chance like this, with so few constraints. However, if you feel you can't do it . . ."

'That was the clincher, of course. Herbert practically jumped out of his seat. Of course we could do it! He loved the analogy to a ship! And, after all, the new project would establish a new scale and indeed *language* for the whole neighbourhood.

'So we agreed I'd prepare sketch drawings showing three alternative design approaches for another meeting two weeks later.'

Jones shifted uneasily in his seat. 'I'm getting a bit cold,' he said. 'How about you? It's the air-conditioning in here. Always gets it wrong.' He got to his feet and fiddled with a thermostat on the wall. Kathy and Brock watched him, saying nothing as they waited for him to settle again.

'I didn't feel any happier at the end of the two weeks. It was clear they were trying to get a very intensive level of development on the site. A million square feet on that area would give a plot ratio in excess of ten to one, which was more like Manhattan than London. The idea of trying to fit that amount of building in without any idea of what lay around it was just ludicrous, and I didn't really take it seriously. I went through the motions, though, and Slade seemed pleased enough when we met the second time. He brought his agent, Quentin Gilroy, with him, which is always a sign he's getting serious. They agreed I should develop the ideas a bit further and we'd meet again in another couple of weeks. But he still wouldn't tell me any more about the location.

'Well, I was finding this a bit hard to take. And when I thought about it, I realized it really wouldn't be too hard to find a central London synagogue that was on the list of buildings of historic or architectural interest, and that was also in the same city block as an Underground station. It took me a couple of hours to trace it, and on the way home that evening I paid my first visit to Jerusalem Lane.

'My first reaction was one of relief. There really wasn't any strong architectural character to the surrounding streets, and the buildings within the block were a mixed bag of structures that seemed to range from scruffy to downright dangerous. I didn't think the synagogue would be any great loss, and on the whole I was inclined to think that wholesale redevelopment would the best option, although the Lane itself intrigued me – it was such an odd thing.

'A couple of days later I went back at lunchtime for another look. I sat in the Balaton Café, looking out into the Lane. There were two old men in the café having an argument about whether it was Chopin or Liszt who was kissed by Beethoven – apparently it was Liszt. Then that rather formidable woman who runs the flower shop on the other side of that little square in the centre of the Lane came over and they had a discussion with her about whether she could find them a black rose for some anniversary that was coming up. Other people called in, taking up conversations with each other they must have started the day before, or maybe twenty years before in some cases. And gradually I began to get an idea of what an extraordinary crowd they were. There was a doctor, I remember, an odd-looking bloke – at least, I assume he was a doctor, because he practically set up surgery in the corner table. People would wander over and show him something and he'd shove his soup to one side and pull out his pad and give them a prescription!'

Jones laughed. 'Do you know them? Do you know what I mean?' And Kathy smiled, recognizing them immediately from his description.

'After lunch I had a closer look at the buildings along the Lane. They were every bit as eccentric as the people who lived in them really, but it was interesting how, in their arrangement, how they all fitted together to form this compact little *place* right in the middle of the city – part of the city, but also private and protected. And what went on inside the buildings was so varied too, little businesses that had probably been running on a shoestring for years all mixed up with flats and offices and a couple of small workshops.'

Kathy nodded, responding to the enthusiasm which lit up his face. Then abruptly it passed and he frowned.

'When I got back to the office and saw again the drawings I'd made, I began to feel very uneasy. The existing buildings might be inconvenient, impossible to modernize, an underdevelopment of a prime site. But to replace them with acres of dead standard office floors seemed somehow obscene. Talk about monoculture! After a couple of hours in the real Jerusalem Lane, the idea of trying to breathe life into those dead drawings seemed just hopeless.'

Out of the corner of his eye Jones saw Brock glance at his watch.

'Anyway,' he went on, 'I called in at the Lane a couple of times over the next week or so, trying to figure out what to do, and one of those times I found myself outside the second-hand bookshop up at the top end of the Lane. It would have been the seventeenth of July, because I remember it was the first anniversary of my divorce. It's funny, isn't it, that I can remember that date when I could never remember our wedding anniversary. Anyway, I thought I might find an architectural book as an anniversary present to myself. I didn't have much success. The place was a jumble, and even the bloke who owned it – Kowalski was his name, a Pole – didn't seem to have much idea of what he had, or where it was. I worked my way back through the rooms of the shop, all piled with books in shelves and boxes, the way you do in old bookshops – you know, imagining you're going to turn up an old Wendingen edition of Wright or something – until I came to the back room. There was a whole stack of old music scores in there, I remember, and books were heaped anyhow on the floor, and above them there were a few framed prints. One of them caught my eye. It was the frame I noticed first, quite an ornate thing. It contained what at first I thought must be an abstract drawing, a bit like a Paul Klee perhaps, made up of a grid of lines scribbled in black ink on dirty white paper.

'Mr Kowalski took it down from its nail on the wall and brought it through to the window at the front of the shop, to let me see it more clearly in the light. He used his handkerchief to wipe the glass on the front, I remember, and I saw that the scribbled lines were in fact lines of writing, done in a hurry with an old-fashioned steel pen, with spots and splashes of ink in places. Kowalski pointed to a date in the top corner, which we were able to decipher as "30 April 1867". The word beside it might have been "Hanover", but the script was so untidy and illegible that it was impossible to make anything else out. Kowalski explained that it was a letter, written in a way that was sometimes done in those days, to economize on paper. Its author had written first in one direction in the normal way, and then turned the page through ninety degrees to cover the sheet with a second layer of writing, which, if the script itself had been more intelligible, would have been quite readable against the first.

'I was rather taken with it. I liked the strong abstract grid pattern and also the puzzle of a text that might be decoded. I bought it from Mr Kowalski for a tenner, which I thought was probably a lot less than the frame would have been worth on its own.

'That evening I sat down with a magnifying glass and tried to decipher the letter. Some phrases were legible and it seemed that the writer was suffering from "carbuncles".' Jones grinned. 'I rather liked that. A couple of names were clear as well. There was a "Dear Fred" at the beginning, and a "Gumpert", who seemed to be advising the writer to take arsenic for the carbuncles. There didn't seem to be a signature, so I guessed the letter continued on the other side. I opened the back of the frame, and found I was right.

I suppose I'd been hoping it might have come from someone famous, and I was a bit disappointed to find it signed by someone called "Mohr". I still couldn't make much sense of what the letter said, anyway, because at least half of it was in German.

'I gave up, but the next day I phoned a friend who works for Lufthansa and speaks German. I faxed the two sides of the letter through to her, and she worked on it over her lunch hour. In the afternoon she faxed back her reply.' He looked round. 'We should have a copy here, actually. Since we started to do so much work through the fax machine, Sophie automatically keeps a copy of all incoming and outgoing faxes in a central file. I'm terrified about site instructions and sketch details and so on flying around unrecorded and going astray. I should be able to lay my hands on the translation if you can just hang on.'

'Mr Jones,' Brock broke in, sounding somewhat weary, 'is this all absolutely relevant, this letter? I think you lost me somewhere back there.'

'I'm sorry' – Jones took a deep breath – 'but yes, to be perfectly honest, it is relevant. Shall I fetch us some more coffee while I'm up?'

When he left the room, Brock muttered, 'I always worry about people who keep saying "to be perfectly honest" and "to tell the truth". It sounds like the verbal equivalent of crossing your fingers when you tell a lie.'

'Do you think he's lying?' Kathy asked. But Brock only grunted and got to his feet, stretching his back stiffly.

13

DEAR FRED,

Your letter arrived this morning and greatly cheered me after another wretched night suffering from a sudden outburst of carbuncles in places that make it intolerable to sit for more than a few minutes at a time. How I shall survive the journey back to London in a week or two with those swine eating into my behind I cannot conceive. I am quite resolved to take Gumpert's advice and resume taking arsenic, although it makes me stupid. At least the book is off my hands at last and I need not keep a clear head for that any longer. How great a weight lifted from my shoulders! Tonight I shall take your advice and get mercilessly drunk.

Meissner proves to be a quite excellent fellow, despite his dreadful Saxon accent. Printing has already started, and he talks enthusiastically about Volume 2. I discussed our plans for four volumes, contrary to his preference for three which I mentioned in my last letter. He is now quite converted and proclaims the highest expectations for the final volume, which will, he says, assure our immortality and make all our fortunes! I would be quite content with a more modest reward, at least enough to put off those 'gentlemen' who 'urgently' await my return to London. If only they would take my carbuncles instead, and leave me in peace to work. I have no more paper to write. Best compliments to Mrs Burns!

Yours,
MOHR

While Brock and Kathy read the fax, Bob Jones was on his knees in front of a cupboard in a corner of the room.

'Er ... there's a bottle of Scotch in here,' he said. 'It's been a long day. Do you fancy a snifter with your coffee?'

Brock stirred. 'Sergeant Kolla here is on duty, so she'd better not. But I'm more or less an observer, so I'll join you, Bob.'

'Good,' Jones said, 'fine,' and glanced at Kathy who kept her head down over the letter, but raised her eyebrows just a fraction. He brought over the glasses.

'I was sitting here, that evening, reading the fax again. I thought it was a hoot, but it meant nothing to me. Then I thought of Judith. She was the only historian I knew. We had been students together at university, and I hadn't seen her for fifteen years, but I seemed to remember that her thing was nineteenth-century economic history. I had no idea where she was, but I had the home phone numbers of a couple of other people who were in our group at university, and eventually I managed to track her down to Princeton and get her phone number.

'That had also been a long day, I remember, and by then it was well on into the evening. I'd had nothing to eat, and one or two of these' – he lifted his glass – 'and I suddenly thought how nice it would be to talk to her again after all this time. So I rang the number. It was her departmental office, and they said she'd gone home for the day. They wouldn't give me her home phone number, but I did get her office fax number, so before I left that night I sent her the translation, with a covering note asking if she could throw any light on it, and some other stuff which is probably best forgotten, to be perfectly frank.'

Jones noticed Kathy's smile and he shrugged ruefully.

'After a couple of days, when I didn't get a reply from her, I reckoned she wasn't interested, and I forgot all about it. I had plenty of other things to think about, to tell the truth, Jerusalem Lane among them.

'The second design review meeting for the project was held a few days later. I'd pinned up the more developed versions of the drawings of Options One, Two and Three on those walls there, and on this wall here I had some other stuff pinned up, but covered with blank sheets so they couldn't see what they were. After Herbert had made a few remarks about the vital issues, like his fee and whether Slade would have lunch with him, I talked about the three schemes on the wall. Then I suggested that these were perhaps reasonable enough, but I'd come to believe that maybe there was another alternative which might present greater opportunities. Slade pricked up his ears and asked what I meant, and I came over to this wall and ripped off the blank sheets, revealing Option Four.

'It certainly had an impact. Both Slade and Gilroy looked stunned. They recognized the plan form of Jerusalem Lane immediately of course. I started to explain that this option set out to take advantage of the asset already presented by the existing Jerusalem Lane. Slade cut in immediately, his voice very quiet. "What do you know about Jerusalem Lane, Bob?" he said. It was hard to see exactly how his expression had changed. His mouth, his eyebrows, they had shifted position by no more than a millimetre, but some-how it was the biggest millimetre you'd ever seen. Herbert saw it, though I don't think he really followed what was happening.

'I told Slade that I'd spotted the synagogue one day, realized it was close to a tube station, and put two and two together, but I don't think he believed me for a minute. I assured him I hadn't mentioned the location to anyone else, and tried to steer their attention back to the design. My idea was to keep a fair amount of the existing buildings as a sort of human-scale crust around the new stuff which would fill the rear courtyards with modern atrium-type office space. I suggested that the present diversity of building forms and uses and rental levels in the crust could be seen as an asset, enriching the overall development. I was trying to present the thing in positive development terms, you see, rather than negative conservation ones. I spoke about the historical origins of the Lane, and how these could become a selling-point, and I got quite lyrical about the benefits of having the present occupants and the new tenants coexist within a new, revitalized Jerusalem Lane.'

Kathy had put down her notebook, captured again by Jones's enthusiasm as he talked about his ideas.

'When I'd finished, Slade turned to the quantity surveyor who had come to the meeting, and asked him right off what he thought of Option Four. He was in an awkward spot, I suppose. He'd got the commission through us, but it was Slade who was paying his fees. He made a few general noises about imaginative lateral thinking, then pointed out that he'd had the drawings for less than twenty-four hours and hadn't had time to do much more than measure the floor areas for the various parts of the scheme. He passed copies of a list of typed figures round the table, and Slade said immediately, "Less than half a million square feet?" I could see Herbert go pale. I explained that, yes, it was a less intensive development form, but then construction costs would be lower proportionately, and there would be more rent-yielding uses of other types. And I was sure that the planners would be much more sympathetic to that type of approach.

'Slade then turned to Quentin Gilroy for his opinion. He didn't need to be so tactful. The construction cost might come down, he said, but the land cost would stay the same, so the rents would have to be higher for what he considered less attractive office space, with irregular shapes and awkward to let. And if my "crust" was going to wipe its face, there was no way the existing residents or businesses could afford the rents. "My God, have you seen some of those people, Derek?" he said. "Did you know there's an old chap up on the top floor of number 4 who's a signwriter for those lunatics who walk around with sandwich-boards saying the end of the world is nigh? That's all he does. His place is full of these sandwich-boards announcing the end of the world! It's unbelievable! I think our square foot rates might be a bit beyond his means." And Slade chuckled tolerantly. "Haven't seen that, Quentin," he said. "Must have a look next time I'm down."

'I felt the way I can remember feeling as a little boy. You know, you're happily going around pretending to be a rabbit or something, and suddenly some adult slams some great chunk of reality down on you, and you realize how little control you have on any of it. Do you know what I mean?'

Kathy nodded.

'Slade thanked me for the "interesting diversion", and we got back to Option Three. Later, after they had all gone, Herbert called me back into the conference room and closed the door. I could see he was absolutely furious. On the way out, he told me, speaking between clenched teeth, Slade had said that he hoped he wasn't paying us to spend time working on designs that didn't even meet half the brief. He said it jokingly, but he wasn't joking. Then he said that a Canadian developer was coming in on the project, and they felt that North American consultants should be involved, in partnership with us. Slade hadn't been sure at first, but now he was coming round to the view that it would be a healthy liaison. So now, Herbert fumed, they were going to bring in bloody Yank architects to do our job, because I'd been messing around, wasting time on tomfoolery – that was his word, a very Herbert word, actually.

'My performance had been humiliating, apparently, and downright unprofessional. But it wasn't just this project. He was beginning to feel that I was out of sympathy with the whole basic philosophy that they'd been building up at Basingstoke. He had to tell me that he was beginning to wonder if my presence in the partnership was doing either of us any good. He suggested that I give this some thought over the next few days, while someone else got to work on Option Three.

'The thing that really annoyed me, funnily enough, was that I'd got the idea for Option Four from that framed letter I'd bought at Kowalski's shop in the Lane – the idea of a grid contained within an elaborate old frame. The idea had come all of a sudden in the middle of the night, and it had seemed so appropriate that I thought it just had to be right. When it fell so flat I felt, well, betrayed somehow.

'I went back to my drawing board, and there were half a dozen telephone messages stuck all over it. One of them was to ring Judith Naismith, on a London number. I made the call, and immediately I heard her voice it was as if we'd left university only the day before, with only the faintest mid-Atlantic trace to mark the years between. She said she'd been glad to get my fax, but had been in a rush to get herself organized for a conference she was going to in Paris. She had a short stop-over in London, and she'd love to see me if I could spare any time that day.

'Judith was the great unscaled peak among the women undergraduates in our group. All the lads had tried to seduce Judith at one time or another, and none had succeeded. Even Charlie, whose powers of persuasion had cut a swathe from the women's college to the language school and through the nurses' home, had been very subdued in his account of his final great attempt on the north face of Judith Naismith. She was a beautiful enigma, and her reappearance suddenly made up for the disaster of the morning's meeting.

'We met for lunch. She looked absolutely stunning, just as I remembered her.'

Although Kathy was absorbed in the story, Brock gave a little cough of impatience. Bob Jones mollified him by offering another whisky, and then continued.

'We fairly quickly exhausted reminiscences and news of

mutual friends and what we'd done since leaving university. I could see she was a bit edgy, and I asked if she was short of time. She said yes, really she couldn't stay too long, but she'd wanted to find out about the letter I'd faxed her. I explained I'd picked it up by accident in a second-hand bookshop. I kind of rambled on a bit about the anniversary of my divorce, and she stopped me dead and said she'd like to visit the shop, and where was it? Suddenly I had the feeling that all the time she'd been much more interested in the letter than in seeing me again. I asked her what was interesting about it, and for a moment I could see her debating what to tell me, then she shrugged and started to explain.

'"Mohr" means "Moor" in English, as in Moorish – the Arabs, you know? And apparently it was Karl Marx's nickname. His family teased him that with his thick beard and swarthy complexion he was like a Moor.

'His closest friend was Friedrich Engels – "Fred". In April 1867 Marx went to Germany to deliver the manuscript of the first volume of *Das Kapital* to his publisher, Otto Karl Meissner, in Hamburg. He went on to Hanover before returning home to London in May. Gumpert was the name of Engels' doctor in Manchester, and Mrs Burns was his mistress.

'I think I made some stupid joke about it being a pity the letter was written by someone so unfashionable, and that I might have been lucky and found a letter from someone important, like Elvis. But all the time I was thinking about that blue plaque on the wall outside Kowalski's shop, saying Karl Marx used to live there.

'I asked if she thought there could be more. She seemed really puzzled about that. Apparently all of the correspondence between Marx and Engels was supposed to have been collected together when they both died. She said that it was now held in Amsterdam, in the International Institute of Social History. It had been published in nine volumes, and

Judith said she was going to check the volume for 1867 and see how this letter fitted in. She was puzzled as to how it had come to be separated from the rest.

'Then she asked me again where I'd found it. I kind of fooled around, and said that the price of that information might be high, considering how I'd always felt about her. You know, that sort of stuff. She humoured me, for about three seconds. So I paid the bill and we got a cab.

'You should have seen her face when we got to Kowalski's shop and I pointed out the plaque. There was the difference of dates, of course – Marx lived there in 1850, not 1867, but all the same, she was stunned. She said that coincidences like that just don't happen. We walked into the shop half expecting to see the ghost of Marx himself standing behind the counter, waiting for us.

'At first we got our wires crossed with Mr Kowalski. We assumed that the letter must have come from the shop itself, found in the attic or something, and he didn't understand what we were going on about. Eventually he explained that he had bought it not so very long ago. The lady who had sold it to him had also given him a box of books, but no other letters that he could recall.

'"What kind of books?" Judith demanded. "Old books, on history, or socialism perhaps?" He scratched his head and said no, he didn't think so. He thought they were children's books. He didn't know where they would be now.

'We spent a fruitless hour searching the shelves, Judith starting in Politics and History, and me in Children. Finally we spoke again to Kowalski, asking for the name of the person who'd sold him the letter. He was reluctant to give it to us, saying that the woman was elderly and might not want to be bothered. Was the document valuable, then? he wanted to know, sounding rather worried. He'd probably recognized the signs of an over-anxious buyer and thought there might be some money in this. He said he would speak to the seller himself, and see whether she had anything else that might be of interest to us. He took my business card and agreed to call me if anything turned up.

'But it was Mrs Winterbottom herself who phoned me a couple of days after Judith had gone on to Paris. She didn't seem to know what I wanted to talk to her about, so I explained that my friend was a historian, and she was interested in the letter I had bought from Mr Kowalski because it related to the period she was studying. Did Mrs Winterbottom have any other documents from that period? She wasn't sure, but said she'd have a look. Apparently there were lots of old papers and things her mother had left, but whether they'd been thrown out by this time, she didn't know. I told her that my friend would be back in London again in a couple of weeks, and asked if I could phone her nearer the time to arrange a meeting, and she gave me her address and phone number.

'By the time Judith returned from Paris, Herbert and I had agreed to part company. The Lowell Partnership moved to much larger and more prestigious premises in Docklands, establishing a joint project office with a firm of New York architects for the Jerusalem Lane project, which they were now calling "Citicenter One", would you believe. I took over the lease of this place, and set up on my own as Concept Design, with just one job, a loft conversion in a friend's house in Maida Vale.

'I contacted Mrs Winterbottom again, and she agreed to see us at a certain time on this Sunday afternoon – she was quite particular about the time.'

'When was this?' Kathy said.

'It must have been about a month ago. Yes, four weekends ago, I should think. Judith had timed her flights around the meeting. We arrived at 3, and Mrs Winterbottom invited us in to her flat and gave us a cup of tea. We chatted about the weather, and how Judith had been in Paris. Mrs Winterbottom mentioned she'd never been there, although it was so close, but she had been to Sydney, which was so far away, and she laughed at that. I got the impression she was sizing us up, to tell the truth, trying to find out if she could trust us. She chatted away about her family, and how she had a granddaughter who had been to Paris on a school trip, and I could feel Judith getting impatient, but trying not to show it. Then suddenly the old lady got down to business. She started talking about books. She didn't have any herself now, she said, she preferred the telly. But her sisters did have some of the old books their mother had left them. She explained they lived in separate flats upstairs, and would we like to take a look?

'We said yes, if it wouldn't disturb them, and she explained that they always went out on a Sunday afternoon, but that they wouldn't mind if we went upstairs and had a little look.'

'You said she was very particular about when you called,' Kathy said. 'Are you saying she intentionally made it for a time when her sisters would be out?'

'I didn't really think about it. I suppose it's possible. We went upstairs with her, and into a flat with the name "Harper", I think it was. Judith's eyes lit up when she saw the wall of books in the main room inside.

'"Eleanor loves books," Mrs Winterbottom said. "Most are fairly recent, I suppose, but I'm sure there are a few old ones that came from our grandmother to our mother."

'Judith was rapidly scanning the titles, as if she might at any moment be deprived of her opportunity. When she had looked at everything once, she returned to some old volumes on the shelves by the window. She took them out, one by one, turning to the flyleaf and then flicking through the pages. She had her back to me as she examined them, but I could hear her intake of breath as each book was opened.

'I went over and asked her if she'd found something. "Proudhon's *Confessions*," she said. "And look!" Her eyes were shining with excitement as she pointed to the handwritten dedication in the flyleaf. It was in the same black spidery writing as in the letter I'd found, though it had been more carefully scripted, and it was clearly signed "Karl Marx".

'"Are they the sort of thing you'd be interested in, then?" Mrs Winterbottom had been watching us from the centre of the room. I remember that as she turned to answer her, Judith suddenly stopped and stared at an old photograph hanging on the wall. She said something like, "Oh, how extraordinary", and the old lady told her it was their great-aunt, whom her sister admired enormously. "Mind you," she added, "some of our Eleanor's ideas are a bit odd to my way of thinking. She's an intellectual. Both of my sisters are. I inherited the common sense rather than the brain-power. But I'm the one what pays the bills." Then she said, quick as a flash, "And do you think them books might be worth a bob or two, then?"

'She caught Judith off guard, and I began to see that she was probably quite a shrewd old duck.

'"Well, frankly, Mrs Winterbottom," Judith said, "I don't think they would fetch much just left out on the shelves of Mr Kowalski's bookshop. But on the other hand they would be of value to someone like myself, studying the history of that period. I think I could probably persuade my university to come up with quite a reasonable figure for them."

'It sounded to me that she was patronizing the old dear, and I wasn't sure it was going to work.

'"My granddaughter is at the London University," Mrs Winterbottom said innocently. "Is that where you are too, dear?" Judith said no, she was at Princeton, in the United States. "Oh, an American university, eh? They have *lots* of money, I dare say."

'Judith began to look a bit worried. "Well, I don't know about that," she said. "But I think they might be willing to pay your sister . . . oh, perhaps fifty or even a hundred pounds each for these older books."

'"A hundred nicker! Well! That's better than a slap in the face with a cold kipper, eh, Mr Jones?" And she dug me in the ribs with her elbow and cackled happily. Judith said, "But do you think your sister would be interested in selling, though, Mrs Winterbottom? She might be attached to these books?" She sounded pretty anxious.

'"Well, you'd best leave that to me, dear," the old lady said. "She may not want to sell. But on the other hand we have a lot of expenses at the moment, and neither of my sisters contributes much in the way of cash, like. The pensions from their work weren't so good in their day, and they'd always rented, never bought as my Frank used to tell them – which is just money down the drain, isn't it? So these books, which was left to all of us, like, when our mother died, perhaps they're something that my sisters might feel they could now contribute toward the household expenses, now that we're in need. But I'd have to put it to them."'

'So she was quite specific about needing money?' Kathy said.

Jones nodded.

'And you don't think she'd previously had any idea that the books might be valuable?'

'That's right. My impression was that she was pretty sharp, and she probably guessed as soon as Kowalski contacted her that she might have something of value. Presumably she'd insisted on meeting us herself, rather than go through the book dealer. And once Judith started looking inside those books she really hadn't been able to hide her excitement. It was obvious to me, and it must have been to Mrs Winterbottom too.'

'What about Judith's valuation of them? Was it fair?'

'I've no idea. My guess, listening to her, was that they had to be worth more.'

'And if Mrs Winterbottom was as smart as you think, she probably drew the same conclusion?'

'I wouldn't be surprised.'

'Go on, then.'

'We had a look in Peg's flat too, but there were far fewer books there, and none held the same interest for Judith. Then we went back down to the first-floor flat, where we chatted about the weather. We assumed that was the end of our meeting, when Mrs Winterbottom suddenly asked if we were interested in papers as well as books, because she'd had a bit of a look and had come across one or two things. We sat down in her living room again while she disappeared into her bedroom. She waddled back in with two sheets of paper covered with the same black ink scrawl as on the letter. As soon as I saw it, I felt the hairs stand up on the back of my neck. I looked across at Judith and she was frozen in her seat, her eyes fixed on the pages.

'Eventually Judith asked, very quietly, what they were, and Mrs Winterbottom said that they were just a couple of sheets from a bundle of old stuff she'd found among her mother's papers. There were more, but most of them were in store. She wondered if this was the sort of thing Judith was interested in.

'Judith took the sheets carefully from her and studied the writing intently. Just the way she held them you could tell she felt as if she was handling something very precious. The old lady was delighted. "I can't make heads nor tails of it," she cackled. "It's like doctor's writing."

'Judith explained that it was very difficult for her, just sitting there, to tell what it might be. She said she'd really have to take them away and show them to someone else.

'"Oh well, that's all right, dear, I trust you," Mrs Winterbottom said. "Only, you might like to show good faith, like, and leave a small deposit."

'Judith jumped at the offer, then realized that she was only carrying francs and dollars. I had two ten-pound notes in my wallet, and she reached over and pulled both out and gave them to Mrs Winterbottom.

'"Thank you, dear," she said. "I suppose they must be worth at least that? So if there were a few hundred sheets, they'd be worth a few thousand quid?"

'Judith's jaw dropped. "There's a few hundred?"

'"Oh, I couldn't say for sure, dear. Not till I look. But I was saying just supposing."

'"Well, I don't know. Perhaps."

'"Course if they was valuable," the old bird went on innocently, "I mean part of our heritage, like, perhaps it would be wrong to sell them to an *American* university. Maybe I should see if a British university would like to buy them."

'To give her credit, Judith didn't show the panic she must have felt. She gave the old dear a warm smile and said, oh no, it was a specialized field, and Judith was about the only person working in it. She didn't think there'd be any British university interested in that sort of thing. There were so many old papers in people's attics, after all. It was a matter of being lucky enough to find a researcher interested in the specific ones. She said it so smoothly and casually. It was interesting to watch someone that you knew doing that, lying through their teeth.

'Mrs Winterbottom insisted that we drink a glass of port with her to toast our business partnership, as she called it, and then we left. Judith put the sheets between two layers of cardboard which she clutched tightly on her lap all the way back to the airport. She didn't want to talk. She just stared out of the car window, eyes shining.

'We didn't hear anything for a while, then Mrs Winterbottom contacted me again, making the appointment for last Sunday. Judith flew over especially from the States for the meeting, arriving at Heathrow that Sunday morning. She was bubbling with anticipation. The handwriting on the two pages was definitely Marx's, and the text was an excerpt from the draft of an essay on the theory of socialism, to which she hadn't been able to find any reference in any of the text books. In my car as we drove from the airport, and all the time we waited for the meeting, she couldn't stop talking about it. She went on and on about how she hadn't been able to sleep for thinking about the hundreds of pages that might be lying in some store-box somewhere.'

Bob Jones smiled at the recollection, and shifted his empty glass around on the table top.

'I thought she looked just like the agitated student she'd never been at university. I much preferred her this way, excited, enthusiastic . . . vulnerable, I suppose, although I'd have liked it better if she could have transferred some of that excitement in my direction. Oh well.' He shrugged ruefully.

'Anyway, you can understand why we were so disappointed when we couldn't get to see Mrs Winterbottom that afternoon. After we looked around at number 22, we decided to go and have a cup of tea somewhere and come back in half an hour, when she might have woken up. Actually we phoned then, but there was no reply. We tried again after another half-hour, and when there was still no reply, we walked back to Jerusalem Lane. That's when we saw the ambulance there, and somebody in the street said that Mrs Winterbottom had been taken seriously ill. Judith was devastated, but she had to catch the evening flight back to New York and couldn't wait.'

Jones sat back in his chair and took a deep breath. His chin sank on his chest and he seemed suddenly drained, as if completing his account had exhausted him. Kathy looked at him, wondering. She glanced at Brock, who gave no indication of wanting to pursue the interview.

'Did you talk to Mrs Winterbottom about the redevelopment of Jerusalem Lane?' she asked.

Jones shook his head.

'Oh, come on. You knew what was going on in the background, the plans that were being prepared. Surely you must have been curious about how she stood?'

Jones sighed and avoided meeting her eyes. 'To be

perfectly honest, I was embarrassed. I would have liked to know if she and the other residents realized what was going on, but I didn't want to have to answer her questions if she thought I maybe knew things that she didn't. Also, I felt I had an obligation to Slade to keep quiet. And ... I felt guilty, I suppose. The first time we met her I did mention that I'd noticed that the bookshop seemed to have closed down. She said the Kowalskis were leaving the neighbourhood, and I asked her if she had any plans like that. It was as far as I felt I could go. She said she didn't.'

'What about the books and manuscript? Have you got an idea of their total value? Did Judith mention anything?'

'No, no.' He shook his head wearily. 'Those figures I gave you were all that she said to me. She didn't talk about money at all when we met last Sunday, and of course we had no idea how much stuff Mrs Winterbottom was going to come up with.'

Kathy said nothing for a moment, then quietly, 'What were your first thoughts when you read that Mrs Winterbottom might have been murdered?'

Jones looked up at her, and she thought she saw anguish in his eyes. 'I ... I don't know. I suppose I wondered if it could have had anything to do with what Judith was interested in, but it seemed so unlikely. I mean she may not be the only scholar in the world interested in Marxist sources, but it's a bit esoteric as a motive for murder, isn't it? Then I thought ...'

'Yes?'

'I thought ... about the redevelopment project. I thought about that big office in Docklands with all those blokes drawing away like mad. I thought about the cost of servicing the site purchase-funding and the cost of delays ... When I asked Mrs Winterbottom about moving, she said she'd recently had an offer to sell, but she said she never would. She said they'd have to carry her out in a box.'

*

They returned to the car. There had been a short break in the rain, but water still coursed along the gutters.

'Can you drop me off at the Yard?' Brock asked. 'I have some things to catch up on.' He seemed preoccupied.

'Of course.'

They drove in silence for a while. Then Brock said, 'The lawyers would have a great time with him in the witness box. It'd take a week to get through his opening statement.'

'He did go on a bit,' Kathy said, glad to talk about it. 'I didn't really mind, though. I found the background about Slade quite interesting.'

'Hmm.' Brock stared out of the side window, arms folded. 'If it's relevant. You liked him.' It was a statement.

'Oh . . .' Kathy hesitated. 'Well, yes, I suppose I did. I liked the way he was honest about his failures. He was almost painfully open about them, I thought – about trying to seduce Judith Naismith, and the fiasco with his design for the Lane. And I liked his enthusiasm, the way he really believed in what he was doing.' She glanced over at Brock. 'You don't agree?'

'I kept thinking,' Brock said after a long pause, 'that he had an awful lot of overheads to support on one loft conversion in Maida Vale.'

14

Kathy stared up at the reflection of herself in the mirrored ceiling. Against the crumpled satin sheets her body and that of Martin beside her looked as if they had been pinned untidily into some giant specimen case.

'This place is so gross,' she said. 'Why do all your friends have such bad taste? They think "expensive" means "smart".'

Martin stirred and traced a finger down her side. 'Very convenient, though. Two minutes from the office. OK?' he murmured.

'Mmm. Always.' Actually it hadn't been so good. Martin was tense and hurried.

'Lot on?' she asked.

'Oh, yes. Difficult case in court later on this afternoon. You?'

'Always variety, you know. Yesterday we went to the seaside in the morning, a funeral in the afternoon, and heard a long shaggy dog story from an architect in the evening.'

'What was he like?'

'Who?'

'The architect.'

'Oh, I don't know. Quite sweet, I suppose. Except we don't know how much to believe.'

'Never mind. Not long before we get away from all this.'

'I dream about it. Seven wonderful days and nights with you, without an alarm clock or an appointment in court.'

The ostensible purpose of the trip to Grenada was Martin's attendance at an international conference of criminal lawyers, but he would duck out after the first day. He had booked them into a hotel so luxurious that each suite had its own swimming pool.

'How's it going with Brock?'

'Good. He was quite talkative yesterday. Still don't know much about him really, except that he's very gloomy about marriage – and just about any other kind of relationship too, as far as I can gather. "Doomed" was his word, I think.'

Martin laughed. 'What about his big case? Did he say any more about that?'

'Upper North? Yes, he said a bit.' She hesitated.

'Well?'

'I don't think I can tell you.'

'What?'

'What he told me. It was in confidence.'

'He told you not to tell anyone?'

'No. But I don't think he expected me to. You're annoyed?'

Martin had that sulky set to his lower lip which she had once thought appealing, until she had seen it on a photograph of him as a little boy standing next to his big brother who was holding a cricket bat.

'I just wonder sometimes what kind of relationship you can have with someone you don't trust, that's all.'

'That's not fair, Martin. You don't tell me everything about your work.'

'Oh yes I do.' His mood brightened. 'I told you all about the woman with the fish.'

Kathy laughed. 'Yes.'

'And the man who tried to steal the three-piece suite from Harrods.'

'Yes, yes.' He was tickling the soles of her feet.

'Well then, you can tell me all about the fiendish plot to recapture Upper North!'

'No, Martin. Brock –'

But Martin had turned abruptly and pushed himself off

the bed, the joke over. 'Bugger Brock,' he snapped, and strode out to the bathroom.

Kathy rolled over and swore quietly into the pillow.

She met Brock at the south end of Jerusalem Lane, as arranged.

He nodded as she got into the car. 'Productive morning?'

'A bit. Commercial Section are doing checks on Derek Slade and known past associates. Also Herbert Lowell and Bob Jones. Sylvia Pemberton can't be more specific about when she saw Adam Kowalski, but I've arranged for people to check with the book dealer in Notting Hill and the van rental place in Camden Town about the timing of the Kowalskis' movements that afternoon.'

'Yes, good. Thought any more about Jones's story?'

'I have been thinking about it, yes, sir. There are things about it that bother me now. He was very shaken up when we first told him why we were there, but his story didn't give much grounds for that, if it was true. Bits of it just don't make sense, and other bits sound like fantasy.'

'Which bits don't make sense?'

'Judith Naismith wouldn't fly specially here from New York to see Meredith Winterbottom, desperate to see what she had to offer, and then just leave her and have a cup of coffee while the old lady has an afternoon nap. They would have tried to wake her up. If they had phoned and got no reply, they'd have shot straight back to make sure she hadn't woken up and gone out.'

'Agreed, although he did know about the ambulance, so he was surely there after the event as well as before. What about the fantasy?'

'This amazing discovery – the Marx diaries or whatever they are. In the cold light of day the whole thing sounds so implausible. How convenient that we can't talk to Judith Naismith – if she even exists. Sam spoke only about a man in a bow tie, and the same with Adam Kowalski. Neither mentioned a woman. If she does exist, well, some of what he said may be true, but not all of it. Perhaps he did fax her the letter, and then met her in London that first time and found out the letter might be worth something. Then he might have decided to work her into the story of his subsequent visit to Meredith in order to throw suspicion on Judith, just as he threw suspicion on Slade.'

'What was he up to, then?'

'If he is up to something,' Kathy said reluctantly, 'it surely has to be something to do with the redevelopment project. It has to be. He is, or was, the architect, after all. How extraordinary that he should be hanging around the last building in the street that Slade hasn't been able to buy. Perhaps he's trying to embarrass Slade. He certainly did a fair job – "have to carry her out in a box"!' Kathy snorted. 'I think we took him by surprise when we told him he'd been seen going into Meredith's house, and he came up with a half-thought-out story to explain his presence there without mentioning the real reason.'

'Which was?'

'I don't know. He could have been advising her how to fight Slade through the planning process. Or trying to persuade her not to sell out, or perhaps to sell to *him*. I don't know.'

'Well, you seem to have thought it through' – he gave a little smile – 'very objectively. So what do we do?'

'After we've finished here, we should see Jones again. At least he should show us the letter he supposedly bought at Kowalski's. Remember, Kowalski couldn't even recall that it was a letter he sold him.'

They climbed the stairs to the second floor of number 22, passing on the way the silent landing on the first floor. Kathy's eyes were drawn to the locked door along the shadowy passage as if its panels had somehow acquired a residue of the personality whose private place had lain behind it, its paintwork now standing in for her face to the world.

The sisters were in Peg's flat. Through the living-room window the other side of Jerusalem Lane could be seen bathed in the afternoon sun. The room was less severe than Eleanor's, with chintz patterned curtains and armchair covers, and a patterned pink china tea service set out on the chest of drawers opposite the gas fire. This cosy domestic scene was presided over by a dramatically colourful portrait of Lenin hanging above the Wedgwood. It was painted in a social realist style, with the great leader gazing off towards a splendid future somewhere beyond the embroidered tea cosy.

As Bob Jones had said, there were fewer books here than in Eleanor's room. They filled one tall bookcase in the recess to the right of the chimney breast. A number of titles published by such bodies as the Institute of Marxism-Leninism of the CPSU Central Committee were jumbled in with a few Mills & Boon and Barbara Cartland romances.

There was a third person in the flat when Kathy and Brock arrived. Kathy recognized Terry and Caroline Winter's elder daughter whom she had met briefly in her home at Chislehurst, and then seen again at the funeral. Seeing Alex Winter now beside her two aunts, Kathy recognized the same dark, intelligent eyes as Eleanor's, the same serious set to her face and strong line to her jaw. But as yet she had none of her aunt's self-confident dignity and upright bearing. She glowered and turned away as Kathy acknowledged her.

The two sisters welcomed their guests warmly. Peg, a gracious hostess presiding over the proceedings as if over a vicarage tea party, produced from her small kitchenette cucumber sandwiches and thin slices of fruit cake served on Wedgwood plates, and sugar lumps offered with silver-plated tongs.

'We really just wanted to check that you were all right,

and see if there was anything you'd thought about or remembered since we saw you last,' Kathy said, suddenly ravenous after missing her lunch.

'I'd better go.' Alex Winter jumped up abruptly and began to pull on a quilted anorak. Turning to Kathy she said with sudden vehemence, 'You should ask them who's been trying to throw them out on the street!'

'Alex, dear . . .' Eleanor rose to her feet. 'There's no need to worry.'

'Has someone been bothering you, Miss Harper?' Kathy asked.

'Yes. My father!' Alex blazed. 'Less than an hour after cremating his mother he was trying to bully her sisters into leaving their homes!'

'Is that so?'

'It was something he said in passing when we were driving back to Chislehurst after the funeral, Sergeant,' Eleanor said. 'I'm sure he didn't mean to sound quite so forceful. He was upset after the service. We all were.'

'Isn't that just about the most repulsive thing you've ever heard?' Alex glared for a moment at Kathy, then turned to her great-aunts and quickly hugged each of them and ran out.

'She has the inflexible and unforgiving morality which only the young can afford,' Eleanor smiled after her. 'She is in her second year at LSE. Doing very well. I would like her to become a little less intense, though.'

'She is a fighter, dear.' Peg nodded with satisfaction and offered Kathy some cake. 'Meredith made it,' she murmured.

'And Alex is quite right about her father,' Eleanor added sternly. 'I would never have offended Meredith by saying it to her face, but her son is a parasite.' Kathy was surprised at the feeling with which the elderly lady spat out the word. 'He preys upon the vanity of women quite ruthlessly.'

'You *did* tell her to her face, Eleanor, dear. Don't you

remember?' Peg corrected her sister with a sweet smile. She turned to Kathy and added, 'She usually tells people exactly what she thinks. As a matter of fact, we were having a discussion about you, Sergeant, just as you rang the doorbell.'

'Oh dear, am I a parasite too?' Kathy laughed.

'No, you are part of the repressive apparatus of the ruling class, my dear, with which it maintains its grip upon the means of production and distribution and alienates the proletariat, naturally,' said Peg, beaming at her.

'My sister is teasing you, Sergeant,' Eleanor said. 'You mustn't take offence, although what she says is of course quite true.'

'I don't take offence, Miss Harper,' Kathy replied. 'I have an uncle who shares your views exactly. He has told me more than once that I am a class renegade and a carbuncle on the backside of the workers.' Kathy watched their faces carefully, but neither sister gave any sign of recognition of the phrase.

'How splendid!' Peg cried. 'We should meet your uncle. I'm sure we would get on so well.'

'He's not in London, I'm glad to say. He lives in what he likes to think of as the Socialist Republic of South Yorkshire.'

'Oh, but I expect he's proud of you really, and very fond of you.'

'I'm not too sure about that, Mrs Blythe.'

'Peg, dear. Please call me Peg. Eleanor and I were talking about you because I pointed out to her how splendidly well organized you are in the police force. So efficient.'

Eleanor gave a snort. 'My sister has a misplaced admiration for good order, Sergeant,' she said stiffly. 'She refuses to accept that the workers, once freed from one form of tyranny' – and she indicated Brock with a dismissive wave of her hand – 'might prefer to avoid being saddled with another.'

'The role of the Party, and in particular the Central Committee, is one of the principal disagreements we have,' Peg interpreted in a confidential tone. 'Eleanor is such an idealist. A utopian, in fact.'

'Peg! I will not be called such a thing!' She half rose out of her chair, and then, seeing Peg's delight at having goaded her so successfully, subsided and resumed her dignified, straight-backed posture with a sniff.

'Mrs Blythe, concerning your nephew,' Kathy said, 'he has admitted to us that he tried to persuade your sister to sell this house. Did she discuss this with you? You must have talked about it, surely?'

'Yes, she mentioned it, but only to say that she wouldn't entertain the idea. Although she indulged the boy, I believe it was the one thing she wasn't prepared to do for him.'

'Did she mention other people trying to persuade her?'

Eleanor thought. 'No, I don't think so. She didn't really talk to us a great deal about those sorts of things. I'm afraid we weren't of much use to her in practical matters.'

'She did say once that she suspected people were trying to trap her, or cheat her. Do you remember, Eleanor?' Peg added.

Eleanor shook her head. 'Sometimes, in the last months, she seemed a little confused. I think, seeing the Kowalskis leaving unsettled her more than she realized.'

'Did she ever mention the name Bob Jones, or Judith Naismith?'

Both sisters shook their heads.

'Have you ever seen a man who wears a bow tie calling around here?'

Again a negative.

'And did Meredith ever talk to you about selling books or papers to anyone, to make a little money?'

'Well now,' Eleanor thought, 'I recall some while ago, she did speak about getting rid of Terry's old children's books. I don't know if she ever did.'

'Did she, or do you, own any old original documents – handwritten papers, letters or essays – which were left to you by your mother?'

'We have old birth certificates and things like that. And family photographs. We did go through Meredith's papers – on Monday, I think it was – to make sure she hadn't left any instructions about her funeral arrangements. But I don't remember anything like what you describe.'

As they got to their feet, Brock said casually to Eleanor, 'Do you know of a writer called Proudhon, Miss Harper?'

'Of course, Chief Inspector.'

'Only I was advised to read him by someone recently.'

'Were you? I should have thought you'd be better off going straight to Marx. But perhaps you would find something in him. It was Proudhon, after all, who argued that without robbery and murder, property cannot exist.'

'Really? Well, yes, that does sound appropriate. Do you have any of his books?'

'I have an old copy of *Confessions*, I believe, although it's some time since I've looked at it. I'd lend it to you, except that it used to belong to our grandmother, and I wouldn't like to lose it.'

'Of course. Well, thank you very much for the tea. The cake was quite delicious. Now we'd better get back to the tedious job of repressing and alienating the proletariat, if you don't mind.'

Peg chuckled, and Eleanor looked sternly disapproving.

15

They couldn't get any reply when they rang Bob Jones's office, and when there was no answer from his home number in Paddington either, they decided to drive over there.

Regent Gardens was in effect an elongated square, with two long rows of cream-stuccoed terraces facing each other across a central grass strip. A series of columned porticos projected forward from the terraces to form entrance porches. Their front doors were approached across steps built over the moat which provided light to the basement rooms. In 1815 these terraces were among the most sought-after of the new residential developments springing up to the west of Regent's Park. Each portico provided a fashionable Doric address (noble, severe and indomitable, in keeping with the mood after the victory of Waterloo) for a family of the merchants and minor branches of nobility who moved in to speculate on rising property prices, and were soon to be disappointed by the crash which followed. Now each portico sheltered an untidy panel of door buzzers, intercoms and name cards, the steps accommodated ranks of empty milk bottles, and the narrow roads which ran along the front of the terraces were jammed with cars and motor bikes parked on meters.

Bob Jones's flat was on the ground floor. The front door to the building was slightly ajar, and Brock and Kathy went in, pushing past a padlocked bicycle just inside. At the far end of the hall a flight of stairs rose beneath an unshaded bulb, and two tall panelled doors faced each other halfway down the length of the hall. The one on the right was open.

Or, rather, it was hanging from the jamb, its frame

broken and smashed as by a sledge-hammer. They stepped over splintered wood and looked inside. The place had been trashed. Furniture was tipped over, table legs smashed, cushions ripped. Across the far wall of the room a message had been sprayed in black letters a metre high. FUCK YOU YUPPIE PIG. In the centre of the room, sitting on the floor among the debris, was Bob Jones.

'Are you all right?' Kathy asked.

He looked up, slightly dazed. 'Hello ... Look what they've done to my books, the bastards.' All around him were architectural books, their backs broken, pages ripped. 'They were about the only things I took with me when Helen and I split up. I thought I'd start afresh, but I couldn't bear to let go of my books. And now they're gone, too.'

'What happened?'

He took a deep breath and struggled to his feet. Kathy gave him a hand.

'They came back again, didn't they?'

'Who?'

He shrugged. 'The first time was about six months ago. I came home and someone had broken the lock and taken my CD player and the video. So I replaced them with the insurance, and put better locks on the door. Three months later they came again. That time they broke the locks open with a jemmy and took the new stuff I'd just got. So I replaced it again and put locking bolts in the door and a steel angle in the jamb. So this time they didn't bother with the locks, they just smashed the door in on the hinge side and did this.'

'Have they stolen the electrical equipment again?'

He looked around. 'Looks like it. Perhaps it's a regular three-month thing. They've probably got computer files of people who've been done over, with dates of when they're due for another check-up, like the dentist.'

'Were they this violent before?'

'No, not at all. The only damage in the past has been to the door. Maybe they got annoyed at having to work so hard to get in.'

'We'd better call the local CID from the car,' Kathy said. 'Your phone seems to be out of action.'

'What's the point? They'll never catch them. Last time I told them about the gang of kids that terrorizes the street – ten- and eleven-year-olds – throwing stones through the windows, smashing milk bottles, slashing tyres, that sort of thing. The policeman told me I should get an air gun and shoot pellets at them. I ask you.'

Kathy looked around. The flat was one large room, once the main reception room of the house, and tall enough for Bob to have inserted a sleeping deck across one end, with a galley kitchen and bathroom tucked in beneath it. Access to the upper deck was by a stair almost as steep as a ladder. The furnishings were spartan – canvas blinds rolled at the windows, photographic studio lights, industrial book-shelving, a few pieces of cheap Habitat furniture.

'Where's the letter you told us about?' she asked.

'I put it back in its frame. It was hanging over there.'

They looked in the corner he indicated, then among the wreckage, but found no sign of it.

Kathy went out to the car to call for the local police while Jones made coffee and Brock righted some chairs and cleared a space. When they sat down, Kathy spoke.

'They'll be here in a bit. Meantime, perhaps you could help us with the reason we came round here, Mr Jones. We were a little uncertain about a couple of points in your statement yesterday. Could we just go over a bit of it again?'

He sighed. 'Which bit?'

'The bit about finding Meredith Winterbottom asleep. Describe for us again exactly what happened when you arrived at Jerusalem Lane last Sunday.'

'Oh, that bit.' Jones seemed suddenly flat, defeated. He

sighed again, lowered his head and began to recount what
had happened – ringing the doorbell, going upstairs, entering
Meredith's flat, Judith looking round the bedroom door
and seeing Meredith asleep, him going upstairs to check the
sisters. Then he stopped.

'Go on,' Kathy prodded.

He lifted his head and looked at her, then at Brock.

'You know, don't you?'

Kathy got a tingling sensation along her spine.

'Tell us.'

'She wasn't asleep. She was dead. When I got down from
knocking on the sisters' doors Judith met me in the passage.
She seemed shocked, and didn't say anything at first. I
asked what was wrong, and then she told me that she'd
tried to wake Mrs Winterbottom, and she couldn't. She said
she must have had a stroke or a heart attack or something. I
said I'd ring for an ambulance, but then . . .'

'Yes?'

'She said there wasn't any point, and, anyway, she
couldn't afford any delay which might make her miss her
plane. She asked if I could wait until after her flight before
telling anyone. Then she said that as she had come all this
way, she wanted to search the flat to check if Mrs Winterbottom had brought anything for her. I didn't like the idea of
that at all. I said, suppose the sisters come back, how would
it look? So she asked me to go down to the front door and if
anyone came in to act as if I was on my way out for help.'

'Well?'

'That's what I did. No one came. After five minutes or so
I became impatient and called out to her. I started to go
upstairs again, but she came running out and we left. She
said she'd found nothing.'

'Was she carrying anything?'

'Her bag. A shoulder bag. A bit bigger than yours.'

'Then what?'

'I took her to the airport. Her flight didn't leave till 7,

and she made me promise not to do anything myself before then. If anyone asked, I was to say that we'd called on Mrs Winterbottom that afternoon as arranged, but had got no reply. I had no idea that anyone had seen us actually go in to number 22.

'On my way back from Heathrow I returned to Jerusalem Lane, and saw the ambulance. I thought, well, it's taken care of now, there's no point in doing anything more. Then when I read the newspaper report about suspicious circumstances, I . . . well, I just wanted to forget the whole thing.'

'You said you suspected Derek Slade of some involvement.'

'Oh, not seriously. Not when you actually say it like that. It's just something that went through my mind, that's all.'

'Why not Judith Naismith?'

Jones looked at his hands.

'Yes. I thought about that, too. But that's just as absurd. More so. Judith could never . . . kill anyone.'

'Did you see or hear Meredith Winterbottom yourself at any point that afternoon?'

'No.'

'So you can't say whether she was alive or dead at any stage in your visit.'

'No.'

Behind them two detectives from the local CID had arrived at the door.

'We'll go now, Mr Jones. Don't leave town.'

When they got back to the car, Brock said, 'Coincidence?'

'I don't know. It's not like a professional thief to waste time leaving messages and causing unnecessary damage. At least we'd better check if they come up with any finger-prints.'

'Well, anyway, Kathy, this case gets better and better. First we get to go to Eastbourne, now it looks as if you've earned yourself a trip to the USA.'

*

But it wasn't to be.

The following morning Brock and Kathy met in Kathy's office at ED Division. Kathy, furious, was pacing the three metres between the filing cabinets and the door. Brock sat quietly in the steel-framed chair by the window.

'I just can't believe it,' she said. 'Inspector McDonald just told me.'

'Yes, he rang me just before I left the Yard. Did he give you any details?'

'Only that he spoke with the coroner last night, and somebody called Marsden at the DPP's office this morning. They don't think there's any point in proceeding with the case. There'll be an inquest, but the coroner's private opinion at this stage is that Meredith was suffering from depression and committed suicide with the plastic bag after making herself drowsy with the port and sedative. The sisters discovered her either before or after their walk and removed the plastic bag before calling for help. That's not right, Brock! If they discovered her before the walk, they wouldn't have gone, they'd have called for help then. And if it was afterwards, then Judith Naismith would have seen the bag over her head.'

'What did McDonald say to that?'

'We don't know what Judith Naismith saw, and it would be too much trouble to find out. And, anyway, Meredith might just have had a heart attack after all – the forensic evidence is inconclusive. According to Inspector McDonald it simply isn't worth pursuing, not with all the other urgent things needing our attention.' She sighed. 'I'm going to Jerusalem Lane to speak to the sisters, tell them that we no longer think it could have been murder. At least they'll be relieved. Everyone in the Lane will be, except maybe Mrs Rosenfeldt, who was convinced it was all a Nazi plot.'

'Hmm, too bad. It was intriguing, but maybe they're right.'

'Bullshit, sir. You know they're not.'

Brock smiled. 'At any rate, Kathy, it's been a pleasure working with you. I hope we meet again.' He held out his hand.

'Yes.' Kathy stopped pacing and smiled. 'Yes, I hope so.'

Part II

16

He stood in the doorway of the canteen, watching the four woman detectives sitting together over by the window. The air was thick with the smell of fried sausages and chips, and he was reminded that he hadn't eaten that morning. Kathy was sitting with her left profile towards him, the April sunlight from the window reflecting off her fair hair. The women were laughing, and Kathy with them, looking happy and fit, her slender fingers brushing her hair back from her brow as she shook her head at some outrageous story.

Suddenly she turned and looked across the room towards him, as if she had sensed him watching her. She smiled with recognition, pointed a finger at herself and raised an eyebrow. He nodded and she got up from the table, saying something to the others as she left.

'Hello, sir. This is a nice surprise!'

'Kathy. It's good to see you again.'

They shook hands formally, Brock slightly awkward.

'That was terrific about North,' Kathy said, filling the momentary silence. 'Your picture looked good in all the papers.'

'Thanks. Look, you remember Meredith Winterbottom?'

'Of course I do. It was only six months ago.'

'Her sister Eleanor was found dead this morning. No doubts this time. She was murdered.'

'Oh no!' Kathy looked stunned. 'Poor Eleanor,' she whispered. 'That's terrible. I remember so clearly the last time I saw her. I told her that we'd decided that Meredith hadn't been murdered after all, and she was so relieved. Oh, that's awful.'

'I've been given the case, and I'm on my way over there

now. I want you to work with me on it, Kathy, if you'd like to. McDonald says it can be arranged at this end.'

Kathy nodded fiercely. 'Of course I would!'

They got into Brock's car. He didn't start the engine immediately, but instead turned to her.

'You're looking really well, Kathy. Life must be agreeing with you.'

'Oh well,' she said, smiling, 'more or less under control, you know.'

'What about that man you were seeing?'

'No. That didn't work out. We decided to call a halt.' She shrugged, puzzled by his question.

'Good. He wasn't right for you.'

She frowned. Still he made no move to start the car. There was silence for a moment, and she decided to change the subject. 'Well, I was thrilled to see your plan worked with North. That was really great. I didn't see any reference to drugs, though. He tried to make a break for it, didn't he?'

'Yes, he heard that he was going to be arrested, so he tried to leave the country. We were waiting for him when he landed in Lisbon.'

'Oh gosh, so he nearly slipped away again, like the last time.'

'Not really. He was never going to be arrested on drugs charges. We just got him to believe that, through the same source that tipped him off before. His solicitor, Martin Francis Connell.'

Kathy froze. 'Martin!'

Then, carefully, 'Martin wasn't his solicitor, he said he wasn't . . .'

Brock sat with his head bowed, letting her work it out.

'How would Martin have been able to know about the police investigation?' she asked.

'There were two possible sources, both detectives in ED

Division who helped with the original case. One was Detective Sergeant Andrew Rutherford.'

'Andy Rutherford. He was suspended last month.'

'The same day North was arrested.'

A pause.

'And the other one was me?'

Brock said nothing, waited.

'The Winterbottom case,' Kathy said slowly. 'You were never part of it, were you? You were still working on North. It always seemed so odd to me. And you were so casual about the investigation. Not at all how I'd heard you were. I thought you'd mellowed!' Her face was to the side window, her voice gradually hardening with anger. 'But I was working on the case and you were working on me. Martin used me, and so did you. God!' She turned to face him, eyes blazing. 'Couldn't you have told me?'

'I'm telling you now, Kathy,' he said softly, eyes fixed on the foot pedals.

She stared at him, her anger flowing, breathing hard.

'Well, too late!' She reached for the door handle.

'Think about it, Kathy. That's over now. There's no doubt about trusting you any more.'

'Oh, is that right, sir? And how do you think I'd ever be able to trust *you* again?'

At around 8 that evening Brock was caught in a thunderstorm as he stepped out of his car. Both lifts in Kathy's block were out of action, and he had to climb the twelve floors. It was like a steam bath inside his coat by the time he arrived, chest heaving, at her door.

She took so long to answer that he was on the point of turning back when at last her door opened. Her face was pale, without make-up, her hair pulled severely back from her forehead. She was wearing faded jeans and an old sweatshirt. She stared coldly at him, saying nothing.

'Ah, Kathy. Glad you're in.' His amiability sounded

strained, especially since he was still gasping to recover his breath. 'Just thought I'd have another word with you ... about this morning.'

'I'd rather not if you don't mind, sir.' She started to close the door, but he stuck out his foot. She stared at it for a moment, then looked him in the eye. Embarrassed, he withdrew it and raised his right hand. In it was a bunch of blue cornflowers, gift-wrapped with a pink ribbon.

'Did you buy those for me?' she asked slowly.

'Yes, I ... er ...'

'If I had been a male officer, would you have bought them for me? Or did you think that, being a woman, I'd just go all gooey at the sight of a bunch of flowers?' Her voice had a terrible calm. 'If I may say, sir, I think it would be best if you didn't give me those flowers, because I'd just have to waste five minutes feeding them down the sink garbage grinder. I'd have to do that, because if I put them in a vase I'd spend even more time cleaning up the floor, on account of my throwing up every time I saw them. So on balance I think it would be best if you just took them home and gave them to your mother or sister or whoever it is you live with.'

Brock's mouth opened and closed a couple of times. For a moment he was utterly at a loss as to what to say. He was saved by a small voice behind him.

'Everything all right, dear?'

Kathy looked past his shoulder, 'Yes, Mrs P. Everything's fine.'

She looked back at the bulky figure of the Chief Inspector, steaming, dripping and wilting in front of her, and some momentary instinct of generosity overcame her.

'Oh, come in, then,' she said, and turned back into her flat.

He didn't like to remove his coat, nor was he invited to do so. The place was simply and frugally furnished, and he sat himself on an old plastic chair beside an oval timber dining table. The curtains were open, and the window was filled with the blackness of the night, criss-crossed by chains of streetlights on the ground far below, trailing off to the horizon.

He laid the flowers on the table.

'You're right, they were a bad idea. The woman in the shop suggested them. Roses would have been wrong, and the irises and chrysanthemums seemed too assertive somehow. I haven't got a mother or a sister as a matter of fact. I live on my own. Have done for a long time now. I quite like it, really. Got used to getting home to an empty house, going to sleep in an empty bed, and now I enjoy it. The main problem is the food, having to cook for one. I like to cook, but the quantities are too small, and after a while the freezer just fills up with stuff I'm never going to eat. Do you find that? I was married for a while, but it didn't last very long. I think, being a copper, the hours, I don't know. We had one child, a boy. Yes, I know I told you I didn't have any children. I usually do, it's easier. We never kept in touch much. And now I'm not sure where he is. Canada, the last I heard.

'I try not to let the hassles of the job get to me, on a personal level, more than they should. But I feel bad about this, with you. I don't blame you for feeling the way you do, and I just wanted to say sorry. Sorry because I liked you, and sorry because I like to work with the best, and I thought you were a good officer. So, I'll take these and go.' He picked up the bunch of flowers and started to get to his feet.

'Oh, put them down,' Kathy said. He subsided into the chair again. She stood facing him, a hand on her hip.

'Tell me how you knew it was Andy Rutherford and not me.'

Brock shrugged. 'We gave each of you the same information about the drug raid, but then we gave each of you something else. We told Rutherford that we were about to do a deal with the Swiss Government to get at the assets which serious criminals were holding in Swiss banks. North shifted his money out of Switzerland just before he ran. We told you about his son having leukaemia. It was clear when we caught him that he had no idea about that.'

Kathy nodded. She remembered with relief how close she had been to telling Martin, and the thought of him brought the usual sharp stab, smaller now but still there. She shrugged her shoulders in a gesture of resignation and sat down opposite him. 'Martin was very special for me. I know all the reasons why he was wrong, but I can't deny him that. I've got over him now, more or less. Although I wish the bastard hadn't taken his wife to Grenada. I'd offer you a drink, but I'm out of everything.'

'Well now,' Brock said, 'in the faint chance that the flowers didn't work, I did take the liberty of bringing this too,' and he drew a bottle of Scotch from his coat pocket. Kathy laughed and went to the kitchen for glasses and a jug of water.

They stood by the window looking out over the city, sipping the whisky.

'After those five days in Jerusalem Lane last year I became quite discontented here for a while,' she said. 'They have no views like this, nothing except of the street, but they don't need them. They're in a *place*. Here you're on the *outside*. There's no place here. No one knows anyone else. Mrs P only speaks to me occasionally because she needs me sometimes for help with the shopping. People like the anonymity, of course. I did until I spent that time in the Lane, then I realized what we missed.

'They were a real *family*, the three sisters, weren't they? You could tell, from the way they talked. They were talking in a family code that was sometimes hard for an outsider to follow. What they *believed* was a reflection not just of the kind of people they were, but of the part they played in the family. You know, the practical one who put the food on the table, the principled one who kept them on the straight and narrow, the tease who got them over the humps. I was brought up in what passed for a family of three, too — father, mother and daughter. But I reckon the three sisters were able to share more in one afternoon than we managed in fourteen years.'

Brock looked at her in surprise. 'You didn't get on with your parents, Kathy?'

'I don't think it was a matter of me getting on with them. Mum was all right, but her sole mission was to look after Dad. And Dad was, well . . .' She thought for a moment and then smiled. 'I remember Bob Jones used a phrase, when he was describing Judith Naismith: the north face of the Eiger. That was my dad. You don't *get on* with the north face of the Eiger. You either affront it, or you don't exist.'

'Do you still see them?'

She shook her head. 'They're both dead. My father was a civil servant. He entered the Civil Service Commission in 1953, and transferred to the Department of Trade and Industry in 1962. In 1971 he was promoted to Under Secretary.' She spoke as of a stranger she had once investigated. 'He had this one vanity, a large Bentley. I found it excruciatingly embarrassing when I was a little girl, the way all the other kids used to stare at this huge posh car, and I'd try to slide down in the seat so I couldn't be seen, which annoyed him no end. One day, when I was fourteen, he drove it into the pillar of a bridge on the M1. We thought it was an accident until things began to come out about his financial affairs. Apparently he had been involved in some kind of fraud, I don't know exactly what. I have the idea that it was to do with the sale of surplus government land. That was the same year that the Home Secretary had to resign because of corruption investigations, do you remember? Reginald Maudling. I remember the Fraud Squad interviewed my mother a couple of times, and she didn't handle it very well. I've sometimes thought about trying to have a look at Dad's case file, just to find out what it was he did. But then, I'm not sure that I really want to know.' Kathy paused, sipped at her glass.

Brock cleared his throat. 'If you do decide you'd like to find out, let me know.'

She nodded. 'Thanks. After a bit we discovered he'd been speculating large sums of money with some shonky developer who had just collapsed. We had lost everything. The house, the furniture, his pension, everything went. We moved up north to Sheffield, where my mother's sister and her husband took us in to their two-up, two-down terrace.'

'Was that your red uncle?' Brock said. 'The one you told the sisters about?'

Kathy laughed. 'You've got a good memory. Yes, Uncle Tom, the red terror of Attercliffe. He was a bus driver, retired early with a bad back. He thought that what had happened to us was providential retribution – my father's bourgeois greed attracting the proper consequences of the inherent contradictions of the capitalist system, or some such. He couldn't resist reminding us at every opportunity of how far we'd come down in the world. Aunt Mary knew how to deal with him. She could put him in his place with a couple of words. But my mother couldn't cope at all. She sank into a kind of despair. I suppose it was depression.' Again she lapsed into silence, staring out of the window at the lights in the darkness.

'It must have been very difficult for you,' Brock said.

'I'm sorry. You've probably had a hard day. I don't know how we got on to this. I can't remember when I last thought about it.'

'It was talking about Jerusalem Lane, and families. So what happened, Kathy? I'd like to hear the rest of the story. You were, what, fifteen at this stage?'

She nodded. 'Yes. I was getting much the same from the

other kids at school as Mum was getting from Uncle Tom. I talked funny, and I didn't know how to stand up for myself. God, why would I? My only experience of physical aggression up to that point had been a clip on the ankle with a hockey stick. I had a lot to learn.

'Mum was a worry. She'd just given up, turned in on herself. I went to the Council, and pestered the social workers and the housing people until they gave us a flat on our own. I thought if I could get her to make her own home again, she'd begin to come round. It was a high-rise, like this. I liked it because all the rooms faced south, and always caught any sun that was going, unlike at Uncle Tom and Aunt Mary's, which was dark and damp. But I don't think Mum even noticed. She never went out on her own all the time we were there. Aunt Mary had to come and visit her, as if she was an invalid, and pretty soon she was. She lost weight and began to pick up infections, which got more and more persistent. Just before I reached sixteen she caught pleurisy. She died of pneumonia within a couple of weeks.

'As soon as I could leave school, I told Aunt Mary I was going back to London. She gave me fifty quid and the address of the Y. It took me quite a few years before I found my way into the police.

'Yes, I can remember when I last thought about this. It was with you, Brock. We were coming back from interviewing the Kowalskis at Eastbourne. You pointed out how their whole life had been changed by one moment in the war, and at the time I thought, yes, that had happened to my mother and me. My father turned his steering wheel a few degrees and everything changed.'

'Well,' Brock said at last, 'I'd say it was the making of you, Kathy, wasn't it?'

She smiled. 'I hadn't thought of it that way.' Then her brow creased in a frown. 'How did Eleanor die, Brock? You didn't tell me.'

'She had a plastic bag over her head.'
'Oh God.'
'And just to make sure, they'd bashed her head in.'

17

Kathy had a disturbed night. Vague and uneasy images haunted her shallow sleep, and in the waking intervals her brain kept returning to insignificant incidents of her past work which now seemed ominous and foreboding. When the alarm clock beside her bed showed 5 o'clock, she was glad to abandon the attempt to sleep further and got up. With the lights on and a mug of hot tea beside her bed, the sense of unease evaporated. Brock had warned her that the incident room set up at Jerusalem Lane was cold, so she pulled on layers of warm clothing, relishing the prospect of returning to the place which she had not been able to forget during the six months since Meredith Winterbottom's death.

She broke her tube journey to call in at ED Division, where she left some messages and picked up her files on the abortive Winterbottom investigation of the previous September. She skimmed through these, as she waited for the tube to Jerusalem Lane.

When she arrived, she found the main Underground exit sealed off. It was only when she reached street level through the alternative exit on to Welbeck Street that she realized why. Looking across at the near corner of the Jerusalem Lane block, she saw in the dawn light that the tube station and its surrounding buildings no longer existed. She felt a jolt of shock, like the survivor of a night air-raid returning to the surface and discovering a ruined and alien wasteland where the day before had been the intimately familiar landscape of home. A smell of burning hung over the place. Irrationally, she wondered if the man who had been protecting his newspapers with plastic sheeting on that corner had survived, and then noticed him further along on her side of the street.

Crossing over, she came to the north end of Jerusalem Lane and saw through a high chain-link fence that almost the whole of that half of the block lying on the east side of the Lane had gone. Witz's Cameras and Kowalski's Bookshop, Dr Botev's surgery, Brunhilde Capek's flower shop – all had gone. Only the synagogue, its north wall raw and exposed by the surrounding demolition, remained at the far end of a huge hole which dropped away beyond her feet. From the darkness of its depths, where unfamiliar frameworks of scaffolding were already climbing up towards the surface, came flashes of blinding white light, the whine and growl of machinery, and the clanking of metal-tracked vehicles, as if the panzers of an invading force were rousing themselves for another day of action.

At first sight the west side of the Lane appeared intact, but as Kathy walked down towards the south end she saw that most of the doorways and windows were boarded up against the entry of vandals. The doors to the office of Hepple, Tyas & Turton and the flat of Sylvia Pemberton had four-by-twos nailed across their frames, and the windows of the Balaton Café and Böll's Coffee and Chocolates were covered with plywood panels on which cheaply printed posters for rock and jazz concerts were already beginning to look tattered. The two remaining shop windows at the south end.– Mrs Rosenfeldt's deli at 22 and Stwosz's newsagency at 24 – looked fragile and threatened. The shop front of number 20 had also not been boarded up, for now it served as the police's temporary incident centre. The light glowing through its window was the only one on this side of the Lane. A uniformed constable stood at the door, talking to a couple of newspaper reporters whom Kathy recognized.

Inside, the incident centre was remarkably spacious and well-appointed for an on-site facility. The front shop counter served as a reception point, with the area in front used as a waiting area and for press conferences. The room at the rear served as a general office, with telephone and computer links to Scotland Yard, and there was a small kitchen, stocked and operational. Upstairs was Brock's office and an interview room. Brock wasn't expected till after 8, and Kathy decided to use the time to take a look next door, at number 22, where the scene-of-crime crew had finished on the previous day.

The uniformed man opened the front door for her, switched on the hall light, and then closed the door again, leaving her to climb the stairs of the silent house alone. There was a smell of damp and mould which she hadn't noticed six months before, as if winter had been more successful this year in penetrating the cosy sanctuary of the old ladies' home. In Eleanor's flat there were further signs of this: a damp green stain in the corner of her sitting room and paper peeling from the wall in the small bedroom. The frugal simplicity of her taste now made her home seem forlorn and cold, the cell of an ascetic nun. Only the wall of books in her sitting room retained a sense of having belonged to an individual rather than an institution. Kathy went carefully through the flat, trying to compare it in her mind with her memory of the place six months before.

When she returned next door, Brock was emerging from the rear kitchen with a mug of coffee. He waved her upstairs and she followed him a moment later with a cup of her own. The lights of his office were on against the gloom of the morning, and a fan heater was humming in a corner.

'Well, this is pretty good, isn't it?' Brock beamed, leaning back in a battered old steel chair. 'I reckon this is the most luxurious incident centre I've had for years. They had no room at the nearest nick and all these empty buildings around here seemed too good to waste.'

Kathy's eyes had fixed on the colour photographs taped across one wall.

'Yes, have a look.'

Her attention had been taken by a series of pictures at one end showing the top of a woman's body. The head was wrapped in a crumpled plastic bag, but it was difficult to identify the face because part of the inside surface of the bag was red with blood. Eleanor had been wearing a plain white cotton nightgown, and her shoulders and arms were almost as white as the material.

Like a bride, the thought came unwelcome into Kathy's head.

'What does the pathologist say?'

'Probably suffocated, then bashed on the forehead with proverbial blunt instrument just to make absolutely certain.'

Whacked on the head, she thought. *Who was it said that?*

'Most of my manpower yesterday had to be wasted looking for the damn thing.'

'No luck?'

Brock shook his head. There was a tap at the door and Brock spun round.

'Come in, Bren! Meet DS Kathy Kolla. This is DS Brendon Gurney. Have you met?'

Sergeant Gurney shook his head and smiled at Kathy, shaking her hand. 'You were in charge of the sister's murder, Kathy?' He was a big man like Brock, though twenty years younger, with a deep, slow, West Country voice which Kathy immediately trusted.

'Yes, although at the time we couldn't be sure it was murder.'

'Well, this surely makes it look more certain, unless someone is just trying to make it seem that way.'

She nodded. The two men looked as if they could have been father and son, and she had a momentary mental image of two large furry creatures, bears perhaps, or badgers, ambling through the wild wood, immensely dependable and strong. Bren Gurney actually made Brock seem quite agitated and quick in comparison with the figure she remembered from the earlier case. Or more likely, she thought, he's taking this one seriously. At any rate, he was rubbing his hands, pacing up and down, and shouting down the stairs to a couple of DCs, telling them to come up for a review of the previous day's progress.

Sergeant Gurney began with a summary of the circumstances surrounding the discovery of the body. As significant points were mentioned, he noted them with a blue felt pen on a white board propped against the wall. Brock sat back on his metal chair with his feet up on the desk, his head propped on his hand, fingers spread across his face, occasionally clawing his beard.

'Mrs Peg Blythe discovered the body of her sister, Eleanor Harper, at around 7.30 yesterday morning. Although they had separate flats, they were in the habit of having breakfast together, usually at Eleanor's. Since their sister Meredith had been killed six months ago, they had kept their front door locked, and Peg opened Eleanor's with her key, after there was no reply to her knock. She found her sister in her bed' – he waved at the photographs – 'screamed, phoned the police. ED Division responded, and they asked for our assistance as soon as the link with the earlier death was recognized.

'The pathologist doesn't think he'll be much help with the precise time of death. It was obvious she had been dead some time, but her electric blanket was on, making the normal signs unreliable. So far he can only say five to fifteen hours before 8 a.m. Peg says she and her sister spent the evening together in Peg's flat, reading, after she'd cooked supper – toasted cheese with tinned spaghetti on top, her favourite. They parted to go to bed at around 9.30 p.m.

'Yesterday we concentrated on trying to find the hammer or whatever was used to hit the old lady, and on door-to-door inquiries. As you'll have seen, almost nobody lives around here any more, and we haven't had any results so far with either line of inquiry, but I assume we'll continue today, sir? Yes.

'Two further circumstances which came to light yester-day, which may or may not be relevant. First, local CID tell us that there have been fourteen separate reported incidents at 22 Jerusalem Lane over the past five months, reported either by the sisters or by Mrs Rosenfeldt downstairs.'

He picked up a print-out.

'Brick thrown through window, water main cut off, super-glue in the front door lock, an intruder tapping on the windows in the middle of the night, and so on. No actual break-ins. Minor damage, but terrifying for elderly ladies in a place like this. That doesn't include the nasty phone calls. They went on until British Telecom started intercepting the calls a week or so ago. CID sent a crime prevention officer round here to talk to the sisters, and they put security catches on the windows, but not an alarm system. However, Eleanor's bedroom window was open when Peg found her yesterday morning.'

'It's an old vertical sliding sash window, isn't it, Bren?' Kathy said.

'That's right. The security fixture was one of those bolts drilled through the side frame of the lower window, meant to slot into a hole in the other window's side frame a few inches up so you can have a little bit of ventilation without anyone being able to get in. But the bolt was hidden by the curtains, and it's possible she just opened the window a crack without remembering to push it home. Outside is the metal fire-escape stair down to the rear yards below. No indication yet of prints or other signs of an intruder.'

'We checked both flats for signs of forced entry, didn't we, Bren?'

Gurney nodded. 'Nothing obvious.'

'All right,' Brock said. 'You mentioned that there were two things that came to light yesterday, Bren?'

'Yes. The other was a couple of phone calls yesterday for the sisters from people who wouldn't identify themselves. The phone used to be downstairs, I understand, in the first sister's flat while she was alive, then it was moved up to Peg's. Well the first call was from a woman who asked for Eleanor, but then hung up when the WPC asked who she was. An hour later there was a second call, from someone who didn't speak, and rang off after listening to the WPC's voice.'

'Didn't British Telecom intercept the calls?'

'No, we needed the line so we told them not to.' Gurney wrote the words 'anon phone calls' on the board.

'OK, let's move on to lines of inquiry, then,' said Brock, easing himself upright in his chair. 'Kathy, why don't you give us a summary of what your investigation threw up last autumn?'

Kathy got to her feet and went over to the board while Sergeant Gurney sat down. 'The most promising line then, and obviously more so now, concerns the redevelopment of this area and the refusal of Meredith Winterbottom to sell out to the developer, Derek Slade of First City Properties plc. According to Slade he didn't really need number 22 in order to proceed with his development, but I don't think we know the full story. The fact that Meredith was the one person in the whole block refusing to sell surely had to be more than a coincidence.

'Then there was her son, Terry Winter. He seemed to be living beyond his means and on the verge of facing an expensive divorce. At first he'd tried to persuade his mother to mortgage her house, then he suggested that she sell it. Slade said that First City had offered Meredith a quarter of a million, but that if the development went ahead without her property it would eventually be worth next to nothing. Whether or not that was just a negotiating ploy, if Winter had believed it he would have had a strong incentive to get his mother out of that house quickly. Terry's alibi for the afternoon his mother died depended on his mistress, Geraldine McArthur. Although he inherited his mother's house when Meredith died, she had arranged it so that her sisters could remain there, rent-free, for as long as they wanted, so his motive remains, and in fact becomes stronger as time passes.

'There was also the architect, Bob Jones. He was the last person we knew of to enter Meredith's house before her body was discovered by her sisters. At first we assumed his visit must have had something to do with the redevelopment, but when we tracked him down he claimed not. Instead he came up with this strange story about valuable historical documents which Meredith owned, and which a friend of his, Judith Naismith, was anxious to get hold of. At first he lied to us about Meredith being asleep when they called, and later admitted he knew she was dead, but we had nothing to corroborate his story. We didn't even know if Judith Naismith existed, and a letter written by Karl Marx, which Jones claimed was the start of their treasure hunt, was conveniently stolen just before we arrived at his flat.

'Incidentally, sir, when I went into Eleanor's flat just now, I looked for the old books which Jones claimed they saw in her bookcase and which Judith got so excited about. There was one title he mentioned . . .' She thumbed through her notes.

'Proudhon's *Confessions*,' Brock said. 'Yes. I looked for the same thing yesterday, Kathy.'

She looked at him in surprise. He hadn't taken notes during the case and hardly seemed to be paying much attention.

'I had a DC check the whole bookcase, and then go through the rest of both Eleanor and Peg's flats. There are no nineteenth-century editions in the house, and no books with handwritten dedications by Karl Marx.'

'Well, that just makes the whole of Bob Jones's story more implausible, then,' she said.

'Quite possibly.' Brock scratched his chin.

'You were worried by Jones, weren't you, sir?'

'Yes. The property motive is obviously a powerful one, and a murderer within the family makes sense in statistical terms. But this other story of his is so much more intriguing. How on earth would these old ladies, improbably extreme Marxists themselves apparently, living in a street where Marx himself once lived – how would they have original letters and books and belongings from the great man in their possession? Would anybody invent a story like that? It seems so implausible. But if you did come upon such an improbable treasure, and you had just set up in business on your own, short of cash, and if you knew that the whole area would soon be redeveloped, and the treasure probably gone . . .'

'I remember I had the feeling that we had caught him on the hop,' Kathy said. 'He took ages to tell his story, almost as if he was feeling his way through it without having had time to plan it.'

'Well, there are certainly things about it that we should check. If only to give you a trip to New Jersey, Kathy.'

'Yes, sir,' Kathy smiled. 'And then there's the Kowalskis and the Croatia Club, and their feud with Meredith Winterbottom. I suppose Eleanor's murder makes their involvement less likely now. It always seemed an unlikely motive for murder.'

Brock nodded. He went over to the board and drew two overlapping circles, one with a bold line, the other dotted.

'Two fields of inquiry,' he said. 'One, the property matter. Very plausible.' In the solid circle he wrote the names 'Slade' and 'Winter'. 'The other, the Marx papers. Very tenuous.' In the dotted circle he wrote 'Naismith' and 'Kowalskis'. 'And where they overlap, Mr Jones, who seems to be involved in both.'

They spent the next half-hour brainstorming possible lines of attack on these areas, before Brock and Kathy left to drive down to Chislehurst, where Peg had been taken to stay with the Winters. Sergeant Gurney remained at Jerusalem Lane to supervise the area teams there.

18

Kathy was preoccupied as she drove herself and Brock down the Old Kent Road through South London. 'Isn't Peg staying with Terry Winter a bit like Little Red Riding Hood boarding with the wolf?' she said eventually.

'Yes.' Brock had been thinking about the same thing. 'There wasn't much we could do yesterday when Winter arrived. The old lady was very shaken up, and they both decided she should go home with him. At that stage we hadn't heard about all the harassment the sisters had been suffering. I must admit I don't like the fellow any more than you do, and she's now the only thing between him and a quarter of a million.'

'I know. It must have been horrific for them in that house with everyone leaving and the demolition going on around them, and then the phone calls, the attacks . . . I'm surprised they held out for so long. At best Winter will only put more pressure on Peg to move. At worst she might have an accident on the stairs, or take an overdose or something.'

'But until we're prepared to arrest Winter . . .'

Winter opened the door, looking fleshier than Kathy remembered. He was unshaved, with greasy hair and crumpled clothes. He looked uneasily at Kathy and led them into the lounge room, where she noticed a roll of blankets and a pillow pushed into a corner behind the sofa.

'My aunt's upstairs in bed. She's not well. The doctor's said she has to rest.'

'We'll see if she's awake, then,' Brock said, turning to the door. 'We'll speak to you when we come down, Mr Winter.'

'I want to be there when you talk to her.'

'Why?'

'To make sure you don't upset her, that's why!'

'That's not necessary. We'd prefer to see her alone. You wait down here. Is your wife in?'

'Not at the moment. She had to go out.'

Peg was sitting up in bed, propped up against a mountain of Laura Ashley pillows. Her cherubic face was pale and drawn, and her body appeared to have shrunk inside her quilted satin bed jacket, so that the wrists and hands which emerged from its hot pink cuffs and clutched a large tapestry bag seemed made to a different scale. She peered at them, looking vague, clearly not recognizing Brock from the day before. He introduced himself and Kathy, and she smiled bravely up at them, nodding her head.

'Do sit on the bed, Inspector, and you too, dear. I don't take up much room.' Her voice was disturbingly weak and on a distinctly higher pitch than Kathy remembered it.

'How are you feeling today, Mrs Blythe?'

'How could I feel, Inspector?' Her eyes grew watery and a large tear swelled against a lower lid. 'It's been such a nightmare.' The tear trembled on the lashes a moment, then tumbled down her cheek. She sniffed and dabbed at her eyes with a tiny lace handkerchief.

'I didn't appreciate when I saw you yesterday what you and your sister had been going through these past months, what with the vandalism and the telephone calls and the like.'

'Oh yes.' Her voice was a whisper. 'They've told you about that.'

'It must have been very worrying for you both.'

She nodded. 'Eleanor was so brave, but it was upsetting us both. Each night, we just didn't know what . . . I really don't know whether I can cope with it now, on my own.' Her lip trembled in a sob.

'Do you have no idea who might have been responsible? You didn't recognize a voice on the telephone or a face at the window?'

She shuddered and shook her head.

'Could it have been children perhaps, or men from the building site, or even someone you knew?'

'Someone we knew?' She stared at him in horror.

'Perhaps someone who wanted you to leave Jerusalem Lane?'

'Oh . . .' She clutched the bag and pulled it to her face, moaning quietly, as if trying to hide from something.

'What is it, Mrs Blythe?'

After a moment she lowered her hands and spoke in such a quiet whisper that they had to bend their heads to her. 'Eleanor said . . . but I never liked to think about it.'

'She said what?'

'She said that *the parasite* . . .' – she looked at them with wide eyes, pointed downwards with a finger and mouthed Terry's name silently – 'wanted to get us out, so that he could sell the house. She thought he might have something to do with the things that were happening. It made her more determined to stay – to spite him, you see. But I didn't believe he would do such a thing, dear little Terry, he was such a sweet boy. And then I saw him at the window that night.'

'You saw Terry at your window in Jerusalem Lane?'

'No, no. I don't know that it was him. It was in the middle of the night.' Her fingers fiddled in agitation with the handle of the tapestry bag as she remembered. 'Eleanor woke up with the noise of something tapping at her bedroom window. She got up, pulled back the curtains, and there . . . there was a creature at the window!'

'A creature?'

'Yes! A monster! With hideous eyes and huge teeth and blood running from its fangs!' She shuddered. 'At least, that was how Eleanor described it, and later, when we told the policeman, we realized it must have been a man in a horrid mask.'

'What did Eleanor do?'

'Oh, she was very brave. I would have hidden under the bedclothes, but she ran out of her flat and rang my doorbell until I woke up and let her in. After a little while we went back into her flat and put on all the lights and looked out of the windows, but we could see nothing. I insisted that Eleanor spend the rest of the night in my flat, and we turned the lights off again. Eleanor went to get something from her bathroom and I waited for her in her sitting room. I looked out of the window again, and there, in the yard at the bottom of the fire-escape stair, I saw a man standing in the moonlight, staring up at me. I nearly died of fright. I closed my eyes tight and opened them again, and he was gone. Then I wasn't sure I really had seen him, or if it was just a trick of the light, or my imagination. But when Eleanor said that about . . .' – she mouthed the name again – 'I thought suddenly, yes, that was him, the same build, the same way of standing.'

'Could you swear now that it was him?'

'Oh no!' She looked up at them with terrified eyes. 'I don't know, you see, I don't know.' She gave a few more sobs and looked at Brock. 'I wonder sometimes if I've imagined everything . . . like the other night.' She screwed up her eyes and shuddered.

'What was that?'

'In the middle of the night again. I woke up suddenly and . . . I thought . . . I thought there was someone standing at the end of my bed.'

She was trembling now and Kathy moved to her and put an arm round her shoulders. 'I think we should get the doctor back,' she said quietly to Brock.

'No, dear, don't worry. I'm all right,' Peg whispered, and took a deep breath.

'You didn't report this before, did you, Mrs Blythe?' Brock asked.

She shook her head. 'It was only the night before last. And I wasn't sure. I closed my eyes and when I opened them again there was nothing. Do you think it could have been . . . *him*, Inspector?'

'I don't know, Mrs Blythe. But perhaps you might feel more comfortable, once you're fit enough to get up, if we found you a nice hotel room for a few days, rather than staying here. Would you like us to arrange that?'

'Oh yes, yes. I think I would like that, Inspector. How kind of you to think of that. I just haven't known what to do.' She beamed relief at them like a fearful child rescued by a grown-up.

'There are a couple of things more we need to ask you just now, if you're strong enough.'

'Yes, Inspector.'

'Has anyone from the company that's rebuilding Jerusalem Lane had any contact with you or Eleanor recently?'

'After Meredith died, a young man did come to see us. He offered us ten thousand pounds each if we would agree to move away and sign a document. He was quite pleasant, although we refused straight away. He told us what was going to happen in the Lane, when the other side of the street would be knocked down, and when they would start building the tower monstrosities they're planning.'

'Would you remember the young man's name by any chance?'

'Oh, I'm not sure. Something from Walter Scott, I think . . .'

'*Quentin Durward?*' Kathy suggested at last.

'That's right! Quentin.'

'Quentin Gilroy.' Brock nodded.

'Didn't you ever think that perhaps it would be better to move away from the Lane when everyone else did?' Kathy asked.

'Oh no, dear,' Peg said with surprising firmness. 'Eleanor and I have never been afraid to go our own way, to believe what we understand to be right, and to act upon it.'

'Another thing, Mrs Blythe. Has anyone approached you to buy books or papers that you might have?'

'Well now,' she said slowly, thinking, 'that does ring a bell. I do believe that Eleanor said that someone had contacted her about something like that, about Christmas time I think it was, wanting to buy her books or something. She was quite annoyed about it. She's very attached to her library.'

'So she didn't agree to sell anything?'

'Not as far as I know. No. I'm sure she wouldn't have.'

'Were some of the books signed by Karl Marx?'

'Yes. How clever you are to know that, Inspector! They were Eleanor's treasures. She was so proud of them.'

'Do you know where they are now?'

'Well, in her bookcase, I suppose.' She saw Brock shake his head. 'Well ... I have no idea ... You mean they may have been stolen by the murderer?' She clutched her bag more firmly to her chest.

'It's possible. But are you certain that Eleanor still had them during the last six months?'

'The last six months? Since Meredith ...?' Peg was looking confused. 'I don't really know ... She had so many books ...'

'But original editions of books signed by Karl Marx would have been very valuable, wouldn't they, Mrs Blythe? Eleanor must have known that? And you too, surely?'

Peg stared up at his face, uncomprehending. 'Valuable? They meant a great deal to Eleanor, certainly. But in money terms, I have no idea, Inspector.'

Brock straightened up. 'Well, we'll leave it at that for today. If you think of anything else that might help us, here is our telephone number.'

'Oh ...' Peg looked suddenly anxious again, and her voice dropped to a whisper. 'Are you going to leave me alone in the house ... with him?'

'We have to speak to him now. We'll wait until Mrs

Winter returns. Will that be all right? Then we'll send a policewoman down with a car this afternoon to take you back to a hotel, somewhere near Jerusalem Lane.'

Her face brightened, and some of the former colour returned to her cheeks as she settled herself back into the pillows.

'Thank you,' she whispered. 'You are so kind.'

'Oh, one last thing.' Brock paused at the door. 'After the crime prevention officer came to see you, did you get the locks to your flats changed?'

'No. He said they were good locks, although they were quite old.'

'And who has keys?'

'Mrs Rosenfeldt has a set. That's all.' She thought a moment and then her face dropped. 'Oh . . . and *he* does, of course. He has his mother's set.'

Winter was sitting forward on the edge of the sofa when they returned to the living room, giving the impression of someone who didn't really belong there. Kathy suspected that he probably wouldn't have known where things were to make them a cup of coffee, even if he had wanted to.

'Well?' he scowled at them.

'She's quite upset, Mr Winter, as you said. She feels she should be nearer her home in Jerusalem Lane, and I've said we'll arrange a hotel room for her. Someone will call for her this afternoon. We'll make sure someone keeps an eye on her for a few days.'

Winter stared at him in surprise, and it took him a few seconds to respond. He started to frame some objection, but Brock abruptly cut in.

'What were your movements on Tuesday night, then, Mr Winter? Here with your wife?'

Winter looked away. 'No, no. If you must know, Caroline and I have split up. I only stayed here last night because of Aunt Peg.' His eyes strayed over to the blankets in the corner.

'Ah. With Ms McArthur, then?'

Winter hesitated. His thinking processes seemed to have slowed down, and the cockiness they'd experienced six months before had gone. He raised his chin slowly, in some gesture of defiance perhaps.

'I have my own place s'matter of fact.'

'Really? You've broken off with Ms McArthur, have you?'

Winter's jaw had locked, and he was speaking through his teeth. 'No. We're still good friends. We're just reassessing the situation, that's all.'

'So, where were you on Tuesday night then, from, say, 9.30 p.m. through till the following morning around 7.30?'

'I was at my flat, 3d Rye Gardens, Peckham, next to Peckham Rye Common, all that time.'

'Alone?'

'No. I had a friend with me.'

'Name?'

There was the sound of a key in the front door and Winter's speech suddenly speeded up. 'Shirley Piggott . . . No. Two "g"s and two "t"s . . . She works in my Peckham salon. You can reach her there.'

Kathy got up and went out to meet Caroline Winter and head her off to the kitchen while Brock continued with her husband. 'I want to talk to you about these disturbances that have been going on around 22 Jerusalem Lane for the past five months or so.'

Winter avoided Brock's impassive stare. 'Yeah, sure,' he muttered, and developed a sudden interest in wiping some carpet fluff from the heel of his shoe.

From his inside jacket pocket Brock pulled out a copy of the print-out Gurney had provided and unfolded it slowly. 'What's your theory about these, Mr Winter?'

Winter shook his head. He finished with the shoe and his right hand began to play with the gold rings and Rolex watch that he wore on his left.

'Kids, maybe. Vandals.'

'Kids or vandals, you think?' Brock slowly took his half-lens glasses out of their case and perched them on his nose. He read from the list. '"Night of October 12th: water stopcock in yard broken off. Water Board took two days to find the fault and restore water supply. Night of October 16th: dog dirt pushed through letter box. Night of November 2nd: lighted fireworks pushed through letter box . . ." Pretty sick kids, wouldn't you say, and unusually persistent? Sounds more like a calculated campaign of intimidation to me. Look at this. Christmas Eve: three abusive phone calls saying this was the last Christmas the old ladies would ever see, plus broken glass left all over the front door step. You must have been pretty worried, weren't you, sir?'

'Yeah, yeah, I was. I told the police they weren't doing enough.' Winter fumbled in the pocket of his silk shirt for a packet of cigarettes, then stopped and pushed it abruptly back.

'And after the New Year we start to get personal appearances: the face at the window in the middle of the night. When was it you set up on your own in Peckham, Mr Winter?'

Winter shot Brock a startled look. Then his eyes darted away and he made a show of thinking.

'January, I guess. Why? You mind if I smoke?'

'Not at all. It's your house.'

Winter got up and started roaming round the room looking for an ashtray. Eventually he returned to the sofa empty-handed.

'That's an unfortunate coincidence, you see, Mr Winter, you being an obvious suspect.'

'What?!' he protested, half rising off the sofa again.

'Well, of course. You must have known that. You have the obvious motive, don't you? To get your aunts to leave Jerusalem Lane so that you could sell the place to the developers. You must have spoken to them about that, didn't you, tried to persuade them to leave?'

'Yes, but in their own interests, I . . .'

'Naturally. And you spoke to the developers again, didn't you, to get their help to persuade the old ladies?'

'I did it for them, tried to get extra money for them . . .'

'Of course. But when all these things didn't work, and they remained so stubborn, well, you can see the conclusions people could draw.'

Winter didn't reply. He flicked a gold lighter and held its trembling flame to a cigarette. He took a deep lungful.

'Forty per cent of murders are committed by someone within the family, Mr Winter, and another forty by people who know their victims.'

'Oh Jesus! You're not going to . . .' Smoke came belching from his face as he jumped up again.

'So it's important that we clear up any doubts in that area as soon as possible. For your sake. You agree?' Winter stared at Brock. 'I want two things. First, I want you to agree to an officer searching your flat in Peckham. We can get a warrant, of course, but it will look better for you if you give your consent.'

Winter hesitated. 'I'll be back there this evening. If you want to send someone round then.'

'No, I want to do it straight away. All right? They'll be very careful not to break anything. You won't even know they've been. I'll get you to sign a note of agreement here, just so I don't get into trouble.' Brock chuckled and wrote a few lines on his notebook and passed it over for Winter to sign.

'I don't know.' Winter looked worried.

'Better if you do,' Brock said reassuringly.

'They won't have a key.' Winter protested again.

'Not a problem, Mr Winter.'

He bowed his head, took another drag at his cigarette. 'I didn't kill her,' he said.

'I dare say not,' Brock replied gently, as he gave Winter a pen. *But you've done something you don't want to talk*

183

about, he thought, as Winter scrawled his signature on the pad.

'And the second thing is that I want you to sit down with this list of dates and prepare a statement of your whereabouts at each of these times. I'll give you an address, and I want you to go there later today and make a statement to my Sergeant Gurney with that information. All right?'

Winter nodded. His ash fell on the carpet.

'He's smoking again, isn't he?' Caroline Winter spat out. 'I warned him I wouldn't have him smoking in here again. The place stinks for days afterwards.'

'I know what you mean,' Kathy nodded. 'The new kitchen looks terrific, Mrs Winter.'

'Oh yeah, do you like it? I thought I'd get it done right before I finally threw the bastard out.'

'Yes, he mentioned you were having a trial separation.'

'Trial nothing!' she laughed. 'This is it, baby. Finito. Kaput. The end. I put up with Mister Wonderful playing around with those tarts he employs for long enough. God, it used to make me physically ill going into one of his bloody salons with him, you know what I mean? The way he talked to them and teased them and touched them up. He thought he was God's bloody gift he did. A heat-seeking dick. He thought he'd found fucking paradise, prancing around from one salon to the next. Well' – her eyes glittered with malice – 'now's the time to pay, lover boy.'

'He did seem rather chastened today, compared to when we saw him last.'

'He doesn't know the half of it, luv. I've 'ad a solicitor and an accountant working on this for months. I'd never have let him through the door today except for Peg. When he phoned, I told him he'd have to bring her here – he'd never be able to look after her in that pigsty he's got in Peckham. But once she's out of here, so's he.'

'We thought we might take care of that, Mrs Winter,'

Kathy said. 'We're going to look after her for a few days. Just to be on the safe side.

'Has he stopped hitting you, then?' Kathy added.

Caroline looked sharply at her.

'Who told you that?'

'Nobody told me. I thought I saw some marks on your face the last time we met. Is he a very violent man?'

Caroline took a deep breath and stared out of the window. A family of thrushes was splashing innocently in a birdbath on the terrace outside. She watched them for a minute, then said, 'What's "very"?

'Anyway,' she shrugged, 'like a few other women in my situation, I've discovered the ultimate revenge. It's called money.'

'And he has been worried about money for some time, hasn't he?'

'Oh, I see what you're getting at. Well, I'd like to help, believe me. Nothing would suit me better than to have him put away for twenty years – after I've stripped him clean, that is. But I'm not sure I can. He's always been a chancer with money, you know, wanting it all, borrowing, leasing, gearing. Yeah, I suppose the last year has been worse for him, though. I think he was hoping to set up that bitch Geraldine whatsit in a nice little love nest at one point, and then when I told him he could clear off as soon as the kids had had their Christmas, he must have seen the writing on the wall.'

'One thing you can do for me, Mrs Winter, is to go through this list of dates, and see if you can vouch for his whereabouts on any of them.'

Caroline's lip, its scarlet outline defined with the precision of a razor, curled with amusement. 'Will it get him in more trouble if I say I can or I can't?'

'Just the truth, please, Mrs Winter.'

'Don't worry, darling,' Caroline laughed. 'You know I couldn't tell a fib.'

She glanced down the list.

'You 'aven't got the 8th of March down here.'

'A week ago? Why should we?'

'That's when I had my break-in.'

'This house was broken into?'

'Yeah. And it was that bastard what did it. I changed the locks when I kicked him out, and this was him having a go at me. He pinched things of mine. Some jewellery he'd given me, stuff like that. He made it look like a burglary, broke a window downstairs, but I knew it was him.'

'How?'

'It was a Thursday afternoon, and he knows I always go and see my mum on a Thursday afternoon. The answering machine was on when I got back, and there'd been a couple of calls with no messages. You know, he was just checking.'

'Anyone could have done that.'

'Yeah, well, it was him, all right. I smelled him, didn't I, in the loo.'

'What, his aftershave?'

Caroline laughed. 'No, dear. His piss. He'd gone to the lavatory and not flushed it. And he'd been drinking. I could smell his stink. That was him all over, Prince bloody Charming.'

'Did you report this?'

'Yes. The coppers came round and took a list of the things that were missing, and fingerprints and everything.'

'They fingerprinted the bathroom?'

'Yeah. But then he'd been round the previous evening, hadn't he, so his prints would be everywhere. After they'd gone I thought about it. I phoned up the coppers and told them not to bother. I didn't want to give him the satisfaction of thinking I was worried.'

'If he'd wanted things, couldn't he just have taken them when he called round?'

'I'd never have let him, or I'd have got the solicitors on to him. Also, he wanted to frighten me. I know him.'

'What about your alarm system?'

'Yeah, well, I never turned it on, did I? It was raining and so I left the cat inside, and she would have set it off. But Terry knew I did that, you see.'

Kathy nodded, thinking. 'Was there a lot of mess?'

'Not really. I hardly noticed it at first. And nothing electrical taken. That's what made me suspicious.'

'What about in here?'

'The kitchen?'

'Yes. Where do you keep your freezer bags, Mrs Winter?'

Caroline stared at her for a moment, stunned. Then, without a word she went over to a cupboard. She opened it and stepped back. There were half a dozen different types and sizes of packets of plastic bags inside. Kathy took out a green bin liner and dropped a number of the packets inside.

When she straightened up, she saw Brock standing by the kitchen door.

'Ready?'

'Can I have a word, sir?'

They went out into the hall and she quickly told him about Caroline's break-in.

'Right,' Brock said. He led her back into the living room where Winter was still poring over the list Brock had given him. 'You have a set of keys to 22 Jerusalem Lane, don't you, Mr Winter?'

Winter looked at him warily. 'My mother's keys, yes. Why?'

'Where are they?'

Winter shrugged. 'Upstairs. I've got a drawer of odds and ends in my . . . in the bedroom.'

'Shall we have a look?'

It was a small drawer in the dressing table by the window. He opened it and stared. It was quite empty. He turned angrily to his wife, standing by the door. 'What have you done with my stuff? There was a gold cigarette case in here.'

Caroline shook her head, her mouth turned down in exaggerated disbelief. '*I* haven't touched it, Terry.'

He turned to appeal to Brock. 'This is where they were, Inspector. This drawer was full of stuff.'

There was a moment's heavy silence as they stared at him.

'Tell you what,' Brock said at last, 'I'll get my Sergeant to come down here straight away. He can take you back up to town. Save any problems.'

19

From the front garden of the Kowalskis' house the Channel was invisible in the fog which shrouded Sussex south of the Weald. Foghorns sounded from the white blanket, mournful and threatening.

At first Mrs Kowalski seemed the same as before, determined to be as obstructive as possible, but as they talked to her in the narrow hallway of her house Kathy began to notice a weariness, as if the woman were condemned to play a part she had grown tired of. She kept repeating things she had said only a short time before. And when Brock told her that Eleanor Harper had been found murdered on the previous day, the news literally knocked her flat. For a moment she stared blankly at his face, and then abruptly crumpled at the knees. They lifted her through into the downstairs sitting room, and Kathy fetched a glass of water from the kitchen. Brock told Kathy to stay with her while he went upstairs to see her husband.

Adam Kowalski was sitting in the same chair and in the same position as when they last saw him, but looked as if he had aged six years rather than six months. His face had no more colour than the fog beyond the window pane.

'Your foot recovered, Mr Kowalski?' Brock said heartily.

'Thank you, yes.' His eyes were watery-pink and his voice hoarse.

'I don't suppose you've been travelling much lately, though. To London, say.'

Kowalski frowned and shook his head slightly. 'Are you alone, Inspector?' he whispered. 'Where is my wife?' He looked beyond Brock towards the door, confused.

'She's downstairs with Sergeant Kolla. She fainted when we told her the news about Eleanor Harper.'

'News?' His eyes widened, apprehensive.

'She was murdered yesterday, Mr Kowalski.'

The old man gasped, his eyelids closed and his head went back, and for a moment Brock thought that he too had passed out. But one attenuated hand, scrawny as a chicken's claw, crept up over the blanket on his lap and made a long and difficult journey up to his face, where it scrabbled awkwardly at his eyes.

'Who . . . was responsible?' he finally gasped.

'Perhaps you can tell me, Mr Kowalski.'

The eyes flicked open again, fearful, anxious. 'Me? No . . . no.' His head shook.

'But you can help me, can't you? You were less than helpful when we spoke the last time I was here.'

'In what way?'

'The man with the bow tie, for example. You seemed to be able to remember almost nothing about him. You didn't even mention the lady he was with. Nor did you mention the connection between him and Meredith Winterbottom.'

When he heard the name, Kowalski's eyelids fluttered as if he were in pain. 'Ah . . .' He stared at Brock for a moment through his watery eyes and then sighed softly. 'It was in the weeks before we moved here . . . There were so many things to think about. I had forgotten. Since you came here,' he added hesitantly, 'I have recalled their visit a little better.'

'This was the man's second visit. When would that have been?'

Kowalski thought. 'A month or so before we moved, which was the 26th of August.

'The man wanted to know if I had any more material like the thing I had sold him on his first visit. I couldn't remember what it was, but when he described it I realized it was something I had bought with some children's books from Meredith Winterbottom . . . oh, perhaps a year before. He had a woman with him, Scandinavian-looking, very striking. She was quite impatient, I remember, and they searched through the shop for some time, although I knew they wouldn't find anything that Meredith had sold me. In any case, I was puzzled because they weren't interested in children's books and kept asking about old books on politics and history. Then the lady demanded to know who had sold me the framed letter. I thought that Meredith wouldn't want to be disturbed by these people, so I said I would speak to her first.'

'You were the dealer after all.'

Kowalski acknowledged this point with a little tilt of his head. Then he turned to stare out of the window, a long, stick-like forearm propping up his head. His pale skin was cracked with pink fissures, and a number of clear-plastic adhesive dressings on his hand looked as if they were holding the skin together. There was silence for an age. Brock thought the old man must have fallen asleep, but then his voice, distant and tired, began again.

'After I closed the shop, I decided to call on Meredith. I could tell that she was surprised to hear my voice on the intercom, in view of the unpleasantness which had arisen between our two families, but she let me in.

' "Well, Adam Kowalski," she said when I was seated in her lounge, "have you come to apologize for the rudeness of that wife of yours?" This was the way she spoke. She was very . . . straightforward.

'I explained that Marie only wanted to protect me. I reminded her how some people still felt about the old days, and I begged her that we should forget all that.

'She acted as if she was still annoyed with Marie, but she had a good nature really, and I think she accepted what I said. Then she asked why I had come, and I reminded her how she had sold me some books a year or so before, and I wondered if she had any more, historical perhaps, or political.

'She asked why I was asking, so I explained about the customer who had bought the old letter in the frame, and how he'd come back looking for anything similar, old documents or books. She asked me what sort of price they might fetch, and I said I might be able to get five or ten pounds each for such things.'

He paused, gathering strength to continue.

'She promised to have a look. Then she said that it would be best if she could discuss directly with the customer exactly what he was looking for. She said I should give her his name, and in exchange she would forget all about Marie's rudeness.'

Kowalski sighed and spread his long fingers.

'This was not what I had intended, but I couldn't refuse her the name and telephone number. I just wanted some peace. Both women were quite . . . implacable.'

He raised his eyebrows to Brock guiltily. There was another long pause, and again Brock was on the point of giving up when Kowalski's faint voice resumed his story.

'Some while later, just before we moved, Meredith came to me again. It was the last time I ever saw her. She had a book. She wanted to find someone who could value it for her. I gave her the name of a friend. Later I spoke to him. He told me what he had told her.'

More silence. Brock waited patiently for him to continue.

'It was a first edition of a book by Karl Marx: *The Fourteenth Brumaire*. In itself that was something. But inside there was a dedication from Marx himself, to "Tussy", his youngest daughter, which made it worth much more than it would have been otherwise. He thought she might get four or five thousand for it. She had told him there were others. A dozen.'

'It's as if they'd been cast adrift,' Kathy said as she drove slowly back through the fog. 'Apparently he just sits up there all the time staring out of the window, wasting away.

She said he was like a plant that'd been pulled up by the roots and left to wither. It was about the only thing I could get her to talk about.'

'He's sick,' Brock grunted. 'She didn't look her old self, either.'

'I think she's declining in response to him. She'd probably be lost without his life to screw up and protect. She's still very bitter towards Meredith, though.'

'Difficult to see why.'

'It seems the people who held out longest got the best price for their properties. The rumour was that Brunhilde Capek got a hundred thousand more for her place, which was the same size as the Kowalskis', because she held out for another six months. Marie Kowalski feels they could have done the same if the fuss Meredith started up over Adam's past hadn't driven them to sell when they did.'

The incident centre at 20 Jerusalem Lane was humming when they returned, its illuminated shop front the only light shining in the dark street. From the front counter where they took off their coats Kathy could see Sergeant Gurney in the back room, moving among his officers and a couple of civilian staff, checking, chatting, pondering. He had the build of a prop forward, and a face that looked as if it had been squashed in a scrum. His hair was slicked back as if still wet from the changing-room showers. She noticed that he had a nice smile and a twinkle in his eye when he spoke to the women. He had been a Navy pilot before joining the force, flying Harriers from *Invincible*.

Gurney was evidently pleased with the results of his day, and they settled in the upstairs room with coffee to hear his news. A partial report had come in from the pathologist, confirming that Eleanor Harper could have been smothered by the plastic bag. The two blows to the forehead had come after death, and were of token force, barely fracturing the front of the skull. There were no other signs of violence to the body. The time of death couldn't be placed more precisely than somewhere between 6 p.m. Tuesday and 4 a.m. Wednesday.

There was a possible lead in the search for the weapon used to inflict the two blows. That morning an old hammer had been handed in by the scaffolding crew to the office on the construction site across the Lane. It was possible that it had been thrown into the site from the Lane and might have been there for some time before it was found. The pathologist was now examining it.

'This is a summary of the results of door-to-door inquiries so far.' Gurney handed Brock a couple of sheets. 'Actually I think we've just about exhausted the possibilities there. The blokes on the site were the most useful, I'd say. We've interviewed them all now, including the drivers of the concrete mixers and other delivery trucks. You'll notice that they seem to remember women more than men, and young women more than older women. An interesting gestalt phenomenon, I'd say.'

'That's one way of describing it,' Kathy said dryly.

'You'll notice the attractive blonde who appears twice there at the beginning of the week, Monday or Tuesday. Then we've got the list of the employees of First City Properties and all the people from other organizations involved in the development project here. Mr Slade spoke to me on the phone about it after I'd left the request with his secretary. He insisted on knowing why we wanted the list, so I told him about Miss Harper. He sounded shocked – hadn't read it in the papers this morning. Said he'd cooperate in any way. He offered his congratulations on catching North, by the way, sir. So much for that.'

Gurney set the documents to one side and reached for another set of typewritten sheets with the look of an amateur magician moving on to a much more interesting trick. 'Now, Mr Terence Winter.' His eyes scanned the sheet with satisfaction. 'Transcript of interview with his alleged girlfriend, Ms Shirley Piggott. She claims she didn't spend last Tuesday night with him. In fact claims she's never slept with him.'

Gurney passed the transcript over to Brock.

'Actually, I wouldn't be surprised if she's lying. She mentioned that both her mother and her boyfriend would be highly displeased if word of her having it off with Terry Winter got around.'

'What's she like?'

'Eighteen going on sixteen. Silly little thing, all giggles and big eyes. I wouldn't be surprised if she changed her story later, if things got a bit hot for Terry. But still, it could be useful to put the wind up him.'

'Poor Terry.' Kathy shook her head. 'It's not his week.'

'Does he know this?' Brock asked.

'No. When I brought him back here, we left him alone for an hour with that list you gave him. Then I went through it with him, and for most of the times he has no alibi at all. A couple he claims he was with someone, but we haven't been able to check them yet. The only times I'd say he might be covered for are those of some of the phone calls, but again, we're still checking.'

'Where is he now?'

'I thought you might like to have a go at him, sir, so I sent him back to the Yard with DS Griffiths.'

'Good. What about his flat?'

'Yes, well, I'm not sure what to make of that. There was a tube of superglue, and a few tools which would have been about right for the damage. We sent the blunt instrument types – a hammer and a monkey wrench – down to the path lab for checking against the wound.'

'What else?'

'Well, no diary with red crosses against the appropriate days, I'm afraid. There were enough condoms to stock a chemist shop.' Gurney grinned. 'This bloke believed in buying in bulk – a real optimist. Not many seemed to have been used, though. Nothing else incriminating. Then it occurred to me, when we called in at his Peckham salon to speak to Shirley Piggott, which is just round the corner from his flat – it occurred to me to take a look at his office there.'

'I don't think I heard that, Bren.'

'His receptionist was extremely helpful. I explained that I was trying to find a set of keys that Mr Winter had apparently mislaid. She opened up the drawers of his desk and filing cabinet for me to look inside. In one of the drawers we found this . . .'

He got up and went over to a cardboard box in the corner of the room. From it he took a transparent plastic bag. Kathy gave a little cry as she saw inside it what looked like a severed head.

'Gruesome, isn't it?' Gurney brought it over to the table. It was a plastic mask of a monster's face with vivid scarlet blood dribbling from its fangs.

'Oh dear, oh dear,' Brock sighed. 'Terry has been a very naughty boy.'

'That must have scared the life out of Eleanor,' Kathy said with disgust. 'No wonder Peg was petrified.'

'We'll have to show it to her before we see him.'

'She's been booked into the Bedford in Southampton Row, down the road. There's a WPC with her still.'

'And no keys to number 22?'

Gurney shook his head. 'I think we should get a search warrant for all his salons.'

'All right. Well done, Bren, we're getting somewhere. We'll get over to Peg and then to the Yard and speak to the monster Romeo again. I'll fill you in on our day as we go. Kathy, I'd like you to check something else if you would.' He pointed to the diagram on the white board where the two circles overlapped. 'Bob Jones. Let's just make sure he hasn't got any more to tell us.'

20

By the time Kathy reached the architect's office, Bob Jones's secretary, Sophie, was tidying up her desk for the night, getting ready to leave. She buzzed her boss and gave Kathy a sharp look when she said that she was there on a private matter.

'You're not a rep, then. Only Bob gets annoyed if reps call without an appointment.'

'No, I'm not a rep.'

'I didn't think so.'

'Could you tell?'

'Oh yes, the women reps tend to be very sharp dressers. Oh' – she blushed – 'don't get me wrong. I mean I think you're more like me, you like to be smart but comfortable too. But they go a bit over the top, you know, all power dressing and shoulders and heavy make-up and enough perfume to knock you over.'

Kathy smiled. The other woman was wearing a red and white polka dot dress with a wide, white collar, and Kathy didn't really feel that being told she had the same taste in clothes was much of a compliment.

'Have you been working with Bob since he set up on his own?' she asked.

'Oh, much longer than that.'

'You didn't decide to go with the other company to their new offices when they split up, then?'

'Oh no. I like working with Bob. I mean they were a good firm and everything, but I couldn't work in an office like that. It's so bitchy, and some of the girls are hopeless. That Janine! Mr Lowell thinks she's wonderful, but she used to drive Bob crazy. He said she was deaf in her telephone ear, too vain to wear glasses, couldn't walk properly because of those stiletto heels she wears, and her brain was preoccupied with her latest affair, so the result was that the partners kept getting messages all scrambled up, and turning up for meetings on the wrong day and everything, and no one could ever work out why!'

They both laughed. Kathy wondered if Sophie was in love with her boss just as it occurred to Sophie that Kathy might be thinking that. 'Oh well,' she said briskly. 'I must push off now. My boyfriend and I have got tickets to *The Phantom of the Opera* tonight. Have you seen it?'

Bob's head appeared on the spiral stair up from the drawing office, and he called out, 'Sergeant! Hello, I didn't think I'd have the pleasure of seeing you again.'

Sophie blinked with surprise and stared after Kathy as she and Bob disappeared into the conference room.

'My God! I had no idea.' Bob Jones looked appalled. 'I haven't read a paper for a couple of days. Miss Harper! She was the upright, dark one, wasn't she? I thought she had an air of tremendous natural dignity about her. That's just awful. Is this some kind of serial killer or something?'

Kathy looked puzzled. 'But you never met her, did you?'

'Yes, briefly. Just as Meredith was showing Judith and me out of Eleanor's flat that time, the other two sisters returned. It was a bit embarrassing really, coming out of someone's flat when they hadn't invited you there in the first place. She was quite pleasant, but I was uncomfortable all the same.'

'Oh.' Kathy was still puzzled. 'Did you mention the books or documents to her or the other sister?'

'No, we left that to Meredith to bring up. Is that why you're here? Or was it just an excuse to see me again?' He grinned, and then, seeing her expression, coughed and looked serious. 'Sorry, that was stupid. Only I've often thought about you and that other chap you were working with. You never found out who killed Meredith, I take it?'

'No. But with the new murder we're reopening that inquiry. We thought you might be able to help us in a few areas, actually. First of all, can I ask you if you have any involvement now in the Jerusalem Lane redevelopment project?'

'The dreaded Citicenter One? No, not any longer. I was upset about the whole situation when we split up, and I don't suppose First City Properties are likely to put any work my way for a bit. All the same, I've kept in touch with some of the people there, and architects are incredibly busy at the moment, so you never know. When some of the fit-out work comes along, I might get a look-in. Can't be too proud when you have to pay the rent at the end of the month. Why?'

'Would you be willing to give us your opinion on one or two things – just advice, not formal evidence? We need a better insight, you know.'

'I don't see why not. Depends what the questions are, I suppose.'

'Well, try this one.' Kathy fixed him with her wide green eyes, which he found somewhat unsettling. 'Can they build this development around number 22 without buying it?'

Jones scratched at his chin in a gesture which reminded her of Brock when he was thinking.

'Anything's possible, but I'm sure Slade would hate it, and so would everyone else – Herbert Lowell, the Canadian developers, the American architects. The whole aim of the development is supposed to be a corporate identity for the twenty-first century, whatever that means – you know, part of London after the big bang, twenty-four-hour trading round the globe between New York, Tokyo and London, all that stuff. Old Mrs Winterbottom's house falling apart in the middle of it all would spoil the image a bit, I should think.'

He thought some more. 'Have you got plans of the development?'

Kathy shook her head. 'I suppose we could get them.'

'Never mind. There was a review of the project the other week in *The Architects' Journal*. Hang on. I'll see if I can find it.'

He returned in a moment and laid the magazine open on the table, sitting down beside Kathy.

'Here we are. These will do. There are basement-level and podium-level plans here. The existing number 22 isn't shown, but let's see' – he drew on the plans with his pencil – 'that's the line of Jerusalem Lane, and number 22 must be about there. Well, yes, that completely screws up the entrance road down to the underground service areas and car park.'

'Couldn't that be moved over to avoid the existing building?'

'Have you ever thought about becoming an architect, Sergeant Kolla? I could teach you how to draw if you like ... Sorry. Where were we? Oh, not really. That would bring the entrance too close to the street junctions at the corners of the site. The highway engineers wouldn't allow it. That was one of the constraints – the service and car-parking traffic had to be taken in off Marquis Street, and had to be just so far back from the street corners.' He shook his head. 'Tricky.'

'All right. Next question.' Kathy found it disconcerting to have him sitting on the same side of the table as herself. 'Here's a list of all of the people who work for First City Properties or are involved with the project among the consultants' firms. If Derek Slade wanted to get rid of Meredith Winterbottom and her sisters, who would he get to do it?'

Bob Jones blinked at her. 'Are you serious? Yes, I can see you are. Wow.' He shook his head and got to his feet. He started to pace round the room, looking at the list. 'I don't know that I can help you with this, Kathy. Can I call you Kathy?'

'You've got a good memory, Mr Jones.'

'Bob, please, since I'm not a suspect. Look, I can't see Derek Slade ever doing such a thing.'

'Why not? Aren't all developers rapacious, rotten and ruthless?'

'No, of course not. Slade is quite a gentleman actually. First City isn't one of these new high-risk development outfits that have sprung up in the last few years. And they're not the Mafia either. They've been around in the City for a long time. Slade's father started after the war with his fifty-pounds demob money and built First City up to be one of the biggest development companies in the country. They don't need to prove anything. There's no way Slade would be involved in something like that.'

'All right, not Slade, then. One of his people who can see a problem and would like to get it out of the way.'

Bob frowned and stared at his red shoes.

'Come on, Bob.'

'Well, I'm sure he wouldn't, but there's only one bloke here would have the nerve, I reckon.' He came back to the table and pointed to a name on the list. Danny Finn.

'Launching a big building project is like, I don't know, launching a war. There's a lot at stake, and a lot of people who have to perform. Just walking down Jerusalem Lane now you can feel it, can't you? A great powerful machine in motion, the feeling of things in progress, of important choices and decisions being implemented. And the machine has to be controlled.

'Slade is above all that. He's the boss, shaking hands, making deals, negotiating with the people outside, the banks and tenants. And people like Quentin Gilroy, and us, the consultants, are too much a part of it, building it, trying to solve the problems it presents. So First City needs someone who can get in there and make sure that everyone else is performing. Someone who is close enough to the machine to feel it tremble, hear it cough, who has oil on his hands and a pair of big boots on his feet for kicking people when the times demand. That's Danny Finn. He's a Glaswegian, and you've got a lot of ground to make up with him if you haven't been born in the Gorbals, haven't been thrown out of work at least once on Christmas Eve, and haven't had to fight your way out of a waterlogged trench against a drunken navvy swinging a shovel at you.'

Bob sat down and spread his hands out on the table in front of him.

'I've got a lot of time for him.' He smiled to himself. 'He likes to go on a bit, usually in the pub, about his underprivileged origins, although now of course, being worth a lot to First City, he lives in an expensive house in Esher. I teased him once that he was a traitor to his class, and he was outraged. "A traitor to the working class, laddie? Never!" and I said "No, Danny, I mean the middle class." He never forgot that. Always mentions it when we meet: "Here's the laddie called me a member of the fucking middle classes."

'He has a heart of gold in many ways, if he likes you. But he can also be a rough bastard. I remember what he did to Herbert Lowell once. Herbert was doing some building for them, and was being even more pompous than usual, throwing his weight around, and he'd complained a couple of times to Slade about Danny getting out of line. So Danny decided to punish him. We'd arranged a site visit to the project, which was half built. I remember it was a bitterly cold day and dark, with a wind so that you couldn't unfold the drawings outside the site hut. Danny had noticed on a previous occasion that Herbert wasn't very good with heights, so he insisted that we go up to the top, up one ladder, then another, then a third.

'At the top there was a gap between two parts of the building, about six or seven metres wide, with this beam across it, maybe so wide.' Bob spread the thumb and little finger of his hand apart. 'Danny marched off across the beam. There was nothing to hold on to. Herbert hesitated, and I could imagine what was going through his mind. The wind was cutting into us and there were flurries of snow in the air. I was right at his shoulder and there was no room to turn. Finally he set off, concentrating on the beam, trying not to look beyond it into the void.

'Halfway across, Danny suddenly stopped, and turned to face Herbert. "Well, Mr Architect," he said, "what's your opinion about that manhole down there?" and he pointed to the ground that seemed miles below our feet. Herbert looked, and just froze. He simply couldn't move. He was totally paralysed.

'We had to organize a crane with a big bucket on the end to come up for him. The whole site came to a stop to watch the architect being lowered to the ground in a concrete bucket. It made a terrible mess of his cashmere coat.'

'I see,' Kathy said, 'but would he terrorize some old ladies who were holding things up? Or even bump them off?'

'No.' Bob hesitated, shook his head. 'No, I'm sure he wouldn't.'

He frowned and stared at his hands.

'Well, thanks anyway, Bob. One other thing. Did you hear any more about those books you saw at Eleanor's flat that time – the ones that your friend Judith was so interested in?'

'Well, yes, I did in a way. A couple of months ago somebody rang me up about them. The call came out of the blue. A man. Said he was a book dealer. He said he had bought these books, and understood I had been interested in them, and was I still? I told him it wasn't really me who was interested but my friend, and I gave him Judith's name, address and phone number at Princeton. He didn't tell me who he was.'

'Did you recognize the voice? Could it have been Mr Kowalski?'

'The owner of the bookshop? No, it certainly wasn't him. I didn't recognize the voice at all.'

'We may need to speak to Judith. You'd better give me her address too.'

'Sure, but she's here, you know.'

'Here?'

'Yes, in London. At least she was a couple of days ago. I got this message from her on my answering machine wanting me to contact her. She was staying at a hotel in Knightsbridge. I rang back and she wasn't there, so I left a message. Then when she didn't get back to me I tried again later that evening. They said she still hadn't got back and I asked them to give her the message to ring me whatever time she got in. She never did, and after that I didn't try again. To tell you the truth I felt I'd done enough running around for her the last time she was over here.'

'Which evening was it you rang the hotel?'

'Night before last. Tuesday.'

'Have you got the number? I'd like to try it now, please.'

'Sure.' Bob found it for her and brought a phone over from a side table.

The hotel receptionist was helpful. 'She checked out this afternoon, madam.'

'Oh, I'd been hoping to catch her this evening.'

There was a pause at the other end while the woman looked something up. 'Yes, she had booked to stay another couple of days, but apparently she had to return to the United States earlier than expected.'

'She went to the airport?'

'I believe so, madam.'

Kathy rapidly dialled the airport police at Heathrow and identified herself. Judith Naismith had booked on the 7.10 p.m. British Airways flight to New York, boarding in twenty minutes. She had already checked in and passed through to the departure lounge.

'Hold her there, will you? I'll get back to you within ten minutes.'

She dialled again, this time the Yard, and spoke to Brock.

'Right, Kathy,' Brock said after she'd explained, 'tell them to pull her off the flight and hold her till we get there. I'll pick you up where you are as soon as I can.'

Brock peered through the glass panel in the door of the detention room. Beneath a bright fluorescent light a uniformed policeman sat impassively at a bare table with arms folded. Opposite him stood Judith Naismith. She leant over the table, one hand propping herself up, the other resting on her hip. Although only a murmur could be heard through the door, she was clearly haranguing him. She had straight, shoulder-length ash-blonde hair, and was of similar build to Kathy, slim and of medium height, but her body was more angular, her gestures more explosive. When they went inside, Brock noticed her sharp and humourless eyes, and decided that Dr Naismith was going to be a formidable customer.

He introduced Kathy and himself.

'What exactly is the problem here?' she demanded, folding her arms. 'You do realize I've missed my flight?'

'I'm sorry about that, but we're investigating the murders of two women which have occurred recently in central London, and we believe you may be able to help us with our inquiries. We only just learned of your whereabouts, and under the circumstances it seemed the only course open to us.'

He gave her a conciliatory smile and began to take off his coat. Her face had given no flicker of response to the mention of murders. Brock indicated to the uniformed man that he could go, and took his place at the table. Kathy waited by the door.

'Please.' Brock indicated the chair opposite him. 'Sit down, Dr Naismith, and we can sort this out.'

She stared at him for a moment without moving and then turned to Kathy. 'I hope you people are within your rights.' She looked at Kathy slowly from head to foot, then back to her face again. Her stare was rude, intended to intimidate. Kathy returned it calmly, not showing the embarrassment which, to her annoyance, she began to feel.

Brock reached into the inside pocket of his jacket and pulled out his notebook and Judith Naismith's passport. 'Come and sit down, Dr Naismith,' he repeated absently, flicking through the pages of the passport. She still made no move, and he began to write in his notebook. Finally she sat down abruptly in the chair, half turned away from Brock with one arm hooked on the chair back, her legs crossed, in an attitude which suggested great self-control in the face of outrageous provocation.

'Why are you leaving now, Dr Naismith? I understand you were planning to stay longer.'

She slowly turned her head towards him. 'What business, exactly, is that of yours?' She enunciated the words slowly, as if to someone with limited understanding.

Brock stared at her for a moment.

'We'd like you to tell us about all of your recent contacts with Miss Eleanor Harper, of 22 Jerusalem Lane, WC2. Let's begin with the last time you actually saw her.'

There was silence for a moment before she said, with the same exaggerated patience, 'Am I under arrest?'

'No, you're not, Dr . . .'

'Am I then free to go?'

'Are you saying that you refuse to co-operate with us?'

'Am I free to go?'

Brock sighed, closed up her passport and placed it back in his inside jacket pocket. 'Where will you be staying in London?'

'I'd like my passport, please.'

'I'm afraid that's impossible. You won't be able to leave the country until you've answered my questions.' She looked at him with surprise as he got to his feet and pulled on his coat. 'If I were you, I'd get myself a good solicitor, Dr Naismith,' he said, and headed for the door.

'That's exactly what I'm going to do!' she called after him, but they were gone before she finished the sentence.

On the way back into central London, Brock, irritated, searched through an address book in his pocket and then made a transatlantic call. The voice at the other end sounded clearer than on a local number.

'Good to hear you, David. Are you coming over?'

'Not this time, Nigel. I need a bit of information quickly, and I thought you might possibly be able to help. It's about an academic at Princeton.'

'If I can. What discipline?'

'Economic history.'

'Oh yes? We have a Search Committee in place at the moment for a senior position in that department here. I could say I'm inquiring for them.'

'Yes, that sounds good. I just want to get some background on the woman. She's a British subject, been over there for thirteen or fourteen years, since doing a doctorate at Cambridge. Name, Judith Naismith.' He spelled it, and, after some perfunctory small talk about the weather and each other's health, rang off.

'FBI?' Kathy asked.

Brock shook his head. 'No. Friend from the army. Went over there twenty years ago. Professor in the Midwest now.' He lapsed into silence and said nothing more on the journey back.

21

During the night, while Brock and Gurney continued their questioning of Terry Winter, unseasonable freezing winds from the north and east displaced the damp, mild westerlies of the previous days, and a bitter change set in. Waking early on the morning of Friday 3 April, the third day of the investigation into Eleanor Harper's death, Kathy shuddered to see that the view from her window of the distant street lights was obliterated by swirling snow. She breakfasted hurriedly on tea and toast, hauled on her long coat, scarf, gloves and woollen hat, and made for the lift.

There was just one policewoman in the office at Jerusalem Lane, minding the phones. She said that Winter had been charged, but she didn't know what with. Copies of statements were on their way over from the Yard, as well as a report from the Metropolitan Police Forensic Science Laboratory at Lambeth Road over the river, on the hammer found in the building site, but neither had yet arrived.

Impatient and edgy, Kathy pulled her outer layers back on and stepped out into the cold dawn of Jerusalem Lane once more. Flurries of snow were gusting through the high chain-link fence which topped the plywood panels of the construction site. Here and there it collected in small drifts. She walked rapidly back up to the north end, head down, and ran across Welbeck Street to the news vendor on the corner. The man had moved his plastic tarpaulin round to the east side of his stall, and Kathy huddled in its shelter. As she searched in her bag for money to pay for the early-morning editions, a red Mercedes sports car pulled over to the kerb on the other side of the street. The interior lit up for a moment as the passenger opened his door, and Kathy saw the driver, a woman, lean over and give him a kiss. He was a big man, who took a moment to haul himself out of the low car, as if his shoulder were giving him trouble. Just before he pulled the collar of his coat up and turned to hurry down Jerusalem Lane, Kathy recognized Brock's bearded face.

The laboratory report arrived shortly after Kathy returned to the incident centre. It confirmed that the hammer was the one used to strike Eleanor's forehead in the moments immediately after her death. It was a ball-hammer, with a rounded head, as used by plumbers. Its shape and size were consistent with the indentations in Eleanor's skull, and scratches on its surface matched impressions found on the plastic bag.

Kathy and another officer returned to Winter's house in Chislehurst to speak to his wife, Caroline. She seemed to find their questions faintly amusing, as if they had no bearing on her own life. She was unable to recall ever having seen the hammer before. Her husband, she said, was not a great handyman.

'Scissors and a comb are about the only tools he's any good with,' she informed the young detective constable with a look that made him blush. 'The last time hammers were mentioned in this house was when one of the builders putting in the new kitchen complained he'd lost one. I can't remember which, though. One of the older men. I didn't pay much attention.'

It was mid-morning by the time Kathy returned to Jerusalem Lane. Bren Gurney was sitting over a mug of tea in the back room, looking exhausted. He told her that Winter's attempts to account for his movements had been a farce. It had been impossible to confirm his whereabouts for any of the incidents that had occurred at the sisters' house, and in the case of the business with the mask, a neighbour had actually seen him leave his Peckham flat an hour before it occurred, although he claimed he had remained at home all night. Peg couldn't be certain that the mask was the one used to frighten Eleanor, since only her sister had seen it, but confirmed that it was just as she had described it.

Despite all this, Winter had refused to admit to anything. Gurney seethed with frustration, and not only with Winter. He was convinced the man was guilty. He had the clearest motive, weak or non-existent alibis, and he was telling lies, at first with a certain amount of assurance, like someone unused to having his lies disbelieved, and then increasingly, as the night wore on, out of sheer desperation. Yet Brock had seemed oddly reluctant to act, and it was only towards 4 in the morning that he had finally agreed that Winter should be charged with a number of offences relating to the incidents at 22 Jerusalem Lane between November and March. These included threatening behaviour and causing malicious damage, but not yet murder.

Gurney sighed and ran a hand across his chin. 'I'd better get myself a shave.'

'Haven't you had any sleep?' Kathy asked him.

He shook his head. 'I hung around to process the charges, then to wait for Winter's solicitor. Brock got an hour or two shut-eye, I guess.'

'Did he go home?'

'Doubt it. He lives down by Dulwich. Probably put his head down at the Yard.'

'Does he have a sister?'

'Yes. Out in Buckinghamshire somewhere, I think. Why?' He looked curiously at Kathy.

'Oh, when I was buying the papers this morning I saw him arrive. A woman brought him, in a red Merc sports.'

A little smile creased Gurney's tired eyes. 'Don't suppose you got the number?'

Kathy reached across and wrote on the pad in front of him. Gurney tore off the sheet and left the office. Half an hour later he strolled back in again, washed, shaved and considerably more cheerful. Without a word he placed a note in front of Kathy. On it was written the name Mrs Suzanne Chambers, a telephone number and an address in Belgravia, barely two hundred yards from Scotland Yard.

At that moment Brock appeared in the doorway behind them. 'You two want to bring me up to date?' he said, and then, seeing the note in Kathy's hand and the smile on her face, 'Good news?'

She shook her head quickly. 'Nothing, really.' She stuffed the note into the pocket of her trousers and followed the two men up the stairs.

It was only when they were seated that Kathy saw that Brock was as tired as Gurney. He had dark circles under his eyes, and he suppressed a yawn as Gurney spoke.

'Winter will appear this afternoon,' he said. 'We're opposing bail, of course, but I don't think the court will wear it. Especially not with the solicitor he's got himself.'

'Who is it?'

'Two of them. A little old guy called Hepple.'

'The sisters' solicitor?' Brock said, sitting up sharply. 'That's odd.'

'Yeah. He was really enjoying himself. I must say I could have done without his jolly repartee this morning. But his mate's the bad news. Apparently Hepple isn't representing Winter, he just came along to introduce him to this brief that he'd found for him. Your old friend Martin Connell, Brock.'

Kathy froze. She didn't hear the next part of their conversation, but as their voices began to register again she was suddenly filled with an enormous sense of gratitude to Brock – first because he studiously avoided looking at her, and then because it was clear that Gurney knew nothing about her connection with Connell. Her hand closed around the message in her pocket, and she screwed it into a tight little ball.

'But how the hell did either Hepple or Connell come in on this?' Brock thumped his fist on the arm of his chair.

'And how can Winter afford him?' Gurney added, shaking his head. 'The only good thing is that we know for sure that anyone Connell represents has got to be seriously guilty. Otherwise it's all bad. Christ' – he rubbed his forehead wearily – 'he even knew about me getting into Winter's office at Peckham without a search warrant. He let it drop that he was going to pin me on unlawful entry.'

Brock swore, pulled himself to his feet and strode over to the window. He stood there for a minute, staring at the snowflakes swirling outside, then walked slowly back to his seat.

'I spoke to the lab just now,' he said. 'It looks as if the plastic bag used on Eleanor was the same type as in one of those packets you brought back from Winter's house yesterday, Kathy. But it's a common type, in every supermarket, and Winter's prints weren't on the packet we picked up, which isn't to say that he didn't take another one. It's not the same type as was used on Meredith, which came from a packet in her own kitchen. So we'll have to pursue the hammer as another way of tying Winter in.'

Kathy reported her conversation that morning with Caroline Winter, and that they were in the process of tracing the kitchen contractor whose plumber might have lost a hammer at the Winters' home.

Brock nodded. 'Now, about the first murder. We'd better have another word with the woman who provided Winter's alibi then. What was her name?'

'Geraldine McArthur.'

'Yes. In view of their falling out, she might be less keen to protect him now.'

He paused, rubbing his eyes. 'Bren, go home and get some rest, will you? I cannot stand people falling asleep when I'm talking to them.'

Gurney shook himself and protested that he was only thinking with his eyes closed. Then, seeing Brock's expression, he got to his feet.

'Yeah, I wouldn't mind a couple of hours, chief.'

'See you later.'

When he had gone, Brock said quietly, 'Bren is convinced we can pin everything on Winter. I'm not so sure. So, what are the alternatives?'

'We've just got the results of the check Bren organized on that list of names from the developer's office and the others involved in the building project. Only one with a criminal record. Guess who?'

'Bob Jones?' Brock asked wearily.

'No, of course not.' She smiled. 'Danny Finn. They call him their Project Manager.'

Brock nodded. 'Well, we'd better have a word with him. See if you can find out where he is.'

Kathy phoned First City Properties, who told her he was on site. She rang the site office, but when she put the phone down she looked both puzzled and worried. 'They say he left. He had an appointment – at the Bedford Hotel.'

'But that's where we put Peg Blythe, for God's sake!'

'Yes.'

'Who knew where she was?'

'Nobody. Nobody knew.'

'What the hell is going on around here!' Brock was on his feet, reaching for his coat.

Kathy quickly punched the hotel telephone number, spoke a few words and returned the receiver. 'He arrived there ten minutes ago. Peg has just phoned down and ordered coffee and chocolate biscuits, for two.'

Brock shook his head in disbelief. 'Let's go and join them, then. What did Finn have on his record, Kathy? Is he a thief?'

'One charge of theft as a juvenile. Since then GBH, resisting arrest, and, most recently, about ten years ago, assault. A charge of attempted murder was dropped.'

She ran after Brock as he thundered down the wooden stairs.

*

Peg answered Kathy's knock, looking fresh and with her morale restored. She was wearing a burgundy knitted suit with flowery blouse and pearls, her white hair carefully coiffed, and she welcomed them with a delighted smile, as if they were old friends she hadn't seen in years.

'How lovely of you both to come and see me again. And in such terrible weather! You're just in time for morning coffee to warm you up.'

'We just wanted to check how you were, Mrs Blythe. Are you alone?' Kathy was looking over the top of her head into the room.

'Peg, dear, please.' She put a neatly manicured, arthritic hand on Kathy's arm and spoke in a confiding whisper. Kathy bent her head to hear, and smelled her lavender cologne. 'I have another visitor, a dear friend of mine that I invited to visit me.' She looked at Kathy with a twinkle in her eye and patted her arm. 'Come in and meet him.'

Seated in an armchair was a wiry little man of about fifty, with a badly broken nose. In one hand he held a teacup raised to his lips, and in the other the saucer upon which was perched a chocolate biscuit. He put these encumbrances carefully down on the coffee table in front of him and rose to his feet.

'Danny, I'd like you to meet the charming police officers I was telling you about. Kathy and . . .' – she hesitated – 'Chief Inspector Brock. This is Mr Danny Finn.'

Finn put out his hand. 'How d'ye do. Peg's been telling me about ye. Come away and sit down.' He turned to Peg. 'Peg, hen, I'll be on my way. Ye'll have things to discuss with the officers, an' I need tae be gettin' back anyhow.'

'Actually it was you we really wanted to see, Mr Finn,' Kathy said coolly.

Finn looked at her carefully. 'Oh, aye?'

'But you will take a cup of coffee, won't you?' Peg lifted the phone. 'Now I remember you take black, Inspector,' she said flirtatiously, 'but what about you, Kathy, dear?'

'No, really, Mrs Blythe, we won't stop for coffee,' Brock said.

'Of course, you're so busy. Well, do please sit down for a moment. Danny here has been such a help. I find it so useful to talk things over with him. He's been giving me advice on security for when I return to my flat. He feels I need better window locks. What do you think, Inspector?'

Brock grunted, 'Very likely. We'll get a Crime Prevention Officer to call again. But you mustn't be thinking of that until we find who was responsible for the death of your sisters. Surely you must understand that.'

'I do so appreciate your concern, Inspector. Have you no clues at all?'

'We believe that Mr Winter was responsible for the acts of vandalism and the attempts to frighten you and your sister in the past five months. We charged him this morning.'

Peg put her hand to her mouth, her eyes wide. 'Oh no. Poor Terry. I know you suspected him . . . Poor Caroline too, and the girls . . .' She shook her head.

'I'm not surprised,' Finn said. 'I said as much to ye weeks ago, did I not, hen?'

Peg nodded. 'Yes, you did, Danny, and I didn't believe you. I just couldn't imagine that Terry would really do such a thing. To his aunties! He was such a dear little boy. Meredith did spoil him, I know. We all did . . . But surely, Inspector, you don't imagine that he could have' – her voice dropped to a whisper as she struggled to articulate the awful thought – 'murdered his own mother . . . and his aunt!'

'We don't know, Mrs Blythe. He hasn't been charged with that. And that's why, until we are satisfied that we've got the person responsible, you shouldn't think of going home. Nor of telling anyone where you're staying. That's the whole point after all, isn't it?'

She didn't seem to understand at first, and then she looked at Danny Finn and blushed.

'Oh dear! You mean . . . Oh, but Inspector,' she recovered herself with a tinkling laugh, 'you can't mean Mr Finn. He is a good friend. With him I feel as safe as houses.'

Danny Finn returned with Kathy and Brock to the interview room upstairs at 20 Jerusalem Lane.

'How long have you known Peg Blythe?' Brock began. Finn seemed quite relaxed, taking an interest in all the activity going on around him in the incident centre. He was dressed in an anonymous business suit, pale blue shirt and dark tie, with a diary and gold pencil forming a bulge in his shirt pocket.

'Oh, let me see. The demolition contractor moved on tae site at the beginning of November last, and I came round tae see the two sisters maybe a week or two before that.'

'Why?'

'Well, they were the last people on the site who hadn't agreed tae sell up and go, and I was concerned we might have some trouble from them. You know, complaints about noise and the like. So I went round tae see what they were like, and try tae explain what was goin' tae happen.'

'You befriended them.'

'Aye, I suppose ye could put it like that. Tae tell ye the truth I liked the old dears. They're real characters. Ye know about their politics? Make Wedgie Benn look like a rabid Tory.'

'And no doubt you could give them disinterested advice on whether they should sell up or stay here?' Kathy's voice was cold with scepticism.

'Look, lassie, I don't like sarcasm. If ye have something ye're trying tae say, you just say it.'

'Well, Mr Finn, I suppose what I'm trying to say is that it seems to me your main purpose in befriending the two sisters was to persuade them to sell up to your company.'

'Aye, that's exactly right. Look, I like things simple, and it was obvious that those old dears livin' in the middle of a building site wasn't goin' tae be simple. It seemed obvious tae me that they should sell up. But equally it seemed obvious that yon wallies at Jonathan Hockings had made a pig's ear of negotiating with the ladies, an' I can imagine that greedy wee Terry only made things worse. So I decided that it needed someone tae talk it over sensibly with them.'

'Someone impartial, like you.'

'Someone like me who understood what the score was, yes. I made no pretence about where my loyalties lay, but equally I told them how they could get the best deal from First City. They weren't under any illusions, don't you worry.'

'And now, you're still negotiating?'

'Mrs Blythe phoned me today, Sergeant. Not the other way around.'

'From what you said earlier, Mr Finn, you knew Terry Winter,' Brock said. 'How come?'

'He was goin' spare when it turned out that his aunts wouldn't leave even after his mother died. He an' yon Quentin Gilroy' – he pronounced the name as if it were a weak joke – 'got together, an' Gilroy suggested Winter speak tae me about ways tae persuade the old ladies tae leave.'

'Why would he suggest your name, Mr Finn?'

'Because he knows my reputation as a total bastard, I expect, Chief Inspector.'

'Or perhaps your record of violent crime, Mr Finn.'

Finn laughed. 'Well, I don't think that Quentin knows about any imaginary "record of violent crime", though no doubt if he did it would only go tae enhance my professional reputation.'

'"Imaginary"? Theft, assault and attempted murder don't sound too imaginary, Mr Finn.'

'Chief Inspector, no young lad with any gumption came out of the Gorbals in my day without a record. When I was fourteen I had a nice wee business supplying plumbing materials tae a builder's supply yard. At night me an' my pal would climb over the wall and pinch the pipes, and next day we'd take them back an' sell them tae them again.' He chuckled at the memory. 'I was a budding entrepreneur, that's all. A Thatcherite ahead of my time. Later on I got in a bad fight in a pub, an' that was where the GBH an' resistin' arrest came from. It was all a long time ago.'

'What about the assault on the tourist ten years ago?'

'Och!' Finn ran a gnarled hand through the unruly tuft of thinning hair that stuck out of his scalp. 'Ten years ago I was made redundant for about the fifth time. We were up north and I had a young family. I was a trained chippie, but there was no work for carpenters there. I was made redundant that last time on Christmas Eve. Have you ever been sacked on Christmas Eve yourself, lassie? No, well . . .' He looked perplexed for a moment as he thought he caught the faintest trace of a smirk on Kathy's face. 'Well, anyway, I got a job sweeping the service roads underneath one of the shopping malls in the town. Part of the job was to stick a label on the windscreen of anyone who parked illegally down there, telling them they'd be prosecuted if they did it again. One day this big car parked, and I stuck on the label. Next thing, the driver, some foreign character, starts abusing me. I didn't like the way he talked tae me, as if, because I was sweeping roads, I was no better than dirt myself. He told me tae get the label off his windscreen, so I said all right, Jimmy, if that's what ye want, an' I put my broom through the bloody windscreen.'

He shrugged. 'I felt better, I can tell ye, but of course, next thing he's got the centre manager down there insisting they call the police, and swearing I'd tried tae kill him, which of course was all a load of nonsense. The centre manager didn't know what tae do, and he got on tae Mr Slade, whose company owns the centre. They paid off the tourist, an' once he'd gone back home the charges against me were dropped. They had tae sack me of course, but the next time Mr Slade was up north he asked tae see me. We got on like a house on fire, an' the end of it was that he offered me a job down here in London.'

'What about Terence Winter?' Brock persisted. 'What did you discuss with him?'

'He came into the office one day. He saw Mr Slade, who couldn't do much except tae sympathize with Winter's predicament. Then Winter asked for me. He said he'd heard from Gilroy that I could get things done. I thought he was jokin', an' I told him about the tricks we used tae play when I was a lad, terrorizing old ladies in the street, like tying the door knockers on opposite sides of the close together with string, then knocking one, an' when they opened their door they'd cause another knocker tae go, an' then that one would get another going, an' so on until the whole close was in an uproar. As I say, I thought he was jokin'. I had no idea he'd actually try tae get them tae leave that way.'

After Finn had left, a WPC passed on a message to Brock from Sergeant Griffiths, who had been sent to bring in Geraldine McArthur, Winter's former mistress. McArthur had not been seen since leaving work the previous afternoon. The WPC added that a Dr Naismith and her solicitor were waiting to see him.

Brock asked her to show them up to his office, rather than the interview room at the back, because it was warmer and he wanted Judith Naismith to see the grisly photographs of Eleanor Harper's corpse pinned up on the wall. But if she saw them as she came in, she showed no sign of it. Her face was set with determination as she and her solicitor, an elegantly dressed man in his late thirties, sat facing Brock and Kathy.

'It is essential for reasons of her work that my client return immediately to the United States, Chief Inspector. Unless you can provide some very convincing reasons for continuing to hold on to it, we must insist that you return her passport to her and allow her to leave the country forth-with. She has made a booking for a flight this afternoon, and she intends to catch it.'

'I see.' Brock scratched his beard. 'I take it then that Dr Naismith now intends to answer my questions?'

'She does. Indeed she would have done so last night if you and your officers had been more, what shall we say, considerate in your treatment of her.'

'Well then, tell us about your contacts with Meredith Winterbottom, Miss Naismith.'

She told them, in a clear, measured tone, without any unnecessary words or gestures, of the two meetings she and Bob Jones had arranged with Meredith, confirming his account of both.

'You had no contact with her independently of Mr Jones?'

She shook her head.

'And what about Eleanor Harper?'

'I met her briefly on that first occasion. Otherwise I've had no contact with her.'

'Really?'

She stared back at him steadily. 'That's correct.'

'Tell us about the books you saw in Eleanor's flat – the older books that interested you particularly.'

'They were a few first editions, and some books with dedications written apparently by Karl Marx.'

'How valuable, would you say?'

'I couldn't say. I'm not a book dealer. But certainly of interest to a historian like myself.'

'Interesting enough to make a special trip across the Atlantic.'

'Oh, come, that's not such a big deal. It's very cheap. A pleasant weekend trip, that's all. And I had other business in London.'

'What about other documents?'

'Mrs Winterbottom gave me a couple of handwritten

pages. One was a letter, the other a piece of text of some kind. She was unclear as to whether there was any more, and on their own they didn't amount to much.'

'Has anyone been in touch with you recently, offering you the books or other material?'

'No.'

'And did you make any attempt to contact the two sisters in the last few days, by phone or in person?'

'No.'

'When did you first learn that Eleanor Harper had been murdered?'

'When my solicitor here told me this morning.'

'And where were you on the night of Tuesday last, the 31st?'

'In my hotel. The Connaught, in Kensington High Street.'

Brock became silent, staring at the papers in front of him.

'All right, Chief Inspector? All in order? Can we be on our way?' The solicitor eased forward in his chair as if to stand up.

'Yes, you may as well.' Brock's voice was flat, his face tired. 'And perhaps you would advise your client not to bother coming back to waste my time until she's decided to be honest with me.'

After a second's pause, Judith and her solicitor both began to protest at Brock's bowed head. When they had finished, he looked up and fixed Judith in the eye.

'I find it inconceivable that you would come all the way to London to buy documents from someone and then go home empty-handed without making any subsequent attempt to contact the owner of those books. I don't believe that you are being honest with us about the significance of the documents. And your hotel tells us that you did not return to your room on the night of the 31st of March. Now, please go away and consider this matter a little more seriously. This is a murder inquiry. You will remain in this country until I consider that we are getting your full co-operation.'

Judith had become even paler than usual. She turned to her solicitor, who said hurriedly, 'I'd like to have a few private words with my client, Chief Inspector.'

'Be my guest.' Brock flapped his hand at the interview room across the landing. Kathy noticed that the weary droop to his shoulders lifted as soon as they left the room, and a little smile came into his face.

After a few minutes they returned, and the solicitor spoke. 'It appears, Chief Inspector, that Dr Naismith had personal reasons for concealing her whereabouts on Tuesday night. She did indeed not return to her hotel room that night. In fact she spent the evening and the night in the company of a close friend. The friend is married as it happens, and Dr Naismith feels that it would cause considerable unnecessary distress if the family became involved in this matter.'

'Oh dear,' Brock sighed, 'we seem to have an epidemic.'

'Pardon me?'

'Could you give us his name and address, please?'

The solicitor looked questioningly at Judith, who shook her head abruptly.

'I understand that it is an extremely sensitive situation, Chief Inspector. Surely you can appreciate –'

'Sorry.' Brock got to his feet and moved to get his coat from behind the door. 'Not good enough. Now, if you'll excuse us, we've got work to do.'

22

They were sitting in the darkened motel room, Terry in the armchair and Geraldine on the floor at his feet, her arms wrapped round his legs, her head resting on his knee. He felt stiff and uncomfortable – and a little ridiculous, as if she'd just brought him down with a flying rugby tackle. His brain was unnaturally active, too terrified to feel tired.

When the word had gone round the salons the previous day that Terry had been taken to Scotland Yard and the police had searched his Peckham office, Geraldine had not known what to do. Then she remembered that Terry had mentioned a solicitor in Jerusalem Lane who had been helping him. She found the name in the Yellow Pages and, even though the number was now disconnected, managed to get the firm's other number in Croydon, and so eventually made contact with Mr Hepple.

At first Hepple had said he was unable to help, but she was so insistent, so distressed, that he asked for a little time to see what he could do. And at that point his famous sense of mischief and wit inspired him with a brilliant idea. How wonderful if Martin Connell, who as Upper North's solicitor had been all over the papers as the adversary of the famous Chief Inspector Brock, could now be persuaded to take on the great man once more in the service of Mrs Winterbottom's unworthy little boy! Hepple was surprised and delighted to find Connell more than willing to consider the proposition, even although he had to make it clear that it might be some time before Winter would be in a position to pay anything like Mr Connell's usual fee – although the lady who had contacted him had assured him that she would meet any obligation.

And so it was that, when Winter was finally charged at 4.20 a.m. the next day, he found – to his great surprise and the police's – both Mr Hepple and Martin Connell waiting for him. Geraldine turned up at the court hearing in the afternoon and guaranteed his bail, which the magistrate granted despite the opposition of the police.

She had rescued him. She smiled to herself and tightened her grip around his legs, a grip which, it occurred to Terry, was a far stronger restraint than any to be found in Her Majesty's prisons. He put out his hand and stroked her hair, hoping to placate her need for him. She snuggled against his leg and clung to him even more tightly.

It was really very difficult to believe that not so long ago he would have gone to so much trouble to get this close to her. How desirable those shoulders, that hair had seemed then! Now he saw only the lines around her eyes, and was irritated that someone in their sort of business didn't make more of herself. It was a source of continual wonder to him how this happened, time after time, this ebb and flow of desire, from craving to indifference, so that the same woman could seem so completely irresistible one week, and so embarrassingly unappealing the next.

He looked around the cheap furniture of the motel room, lit by the table lamp, and remembered Geraldine's miserable little flat. How threadbare it was compared to what he had left behind in Chislehurst! He had a vivid recollection of the carpet frayed by the door, the clutter of cheap plastic toys left in a corner by her two little brats, the Woolworth's crockery, the smell of the homemade soup which always clung to the place. How would he be able to stand it?

Into his mind came a picture of a plastic bag enveloping this head upon his knee, of a hammer thudding into its skull. He shuddered and closed his eyes, and the nausea which had been with him now since the police arrived yesterday morning, returned, welling up in his stomach.

'Darling?' She was looking up into his face, concerned. She reached up with one hand and took his, gripping it tight. 'Don't worry! Everything will be all right now.'

He groaned. 'How can you say that?'

'Because it's true! Look. You'll admit the things you did to frighten your aunts. You'll say how stupid it was, how sorry you are, but you were driven to it by your financial worries. It all got out of hand. But at least you didn't physically hurt anyone. And you'll make a clean breast of it with your Aunt Peg, and tell her how awful you feel and beg her forgiveness. And she *will* forgive you, because she's always been fond of you. And then she'll tell the court how she's forgiven you, and no harm's done, and they won't be able to punish you. You've never been in trouble before.

'As long as they don't think you had anything to do with the death of your mother and Eleanor – and they can't if I can tell them that you were with me at the time your mother must have died. And you know' – her voice became a whisper, intense and intimate, and her hand slipped out of his and gripped his thigh uncomfortably tight – 'you *know* I will say that, don't you, darling, that I won't mention the hour you were away . . .'

'It was hardly an hour,' he said weakly, 'and it was to check the salon, you know that.'

'Of course, but we didn't tell them last time, so we can't bring it up now, can we?'

He shook his head obediently. It wasn't she who was going to suffocate; it was he, and not in the folds of a plastic bag but in the smothering embrace of her love. Perhaps after all it was inevitable. He had always felt that his freedom with women was illusory. When it came to the big decisions, it was his mother, his wife and now Geraldine who took the reins. Men, after all, were putty. A woman might leave her husband because she wanted something better, whereas a man would fool around, pathetically hoping for the best of both worlds, and finally make a move only when his wife or his mistress forced him to jump. For a short time in the inevitable transition from Caroline to Geraldine he had managed to slip the leash, to become a single man again, but he had messed it up, as he inevitably must.

Geraldine saw the worry in his eyes. Yet, terrible as this was, it would be the thing which would save them both. She would lead him out of this tragedy, and their relationship would thenceforth be unique, not the outcome of one of his affairs, but a new contract, a new bond. She would have saved him and would have put herself beyond betrayal. But first he must sink to the very bottom. Already two salons had gone, and Caroline would take as much of the rest as she could. And his experience with the police through last night and today must have been terrifying.

She had never doubted that he would come to her in the end. At first she had pretended that, like him, she wanted a casual, enjoyable affair. But her heart, frozen hard through eight bitter years of her husband's indifference, of watching him being stolen away by another woman, of divorce, and of steeling herself to lonely independence, this heart, being melted at last by Terry's confidence and passion, did not want a passing romance. So fast that she hardly realized it was happening, she found herself in the grip of what in her childhood her mother had described to her with dread in her voice, as a 'grand passion', the kind of passion that takes over your life, and, like some exotic tropical disease in the blood, never ever leaves you.

She would lead him out of his present despair, and when things had settled down she would speak to Peg, and they would agree on a way to sell the house to the developer. And then she and Terry would start again, from the bottom, building together. They might have a baby – she wasn't too old. He would come to regard her boys as his own. And they would start a little business together. But not hairdressing. No more girls, no more temptation. He was a mess now, falling apart at the seams. But like an unruly plant which had been neglected and left to grow wild, he could be pruned and shaped and nurtured, and in a season or two he would be transformed.

Terry felt the strain across his shoulderblades. He breathed deeply, trying to relax. Perhaps, after all, she was right. Perhaps things weren't so hopeless. He would just have to face the music over the stupid games he'd played, if they would only leave it at that. And afterwards, who knew? Geraldine's little flat wasn't so bad a place to shelter from the storm, and at least she was a much better cook than that bitch Caroline had ever been, for all her German kitchens. Two salons had gone, and a third on the way, but at least one of the other two might be saved, and he could build up again, learning from his past experience. In a year or two he would be back on his feet again, hiring girls. He smiled to himself. There was that pretty young black girl who had started just two weeks ago at New Cross. He'd never been to bed with a black girl.

23

The next morning Brock received a call from Judith Naismith, who wanted to meet him. He said that he and Kathy
would come to her hotel room at 10. Just as they were
about to leave, a transatlantic call came through.

'It turned out our Search Committee had actually considered
Judith Naismith, David, so I have some information on her.'

'Perfect timing, Nigel. Let's have it.'

'She got off to a very strong start at Princeton when she
arrived here, mostly developing the areas she worked on for
her Cambridge doctorate – a study of nineteenth-century
women who had contributed to the development of economic theory. Her first five years – that's '77 to '82 – she had
a dozen strong papers published in refereed journals, about
the same number of conference papers, and a book. She was
highly regarded, went on tenure track in '80 and got tenure
in '83. Then things started to dry up. There's been very
little publication since, and the word is she's lost her way.
The advice of referees to our committee was that she was
living on that early reputation. There was also a bit of
scandal a couple of years ago about an affair with a student
who took an overdose.

'So, one way or another our people decided not to take it
any further. I understand, though, that she has recently
been applying for big funding from foundations – well, big
for historians, anyway, six figures – but I don't know what
for exactly. So maybe she has some new project on the
blocks. That's about it.'

'That's terrific, Nigel. Most obliged. Fills us in nicely.'

'Oh, by the way, that student who OD'd was a girl.'

*

Judith seemed slightly flustered when she opened the door to them. 'You're early,' she said. The bed was unmade and articles of clothing scattered across the floor. 'Would you mind sitting over there by the window? I'll be a sec.'

They sat together on a grey settee and looked at the tastefully vapid lithographs in gold frames bolted to the wall, while Judith rapidly swept some order into the other end of the room. Finally she came over and sat in an armchair facing them. She crossed her legs, lit a cigarette, and took a deep breath.

'This is very difficult for me,' she began.

'I understand,' Brock said. 'You've talked things over with your friend?'

'No. It's not that.' She frowned and flicked the ashless cigarette impatiently in the direction of the glass table. 'You probably passed her in the corridor just now.' She shrugged. 'She was splitting up with her husband, anyway.

'Look, supposing . . . supposing you had some case where there were industrial secrets involved. Something like that. You could understand, couldn't you, how difficult it might be for someone involved to talk about it, without giving out information that might find its way to a competitor?

'In a way, for me, source materials are a bit like that. I know a professor over here, an economic historian, who was walking home one afternoon thirty years ago, and he passed a site in South London where they were demolishing old buildings. He noticed a pile of old books scattered about on the floor of a half-demolished building and went in to investigate. They turned out to be the complete account books for the building company which had had its offices there for an unbroken period of a hundred and ten years. That find totally changed his life.'

She stared intently at them, willing them to understand.

'His whole subsequent academic reputation and career grew out of his work on the nineteenth-century economy of South London based on the interpretations and computer analyses of the figures contained in those ledgers. They were his private gold mine, which he spent the rest of his life excavating. If somebody else had noticed them first, and another historian had got hold of them, he might now be just another embittered lecturer in a minor department, instead of the internationally revered father of studies in the economy of Victorian cities.'

'And you've found something similar here?' Brock asked.

'Maybe. I'm not sure. If . . . if I tell you about it, is there any way I can guarantee it won't get passed on . . .?'

'To one of your academic competitors? Dr Naismith, if your information is relevant to this murder investigation, there's no way you are going to be able to keep it to yourself.'

She nodded, took another shallow drag on the cigarette and flicked it.

'It began with that letter that Bob Jones found.'

'We were beginning to doubt its existence when it couldn't be found in his flat.'

'Oh, it existed, all right. I saw it. The mystifying thing is what it was doing there. You have to understand that when Marx died, all his papers and books were gathered together, and carefully preserved. They called the complete collection the *Nachlass* – you know, the *Estate*, almost like the shroud, or the grail, or the true cross or whatever. It was in the care of Engels at first, who continued working on his friend's papers and preparing the second and third volumes of *Das Kapital* for publication in the period up until he died in 1895, twelve years after Marx. Now Engels gathered together the correspondence he had had with Marx over forty years, and, so we're told, preserved all but a few excessively intimate letters from his friend. They take up nine volumes, each about four or five hundred pages, in the collected edition of Marx and Engels' works.

'How then had this one solitary letter gone astray? And was it in fact solitary? At first I thought it an amusing puzzle, but when we met Meredith and she showed me the books in Eleanor's bookcase, I began to take it seriously. There were maybe ten or a dozen books that really interested me – I could give you most of their titles. The thing about them was that they all seemed to have belonged to Eleanor Marx, the youngest of Marx's children, and his favourite. I am *very* interested in her. She was a significant figure in the development of socialism at the end of the nineteenth century, as well as being important for the work she did on her father's manuscripts. Some of the books were hers, inscribed with her name, and some had been given her by her father with handwritten dedications from him to "Tussy", the pet name he gave her.

'I was intrigued by how these could have come into the possession of Eleanor Harper, who not only had the same first name as Eleanor Marx, and actually looked rather like her, but also had a picture of Eleanor Marx hanging in her living room.'

'Her great-aunt,' Kathy said.

'That's right. It took me some time to work it out, because the connection wasn't through any of Marx's six legitimate children. But in 1850 the Marxes' maid, Hélène Demuth, whom they called "Lenchen", or sometimes "Nimm", had a baby boy, Frederick Demuth, who was assumed at the time to be Friedrich Engels' illegitimate son.'

'Yes, he was born in Jerusalem Lane,' Kathy said, recalling the account which Mr Hepple the solicitor had given of the history of the Lane.

Judith Naismith stared at her, astounded, 'You know, then?'

'Not everything,' Brock interjected. 'Please, go on.'

'Well, the baby wasn't brought up in the Marx household, and he became a manual labourer when he grew up. But just before Engels died, he revealed that Marx had been the father of the child, not himself. Eleanor was shocked that her beloved father could have first deceived her mother and then abandoned the child, but she got over it and became quite attached to her half-brother, and helped him in various ways before she died in 1898.

'The year before that, Frederick Demuth married a young woman, Rebecca Jacobs, who was a friend and acolyte of Eleanor's. They had a daughter, Mary, who married one George Harper, and they had three daughters, Meredith, Eleanor and Peg.'

'So they were the great-granddaughters of Karl Marx,' Kathy said.

'Yes. Even so, it was puzzling that they should have inherited books and papers from Eleanor Marx. She didn't have any children of her own, but still, there were others to whom she would have been more likely to have given things like that than to the labourer Frederick – her sister Laura, for instance. It was the other papers which Meredith gave me that made me begin to suspect the reason.'

Judith got abruptly to her feet and lit another cigarette. She strode over to the window and stood for a moment, arms folded, exhaling smoke. They waited, and after a while she said, without looking back, 'Would you like a coffee or something? I wouldn't mind one. There's a kettle and cups over there.'

She made no move, and Kathy said to Brock, 'Shall I?'

'Would you mind, love?' Judith said from the window, still not turning round.

Kathy glared at her back and got up. No one spoke until she returned to the glass table with three cups of black coffee, together with some small tubs of long-life milk and packets of sugar. Judith then sat down again and continued her account.

'One of the pieces of paper Meredith gave me was another letter, this time from Engels to Marx, and dated a couple of years after the first one. The thing it had in common with the first was that it also mentioned the fourth and final volume of *Das Kapital*, and referred to it as *das Endziel*, that is, the final "aim" or "goal". I thought at first that this was a term which Engels was using to describe the last volume. I couldn't recall the word being used before at all. But then I looked at the second piece of paper that Meredith had given me. It was a page of a manuscript handwritten in Marx's usual chaotic script, with corrections and insertions, like the draft of an essay. Written across the top, in a different script which I later identified as Tussy's, was a message which read, "To my dearest Rebecca, this is our true *Endziel*. Treasure it. E.M."

'It was dated 31 March 1898 – the day Tussy died.'

Kathy and Brock waited, still uncertain where all this was leading, while she lit another cigarette from the stub of the last.

'You have to understand the circumstances then,' Judith went on. 'When Marx died, there was great concern and rivalry between the various socialist factions about his *Nachlass*, so much so that the German Social Democratic Party actually planted first a housekeeper, Louise Kautsky, and then a doctor, Ludwig Freyberger, in Engels' household in order to make sure that when Engels died, everything would come to the German Party. The year before he died, Eleanor discovered that they had persuaded him to change his will so that the German Party would inherit all his books, manuscripts and letters, including all of Marx's own books which Eleanor had given to Engels when her father died to help him with his work. Tussy was furious and had a terrible row with him, which eventually came to a head on Christmas Day 1894, when Engels promised to leave manuscripts in Marx's handwriting to her, along with family letters.

'But Tussy was still terrified that the Freybergers – the two spies had married by this stage – would persuade him to change his mind, or would appropriate manuscripts in his possession. They tried to prevent her having access to Engels' house, and her suspicions were further heightened when there was an announcement in the paper of the German Party, *Vorwärts*, that volume four of *Das Kapital*, which she was actually working on, would not be issued. She even begged Engels to allow her to copy her father's rough draft of volume four herself, or with her sister Laura, in order that it not be lost before she had completed the task of preparing it for a publisher.

'Eventually it was published, after Eleanor was dead, under the title *Theorien über Mehrwert*, but curiously, before she died, Tussy described it in a letter as being "*not* in the ordinary sense the fourth volume, being only certain notes which the editor has to work from". In other words it was very far from being the *Endziel*, or "the final volume which will assure our immortality and make all our fortunes", as Marx wrote in that first letter in 1867.

'I began to wonder if Tussy had herself appropriated documents from Engels' house in order to prevent them from falling into the hands of the Freybergers – her father's manuscript of the true *Endziel*, perhaps, and those letters from his correspondence with Engels which referred explicitly to it.'

Judith was talking now with total absorption, as if she were still struggling with the enormity of the theories which had grown in her brain.

'It sounds absurd, doesn't it – a whole book, the final and most important book written by the most influential thinker of our age, totally lost, its very existence unsuspected, lying in an attic in Jerusalem Lane.

'I wondered if Tussy had been behind what had always seemed the unlikely match between her dedicated student Rebecca, a committed socialist and intellectual, and her half-brother Frederick – for this purpose, to provide a safe future home for the precious material. Frederick after all was twenty-five years older than Rebecca, and had been married to a woman who had left him years previously before Tussy took him under her wing, and got him to formalize his separation from that first wife in a divorce. At any rate that does seem to have been the route which the documents Meredith showed me had taken, from Tussy to Rebecca, and from her to her daughter Mary, and then to Mary's daughters Meredith, Peg and Eleanor, each time passed on, a private *Nachlass*, down the female line of the family.'

She shrugged. 'I guess I maybe got carried away. After all, there really was very little evidence for the existence of the *Endziel* I imagined. As you suspected, I did try to contact Eleanor and Peg after that abortive visit to Meredith. I phoned them from the States, and I came over again, around Christmas time, and tried to get them to talk to me about it. Actually they got quite short with me. I can't blame them really. I guess I was pestering them. They said they knew nothing about further documents, and kind of suggested that I'd put pressure on Meredith to steal Eleanor's books to sell to me, which wasn't true.'

'Did you come over this time to try to speak to them again?'

'No, I'd more or less given up on them. I did try to call on them a couple of times at the beginning of the week, but they wouldn't see me. But a few months ago I got a phone call from a book dealer in London, who said that the books Meredith had shown me had come into his possession, and were now for sale. I assumed Eleanor must have sold them, and I said yes, I wanted first refusal. He had a much more realistic idea of their worth, and was asking five thousand each. That's pounds, not dollars. He sent me photocopies of the flyleaf of each book, with the handwritten inscriptions, and I set about trying to raise some funds in the States to buy the collection.'

'Who did he tell you he was?'

'He didn't, and he said I couldn't contact him, and this really presented a problem for me. You see, the chain from Marx forward to the present had been broken. I mean I could readily accept that an old inscribed book on the shelf of Karl Marx's great-granddaughter would be genuine, but how could I be sure the same would be true of a book sold to me by a mysterious dealer who wouldn't identify himself? The photocopies did look identical to those I'd seen in Eleanor's room that day, but for all I knew he might have had half a dozen versions forged into ordinary copies of those books, which would be worth only a few hundred dollars, and be selling them to universities around the world. Ever since the *Hitler Diaries* fiasco we've all been paranoid.

'The only way I could see of testing him was to tell him something about the manuscript of which Meredith had given me that first page. So the next time he called me I said that that was what I was really interested in, and if it was what I expected, it would be worth hundreds of thousands to my research sponsors. But I didn't mention the word *Endziel*, or my theory about the fourth volume of *Das Kapital*, and I could see no way that anyone could work that out in order to forge something.

'We arranged that I would come over to London this week to see the books and anything else he might have been able to get hold of, and he would contact me here at the Connaught. He never did, but when I saw a newspaper on Thursday saying that the second sister had been murdered, I took fright and booked out on the next available flight.'

'You assumed he would have been responsible?'

'Well, it was one hell of a coincidence if he wasn't.'

'If what you say is true, Dr Naismith, and the manuscript of your fourth volume does exist, and your mystery dealer doesn't have it, then the remaining sister, Peg Blythe, is still very much at risk.'

'Yes. I wish I could say that that was my reason for telling you all this now.'

'But instead you just wanted to go home.'

'Actually, no.' She looked up at Brock defiantly. 'The

reason is that I realized that if the dealer, or anybody else for that matter, ever does get their hands on the manuscript, the thing that's going to prove its provenance – its unbroken line back to Karl Marx – is your investigation. You may think that you're trying to find a murderer, Chief Inspector, but to my mind you're doing something much more important. You may find Karl Marx's *Endziel*, and when you do, I'd like to be around.'

24

Bren Gurney was back in top gear when Brock and Kathy returned to Jerusalem Lane, issuing instructions over the phone in Brock's office while munching something held in his big paw.

'Brass monkeys weather,' Brock complained as they bustled in. He stopped and sniffed the air. 'That bacon sandwich smells good, Bren. Where'd it come from?'

'Mrs Rosenfeldt's Sandwich Bar next door, chief.' Gurney put down the phone. 'Chip butties and mushy peas the *spécialités de la maison*.'

'What! That's sacrilege! What happened to Rosenfeldt's Continental Deli?'

'Swept away by market forces, chief. She did a careful market survey among the DCs here and the lads on the site over the road, got a few recipes from them, did a few sample tastings, and now she's flogging greasy bangers and mugs of hot soup as fast as she can churn them out. She's taken on two girls and she's making a killing.'

'Unfortunate choice of words,' Kathy said, smiling.

'You're allowed to use phrases like that when you're in Serious Crime, love. Sets people's teeth on edge.'

'Never mind about that,' Brock said gruffly. 'Get someone to fetch me one of those bacon sandwiches. No, better make it two.'

'Yuck.' Kathy curled her lip in disgust, and Brock began shuffling guiltily through the mail on his desk.

When Gurney returned, Kathy told him about their meeting with Judith Naismith.

'You believe her?' he asked sceptically.

'Yes, I do. At least I believe that what she told us was

probably true, although it may not be all she knows. I think she sees us now as being at least a possible route to the stuff she wants, and probably the only way of authenticating it when it turns up.'

'Do you have a list?'

Kathy gave him the list of book titles that Judith had written out for them.

'Mmm,' Brock said, speaking with his mouth full. 'Better get it typed up and some teams out straight away. Every second-hand and antique book dealer. That's got to be top priority.'

Kathy nodded.

'I don't know.' Gurney was still unconvinced.

'A dozen books, Bren,' Brock said, 'worth five thousand pounds each. That's a reasonable motive for putting a couple of old ladies to sleep.'

'But so traceable,' Bren objected. 'What professional dealer is going to get involved once they realize where they've come from?'

'Hence the need to contact Judith Naismith. Get rid of them out of the country.'

'But what do we really know about this dealer? That he's male and that he knew how to contact Bob Jones. How? In fact how do we know it wasn't Bob Jones?'

Kathy shook her head doubtfully.

'All right, then,' Bren continued, the bit between his teeth, 'whoever it is, he contacts Naismith and she tells him that she really wants something else, something that Meredith had that was even more valuable than the books. A manuscript, probably wrapped up in old newspapers or something so you wouldn't even realize you had it. What does he do? He tries the sisters, and they tell him they haven't got anything and to get lost. So then he contacts . . .?'

Gurney raised his eyebrows and looked at Kathy.

'Meredith's next of kin,' Kathy said.

'Mr Terry Winter, exactly.' Gurney folded his arms with

satisfaction. 'So now our Terry knows about the manuscript. And he knows *he* doesn't have it. So it's got to be at Jerusalem Lane. He tries every way to get in there to search for it, but the old dears hardly ever go out. Eventually, as the date for Naismith's trip gets closer, he has to break into his own house in Chislehurst to get his keys to Jerusalem Lane, and then pay his aunts a night-time visit. Eleanor's the best bet for having the stuff. It was probably in a suitcase under her bed. She wakes up and sees him groping around, and he has to kill her to silence her. Then he makes off with the manuscript. It's too late to get to Naismith or the book dealer by this stage, but it doesn't really matter. He can wait. And the beauty is that when he finally does produce it, he can say he inherited it directly from his mother, and Naismith's provenance is intact. No wonder he can afford Connell!'

Brock wiped his mouth and beard with a paper napkin appreciatively. 'Good as far as it goes, Bren. Where is the manuscript now, then?'

'In a security box in the bank, or a left-luggage locker, or with a friend – the missing Geraldine maybe. It's the first murder that bothers you in casting Winter as the villain, isn't it, chief?'

Brock nodded. 'Winter is a spoilt boy who's never really grown up. I think his mum was still number one. He might try to manipulate her, exploit her, even bully her, but I can't see him killing her. And besides, he's got a plausible witness who says he was never within five miles of Jerusalem Lane at the relevant time.'

'All right. But we've been assuming that both sisters were killed by the same person. Why? If Winter did the second, he would want it to look like the first, for which he has an alibi, right?'

'Who killed Meredith, then?'

'I don't know. I think we've got to start from the beginning again with that one.'

Brock frowned. 'Kathy?'

'There's something in what Bren says, sir. I've always been uncomfortable about not getting to the bottom of what was happening to Meredith before she died. Of course her depression could have been due to Terry putting pressure on her, but I always thought it was more than that – something to do with her life here in Jerusalem Lane. It's difficult to imagine it now, with them all gone, but the atmosphere was so real, and so intense. They were like characters from some weird melodrama, all so passionate, and all locked together in this little street. Do you remember Dr Botev, and the impression he gave that he knew what had happened to Meredith? And Mrs Rosenfeldt and her dark hints about the Nazis? We put all that to one side. But maybe . . . I don't know.'

'Go on,' Brock said.

'Well, maybe they all knew things were coming to an end here, and maybe someone had some final score to settle with Meredith.'

They were silent for a moment, until finally Brock spoke. 'All right, we know where Mrs Rosenfeldt is. See if you can trace Botev, Kathy. Bren, we'd better get hold of the records from the local CID of that break-in at the Winters' house. And let's find those damned books!

'One other thing,' he added as they got to their feet. 'If your theory is right, Bren, about Winter stealing the papers from Eleanor, he probably has to assume that Peg knew Eleanor had them. In which case he won't really feel safe to sell them until Peg is dead, too.'

Peg received them with her usual radiant composure. She was seated at a table by the window of her hotel room, letters and sympathy cards spread over its surface.

'People are so very kind,' she sighed, picking up a card. 'The Stoke Newington Socialist Guild. How very thoughtful of *them* to write.'

Kathy felt not for the first time that Mrs Blythe was rather enjoying all the attention coming her way. 'Peg,' she began, 'we were speaking to Judith Naismith this morning.'

The old lady smiled blankly at her. 'Naismith? Should I know her?'

'She came to see you and Eleanor, about your books and other papers.'

'Oh, the dreadful American academic woman!' She frowned. 'I'm afraid we had very little time for *her*.'

'She told us about her theories. We had no idea you three sisters were the descendants of such a famous man.'

Peg puffed up with pride. 'Oh,' she preened coyly, 'we didn't advertise it, you know. And these days, being the great-granddaughter of Karl Marx is rather like what it must have felt twenty years ago to be the last descendant of the Tsar Nicholas – you know, a historical relic from a bygone, irrelevant and very unfashionable age.'

Brock smiled. 'You don't believe it's irrelevant, though, do you, Peg?'

She returned his look. 'No, Chief Inspector, I do not. But' – she gave her tinkling laugh – 'from what one reads these days, I am almost the only one left.'

'But the wheel will turn, eh?'

'Ah, yes.' Her eyes were bright as she answered him. 'How short people's memories are!'

'What did you make of her notion that your mother might have passed down to you important documents which came from your great-grandfather?'

'Nonsense!' she chirped, her eyes still unaccountably shining. Kathy wondered if she was flirting with the old man. 'She was full of silly theories, like all academics. Eleanor recognized her type straight away. She used to meet them all the time when she worked in the British Museum. So bossy, and so insistent, you know, like those awful American religious people who knock on your door. It was distressing, especially for Eleanor. She thought Eleanor had something hidden, something about her books.'

'Did Eleanor feel threatened by her, would you say?'

Peg frowned and shook her head, 'Eleanor did not feel that she needed to be protected, Chief Inspector,' she said quietly. 'She was a strong person. Of all of us she was the strongest. Perhaps that was why she believed, like our great-grandfather, that you do not need a strong Party, because they themselves were so strong and good.

'But I' – and the persona of the sweet, frail and brave Queen Mother slipped back over her again – 'am not strong or good, and so I believe that we must have strong leaders and a strong Party to keep us upon the true road.'

Brock looked thoughtfully at her for a moment, and then nodded. 'Well, Mrs Blythe, I believe that you at least *are* in need of protection. I am going to have to insist that you tell no one else where you are staying. And I am going to arrange for a woman constable to stay here in this hotel with you. If you would like her company, that's fine, otherwise she will stay out of your way. But she will be here.'

'I am sure that isn't necessary, Chief Inspector, but I do appreciate your concern. Of course I would be delighted to have her company.' And then, as she showed them to the door, 'Eleanor's model was her great-aunt, you know, another Eleanor, whose picture she hung upon her wall. Our Eleanor lived as noble a life, and died as noble a death, as that model she revered. I do have a great fear that when the time comes for me to join them, I shall not be as strong. I should so hate to let them down.'

'Answer the door to no one until our officer arrives,' Brock said. 'She will phone you from the front desk first, and identify herself.'

25

There had been a slight thaw the previous afternoon, followed by a sharp drop in temperature during the night, so that the snow and slush had now solidified into rutted, glazed mounds of ice. When she got out of the car, Kathy had to pick her way carefully across the pavement and down the short drive leading to the front door of the semi-detached house. Like most of the originally identical pebble-dash houses on the street, this one had been through several cycles of improvement, the original timber casements of its bow windows replaced by modern aluminium windows with mock diamond pane patterning, and a recent bedroom extension inserted into its tiled roof. The drive was almost the only one on this Saturday morning not occupied by a car, and its surface had not been cleared of snow.

It took Dr Botev so long to come to the door that Kathy almost gave up. Then she heard a shuffling from the inside, the door opened a little, and the doctor's thick lenses peered out at her.

'Kathy Kolla, doctor. From the police. I phoned half an hour ago.'

He led her through a small hallway made almost impassable by open cardboard removal cartons, and into the front room where more boxes were heaped so that an orange settee and armchairs resembled life rafts floating in a sea of wreckage. He sat down heavily without a word, leaving her to clear a pile of old towels off a seat opposite him. After the cold outside, the warmth of the central heating was suffocating and she unbuttoned her coat.

'Nice street,' she smiled at him, hiding her shock at seeing him so changed. He had lost at least twenty pounds, his shoulders sagged, his complexion was grey, and the stubble on his chin had grown into a bristly white beard stained yellow around the mouth.

'How long ago did you move in?'

He stared at her for a moment, then mumbled, 'October.'

Five months, she thought, *and not a single box unpacked.*

'What are the neighbours like?'

He shook his head vaguely and seemed to withdraw into the cushions of the armchair. Kathy wondered if it had been a mistake to sit down.

'Look,' she said as she got to her feet, 'would you think it rude if I made us a cup of tea? I'm gasping for one.'

He looked up at her, vaguely surprised.

'Could you show me where the kitchen is?'

He didn't move, so she went out herself, through the cluttered hall and found the kitchen door. It wasn't as bad as she had feared – probably, she guessed, because not a lot of food got prepared there. There was a cup and saucer on the draining-board, half a dozen empty milk bottles in a corner, a bowl of half-eaten cornflakes on the small kitchen table. And in the fridge there was a homemade apple pie, with a slice removed.

She heard his shuffling footsteps behind her. 'The apple pie looks good. Did one of your neighbours bake that for you?'

She was surprised when he answered, his voice quite clear, heavily accented and with that unexpectedly high pitch. 'We always had apples. Even at the end of the winter, when everything else was gone, there was always an apple left at the bottom of one of the boxes.'

'When was that, Dr Botev?'

'After the war came to an end.'

'Ah yes. Were you married then?'

He looked at her, puzzled. 'No, no. The Great War.'

'Oh . . . You must have been very young.' She plugged in the kettle. 'I wanted to ask you about Meredith again. You remember we talked about her last September? After she died?' She turned and looked carefully at him to see if he knew what she was talking about, and was relieved to see a little of the old belligerence returning to his face.

'Did you arrest someone?'

She shook her head. 'We're still looking. We need your help. I wondered if there was more you could have told us, about why Meredith was depressed, for example.'

He sat down on the only chair at the table and studied the cornflakes while Kathy found an open packet of tea.

'The past,' he said at last, 'is a jealous mistress. No! A jealous mother!' He corrected himself and nodded his head vigorously. 'I remember every day more clearly the village where I was born. Pentcho and Georgi, Dora and Bagriana. The smell of the fires ...' For a moment he was lost, his face twitching between a smile and a frown. Then he continued, 'But as to yesterday, or last week, or last September ...' He shook his head hopelessly.

'But you do remember Meredith?'

He nodded. 'She was so innocent. How could she be otherwise! She was English. The English are innocents. They have not had our experience.'

He thought some more. '*Her* past was a jealous mother, all right. More jealous than most.'

'Meredith's?'

He looked at her, puzzled again. 'No, Becky's.'

Kathy's heart sank. More distant memories. She put a cup of tea in front of him. 'Who's Becky, doctor?'

He shook his head. 'She always listened to Becky.'

'Who did? Meredith? Your mother? Who?'

He looked at her vaguely, and then seemed to come to a decision. He got firmly to his feet and said sharply to her, 'Come!'

He led her into the other downstairs room which faced, like the kitchen, towards the snow-covered back garden. This time it was a bed which was crammed in among the

246

boxes. He crouched and drew out a small suitcase from underneath it, and set it on the quilt. It was full of old photographs, all black and white.

'Here.' He indicated to Kathy to sit on the bed, and pulled a picture from the pile. 'This is Dora. When she was sixteen. You see how she hated to wear shoes? It was the next spring that the soldiers took her.'

He handed it to Kathy, his eyes full of tears, and reached for another.

Depressed and no wiser, Kathy returned to Jerusalem Lane. It was past noon, and a steady stream of building workers and police were filing into Mrs Rosenfeldt's shop with lunch orders. At least the old lady's mind was entirely in the present, Kathy thought, even if she didn't welcome the interruption.

'This is coming up to my busy time,' she grumbled. 'Can't you come back later?'

'No, I can't,' Kathy said, making little attempt to keep the exasperation out of her voice. 'Let the girls cope with it for ten minutes. I need to speak to you now, in private.'

Mrs Rosenfeldt shrugged and led her through to a small storeroom at the back of the shop, in which there was a scrubbed wooden table and two chairs. They sat down facing each other across a pile of invoices and receipts.

'I've told you all I know about the vandals. There's nothing else I can say about Eleanor's death.'

'Not Eleanor. I want to talk to you about Meredith.'

Mrs Rosenfeldt raised her eyebrows. 'Six months, and suddenly it's so urgent?'

Kathy hardly knew how to begin. After Dr Botev's ramblings, and surrounded now by the bustle of a changing present, the ghosts of the past seemed increasingly irrelevant.

'Do you know anyone called Becky?'

'Becky?' Mrs Rosenfeldt's eyes glittered suspiciously through her steel-rimmed glasses.

'Yes. A friend of Meredith.'

'Of course. I am Becky.'

'You? Ah.' Kathy smiled. She would never have associated the name with this severe little woman.

'Why?'

'We heard she had a friend called Becky, but didn't know who it was. It doesn't matter.'

It does, Kathy thought, *but how? What thing from Mrs Rosenfeldt's past could have touched Meredith?*

'When you first spoke to us, you said we should look out for Nazis. Did you really mean that? Surely all that was far in the past?'

'Really?' Mrs Rosenfeldt snapped. 'You think Nazis disappeared because the war came to an end? They never disappear. Don't you read the papers?' She rubbed a stick-like thumb angrily on her bony wrist.

'But not in Jerusalem Lane, surely. I mean, I know Meredith discovered that business about the Kowalskis' past during the war, but that was, well, a tragedy. They were victims too, weren't they?'

'Oh, you think so?' Kathy could see that Mrs Rosenfeldt was holding herself tight as a spring.

'Don't you?' She smiled innocently at the rigid face. She thought for a moment that the old lady wouldn't respond, then she saw the thin lips open.

'Don't tell me about *victims*, young woman!' She spoke with an intensity that made her frail body shake. 'I have seen *victims*! Adam Kowalski was never one. His students were victims. He was one of *them*. I know. I can smell *them*, the way you can smell *dogshit*.'

Her vehemence unnerved Kathy. 'He's a frail old man,' she protested.

'So? Even Nazi murderers get old.'

'And you told Meredith this? That Adam Kowalski was a murderer?'

Mrs Rosenfeldt bowed her head in a gesture which Kathy thought rather evasive.

'What has this got to do with Meredith's death, really, Mrs Rosenfeldt? What did Adam Kowalski do to Meredith?'

Kathy saw from the woman's dismissive shrug that this was not the right question.

'Marie Kowalski, then?'

Warmer. Mrs Rosenfeldt's fingers had developed a sudden interest in the paperwork on the table.

'What do you know about Marie Kowalski?'

The gaunt figure didn't respond, and Kathy felt herself become angry. She got abruptly to her feet and leaned forward across the table. 'What about Marie Kowalski, Mrs Rosenfeldt?' She was aware that her voice was loud, almost shouting. 'Did you see something?'

When the old woman looked up to meet her eyes, Kathy saw, somewhat to her shame, that they were filled with fear.

'She came . . .' Mrs Rosenfeldt began, and then hesitated.

'To see you?'

She nodded, lowered her eyes.

'Marie Kowalski came to see you. Yes?' *Come on.*

With a small effort at bluster, Mrs Rosenfeldt tossed her head. 'And I told her. Of course I told her. They couldn't escape just by running away to the seaside!'

Kathy sat down slowly and stared at her. *Is that it?* 'You told her that Meredith would go on telling people about them?'

Mrs Rosenfeldt's head dropped low so that Kathy found herself staring at the silver bun of her hair. It was a nod of acknowledgement.

'When was this?'

'That afternoon.' The voice was a whisper. 'The afternoon she died.'

'Marie Kowalski called on Mrs Rosenfeldt shortly after 2 that afternoon.'

Brock put down the draft report he had been reading to listen to Kathy, who was slightly out of breath from the speed with which she'd taken the stairs.

'She came to say goodbye,' Kathy continued. 'She had never realized that it was Mrs Rosenfeldt who had been stirring the pot over Meredith's discovery. For months Mrs Rosenfeldt had been telling Meredith she should do something about it, to unmask the Kowalskis. I think that's what had been getting Meredith down. She didn't know what to do for the best. Mrs Rosenfeldt was pretty formidable once she got an idea in her head.

'That afternoon she just couldn't let Marie get away without putting the knife in. She told her that she could expect big trouble. Their names would be in the papers. Meredith would see to it. Marie left at around 2.15 in a state. Three hours later Mrs Rosenfeldt heard that Meredith was dead, and drew her own conclusions. But she couldn't tell us directly without revealing that she had inflamed the problem. I think she feels as guilty now as if she'd killed Meredith with her own hands.'

'The past is a jealous mother.' Brock repeated the phrase and shook his head. 'It doesn't sound like Dr Botev.'

'I think he was quoting. An old Bulgarian proverb probably.'

'Well, we'd better find out PDQ exactly what the Kowalskis' movements were that afternoon.'

'I think we know, sir.' Kathy frowned. 'I'm sorry. It's in the file and I never realized. DC Mollineaux was still checking when the investigation was closed. His report was added to the file later, and I didn't know it was there. I phoned him just a moment ago, and he told me.'

She opened the file she was carrying.

'The book dealer in Notting Hill where Adam Kowalski and his son Felix went to dispose of the final load of books confirmed to Mollineaux that they arrived around 1.45 p.m., and were there for about thirty minutes. Then the van rental place in Camden Town turned up their records which showed the van was returned at 3.05 p.m. Marie must have been on her own in the Lane from about 1.30 p.m. to 2.30 p.m. or a bit later.'

'That was what Adam Kowalski told us, wasn't it?'

'Yes. It was Felix who said they were back around 2.00 p.m.'

Brock looked at his watch. 'Looks like another trip to the seaside, Kathy. Let's grab one of Mrs Rosenfeldt's meat pies before we go. Bren says they're excellent.'

26

İt seemed that each time they drove down to the coast the weather became more threatening. Now the sky was filled with oppressive dark snow clouds, and the sun, when it did manage to break through, was a baleful red disk, the eye of Lucifer observing their progress across the frozen grey countryside.

They had phoned ahead to make sure the Kowalskis were at home, and when they arrived at the doorstep they could see the two of them through the window, sitting in the front lounge, dressed in their Sunday best like a pair of refugees waiting stoically for their deportation orders. Marie opened the front door and led them without a word into the room, where they all sat formally facing each other. There was an indistinct, unpleasantly sweet odour in the air, and Kathy loosened her coat, feeling suddenly nauseous. She looked at Adam, who sat to attention beside his wife on the settee, his watery eyes fixed on a framed photograph hanging on the opposite wall, of the two of them on their wedding day. His suit, and the starched collar and cuffs of his shirt, hung absurdly loose about his gaunt frame. Brock began by trying to separate the two old people, and take statements in different rooms, but Marie refused to say a word if they were split up, and Brock relented.

There was no satisfaction in listening to Marie's confession. On the contrary, it made Kathy feel deeply depressed. She had immediately sensed a great tension in the little woman, and as soon as Brock made it plain that they knew about her visit to Mrs Rosenfeldt on the afternoon of Meredith's murder, the words began to tumble out of her in a low, breathless torrent, as if the effort of holding them back had become unbearable.

She had called on Mrs Rosenfeldt to pass the time until Adam and Felix returned. Their relationship had never been warm, rather distant in fact, but Marie thought it only polite to say goodbye to her neighbour. She was shocked to discover the depth of Mrs Rosenfeldt's hatred of her husband and herself. It was like a physical blow, which left her for a moment stunned.

Then Mrs Rosenfeldt said that Meredith Winterbottom felt the same way. That Meredith was determined to expose her husband's war crimes. Those were the words she used. No matter where they went, the evil of their past would, one day, be exposed for all the world to know.

Marie left Mrs Rosenfeldt's apartment in a state of shock, and walked slowly back to Jerusalem Lane. Gradually, the terrible injustice of Mrs Rosenfeldt's accusations filled her mind. At first she couldn't believe that Meredith – an intolerable busybody certainly, but not malicious or vindictive – could really intend to persecute them in this way. Then the prospect of their retirement haunted by such ghosts rushed through her imagination. She was overwhelmed by despair, then indignation, and finally anger. She determined to have it out with Meredith. She marched down to number 22, rang the bell, and when no one answered, opened the door and stormed straight up to Meredith's flat.

At this point Marie paused in her account. She looked rapidly at each of the other people in the room, at Kathy writing in her pad, and her husband staring fixedly at the wall, and finally came to Brock who held her gaze, looking, so it seemed to her, straight into her soul. The hands clasped upon her lap shook. When she began to speak again, it seemed the words no longer wanted to come, but had to be forced, struggling and shameful, out into the room, where they were frequently interrupted by choking sobs.

She described how she found Meredith asleep on her bed.

As she looked down at the still figure it occurred to her that there was only one way to ensure that her husband's last years would not be haunted by the past. She thought of using a pillow, but then recalled the television advertisements that warned of the dangers of children playing with plastic bags. She went into the kitchen, and put on a pair of pink rubber washing-up gloves beside the sink so that she wouldn't leave fingerprints. Then she found a plastic bag in a drawer. She returned to the bedroom and slipped it over Meredith's head without difficulty. Meredith passed away peacefully within a few minutes.

On her way out Marie noticed a plastic carrier bag tucked under the bed, containing books. She looked inside and thought she recognized the old and valuable books which Adam had told her about. On an impulse she took them with her. She didn't mention the books to Adam or Felix when they returned, but later contacted a dealer through the Yellow Pages and sold them. She couldn't recall his name.

Throughout all this, Adam had sat without moving. It was as if he had heard nothing, although Kathy thought she could detect tears in his eyes.

Brock made Marie repeat the final part of her story, from when she had left Meredith's bedroom. She used almost exactly the same words as in her first account.

Brock charged her formally with the murder of Meredith Winterbottom, and told her that they would take her back to London with them, where she would be held. He advised her to contact a solicitor. Inevitably this turned out to be Mr Hepple. She had to be helped out to the telephone in the hall to leave a message with his answering service.

When she returned she said, 'Felix must look after his father now. You must tell him to come.'

Kathy made the call to Enfield. A tentative female voice answered.

'Mrs Kowalski? Can I speak to Mr Kowalski, please?'

Felix's wife was hesitant. 'Who is this?'

'I'm Detective Sergeant Kolla from the Metropolitan Police. I need to speak to Mr Kowalski urgently.'

'Oh.' More hesitation. 'He's away at present. At a conference.' She spoke uncertainly, as if she found talking on the phone a problem.

'Well, could you tell me where? Maybe we can contact him.'

'I'm not sure. It's at the University of Nottingham ... What is this about? Has he been involved in an accident or something?'

Kathy took a deep breath. 'No. It's his parents, Mrs Kowalski.'

'Oh no. What's happened?' The woman's voice sounded flat, defeated.

'His mother is being detained by the police in connection with a serious offence. She wants your husband to look after his father while she is in custody.'

'Custody?'

'I'm afraid so. Look, would it be easier if we took Mr Kowalski senior back up to London with us? I'll give you an address and a phone number, and you can make arrangements with your husband to pick him up later this afternoon, say around 4.'

They drove back in silence, the old couple like statues together in the back. In the event it was their daughter-in-law who was waiting for them when they arrived, and who took charge of the old man. She hadn't been able to get a message to Felix yet, she explained, as the conference sessions had finished for the day, although they hoped to contact him when he came in for his evening meal with the other delegates. She had a little boy, about four or five, clutching her hand and she looked drained, as if there were already so many things to cope with that she could hardly bear to find out what this was all about. Brock and Kathy left her talking with Mr Hepple, whose cup was obviously brimming over. Brock had some difficulty being civil in response to the solicitor's ebullient greeting.

On their return to 20 Jerusalem Lane they found Bren Gurney in almost as good a mood as Mr Hepple. His earlier hunch had been dramatically vindicated, and he felt entitled to some measure of triumph. He himself had had no luck with his own lines of inquiry. The plumber who had worked on Caroline Winter's kitchen had died of a heart attack just two months before, and no trace of the missing books had been found either, although, as he pointed out to Brock, half the places they visited had been closed for the weekend.

'Yes,' Brock nodded resignedly, 'we're not going to get anywhere further with that until Monday.'

'All the same,' Gurney grinned, 'this clears the way to charging Winter with Eleanor's murder.'

Brock shook his head wearily. 'No Bren, sorry, not yet. You yourself said that his girlfriend will likely as not change her mind about being with him that night. It's all too circumstantial. Let's get that damn book dealer first. Find out who he contacted and how much he told them.'

Gurney made as if to argue, then changed his mind and shrugged. 'All right, chief.'

Brock gave a little nod. 'See you Monday, Bren.'

Kathy gathered her things together to follow her colleague downstairs.

'Eleanor's funeral is tomorrow afternoon,' she said to Brock. 'I think I may go.'

Brock seemed not to hear at first. He appeared preoccupied and unsettled. Then he roused himself. 'I should take a break, Kathy,' he grunted. 'You've had a solid week of it. Tomorrow's Sunday. Go out and have some fun for a change.'

Kathy smiled. 'Easier said than done.'

'Get that architect to take you out to a show or something.'

'Bob Jones?'

'Yes. Much more your type.'

'Than Martin Connell?' She looked at him carefully. 'Don't worry about that, sir. It doesn't bother me. Not any more.'

He nodded. 'I just wouldn't like to think that we were confusing our targets, between Winter and his solicitor.'

'I understand. You're still not sure we've got it right, are you?'

'I'd feel happier if Marie had told us something she couldn't have got from the newspapers. Like that the plastic bag was found in the bin in the kitchen, not on Meredith's head.'

'Yes, but why would she lie? And she did know about the pink washing-up gloves, and the books.'

'Oh, I don't doubt she called on Meredith that afternoon. If only she could have told us the name of the book dealer!'

Kathy nodded. 'What will you do tomorrow?'

'Oh,' Brock shrugged, 'I'm going down to a gliding club on the Downs. A winter picnic, they call it. Must be mad.'

'Do you fly, then?'

'Used to glide. Mainly a spectator now, though. They invited me down for tomorrow.'

'What about Bren? How does he spend his time off?'

'He's a family man, Kathy. Young kiddies.'

When she got downstairs, she bumped into Gurney again who was heading for the door.

'We're making a mistake,' he muttered. 'We should be nailing Winter now while he's still in a panic. I reckon that bastard Connell's beginning to make Brock jumpy.'

'I don't think so, Bren. Is Connell a bastard, or is he just good at his job?' Even as the words came out, she wondered why she was saying this. Did she really want to know why Gurney was so riled by him?

'You'll find out for yourself, I dare say.'

Now she was getting herself in a mess, letting Gurney

think she didn't know Connell. Yet she couldn't face the thought of having to explain. She cursed Martin inwardly for involving himself in this of all cases, and said, 'How about your unlawful entry? Has he made any more of that?'

'Let him try, Kathy,' he snorted. 'Just let him try.' He waved and pushed the outer door open against the bitter wind.

27

Spared the necessity of having to go to work, most of London had decided to stay at home rather than risk the icy conditions outside. The route to the suburban crematorium was deserted and Kathy, arriving early, found herself alone in the car park. She chose the same spot where she and Brock had parked the previous September, with its good view of the entrance to the chapel. She had his Polaroid camera, and when people began to arrive, took pictures of them entering the building. But there were so many of them that she soon realized that she wouldn't have enough film. Moreover, they were all wrapped up heavily in coats and hats and scarves against the cold, and after a while she gave up what seemed like a pointless exercise.

She found Eleanor's funeral an unsettling experience. The crematorium chapel, with its emasculated, ecumenicized forms of liturgical architecture, its medieval-modernist pews, lectern and stained glass, seemed an incongruous setting for the rendering of the *Internationale* which opened the service. The congregation seemed ill-tempered, forming knots and factions of elderly men and women who pointedly avoided looking at each other, on ideological grounds perhaps, or for more personal reasons, and who obviously resented being crushed together. In the front pew Terry Winter sat sullenly on one side of Peg, his wife and two daughters, wearing brave expressions, on the other. Mrs Rosenfeldt, who had closed her new enterprise for the afternoon, was a spectral figure among a pack of mourners at the rear. Only Peg's preference for the colour red in all its shades lent some warmth and unity to the proceedings – the scarlet drape over the coffin, the two vases of red roses on each side of it and on Peg herself the same bright outfit she had worn to Meredith's funeral six months before.

An elderly man, stooping like a black stork over his notes, gave a brief tribute to Eleanor's work for the socialist cause. Peg then took his place at the lectern and thanked all those who had come to pay their last respects to her sister, as well as to those who had written. They would, she said, with an affecting sob, be glad to know that, despite all the changes to the street where they had lived happily for so many years, her sister would find her last resting place there, as she would have wished – indeed on the very spot where their great-grandfather had once lived and their grandfather had been born. The new owners of Jerusalem Lane had kindly arranged that Eleanor's ashes would, together with a few of her most precious possessions, be placed that very evening in a specially prepared casket and sealed into the foundations of the new building. A plaque in the foyer would record these circumstances.

Kathy was as baffled by this announcement as were obviously the rest of the gathering, through whom a ripple of uncertain applause briefly passed.

For all that, Kathy felt her tear ducts sting as everyone rose at the end and sang *Jerusalem* to wish farewell to the departing casket.

Outside she stood alone for a while, uncertain why she had come. She stamped her feet, her breath forming trails of steam in the still cold air. Already it was almost dark. She thought of Brock and his friends on the North Downs, rugged up in their Range Rovers, no doubt, or red Mercedes sports, drinking hot coffee spliced with whisky, and his sensible admonition to her to have fun. Easier said than done, she repeated to herself, feeling her spirits sink miserably towards her frozen feet.

Her gloom was interrupted by a hoarsely cheerful Scottish accent.

'Hello, Sergeant. Was that not grand? There's nothing

like the *Red Flag* and a few verses of *Jerusalem* tae stir the blood. Even if neither of them was written by a Scotsman.'

'Hello, Mr Finn. I didn't expect to see you here.'

'Och aye, lassie. Peg asked me tae come along. Do ye know Mr Jones here?'

'Yes. Hello, Bob.'

'Oh, it's Bob, is it? Did you know that this laddie once accused me of bein' a member of the middle classes? Can ye credit that?'

'Shocking.' Kathy smiled at Bob.

'Well' – Finn rubbed his hands together and stamped his feet – 'I've always maintained that the real point of a funeral is the wee dram at the end, tae restore the spirits of the living, but I think Peg'll be tied up with her friends, so I suggest we retire tae the pub I saw up the road before we get frozen tae the spot.'

Bob nodded his head vigorously. 'I knew we could rely on you for a really sensible suggestion, Danny. Kathy?'

'Why not.'

She returned to her car and was about to start the engine when she heard a tapping at the passenger window. She looked across and her heart lurched to see Martin Connell's face through the glass. She stared stupidly at him for a moment until he banged impatiently on the door again, and she leaned across and opened it.

'Could freeze to death out there,' he complained as he got in quickly and slammed the door. He was wearing a black coat, black leather gloves, gleaming white shirt and an expensive silk tie that Kathy thought just a little flashy for a funeral. He turned to face her, and gave her one of his big, warm, charming smiles, his eyes travelling speculatively over her features.

'You're looking good, Kathy. Really good.'

'What do you want, Martin?' She heard her voice unnaturally flat, and resented him for it. *Even my voice isn't my own when he's around*, she thought to herself.

He smiled and didn't answer straight away, as if he would first read everything that was going through her mind. *Just another bloody lawyer's trick.*

'Well, I wanted to see you, speak to you again. It's been a long time.'

The words weren't important, it was only necessary to use the voice, so confident, so sonorous, to bring to life the well-remembered style, the warm, easy, habit-forming style, as addictive as a drug, which she had allowed to soak deep into herself through long susceptible hours on the phone, in the dark, in whispers and in parked cars just like this.

'No, Martin. I don't want to talk. There's nothing to say.'

He leaned across to her, uncomfortably close in the intimacy of the car, his left arm stretched out with his black gloved fist on her steering wheel.

'We're working on the same case, Kathy. We're bound to see each other.' His voice was intimate, patient, amused. 'We could help each other. One way or another.'

She took a deep breath, glad to feel angry now. 'Clear off, Martin. Just clear off. Find someone else to try it on.'

He drew back with a little smile. *A tactical withdrawal. Try a different tack.* 'You lot are making a hash of this one, Kathy.'

There was something in his voice which chilled her suddenly. The grown-up was telling the child how reality was going to strike her down if she didn't do what was required.

'That Sergeant Gurney, for instance. Left himself wide open, walking into my chap's office like that, and rifling his files, without a warrant. The girl says he pushed her aside, rather brutally actually. He doesn't know how much trouble he's in. And it'll reflect on Brock, of course.'

Kathy clenched her jaw, getting her anger under control.

'Does Lynne know where you are today?' She got some little satisfaction from seeing him blink at the mention of his wife. 'In fact, it only occurred to me the other day, that I never really knew for sure if she knew about us. Did she know, Martin? Did she know that she was the second choice for the trip to Grenada?'

Connell stared at her for a while, his lips pressed tight together, then abruptly turned away and yanked open the car door. A flurry of snow sprayed into the car as he got out. Just before he slammed the door closed again, he stuck his head back in and hissed, 'You are the hardest bitch I ever screwed, you know that?'

Kathy leaned over and banged the lock down on the door. Several small flakes of snow lay on the passenger seat, melting in the warmth he had left there. She gripped the steering wheel, and began to shake.

In the snug of The Crooked Billet, Danny brought them their drinks, brandy for Kathy and Scotch for Bob and himself. He raised his glass.

'Tae absent friends.' For a moment they were quiet, savouring the heat of the spirits slipping down inside. Kathy took a deep breath, willing Connell out of her mind.

'Well,' Danny said, licking his lips, 'Peg will be moving out at the end of the week.'

'What!' Kathy stared at him. 'Is that what her announcement about Eleanor's ashes was all about?'

Danny Finn smirked. 'Aye. It just needed the right negotiator tae make everybody happy. The trouble with most people who try tae get their own way is that they don't bother tae listen tae what the other party wants. Well, I was a shop steward for a while, and I learnt that the first priority in any negotiation is tae understand what the other man really wants – which may not be what he says he wants.'

'What did Peg really want, then?' Kathy asked sceptically.

'She wanted tae do the right thing by her sister Eleanor. She didn't really want tae stay any more in Jerusalem Lane, but she didn't want tae let down her sister. It was Eleanor, ye see, who first brought them all tae the Lane, on account of their great-grandad Karl Marx having lived there, and their grandad, Freddy Demuth, being born there. It's a fascinatin' story. Anyhow, we eventually came to an answer.'

'You conned her, you mean.'

'Don't be so suspicious, lassie.' Danny looked hurt. 'I'm not trying tae rob the old dear. The answer we came tae was this, that Eleanor can stay in Jerusalem Lane, in perpetuity, and Peg can go tae a lovely wee modern apartment that's just been completed in a refurbishment job we've done up in Highgate, not a stone's throw from great-grandaddy's final resting place in Highgate Cemetery, which she likes tae visit every Sunday afternoon.

'Well, Eleanor's stay maybe won't be in perpetuity,' he added. 'I did explain tae Peg that the kind of things we're building now will almost certainly be obsolete and ready for redevelopment in twenty or thirty years, anyway, but she wasn't worried about that. In fact she seemed rather taken with that idea.'

'What about her rent?'

'Hen, she's seventy-two and not that strong. We'll work something out in the purchase price of number 22 with Terry Winter, so she doesn't have tae worry.'

'You're a cunning old bugger, Finn,' Bob laughed. 'Anyway, I'm glad she's going. Jerusalem Lane is no place for her now. What exactly is she going to do with Eleanor's remains, then?'

'Well, I had the contractor's joinery shop make up a nice wee oak chest tae her specification, two feet by two feet by one foot six, and into that she'll put the ashes and so on, and this evening she and I and a couple of the contractor's men will lay it tae rest precisely under the spot where number 3 Jerusalem Lane used tae stand, and which just happens tae be the position for the main lift core of tower A, on which the big concrete pours start in the mornin'. The timing was perfect, ye see.'

*

Kathy and Bob lingered in the pub after Danny left, reluctant to exchange its warmth for the freezing night outside.

'Why did you come to the funeral, anyway, Bob?' she asked.

'In the hope of seeing you,' he said with a lopsided leer.

'I wish you wouldn't do that,' she said, glumly drawing patterns with her finger on the table top.

'What?'

'Try that stupid patter on me.'

'Oh.' He rocked back in his seat and blinked. 'Sorry.'

She gave a little frown. 'Don't get me wrong, I like you, when you're being yourself. But you're hopeless at chatting up women.'

He sighed. 'Yes, you're absolutely right. Always have been. And I haven't had much practice for a long, long time. Apart from a disastrous attempt on Judith Naismith.'

'Well,' she smiled, 'your patter would have had to be miraculous to have got you anywhere with her.'

'The stupid thing is, I meant it.'

'What?'

'About coming here in the hope of seeing you.'

'It's not a very good time . . .' And then, seeing him blush and begin to stutter, she added, 'I mean that I'm sort of preoccupied at the moment with this bloody case. But I wouldn't mind something to eat. Why don't we go somewhere?'

They found a Thai place which had recently opened. Kathy ploughed hungrily into the peppery *tom yum* soup. When she finally lifted her head, she saw Bob staring thoughtfully at her.

'What?'

'Yes, you look like someone who's stuck at the end of stage one.'

'What do you mean?'

'The French mathematician Poincaré said that there are

four stages to the creative process. First is the gathering and absorbing of the data. I don't just mean finding out the facts and making lists, but actually getting your brain to soak the information up and get a feel for it. Towards the end of this stage you're trying to make sense of it – in Poincaré's case trying to devise a theorem, I suppose, for me trying to get a design concept for a building, and for you reconstructing the murder. But the solution is very elusive. You just can't get an answer that *feels* right. And you get to look like you look now.'

Kathy smiled. 'Go on.'

'OK. So you put it out of your mind. You go out to the movies, or go for a run, or get drunk, or whatever. You let your brain get on with it in its own time, and you stop trying to worry the problem to death. This is stage two, the mulling stage.

'Then, one night you wake up with a start at 3 o'clock in the morning with the answer staring you in the face. Or maybe it hits you in the bath, like Archimedes, or while you're on the loo. This is the eureka stage, stage three, and it's wonderful, pure euphoria. You can't understand why you couldn't see it before, it's so obvious, and so beautiful. That's the important thing, the answer doesn't just work, it's also elegant and economical and beautiful.

'At least,' he smiled shyly, 'that's how it can be, when you're very lucky.'

Kathy nodded. 'Brock was trying to tell me to relax this weekend and put it out of my mind. Maybe that's what he meant. He went off gliding or something. Maybe he's decided to move on to stage two. This isn't another of your silly chat up lines, is it, Bob?' she said suddenly. 'To persuade me the only way I can progress this case is by forgetting all about it and going out and getting drunk with you or something?'

'Good heavens.' He looked at her, wide-eyed with innocence. 'I never thought of that. What a brilliant idea.'

'Anyway, you didn't say what stage four was.'

'Ah yes. Very important. Architects sometimes forget it. Stage four is checking that your brainwave really does work, and isn't some seductive chimera that doesn't quite fit.'

'Well, look,' Kathy said. 'This is what we'll do. If stage three strikes, we'll go out and get wonderfully drunk together. A deal?'

Then she added, 'Provided you don't turn out to be the killer, that is.'

Bob dropped a forkful of *masman* curry down the front of his trousers. 'A deal,' he said.

28

Kathy insisted on saying goodnight to Bob at the restaurant, then drove back to Jerusalem Lane. The whole block was in darkness, silent. Ice crystals crackled under her feet as she walked down the deserted Lane to the incident centre. It was locked, abandoned for the night, and she used her key to open the front door, fumbling in the blackness for a light switch inside.

The sense of emptiness, of the absence of Brock and Gurney and their teams, pervaded the building, bringing back the feelings of loss and despair which she had felt at Eleanor's funeral. Unprofessional feelings, she felt, a sign of personal involvement which was dangerous. Underlying them was the sense of the intimate presence of death, of Meredith's death, and Eleanor's, of the death of Jerusalem Lane, and, deeper still, of the other deaths, more distant and less easily acknowledged, of her father and her mother. She knew she wouldn't be able to sleep if she went home, so she went upstairs and turned on the heater, pulling off her hat and gloves, unwinding the scarf around her neck, and opening the front of her coat.

Slowly, with the rising temperature of the room, her mind began to focus on the case again. Her eyes travelled once more over the ugly colour photographs on the wall, the white board, the sheaves of notes and typed pages on the table.

Out of her coat pocket she pulled the Polaroid photographs she had taken at the crematorium, a dozen of them, and spread them across the table. As she'd suspected, they weren't very clear. She recognized a few people she had noticed at the time, and saw several more she hadn't.

Among these was a tall slender woman in a headscarf and dark glasses who might conceivably have been Judith Naismith. It occurred to Kathy that most of the potential suspects for the murder of Eleanor Harper had been at her funeral, and she recalled Martin Connell's gibe that they were making a hash of the case. The thought of their conversation made her throat tighten and brought on the shakes again. She was shocked to find that he could still affect her this way, and she tried systematically, calmly, to trace the source of her reaction. It wasn't just his betrayal of her over North. That had made her angry, but what she felt now wasn't predominantly anger. It was fear. She took a deep breath and forced herself to continue the line of thought.

What is the source of the fear?

It was his manipulation of her which made her afraid.

Why does that make me afraid?

And so she continued, an interior, silent interrogation, knowing always where it must lead, and pressing on until she had admitted the answer to herself, as she had been taught she should. For within Kathy there still lived a young girl, unresolved, unassimilated, misused, still haunted by a dark figure, a man as powerful, as cold, as manipulative as Martin Connell. And the fear was not just the fear of him, but also of the possibility of her own failure to survive without him.

On the other hand, she thought as she shook herself, shivering from head to toe, *Martin may just have wanted to warn me that we are making a mistake*. It was an unsettling thought. And unsettling that it was so difficult to think straight where he was concerned.

She picked out the figure of Danny Finn in one of the photographs, and returned to the question that must have passed momentarily through the minds of everyone at the funeral. What treasures was Peg burying along with her sister's ashes? What would fill an oak box two feet by two feet by one foot six? What did a scientific socialist want to take with her to the other side? Her childhood teddy bears? Her postcards of Moscow? Or the manuscript of the genuine fourth volume of *Das Kapital*? But why would she do that? 'Look what I've brought for you, Great-grandad. We kept it safe for you all those years.'

But perhaps it didn't really matter what was in the box. What mattered was what someone who had murdered once, or even twice, for the *Endziel* might imagine was there. And perhaps it was a message from Peg to that person, an irresistible message, that she was getting rid of the thing they were after, and they must now leave her alone. And if that were the case, tonight would be the only opportunity for that person to retrieve it before it disappeared beneath twenty-five storeys of concrete office block.

She didn't really believe it. But there was nevertheless a reason why she must act upon it, as an act of good faith with herself that, despite the fact that Winter had Martin as his solicitor, she would still pursue any reasonable possibility that he was innocent, and that someone else was responsible for Eleanor's death.

She sighed, hesitated for a moment over whether to have a mug of coffee before deciding against it. She buttoned up her coat again and went downstairs. In the general office she found a heavy torch which she stuffed into a pocket of her coat before locking up the building and stepping out into the cold darkness.

She first walked north up the Lane to the spot where the Kowalskis' bookshop had been, with its plaque commemorating its famous former resident. Here she found a viewing hole in the plywood panels that screened the site. As her eyes grew accustomed to the darkness, she was able to make out a tower crane rising on the far side of the site, and a light in the street beyond it. As a double check she counted the number of viewing holes along from the corner at the top of Jerusalem Lane, so that she could count back from the other side of the hoarding to establish this spot.

There was no break in the screens, and, short of trying to climb over them, she could see no way into the site from here. She walked down to the south end of the Lane, where the synagogue was now almost entirely demolished, and where a site entrance for vehicles opened on to Marquis Street. Lights which had been rigged up on poles overhead formed a pool of brilliance in the surrounding darkness. The chain-link gates were secured by a large padlock, and a printed sign warned that the site was patrolled by guard dogs and security personnel.

She returned to have another look at what was left of the synagogue. In one corner she recognized the battered remains of Sam's cardboard box. Her eyes were again adjusting to the dark after the lights of the entrance gates, and she could make out the name of the German dishwasher manufacturer on its side. She checked to make sure it was no longer inhabited. Behind the box the demolition team had fixed up a temporary site fence using chain-link panels attached to a timber framework with loops of twisted wire. Kathy untwisted two of the loops and eased the panels apart. She slipped through and reattached the wire loosely. It was only when she had done all this and felt her fingers numb with cold that she realized that she had left her gloves behind in Brock's office. She swore and hesitated for a moment, then turned and moved on into the site.

She passed slowly through a forest of scaffolding poles decorated with icy stalactites, and had to take her hands out of her pockets in order not to slide on the furrows of ice which traced the vehicle tracks across the frozen ground. On the other side she found a path of scaffolding boards which appeared to follow the site boundary northward towards the area she wanted. After twenty metres or so she felt a springiness in the boards beneath her feet and guessed that she had left the ground, but it was only when she stopped and stared into the darkness beyond the scaffold rail and made out the dim outline of a dumper truck a long way below her that she realized that she was now five or six storeys in the air above the excavated pit.

Her fingers were aching with cold now, but she had to keep reaching to the freezing steel scaffolding tubes to steady herself on the treacherously slippery boards, upon which her shoes seemed to have very little grip. Over to her right she could make out the silhouette of the tower crane and the street light gradually shifting position behind it as she worked her way closer to the spot, until at last they seemed to be aligned pretty much as she had seen them from the other side of the screen.

She stopped and breathed deeply, lifting her painfully stiff hands to her mouth and blowing into them, willing her pounding heart to slow down. The walk across the icy scaffolding in the dark had been much more difficult than she had anticipated, her eyes and hands and feet straining to pick up every subtle, threatening shift in the shades of darkness all around. Now she just stood still and listened, letting the adrenalin subside, her frozen hands thrust under her armpits.

Silence. So far so good. Now what?

Somewhere on the ground below was the place where the box would have been left, but it was clear that she was too high up to see anything down there. Further along she saw the top of a wooden ladder projecting above the edge of the scaffold platform. She shivered and began to move carefully towards it. Crouching down, with her left arm hooked around the scaffolding rail, she swung herself under it and round on to the ladder, her right foot making contact with one of its rungs as her right hand grabbed its side. As she shifted her weight over so as to move her left foot and hand across, the right foot abruptly slipped off its perch. With a shock that jarred her whole body it slammed down on to the rung below, slipped again and then caught on the one below that.

She found herself muttering, choking, 'Dear God, dear

God,' over and over through chattering teeth as she clung to the ladder, recovering her grip. Then, finding that her arms and legs were aching with the tension of her rigid hold, she eased one foot out, and with infinite care began a slow descent. She reached the next scaffolding platform but kept on going down, step by painful step, clinging to the ladder, her cheek brushing each icy metal rung, until she reached its foot on a third level below. Rolling on to the safety of the boards she crept back from the edge, breathing hard. Her arms and legs were trembling with the effort and her heart was on overdrive again.

After a while she stood up, walked gingerly back to the rail and looked down. Clearer, but not clear enough. She could make out a white form in the centre of a dark hollow below her, surrounded by a grid of grey lines.

Try the same again.

She repeated her earlier manoeuvre on the next ladder, with painstaking caution, feeling like one of the counters on her favourite childhood board game of snakes and ladders, praying that she didn't come upon a snake. Two more levels, twenty-six treacherous steps, then in to the comparative safety of another scaffold platform. *Piece of cake.*

She sank on to her heels, leaning her back against the wall of steel-sheet piles which were retaining the sides of the pit. Gradually her breathing returned to a more normal rate, but she was in no hurry to move. She waited like that, her head tilted up towards the sky hidden above by the layers of dark scaffolding, until she was shaking so much with the cold that she just had to move.

She tilted forward on to her knees. She felt agonizingly stiff, and, reluctant to get back up on to her feet, she crawled forward to the scaffolding edge and looked down.

There were another two levels below her to the base of the pit, but she could make out its features quite clearly now. The pale grey grid which she had seen before was now apparent as a network of concrete beams, and when she focused carefully she could see the carpets of steel reinforcing mesh laid between them. There was something else. Sprouting from the top edges of the beams, and also through the intervening areas of mesh, were hundreds of steel rods sticking vertically into the air, like sprouting shoots of some nightmarish metallic rice paddy. These were the starter bars which would tie the foundations into the next layers of reinforced concrete which would form the base of the lift shaft core.

In the middle of this ferociously spiked floor was a square hollow, shrouded in black shadow except for a pile of milky white plastic sheeting at its centre. Kathy guessed that this must be Eleanor's box, wrapped ready to receive its concrete burial in the morning.

Suddenly she heard a soft rustle from the white plastic shape, and the black shadow around its edge began to move. Her breathing stopped and she strained forward to see what was happening. A figure was detaching itself from the surrounding darkness. For a moment she saw its form against the pale bundle. She heard the soft ripping of a blade through plastic sheet.

She fumbled in her coat pocket for the torch, tugging its clumsy rubber body with her frozen fingers. She had it out now, groping with unfeeling fingertips for the button. She squeezed. Light burst out of the wrong end and the torch jumped out of her hands like a live thing. It dropped away into the void, its beam spinning round through the darkness for a few brief moments before it hit the ground with a crash and the light extinguished.

Oh, terrific.

The torch beam had blinded her. She stumbled to her feet. Another blaze of light hit her, coming up from the centre of the pit below. Too late she jumped back out of the line of sight, slipping as she went and slamming hard against the steel wall.

Someone moved quickly down below. Now the metallic

ring of feet on a ladder. Her brain worked fast. *No weapon,* and the other had at least a knife. *Coming up which ladder?* She couldn't see. *Try to get up to the surface first?* She thought of that long series of rungs, and of someone coming up below her, grabbing her ankle. She turned to the right and moved as quickly as she could, skipping and slithering across the icy planks, hoping to find the ringing ladder. Nothing. The platform came to an end. The ringing had stopped. The other must be behind her. Now she was cut off.

If only there were a weapon. She looked desperately around. Across a five- or six-metre gap she could see the scaffold structure forming the opposite side of the core, and on the same level as her a stack of something – steel tubes or short lengths of timber – piled near the edge. Spanning the gap was a single timber beam, as narrow as the one Bob Jones had described in his story about Danny Finn and Herbert Lowell. She felt a sudden rush of empathy with the pompous architect.

She put her left foot tentatively out on to the beam. It would only be ten or a dozen short careful steps. She put out of her mind the possibility that the beam might be slippery with ice. Two . . . Three . . . Four . . . She kept her eyes fixed carefully on the beam just in front of her feet, and definitely not looking past it to the steel rice-paddy on the ground below. Eight . . . Nine . . . Ten. Must be nearly there. She lifted her head, and saw the hooded figure just an arm's length in front of her.

She yelped.

The dark figure was standing on the edge of the scaffold platform, waiting for her, a length of timber in its hands. As it swung the weapon up to shoulder height the hood of its anorak pulled back and she saw the face of Felix Kowalski, snarling with rage. She automatically put up her left arm to deflect the blow as it came, smashing across her forearm and bouncing up to slam into the side of her head. She saw a flash of light and half turned, stunned, feeling her right foot slide away. Then her other foot gave way. She went down, arms and legs flailing, and hit the beam hard with her left shoulder. Instinctively her arms went round the beam like a baby round its mother's neck. She could hear herself snuffling like a baby. She looked up, past the beam from which she hung, and saw him raising his timber club again. The blow came on her right hand, although she didn't feel it. She just knew that she was flying.

29

Felix Kowalski was led into the basement interview room shortly after midnight. Despite the events of the previous hours, he held his bandaged head high, and appeared alert. His eyes took in the room, the metal office desk and chairs, the flask of water, the tape recorder, with interest. He sat in the chair which Gurney pulled out for him, clasped his hands loosely on his lap, and looked around confidently.

Alerted by Kathy's scream, the two security guards hired especially by Danny Finn had come upon Kowalski, peering over the edge of his platform at her body sprawled down below. He had reacted by leaping to his feet, swinging the length of timber, so that they had felt no compunction in using their sticks to beat him into a more co-operative state, with the result that he now had a heavily bandaged crown, one purple, swollen eye and a bandaged hand. The security men had radioed for the emergency services, as well as for Danny Finn, who arrived on the scene shortly after Brock. By that stage the rescue team had managed to extricate Kathy, badly injured, from the pit, and sent her off in an ambulance. Kowalski too had been taken to hospital, with Bren and another detective, to have his injuries X-rayed and dressed before he was pronounced fit for questioning.

It was Finn who explained to Brock about Peg's box in the foundations of the building, and her announcement at Eleanor's funeral. Together they went down to see where Felix Kowalski had been disturbed as he sliced away the polythene sheeting which had been wrapped around the box. Grunting with effort, Finn pulled the sheeting away to reveal a shiny black cube.

'I thought you said it was a wooden box?'

'Aye, it is. But it's covered with bituminous paint – that black stuff. It's used for waterproofing.' He poked gingerly at a corner of the dark shape and his finger came away covered with black goo. 'You'd get in a real mess trying tae get it off now tae get at the screw heads holding the lid down. Do ye really need tae get into it?' Finn looked doubtfully at Brock. He was panting with his exertions, his breath steaming white in the glare of the arc lights which had been set up overhead for Kathy's rescue, and were now being dismantled.

'What did Peg put inside?'

Finn shook his head. 'I don't know. She came down tae the site office about 6 this evening with this big handbag she carries, and I left her alone for a couple of minutes. I offered her plastic bags tae put the canister of ashes and whatever else she had in, but she preferred tae wrap them in newspaper. I suppose suggesting plastic bags was a bit tactless under the circumstances. Then I screwed down the lid, and the two men from the security firm carried it down here with me. I had a drum of the bitumen paint, and I more or less poured it all over the box tae seal it. It won't set in this cold. Does it really matter what's inside?'

'Probably not. When will it get concreted in?'

'Depends on the weather. Supposed tae be tomorrow, but with this cold, and more snow forecast tonight . . . We'll just have tae see.'

'Will you keep the security men on?'

'Aye. I promised Peg they'd stay till the concrete's poured. I want tae find out where the hell they were when Kathy and that bastard were down here. By the time I've finished with them, they'll never move from this spot again, I can promise ye that.'

Kowalski was talking in a calm, almost amused tone when Brock entered the interview room. Bren stopped him, and had him repeat the earlier part of his story for Brock's benefit. He had been on his way home from the conference he had been attending at the University of Nottingham, he said. When he arrived back in London, he decided to go to Eleanor's funeral before catching the train home to Enfield. He had read the announcement in *The Times* while he was away, and the arrival of his train at Euston just gave him time to catch a taxi out to the crematorium for the service. He wasn't really sure why he had bothered, apart from curiosity. When he heard Peg's strange announcement about her sister's remains, he recalled something his father had once mentioned, about the sisters owning valuable family papers which they were unwilling to part with. He wondered if this was their way to hide them, and thought it at least worth investigating. It was a stupid thing to do, he now acknowledged – he was guilty of trespassing on the building site – but then it had seemed a fortuitous way in which the sisters might repay his parents for the trouble and distress they had suffered through Meredith's meddling. The beauty of it was that, though technically a theft, no one would know that the papers had been removed, and so no one would be the worse for his actions. He paused briefly to look over his shoulder and smile with satisfaction at Brock, then continued his story. The accident with the woman police officer was very distressing. While he was trying to get at the box, he heard her on the scaffolding. The noise alarmed him, and he began to leave. However, when he saw her walk across the plank, then slip and fall, he tried to go to her assistance, but had been prevented by the security men, who without provocation had assaulted him.

Felix Kowalski related these details in a normal voice, and when Gurney probed and questioned his account, responded quickly with an air of confident reasonableness. Nevertheless, Brock, from the other side of the room, thought he detected the unnatural glitter of shock and adrenalin in the man's eyes. And something else. Whenever his interrogator looked away, Kowalski would flick up his eyes and glare at him, only softening his gaze once Gurney returned his attention to him. Brock recalled this vividly from the interview which he and Kathy had had with Kowalski the previous September in his father's empty shop. It was the flicker of an intense anger. Why anger? It seemed an odd, almost involuntary response, as if anger had rooted itself so deeply in the man that it had taken the place of fear, shame and guilt.

For half an hour Brock watched silently as Gurney tried to shake Kowalski, then he got up quietly and left.

There were endless waves of nausea. Each time the brain struggled through the nightmare dark into consciousness it was only to achieve a few moments of agonized retching, hot with curry and bile, and then to slide back into the foul dark again. The eyes wouldn't open, and the struggle went on with her unaware that Brock was there, frustrated at his inability to help her.

When finally the retching stopped, the brain was over-whelmed by a sensation of clammy claustrophobia. It tried to tell the mouth to cry out a warning. *Someone is trying to suffocate me.* But nothing came, and the brain slid away into darkness.

Brock watched her become calm at last, falling back into sleep. He sighed, nodded to the nurse and left.

Brock and Gurney spoke in the corridor outside the interview room.

'I can't shake him on any of it. He's a superior little prick. He talks as if he's not got a worry in the world.' Gurney didn't try to hide his anger from Brock, just as he hadn't from Kowalski.

Brock thumbed through a draft record of the interview to date and nodded. 'Well rehearsed, I should imagine. I'll have a go now, Bren. Does he know about his mother?'

'Doesn't seem to. He evidently hasn't contacted his wife in the past twenty-four hours.'

'All right, let's keep it that way for the time being.'

When Brock took the chair opposite him instead of Gurney, Felix Kowalski gave a little smirk to himself. He believed that Brock and Gurney were intending to use a nice-cop, nasty-cop routine, and he was reassured by their predictability. When Brock asked him what he could possibly find amusing in his present circumstances he looked away without answering.

However, Brock didn't offer him a cigarette, or try to reassure him that his co-operation would somehow be appreciated and rewarded. Instead he went back, coldly and without emphasis, over details of Felix's statements to Bren, of his movements the previous day, and on the day of Eleanor's death and key dates before that. It seemed to Brock, as he studied Felix's face during his responses, that the effect of the adrenalin was beginning to fade and that he was having more difficulty controlling his voice.

They finally reached Kowalski's account of Kathy's fall. Brock paused, staring at Felix with an intensity that made him shift in his chair. When Brock spoke again, his voice remained quiet, yet Kowalski found that it was difficult to focus on anything else, as if it were filling the room.

'The piece of wood you used has fibres of your gloves at one end where you gripped it, and fibres of Sergeant Kolla's coat at the other where you hit her on the shoulder. There is also her blood on that end of the timber, over the fibres, where you hit her the second time, across her knuckles, from which the surgeons have removed splinters of wood, from your weapon.'

Brock was improvising, in the absence of a forensic report, but he had studied the length of timber closely and knew that he was close enough to the truth. Listening to his accuser, a phrase entered Kowalski's head which he could not drive out: *dies irae*, the day of wrath.

The room, which had been formed by subdividing a larger

space into four small offices, was barely large enough for the two detectives to carry out their search without getting in each other's way. When the night security man showed Brock to the place, they had already gone through all the books which filled the metal shelving on both side walls, and were now on their hands and knees, one going through a stack of files and student essays heaped in the corner below the tiny barred window, and the other pulling up sections of the vinyl tile floor coverings. Brock squeezed in and the detective pulling up the floor straightened up to show him what they had so far.

'None of the books on your list, sir. But this one is interesting.'

The officer handed Brock a battered old copy of *Scouting for Boys*. Brock frowned.

'Open it, boss.'

He did so, and found that the centre of the book had been neatly cut out, the hollow refilled with a wad of banknotes.

'Almost a thousand quid, in twenties and fifties mostly,' the detective said.

'Anything else?'

The man shrugged. 'What you'd expect, really – teaching materials, class lists, stationery. Diaries for the past three years, but they only seem to have class times and staff meetings, stuff like that. And a bottle of whisky, nearly empty, in the top drawer of the desk. The one that locks. With his passport.'

Brock took the passport, the old type with stiff covers, issued in 1983, valid ten years. There were visa and entry stamps for Poland for 1983, and an entry stamp for Toronto, Canada, dated 1 September 1989. Brock picked up the diary for the previous year, and thumbed through to the beginning of September. There was an entry 'Scarborough Conference' for 31 August, and the following seven days were crossed through.

*

It was almost 4 a.m. by the time Brock reached Felix Kowalski's home in Enfield. The lights both upstairs and downstairs were ablaze. Three cars were parked at the kerb and in the driveway. Felix's wife, Heather Kowalski, was sitting in the kitchen with a uniformed policewoman, while the detectives with the search warrant roamed about upstairs.

Heather's face was pale and drawn, framed by locks of auburn hair which she tucked wearily behind her ear from time to time. After speaking to the team upstairs, Brock joined her, accepting the offer of a cup of tea from the WPC.

'Your father-in-law is in the room at the end of the landing, is he, Mrs Kowalski?'

She nodded. Her hair fell forward and her fingers went up automatically. Then they dropped to the table and swept away some grains of sugar which had fallen on its surface. Everything in the kitchen was meticulously in its place, Brock noticed.

'I'm sorry, but I'm afraid we'll have to disturb him so that we can have a look in his room. Maybe you could help move him to the back room when they've finished there.'

'He doesn't seem to know where he is, anyway.' She sounded drained. 'They won't need to disturb little Adam again, will they? He took so long to get back to sleep last time. He was frightened.'

'No, they've finished there. I am sorry about this. You've no idea where else we could look for books?'

She shook her head vaguely.

'Has your husband had any particular financial or personal problems lately, Heather?'

She stared at him for a moment. Her plain features seemed permanently set in a look of resignation, now emphasized by a lack of make-up and the pallor of fatigue. Another little shake of the head.

'I do appreciate how co-operative you've been, and I

know how tired you must be, but I want to get to the bottom of this as soon as possible. I think you must want that too. Have you and your husband been having difficulties lately?'

Her eyes winced and slid away. He suddenly wished he had Kathy there with him to do this.

She lowered her head, but said nothing. He waited, sipping his tea.

Eventually she said softly, 'He was very upset by what they did to him in the reorganization at the Poly a few years ago.'

'Really? What was that?'

'His subject was Russian Culture and Politics, you see, in the Department of Russian Studies.' She gave a bitter little smile, as if that should speak for itself. Brock wondered if the gesture was her own, or more likely a loyal imitation of the sort of look her husband would have given.

Seeing that he didn't seem to follow, she explained, 'They closed the department down. The government decided they no longer needed Russian departments. The Poly reorganized all the people they didn't want any more into a new Department of General Studies. Felix ended up teaching things that didn't interest him to all the most stupid students, who were even less interested but just needed to pick up extra units. He's very bitter about it.'

'I see. Still, he manages to get away a bit. At least they send him to conferences from time to time.' She looked up anxiously at him and he held her gaze. 'This last one, at the University of Nottingham, wasn't it? And the one last September, in Canada.'

She looked startled, 'Canada! No . . . No.' She smiled at his mistake. 'Last September he went to Yorkshire – to Scarborough.'

'There's a Scarborough in Canada too, Heather. In Toronto. I rather thought that was the one he went to.'

'Oh no! No, he certainly didn't. He's never been across

the Atlantic. Neither of us have.' She gave a little laugh, with fatigue and relief.

The brain tentatively ordered one eye open. There was Brock.

'What a mess,' he said, sadly shaking his head.

The brain ordered the mouth to do something. 'Bringing me flowers again?' it croaked.

'From all of us. Can I do something?'

'Water,' she whispered. He held the tumbler to her lips, she sipped, felt sick, retched and fell back exhausted. The brain decided that was enough, and switched everything off again.

Felix Kowalski had begun to withdraw behind his bandages.

'Nothing,' Gurney said wearily. 'We've been over it all again. Any news of Kathy?'

'I just saw her. She came out of the anaesthetic at 2 and has been sleeping since. She woke briefly when I was there. They say she'll live. Bloody lucky.'

They went in and Brock took the seat opposite Kowalski again. He noticed the shadow under the unbruised eye, and a slight shake in the unbandaged hand.

'Sit up and drink your tea,' he barked abruptly. 'Tell me about Toronto.'

Kowalski blinked at him in surprise.

'Toronto, yes, Toronto. What did you go there for last September?'

Kowalski's mouth hung open stupidly for a moment as he tried to read Brock's mind. Then he mumbled something.

'What?'

Kowalski cleared his throat. 'Get stuffed.'

'Last September,' Brock persisted, 'just before Meredith Winterbottom died.'

Kowalski snorted, shook his head.

'The time your wife thinks you were at a conference in Yorkshire. I'll find out, Felix. I'll find everything out eventually. Better tell me now.'

He was rewarded by a blaze of anger which burst from Kowalski's red-rimmed eyes. He tried to get to his feet, swearing furiously. Gurney pressed him back down with one hand on his shoulder, and he subsided, trembling. The anger died away, and when he regained control, he muttered, 'You can't connect me to Meredith Winterbottom's death, and you know it.'

Brock paused before answering quietly.

'Well, we know that, Felix. Your mother's already confessed to the murder of Meredith Winterbottom. She was arrested on Saturday afternoon. Didn't you know?'

Felix rocked back in his chair as if he had been struck. His eyes widened and his jaw dropped open. 'No . . . No. That's impossible.'

'Not in the least. We established that the times you gave us for when your mother was on her own that afternoon were wrong. Then we found out about her visit to Mrs Rosenfeldt, and following that Mrs Winterbottom. When we went to see your mother on Saturday afternoon she knew what we'd come for. She confessed to killing Meredith.'

'No,' Felix repeated, shaking his head. 'It isn't possible.' It sounded more a statement of fact than of belief. Brock leaned forward, watching him closely.

'Why? What do you know, Felix? What possible doubt could there be?'

But Felix had withdrawn. He sat rigid in his seat, staring straight ahead with unseeing eyes.

'Felix!'

'No . . .' He shook his head furiously, then said no more. Brock sighed and looked at the wall clock.

'5.35. All right. Give him a bed. I'll see him again at 9.'

He got to his feet as Felix was led away. 'Let's get a couple of hours ourselves, Bren. I'm beginning to feel my age.'

'I might get over to the hospital, chief; see how Kathy is.'

'There's not much point at present, Bren. Why not leave it to the morning? I need you with your wits about you.'

'What do you reckon to him?' Gurney nodded towards the door through which Felix had been taken.

'I think that he's trying to decide whether to save his mother, or just let her drown.'

'You think he can save her? She confessed to cover for him?'

'Something like that. You know, I used to think that organized crime was complicated. It's peanuts compared to this lot.'

Brock, feeling better for a couple of hours' sleep, knocked on the door marked 'Head of Department'. There was an indistinct sound of a voice from inside and he went in. He introduced himself and Gurney. Dr Endicott looked up from the papers on his desk with an anxious, preoccupied frown. His face had deep lines cut around the mouth and brow which contrasted oddly with his smooth skin, as if he had been prematurely aged all of a sudden. He was dressed in the careful neutrality of a businessman.

'Yes?'

'I'd like some information about a member of your staff, Dr Endicott. Felix Kowalski.'

'Felix? Is he in trouble?'

'He's helping us with an inquiry. There's just a couple of things you might be able to confirm for us.'

'I really don't know that I can do that. If he's in trouble . . . a colleague. Also, I'm due at a meeting at 9.15, so I don't have time at present. Perhaps you might make an appointment with my secretary.'

'Important?'

'Pardon?'

'The meeting. Is it important?'

'Ah. Well.' He looked doubtfully at the papers on his desk, about two inches thick. 'A meeting of the Academic Board sub-committee to decide the composition of the Committee on Gender Equity in Selection and Promotion Procedures.'

'Well, ours is a murder inquiry, and I really don't want to take up much of your time, but I'd like to do it now.' Dr Endicott's eyes widened at the word 'murder'. Brock pressed on before he could frame a question. 'Have you been aware of any difficulties Mr Kowalski might have been having lately?'

'Not really.'

'I have the impression that he's not happy in his work. Would that be fair?'

'Not happy? Well. Like many of us, he has had to adjust to changing circumstances. Funding cuts, new priorities, and so on. I think he has found it rather difficult. He was in a particularly hard-hit area.'

'Has he been looking for some alternative?'

'I really feel he should be telling you this himself. But I suppose I can say that I did write one or two references for him some three or four years back. Nothing recently, though. I rather thought he'd, er, become reconciled.'

'Is he a popular member of staff?'

'Ah . . .' Dr Endicott swept some lank hair back from his lined forehead and frowned at his papers as he thought about that. 'He is a challenging colleague, one might say. Abrasive, even.'

'Yes, that was rather our impression. And is that the result of his work frustrations, would you say, or is there some other reason?'

'Oh, I really couldn't say. I always felt there was something . . . fiery in his make-up. Central European, you know.'

'You've sent him to conferences, I believe. One just last week.'

'Really?' Endicott looked vague.

'The University of Nottingham?'

'Ah yes. Not really a conference. More a staff development course, really. "Communication under Conditions of Stress" or something like that. Quite appropriate given our staff–student ratios.'

'And last September?'

'I can't recall him being away last September. I could get the file. Maureen will remember, I'm sure.'

'Scarborough?'

'Oh yes. That was a conference. Not really his field if I recall, but the Departmental Conferences Committee felt rather sorry for him, I think.'

'So he went to Canada?'

'Canada? Good heavens no! Scarborough in Yorkshire! There would have been no way of sending him to an overseas conference with our budget in the state it was!'

'Yet we have reason to believe he went to Canada during the first week of last September.'

'Really? Skipped off to Canada when he was supposed to be at the conference in Yorkshire? Are you sure?' Dr Endicott seemed rather taken with the idea.

'Are you aware of any connection he might have had with North America – friends, relatives, academic connections?'

'Well, no.' He hesitated, then shook his head as if dismissing an absurd idea.

'Something?'

'Well, the only "connection" that springs to mind is that we had an exchange student from Canada in the department last year. Rather personable young woman. But that hardly seems relevant.'

'Felix taught her?'

'Emm, I couldn't say. Maureen would know, our departmental secretary. We might ask her.' Dr Endicott seemed to have forgotten about his committee meeting as he led them out to the departmental office, where Maureen was briskly giving orders to a group of confused students. She turned to deal with the Head of Department with the same determined look on her face.

'These gentlemen are from the Metropolitan Police, Maureen.'

'I know. I told them you wouldn't be able to see them. You were supposed to be at that committee meeting five minutes ago.'

Dr Endicott cleared his throat. 'Yes, well, they need some assistance regarding that Canadian girl who was here last year. Do you remember?'

Maureen ignored his question and turned on Brock. 'Are you the same lot that have been searching Felix Kowalski's office?'

'Searching?' Endicott looked startled.

'We have a search warrant, sir. Look, if you want to go to your meeting now, that will be fine. You've been most helpful. If we can just have a few moments of Maureen's time.'

Maureen rolled her eyes and broke off to give instructions to the photocopier repair man who had just appeared. Dr Endicott hesitated, then regretfully sighed and turned back to his room to collect his papers.

'Well?' Maureen returned her attention to Brock and Gurney.

'Do you recall the Canadian student Dr Endicott mentioned, Maureen?' Brock asked amiably.

She looked suspiciously at him for a moment. 'What is this all about?'

'We're conducting a murder investigation. We'd appreciate your co-operation.'

Maureen's eyes lit up with curiosity. 'You think Felix has murdered someone?'

'He's helping us with our inquiries,' Brock said. 'Do you remember her?'

'Of course I do. She's been writing to him every week since she went back.'

'To him here?'

'Well, I don't suppose he wants her to write to him at home!' She smiled grimly.

'Did you know he went over there last September?'

'No, I didn't know that.' She shook her head. 'But, I do remember a call from a travel agent for him, which I thought was a bit funny. Sometime in the middle of last year.' Her eyes wandered away in the direction of the corridor leading to Felix's room. 'What exactly are you looking for?'

'Some old books. Are there other places we should look?'

'Only . . .' She hesitated, then shrugged. 'He left a box in my store cupboard last year. Just before Christmas term started. I told him to move it somewhere else because I've got little enough space as it is to keep the stationery and departmental records and so on, but he never did.'

She showed him a door in the corner of the office, opening into a small storeroom with shelves crammed with boxes, files and papers. On the floor at the back they found an old box for photocopy paper, sealed with brown plastic tape. Bren lifted it out on to Maureen's table and took the scissors she offered him. From the look of the tape the box had been opened and resealed several times. He folded back the flaps of the box and brought out a wad of Canadian airmail envelopes held together with a rubber band. Then he began carefully to pull out the books. Brock reached for one with a frayed black leather spine. 'Proudhon's *Confessions*,' he said with satisfaction. 'We seem to have found our dealer, Bren.'

'Will he be away long?' Maureen called after them as they left, Bren carrying the box under his arm. 'Only we'll have to rearrange his classes.'

They called in at the hospital on the way back. Kathy was

conscious, gazing through half-open, bruised eyelids at the snow falling past the window against the grey of the morning sky. A tube was in her nose. She creased her eyes in a smile, the unbruised parts of her face as pale as the pillow and the bandages around her head.

'A little better?'

She nodded and wiggled the fingers of her left hand, which Brock, sitting beside her, took in his own. Bren remained standing at the end of the bed, unable to keep the concern out of his eyes. She looked towards the plaster cast on her right arm.

'Haven't told me,' she whispered hoarsely. 'What's the damage?'

Brock cleared his throat. 'Three fingers of your right hand are broken,' he said.

'Anything else?' she asked faintly.

'One of the reinforcing bars went through your right side. Hell of a job to get you out of there. You'd appreciate it, having been in Traffic. Seems some of the bars down there were high tensile steel, and the steel cutters couldn't get through them without making too much of a mess of you. Eventually had to lift you straight off. Lost a lot of blood. Missed the vital organs, though. They operated and stitched you up. It'll be all right.'

She drifted away for a while, then suddenly lurched back into consciousness. 'And?'

'Another bar scraped your left knee. No great problem, but it'll be sore for a while. You were very lucky.'

'How?' she whispered.

'Lucky you weren't a man, that is. The middle bar, in between those two, would have been very unpleasant.'

'Ugh.'

'Your left shoulder was dislocated and badly bruised.'

'Oh.'

'And you banged your head. Possible concussion.'

'Mmm.'

'That's about it, really. Pretty good under the circumstances. You could have been killed.'

She closed her eyes and slipped into unconsciousness.

Felix Kowalski did not seem to have benefited by the break and a hot breakfast. On the contrary, he crouched in his seat with the air of someone suffering from a very bad hangover. He eyed them truculently as they took their seats, Brock in front of him, Gurney to the side.

'You must release my mother,' he said, before they could speak. 'At once. She is not in any way responsible for the death of Meredith Winterbottom. She has only confessed in order to protect me.'

'Really?' Brock said noncommittally, turning the pages of one of the two files he had brought in with him. 'Are you confessing to that murder, then?'

'No, of course not. But my mother obviously thinks I had something to do with it. Her *confession*, as you call it, is absurd.' He was struggling with impatience and seemed slightly feverish.

Brock flicked the file shut and sat back. He stared at Kowalski and then nodded. 'Go on, then.'

'When . . .' Kowalski hesitated and gave a little groan.

'Are you all right? Would you like a doctor to have another look at you?'

'No,' he snapped. 'When my father and I returned from delivering the last of his books to Notting Hill, my mother was waiting for us in the shop. It was about 2.30. She was upset. She told us what that old crone Mrs Rosenfeldt had said to her, and said she'd gone round to see Meredith Winterbottom. She was on her bed asleep, she said, and the thought had gone through my mother's head, upset as she was, to strangle the woman. She even imagined putting on the rubber washing-up gloves she saw in the kitchen, so she wouldn't leave any fingerprints. That's what she told us. Of course she did no such thing. My father was shocked at the

293

idea, and we calmed her down and gave her a cup of tea from the flask we'd brought. Then I left to return the van. When she heard later that someone had killed Mrs Winterbottom, she must have naturally been worried that I might have done it while I was away, to save them further distress. Of course I didn't, but the idea will have been preying on her mind. She's not been well lately. Neither of them have.'

By the time he got to the end of this his voice had sunk to a monotone. There was silence.

'That's it?'

'Yes.'

Gurney snorted contemptuously from across the room. Kowalski looked from one man to the other. 'What else should there be?'

'What about the books, Felix?' Brock spoke very quietly.

Kowalski kept his face blank, his eyes unblinking.

'Books?'

'Mmm, books. Your mother had quite a bit to say about books.'

He appeared to rack his brains, then said slowly, 'I think . . . she did mention something about some books. Under Mrs Winterbottom's bed, I think it was, in a plastic carrier bag. My mother looked inside and saw that it contained some old books. When she mentioned them, I seem to remember that my father said something about them probably being ones that he had valued for her.' He shrugged. 'That's about all I can remember.'

'So your mother didn't have the books with her when she returned to the shop?'

'With her?' He looked startled. He stared at Brock for a moment, searching rapidly for clues in his expressionless face, then groaned and covered his eyes with his hand. 'She said that? She said she took them?'

'Felix,' Brock said, his voice still deadly quiet, 'you don't seem to have taken in what I told you last night.' He leaned forward across the table. 'I will not be lied to. I will discover the truth. You are just making things a hundred times worse for yourself and your mother.'

Kowalski lowered his head. His shoulders rose and fell with his breathing. When he began to speak again, his head still down, his voice came deep, from the back of his throat.

'When I left them, I drove the van round the block to the lower end of Jerusalem Lane. I went in to number 22. I wanted to tell Meredith to lay off my parents, but she was asleep. Lying peacefully on her bed. So I looked at the carrier bag with the books. There were about a dozen of them. The ones I looked in had inscriptions from Karl Marx, just as my father had described. He had said they were worth four or five thousand each. So I quietly put them back in the bag and walked out with them. I took them for my parents' sake. I reckoned she owed them at least that.' A note of anger infiltrated the resignation in his voice. 'I had a duffle bag at the shop to carry the sandwiches my wife had made us, and I slipped the carrier bag into that when I got back. I suppose my mother must have seen. That's why she thinks I killed Meredith Winterbottom. But I didn't.' He looked up to face Brock. 'I swear to God I didn't.'

'Yes,' Brock replied flatly. 'Go on.'

'What?'

'Tell us about what you did with the books.'

'Oh . . . I waited for a while till I thought things would be quieter. Then I told my father a friend of mine had some old architectural books to sell, and asked for the name of the architect he'd mentioned in connection with Meredith Winterbottom's books. I remember now how my mother looked at me when I raised it. He still had the man's business card, and I copied the phone number and rang it later. The architect said it was really a friend of his who was interested, an academic in the States. I contacted her, and it was she who told me about the other documents.'

He looked up at Brock, and for the first time there was a note of supplication in his voice. 'I only stole the books for my parents. That's all I wanted the other papers for. For them.'

'No.' Brock shook his head. 'You needed money, didn't you, Felix? For yourself. To escape. Isn't that it?'

'That's ridiculous.'

'I'd call it a kind of escape. Someone else might just call it a fantasy. Running away. Digging a tunnel out of the prison, to freedom. To Canada. A fantasy.'

A look of panic formed on Kowalski's face.

Brock leaned forward and spoke intently to him. 'I'd like you to appreciate just how impossible that fantasy now is, Felix. I'd like you to acknowledge the truth of the matter with me. There's really nothing left to be angry about. It's not a matter of other people stopping you any more. You've stopped yourself.'

Brock fished his half-lens spectacles out of his jacket pocket and made a bit of a play of examining a page of the file while he let that sink in.

'What about her family, Felix? What's her name? Jenny, that's it, isn't it, the girl in Toronto? What about her parents, her friends? What do they think of her infatuation for a bad-tempered, frustrated, middle-aged, married Englishman, twice her age, who has no funds and no prospects? Pretty daunting for them, I should think. Or do they think it's laughable, that it will all blow over with time? Or do they not even know yet?'

Felix's face had become blotched red.

'She . . .' he began, then stopped himself, clenching his jaw tight shut.

'She what?' Brock prompted mildly. 'She loves you? She's pregnant? I found it rather difficult to decide about that from her letters – whether she was just fantasizing, or whether she really was pregnant. Anyway, it doesn't really matter, does it? Because you were so taken with your fantasy, Felix, so hungry for it, for the money you needed to make it happen, that you killed two old ladies and nearly killed a police officer. And I don't think that even Jenny's love can survive the knowledge of that.'

'I . . .' He seemed to have difficulty forcing the words through his throat. 'I didn't kill anyone.'

'Really? Hard on your wife. And your little boy. How long will they bother to come to see you inside, I wonder? Not the full twenty years, that's for sure. Probably better if there's a clean break now.'

Then, as if changing the subject completely, 'She's a meticulous woman, your wife, isn't she? I noticed that when I visited your house last night. Everything in its place. Obsessively so. Is that part of the cause or the effect, I wonder? Is she so obsessive about the little things because she knows the big things are so askew, or was her obsessiveness one of the things that made you come to hate her so much? She's the sort of woman, I'd say, who would insist that a man lower the seat of the toilet after he's had a pee. Some women are like that, I believe. They find a raised toilet seat offensive because it signifies something about the male member. That's what they say in women's magazines, I'm told. Does your wife do that?'

Felix stared at him as if he were mad.

'Humour me, Felix. I'm all you have now. Does your wife do that?'

He swallowed with difficulty. Finally he nodded. 'Yes.'

'Yes, I guessed that. Because when you broke into the Winters' house in Chislehurst and needed the toilet – nerves, I suppose, and you had been drinking beforehand, hadn't you? – you naturally took off your gloves to undo yourself, and when you finished you automatically lowered the seat, as your wife had drummed into you, before you put the gloves back on. You left a beautiful set of prints' – Brock peered at the second file he had brought in – 'which until today we had been unable to identify.'

Felix's shoulders gave a little convulsive jerk. A sob came from his bowed head. And then he let go. The tears started to stream down his face and his whole body began to shake.

30

He was there, reading, when she looked up.

'What time is it?'

'Two in the afternoon. You've been here thirty-six hours.'

'God, I'm beginning to hurt now.'

'You will. At least they've removed the tube and the drip.'

'Yes. They did that this morning. I just seem to keep dropping off. Could I have some water, please?'

He helped her, and now she was able to keep it down.

'Did you get him, then?'

'Kowalski? Yes. Danny Finn had arranged with two men from the security firm to keep an eye on Eleanor's box through the night. They turned up just after Felix attacked you. Lucky for you they got the medics to you so quickly. They held him and handed him over to us. He's been charged with the attempted murder of you, and the murder of Meredith and Eleanor. You know, you were crazy to go in there unarmed and without telling anyone.'

'I know. I only meant to observe. It wasn't until I got in there that I realized it wasn't going to be so easy.'

'Well, it had the desired effect. Flushed him out. Funny, I hadn't really got my sights on him. Should have spotted his anger, I suppose. And the evasiveness of his parents.' He scratched his beard.

'He was at the funeral apparently, wrapped up in a scarf. Drew the same conclusion you did from Peg's announcement. So did Judith. She's been going berserk trying to stop them pouring the concrete.'

'Did she have any luck?'

Brock shook his head. 'Danny Finn wouldn't hear of it. If Peg wants it buried unopened then he will make sure that's exactly what will happen. I think he sees it as a sort of obligation to his class roots. If the manuscript is down there, it's due to be buried under a hundred tons of wet concrete any moment now. They couldn't do it yesterday because of the cold and snow, but with the mild change today they said they'd probably go ahead this afternoon. When asked, Peg smiles vaguely and says she doesn't understand what everyone's going on about. As far as we're concerned, what's important isn't what actually is in the box, so much as what Kowalski thought was there. I couldn't see us getting a warrant to open it up if Peg didn't want us to. She's returned home to Jerusalem Lane now that Kowalski's been charged.'

Brock stopped talking as a nurse came in to give Kathy more painkillers.

'What's that you're reading?' she asked him when she had got the pills down.

'A biography of the first Eleanor, Eleanor Marx. I'd got it out of the library to do a bit of background reading. Won't need to now, I suppose. I'll leave it with you if you like. You'll have the time for it over the next few days.'

'Days?'

'Oh yes, they want to keep you here a while for observation. To make sure your side starts to heal up properly. And they're a bit worried about concussion, too.

'Best thing.' He smiled at her kindly. 'Now, never do this again, Kathy, but everyone sends their congratulations. You got the result.'

Kathy looked out through a tall window at the grey afternoon sky, breathing in the smells of the hospital and listening to its background noises – the rattle of a trolley, an exchange between two cockney women walking past the door of her room, the squeak of rubber soles on the plastic flooring. Everything was hurting in a dull way that discouraged movement. She thought to herself, *Yes, I did get the result*. Without Brock or Gurney, I found the bastard. But all she felt was anti-climax. Her exposure of Kowalski was nothing like the triumph of the intelligent imagination which Bob had described in his 'stage three'. Her achievement seemed uncertain, a foolhardy exercise in dumb detection, throwing herself into a dangerous situation and seeing who came out of the shadows to hit her down. There was no flash of inspiration, no euphoria. She even felt mildly guilty that what she had discovered disappointed whatever theories Brock had been forming on the case.

She closed her eyes wearily and drifted off to sleep.

In her mind Peg was staring at her with shining eyes, just as she had on the day before the funeral. She said the words she had used to Brock that day, speaking with intensity, as if her words contained a central truth. At first Kathy couldn't hear what she said. Then she heard it clearly.

'Eleanor lived as noble a life, and died as noble a death, as the great-aunt she adored.'

Kathy's eyes blinked open with a start.

Her room was in darkness, although from the lights in the corridor and the sounds of activity elsewhere she could tell that it wasn't late. She saw people walk past the open door carrying flowers. Visiting time.

The picture of Eleanor came into her mind, lying on her bed, dressed in white, a bloody plastic bag pulled over her head. What was noble about a death by smothering with a plastic bag? Cut-price, perhaps – disposable, hygienic, but hardly noble. How did great-aunt Eleanor die? Kathy had got the impression from what Judith had said that it was sudden.

She reached to the pendant light switch on the pillow beside her and put on the light overhead. Brock's book was on top of the bedside cabinet, and with a wince she reached over for it. It was called *Eleanor Marx: a Socialist Heroine's Tragedy*. She turned towards the end and found the passage she was looking for, which described the circumstances of Eleanor's death.

For some years beforehand, Eleanor had been living with Edward Aveling, a socialist activist with an interest in education and the theatre. Although not legally married, Eleanor considered their union a true marriage of free love. Aveling, however, was not a popular figure among her friends, who saw that he took advantage of Eleanor's generosity, spending extravagantly on his theatrical friends the legacy from Engels which was her only capital, while she immersed herself in the hard work of Marxian scholarship, socialist politics and the development of the trade-union movement. On the morning of Thursday 31 March 1898 Eleanor received an anonymous letter revealing that Aveling had secretly married an actress some months before, changing his surname to that of the woman, but continuing to live with Eleanor in order to relieve her of the last of her savings.

Eleanor's reaction was remarkable. She called Aveling and told him calmly that she proposed to commit suicide, and invited him to accompany her into death. While Aveling prevaricated, Eleanor sent her maid round to the chemist with a note requesting chloroform and prussic acid so that they could put down their dog. The maid duly returned with two ounces of chloroform and enough prussic acid to kill several people, together with the book which the chemist kept for purchasers of poisons to sign. Eleanor took the book into the room where Aveling was, and a little later brought it back, signed 'E. M. Aveling', for her maid to return to the chemist. Seeing that Eleanor was determined to go through with it, Aveling announced that he was 'going up to town', and promptly left.

Eleanor then went upstairs and wrote several letters and prepared certain packages, among them, presumably, one containing Marx's manuscript on which she wrote her message to Rebecca Demuth. She gave all these with instructions to her maid, had a bath, dressed herself in white, and retired to bed. By eleven o'clock that morning she was dead.

Kathy let the book drop on to the bedcovers, as she tried to imagine Aveling's reaction to Eleanor's calm demand that he join her in suicide. If her death was noble, it was also impossibly implacable and remote. Suddenly Caroline Winter's reaction to her husband's infidelity, to go out and order a new kitchen, or that of her own lover's wife, whose price had been a week in a luxury hotel in Grenada, seemed comfortingly practical and sane.

What happened to Aveling? She read a little further and discovered that Eleanor's tragedy had had one final twist, when Aveling himself had died no more than a month after her, from a cancer which had been growing all the while in his side. She winced, conscious again of the throbbing pain in her own side.

Eleanor was dressed in white.

And something else. Kathy went back to the beginning of the account and read again until she found it. Eleanor Marx died on 31 March. So also did Eleanor Harper.

Something crawled up Kathy's spine, the adrenalin beginning to feed into her system. Her heart thumped. The thought, blindingly obvious now, flashed into her head. *If Meredith was expecting to meet with Bob Jones and Judith Naismith at 3, why did she take a sleeping pill at 2 that would knock her out for the whole afternoon?*

She lay for a while, thinking, then rang for the nurse and asked for a telephone.

The woman on switch at New Scotland Yard was no help at all. There was no reply on Brock's line, nor on two others she tried. Paging him produced no results. Similarly with Gurney.

'I've already tried Chief Inspector Brock's home number but there's no reply. It's really very important I speak to one of them immediately! I don't have Sergeant Gurney's home number. Could you let me have it, please?'

'I'm sorry. We can't give that sort of information over the phone. They both must have left for the night.'

Kathy's brain was racing. She reached for the buzzer and got hold of the nurse again.

'I'm sorry,' she gasped, the exertion of small movements draining her absurdly.

'Don't worry, dear. What can I do for you?'

'My clothes. Are they around somewhere? There's a telephone number I need in one of the pockets.'

The nurse nodded. A few minutes later she returned with a carrier bag. She grinned. 'Anything else?'

'No. that's great. Thanks a lot.'

Kathy found her trousers at the bottom of the bag, rolled up in a ball, and fished out the screwed-up note which Bren had given her with the address and telephone number of Suzanne Chambers. She hesitated, then dialled the number.

'Yes?' A woman's voice.

'Er, I'm sorry to bother you. I'm trying to contact Detective Chief Inspector Brock on a very important police matter. Is he there by any chance?'

'Who is this?'

Kathy felt a trickle of sweat run down her back.

'I'm a colleague of his. I really am most sorry to disturb you, but this is a matter of life and death.'

'He's not here. Did he give you this number?'

'Thanks. Sorry again.' Kathy put down the receiver. 'Shit!' She bit her lip with embarrassment.

She didn't know what to do, although she knew she had to hurry. She lay helpless, drumming the fingers of her left hand on the white bed linen.

At last she clenched her teeth and reached across her body with her comparatively good left hand and pulled the bedclothes back. With a grunt of effort she eased herself up into a sitting position, then swung round so that her feet could fall off the side of the bed. She saw her bandaged left knee under the hem of the white cotton gown they had given her. Her side was aching more insistently now as she began to shift into position to stand on her wobbly legs. She waited until her head was clear, then tried to stand. A wave of nausea flooded through her, and she put her weight on the side cabinet, ready to reach for the stainless-steel bowl. The feeling passed and she sat again on the side of the bed. Very slowly she bent her trunk forward and pulled the plastic carrier bag towards her, emptying it on to the bed. Inside were the clothes and shoes she was wearing yesterday. Her coat wasn't there.

It took a painful, exhausting age to work her aching body out of the gown and into her underwear and trousers. Then she slipped her polo-neck sweater over her head. She had to stretch the right arm out of shape to get it around the plaster cast, and ease it carefully down over the pad of dressing around her right side. The laces on her shoes were the biggest problem. When she stretched forward to do them up, she gave a stifled yell as an agonizing pain shot through her side. She closed her eyes, gasping, then tried again, controlling the pain just long enough to tie the laces clumsily.

She scribbled a short note for the nurse. The pain seemed to help her to focus. She got to her feet, swayed towards the door, then stumbled down the corridor, blindly following a knot of visitors on their way out. She sensed that people were staring at her. She didn't understand why until she passed a nurses' station with a mirrored panel facing into the corridor, as if for visitors to fix up their smiles before facing the patients. *Who is the weird woman who looks as if she's been hit by a bus?* She examined the mirror more closely. Tufts of fair hair sprouted through a swathe of bandages. The visible part of her face was mottled black and blue.

She found herself in a lift. Someone spoke to her and she mumbled a reply. Then she came to a bright foyer area, passed through swing doors and out into the cold night air. A couple got out of a taxi in front of her. She stumbled past them and collapsed into the back seat, her side on fire.

The man's eyes in the driving mirror looked concerned.

'What you say?'

'Jerusalem Lane.'

'Where's that, then? I dunno it.'

'Marquis Street,' she said urgently. 'Corner with Carlisle Street. East Bloomsbury.'

When they reached the end of Jerusalem Lane, the man had to open Kathy's door and help her out. She screwed up her eyes with pain as she straightened her back to stand on the pavement.

'There's some money in the right pocket of my trousers,' she gasped. 'Can't get it. My arm.' She swung the cast helplessly.

He looked doubtful as he came round behind her right side and reached towards her pocket. Suddenly he pulled away his hand and held it up under the light that illuminated the gates to the building site.

'Jesus! You're bleedin'! Oh gawd!' His mind leapt to the risk of AIDS. 'You need an ambulance, not a bleedin' taxi!' He thought of the blood on his seats.

'Please,' she said struggling to reach into her right pocket with her left hand.

'Forget it.' He was already back in his cab and pulling away.

31

'Kathy?' Peg's voice, mechanically distorted, sounded in surprise from her intercom. 'Come in, dear.'

The door clicked and Kathy limped slowly up the two flights towards the diminutive figure waiting for her at the top.

'Oh my, dear! Is that really you? What a state you are in!' Peg clucked around Kathy who shuffled into the lounge room and sank into an armchair, gasping for breath.

'Should I get you a doctor, dear? You look terribly white! And those bruises!'

'No. I want to talk to you, Peg.'

'Of course, dear. What about?'

'About Eleanor, and Meredith. It's time you told me the truth.'

'Oh . . . I see. Are you up to it, though, dear? You really don't look well. You're trembling.'

'A glass of water would be wonderful.'

'Of course.'

Peg went off to the kitchenette and busied herself for what seemed a long time. Kathy was grateful to be able to remain still and soak up the heat from the gas fire blazing in front of her.

Peg at last returned with a glass, not of water but of a steaming brown liquid the colour of weak tea.

'This is what you need, my dear. Our father was a Scotsman, and this was his infallible cure for any ailment, especially in the winter. A hot toddy. You get this inside you and it'll warm the cockles of your heart.'

She stirred and then removed the teaspoon. She offered the glass to Kathy, who held the potion to her nose, inhaling the fumes of hot whisky. She sipped and almost choked on the burning spirit. She could taste the sweetness of the sugar swirling in the bottom of the glass. Gradually her throat accustomed itself to the whisky as it filled her with reassuring warmth.

'Was it the books, Peg? Is that why Eleanor did it?'

'Did what, dear?' Peg asked cautiously.

'Killed Meredith.'

All of a sudden Peg seemed filled with confusion. She ducked her head, put her knuckles to her mouth, looked this way and that, as if seeking advice from the sisters who were no longer there to give it.

'Oh,' she whimpered. Then she gave a long sigh, plucked a dainty handkerchief from the sleeve of her cardigan and pressed it to each eye. 'How did you find out?'

'Just tell me,' Kathy said.

'The books . . .' Peg began slowly, shaking her head. 'They were only the final straw. Eleanor was so very upset when she discovered that they were gone. But there had been other precious things which Meredith had been taking. At first Eleanor didn't realize. There was a letter in a frame which she kept in an old suitcase under her bed. One day she noticed that it was gone. Then later, one of her books from the bookcase was missing, and more papers from the suitcase. She was quite beside herself. She even thought she must be going senile and mislaying things, although of course she had the clearest mind of any of us. It wasn't until she saw the book in Meredith's flat that she realized that Meredith must have been taking them. When she confronted her, Meredith was quite unabashed.

'How is your toddy, dear? Do you feel any better?'

'It's just fine, Peg. Go on.' She had nearly finished the drink, and the warmth inside and outside her body was easing her discomfort. Even the stabbing pains in her side had diminished to a steady throb.

'One can't really blame Meredith. She just didn't realize

what she was doing. She had become so very worried about money in recent months, and we were very little help to her in that respect. I'm afraid that neither of us was in a well-paid job, and we didn't have the superannuation schemes people have now. Over the past ten years our funds had run down almost to nothing. Meredith saw the problem most clearly, and she was under so much pressure, from Terry, and then from the people wanting to buy the house. And then there were the leaks in the roof, and the wiring. I think she must have felt she was having to hold the world together entirely on her own. So when Eleanor accused her of stealing her things, she was quite brazen. She said that she had been forced to do something, and Eleanor should feel pleased to help. In any case, she said, the old things had come from our mother, and really belonged to us all. You see, she just had no idea of the value which Eleanor attached to those things. She had never been interested in the history of our family, and the things which had come down to us.'

'But to murder her . . . her own sister.'

'I know, dear. It was quite terrible. Terrible.' A single tear ran down Peg's cheeks, leaving a tiny trail of reflected firelight. 'But Eleanor said Meredith simply couldn't be trusted. When she realized that the things were worth a lot of money, she insisted that they must be sold. She said she would get lawyers to take them from Eleanor. She was the eldest sister, and said they were rightfully hers. So like her to say that, just as she did when we were little girls.'

'I don't understand, though, why Eleanor wouldn't be happy to sell them to Judith Naismith's university.' Kathy was feeling much more comfortable. The tension in her body had been replaced by a warm glow. The alcohol had gone to her head a little, and her tongue slurred over the last words of her sentence.

'Oh dear me, no,' Peg clucked her tongue. 'Dr Naismith is an academic. She sees the papers as simply some kind of valuable historical relic, like the Dead Sea Scrolls or something.'

'Well, they are, aren't they?'

'Oh no!' Peg's voice dropped to a whisper. Her eyes shone with the same inner light that Kathy had seen before. 'Do you know what is written on the monument on our great-grandfather's grave? Beneath his famous words "Workers of all lands, unite" is a second quotation from his writings. It says, "The philosophers have only *interpreted* the world in various ways. The point, however, is to change it."'

Kathy stared blankly at her, uncomprehending.

'Eleanor said that the papers belonged to the future, not to the past. Not even to the present, when the works of Karl Marx are so universally misunderstood and misrepresented. You see, our great-grandfather maintained that the revolution could only be achieved in the most advanced societies, not in the backward peasant countries where so-called Marxist revolutions have occurred in the past seventy years. That is logical, you see, because he understood that it was only by passing through the complete cycle of capitalist development that a society would experience its inner contradictions to the full, and thus be capable of transforming itself and achieving the final goal of true socialism.'

Peg was reciting the phrases in a cosy, familiar manner, as another elderly lady might discuss the strategies of contract bridge, or growing roses.

'Now if you understand this, then you can see that the whole history of socialist revolutions in this century, in Russia and in even less developed countries, has been a dreadful mistake, a misguided attempt to take a short cut from feudalism to socialism. Our great-grandfather foresaw that such an attempt would be doomed, and he wrote his final book to describe the true path. His book is a map of the future, but it cannot be used to take a short cut to that future, as were his other books. That is why it cannot be published until the time is ready. And just imagine how people would sneer at it now, when all the world believes that the failure of those false experiments of the past seventy years has proved that Marxism is a path only to poverty, oppression and despair. We must wait, twenty years or thirty, until the memory of these mistakes has faded, and a new generation is ready to understand the true path to the final goal.'

Kathy found it difficult to reconcile this grand vision of human history with the reality of the elderly lady huddled in front of her gas fire, explaining why one of her sisters had pulled a plastic bag over the head of another. The mis-match was too silly to be taken seriously. She felt her weary brain lose focus, and her stricken body withdraw into itself.

'Am I explaining it to you, dear?'

'Not really,' she mumbled in reply. She really was desper-ately tired, and could hardly remember any more why it had seemed so urgent to leave her hospital bed for this nonsense. She couldn't imagine how she was ever going to get out of this armchair again.

'Oh dear. Well, that was how it seemed to Eleanor, anyway. She was so bright, so dedicated. The papers weren't just something given to us by our mother. They were a sacred trust which our family had inherited.'

Kathy tried to rouse herself. 'Why did Eleanor wait so long before killing herself?'

'She was drawn to the anniversary of Tussy's noble suicide, of course, and then she wanted the new buildings to be at the stage where we could put her safely away, where she wouldn't be disturbed, at least for a couple of decades.'

'So that wasn't Danny Finn's idea?'

'No, dear man. He thought it was. I helped him to think of it.'

'And the *Endziel* is down there with Eleanor?'

Peg gave a coy smile, 'Perhaps, my dear, perhaps.'

'Why the hammer?'

'Eleanor thought we should distract you. To give us more time. We saw it at Terry's house one day when we were invited to admire the new work being done to their kitchen. Eleanor thought of it. We knew it would make things worse for Terry for a while, but it served him right. Stupid boy. It was a hateful thing to do to poor Eleanor. But she was already gone, and sometimes one must do hateful things.'

An interval occurred which Kathy couldn't account for. One minute Peg was a few feet away, the next right beside her, her face very close.

'Are you all right, dear?'

'Must have dropped off. Very sleepy.' Kathy's eyelids simply refused to open, but some corner of her brain that was still working reminded her that Meredith must have felt like this, having been given a sleeping pill before she was killed. She made herself speak. '*We.* You said just now, *we.*'

'Of course, dear. We both killed dear Meredith. Why ever would you imagine otherwise?'

Kathy forced her weary lids open a crack and saw the old lady standing over her. In her hands she held a plastic bag.

32

The site workers arriving in the pre-dawn darkness found Marquis Street half blocked with police cars and ambulances, their blue and red emergency lights whipping across the scarred remains of Jerusalem Lane. A crowd of police officers and men wearing donkey jackets and hard hats huddled around the entrance to Mrs Rosenfeldt's Sandwich Bar, sipping steaming mugs of tomato soup.

Upstairs Brock picked his way round the ambulance crew as they strapped Kathy's body into the stretcher. He conferred for a moment with Bren Gurney before going over to Dr Mehta who had emerged from Peg's bedroom.

'My guess would be two or three sleeping pills in the drink to make her sleepy. Then the plastic bag,' the pathologist said. 'There's a foil of Somatone in the kitchen with half a dozen pills missing.'

Brock nodded. He turned back to Sergeant Gurney. 'Have a good look for the manuscript here when the scene-of-crime people are done, Bren. I don't think you'll find anything, but better check.'

Gurney nodded, then indicated to Brock where one of the ambulance men behind him was trying to attract his attention.

'Yes?' he said to the man, a stocky figure with an expression on his face which suggested that he had long since stopped being impressed by disasters.

'We'll get going with this one now, squire.'

'All right.' He looked down at the bandaged head visible at the top of the red blanket. Her eyes were open, staring in the direction of the bedroom, where the photographer's flash gun kept throwing the figure of the old lady on the bed, with the crumpled transparent plastic bag over her head, into brilliant focus.

When they reached the street, the crowd outside parted, staring solemnly down at her as she was lifted up into the ambulance. Behind them, framed by a halo of light from her shop, she thought she made out the frail figure of Becky Rosenfeldt, the last survivor of Jerusalem Lane.

The ambulance was swaying from side to side like a small ship in a heavy sea, but she felt secure within the womb of the strapped stretcher, the old man above her, holding her hand, watching the ambulance crewman who kept checking the drip attached to her left arm.

'Am I still alive, then?' The words barely made it past her lips, but Brock seemed to pick them up. He was saying something about her foolishness, and how long it had taken for her message to reach him. But there was something she had to tell him.

'She confessed to me, Brock. They both killed Meredith, then themselves.'

She blinked her eyes to see his face, but her vision was blurred by tears she couldn't wipe away.

He said nothing, but she felt the pressure of his hand on hers.

At last she spoke again, in a whisper. 'At least Marie Kowalski can go free.'

Brock nodded. 'Yes, but Felix Kowalski will still have to pay for what he did to you. And, much as it hurts to admit it, I'm afraid we'll have to let Terry Winter go. Without the sisters' evidence we'd never make it stick.'

The mention of Terry brought Martin Connell abruptly into her consciousness. She held him there for a moment, then took a deep breath, letting him go.

'I don't care,' she whispered. 'I really don't care.' Then, 'The manuscript *is* in the pit with Eleanor.'

But surprisingly Brock was shaking his head. He didn't think so. Stupid place. Never know when it would reappear.

A red herring to keep us all off the trail. Something about the female line, from mother to daughter, from aunt to niece.

'Terry Winter's daughter, Alex?'

He was shrugging. 'If it exists at all,' she heard him say.

She closed her eyes, feeling terrible. 'What's wrong with me?'

Stitches torn, loss of blood, sleeping pills in the drink, probably die, serves you right.

But when she looked up at him he didn't seem unduly alarmed.

She relaxed into the warmth of the blanket, letting it just happen.

'Tell Bob,' she whispered, and he bent his head to hear. 'Tell him: Eureka.'

FOR THE BEST IN PAPERBACKS, LOOK FOR THE

In every corner of the world, on every subject under the sun, Penguin represents quality and variety—the very best in publishing today.

For complete information about books available from Penguin—including Puffins, Penguin Classics, and Arkana—and how to order them, write to us at the appropriate address below. Please note that for copyright reasons the selection of books varies from country to country.

In the United Kingdom: Please write to *Dept. EP, Penguin Books Ltd, Bath Road, Harmondsworth, West Drayton, Middlesex UB7 0DA.*

In the United States: Please write to *Penguin Putnam Inc., P.O. Box 12289 Dept. B, Newark, New Jersey 07101-5289* or call 1-800-788-6262.

In Canada: Please write to *Penguin Books Canada Ltd, 10 Alcorn Avenue, Suite 300, Toronto, Ontario M4V 3B2.*

In Australia: Please write to *Penguin Books Australia Ltd, P.O. Box 257, Ringwood, Victoria 3134.*

In New Zealand: Please write to *Penguin Books (NZ) Ltd, Private Bag 102902, North Shore Mail Centre, Auckland 10.*

In India: Please write to *Penguin Books India Pvt Ltd, 11 Panchsheel Shopping Centre, Panchsheel Park, New Delhi 110 017.*

In the Netherlands: Please write to *Penguin Books Netherlands bv, Postbus 3507, NL-1001 AH Amsterdam.*

In Germany: Please write to *Penguin Books Deutschland GmbH, Metzlerstrasse 26, 60594 Frankfurt am Main.*

In Spain: Please write to *Penguin Books S. A., Bravo Murillo 19, 1° B, 28015 Madrid.*

In Italy: Please write to *Penguin Italia s.r.l., Via Benedetto Croce 2, 20094 Corsico, Milano.*

In France: Please write to *Penguin France, Le Carré Wilson, 62 rue Benjamin Baillaud, 31500 Toulouse.*

In Japan: Please write to *Penguin Books Japan Ltd, Kaneko Building, 2-3-25 Koraku, Bunkyo-Ku, Tokyo 112.*

In South Africa: Please write to *Penguin Books South Africa (Pty) Ltd, Private Bag X14, Parkview, 2122 Johannesburg.*